Praise for *The Spy Across the Table*

ALSO BY BARRY LANCET

Japantown

Tokyo Kill

Pacific Burn

THE SPY ACROSS THE TABLE

A Jim Brodie Thriller

BARRY LANCET

SIMON & SCHUSTER PAPERBACKS

New York   London   Toronto   Sydney   New Delhi

This one is for Renee, Michael, and Haruko

And for Melbourne Weddle, family, friend, fan, Korean War veteran,
Dashiel Hammet enthusiast, and so much more

Fall down seven times, stand up eight.

—JAPANESE PROVERB

CHAPTER 1

DAY 1, SUNDAY, 3:00 P.M.
THE KENNEDY CENTER, WASHINGTON, DC

M IKEY was shot because he begged me for a favor and I complied. My old college buddy and I stood in the wings of the Kennedy Center's Opera House theater, watching a Kabuki play unfold in front of a sold-out crowd. VIPs were abundant.

Mikey was starstruck. While everyone in the audience tracked the mesmerizing movements of the Japanese players in their colorful robes, Mikey focused on the bigger picture. Yes, he took in the artistry of the actors, but his expert eye also cataloged the exquisite details of the backdrops, the exotic sweep of the pageantry, and how each played off the other.

"Her costume and makeup are perfect," Mikey said in a low voice. "Is that really a man under there?"

My friend's emerald-green eyes sparkled as he soaked up the spectacle. Onstage, snowflakes wafted down. A woman in an elaborately embroidered kimono cooed plaintively for her lover. The expression of emotional turmoil on her face was sublimely complex, half-hopeful even as it plunged toward despair.

"Yes," I said.

Early in seventeenth-century Japan, the shogun famously banned women from the Kabuki stage. The elegantly clad females proved too much of a temptation for aristocratic samurai, who were expected to set an example for the common people by staking out society's moral high ground. Over time, the long-standing men-only policy evolved into a tradition that persists to this day.

Mikey remained incredulous. "Are you absolutely sure?"

"I'm certain of it."

Kabuki troupes wasted no time in seeking men with the prowess to play women. Costumes were upgraded. Makeup was subtly altered. Gestures demure and flirtatious were endlessly practiced and refined, then perfected. The Kabuki experience reached new heights. Even today, Kabuki continued to win converts. Transfixed, Mikey was clearly another. Before him, an actor in snow-white makeup, coiffed wig, and ruby lips uttered a soft lament.

"What'd she say, Brodie?"

She. I told him.

"Brilliant," he whispered. "The mood of the lighting and even the set itself echoes her sentiment."

Michael C. Dillman was a production designer. He created sets for movies. Tonight he was a kid in a candy store. We'd run into each other at San Francisco State, where we shared the same artistic sensibilities. Mikey funneled his into set design. I channeled mine into a store selling Japanese art and antiquities out on Lombard, west of Van Ness Avenue.

"How is it you two never met?" I asked, a reference not to the "temptress" onstage but to Sayuri "Sharon" Tanaka.

My old college buddy blushed. "I . . . I just never found the time."

I smiled at his transparent evasion.

Mikey was shier than shy, even with two Oscar nominations and one win under his belt. Sharon Tanaka was a famed Japanese designer for stage and screen and had been hired to create special backdrops for the Kennedy Center production.

"Did I thank you for getting me in to see her, Brodie?"

Mikey was a longtime admirer of Sharon Tanaka's work.

"Yes. More times than I can count."

Sharon and I were friends and frequented some of the same art circles in Tokyo. When Mikey had heard she would be traveling to Washington with the Kabuki troupe, he asked me to arrange a meeting.

"This is a dream. Thanks, man. I owe you."

"No, you don't," I said.

From under a disheveled bush of auburn hair, his eyes glowed with a gratefulness I found embarrassing. I glanced away, recalling the first time I'd seen the look. We were college roommates for a while, sharing a near-campus apartment. I got a dose of the look when I gave him the larger bedroom, because even back then he was hauling around cumbersome stage paraphernalia.

Mikey checked his watch. "Time to go see the grand lady. Thanks again, man."

"Stop saying that. Maybe one day you two can collaborate."

Mikey grew wistful at the thought. "That would be nice. Wish me luck."

"You don't need any. Just enjoy the get-together."

Turned out I was wrong.

He needed luck in the worst way—and didn't get it.

CHAPTER 2

THE muffled sound of a gunshot reached my ears during the fireworks scene, and momentarily my thoughts strayed from the spectacle before me to Mikey and Sharon.

Onstage, faux Roman candles shot glittering starbursts into the air. The bouquets of color enthralled onlookers and temporarily deafened performers.

In the wings, the echo of gunfire alerted all who could decipher the backroom volley. Which turned out to be two wired-up Secret Service agents and me. An American staffer from the running crew turned her head toward the distant pop, then dismissed it.

The Secret Service agents reacted instantly. Their presence confirmed the attendance of VIP heavyweights. With an event as rare as a Kabuki performance all the way from Tokyo, a heady cocktail of luminaries was guaranteed. No doubt a good sampling of senators and cabinet secretaries and ranking diplomats were in the theater. Rumors placed members of the White House family on hand as well.

The discharge had been partially muted either by distance or a closed door. Possibly both. The direction suggested the vicinity of the dressing rooms.

Where Mikey was meeting his idol.

Maybe I should wander back and check on my friends.

I cast a last look at the actors onstage. The woman character, wrapped in kimonoed elegance, collapsed to her knees in slowly unfolding agony. Her samurai lover brandished his sword with justifiable fury, hoping for a chance to strike down the villain who, by pulling political strings from the shadows, had snared the twosome in his web. Having set a trap of their own, the star-crossed pair hoped to lure him from hiding, but to the end he'd outfoxed them.

Saddened, defeated, and resigned, the couple froze, assuming a final dramatic pose. The moment was poignant. Into the stillness of the scene, a new round of fireworks released a climactic series of thunderclaps, sending out rivers of sparks arching over the heads of the doomed lovers. More than one jaw in the crowd slackened. More than one eye glistened.

In the midst of this fresh cascade came a second gunshot.

The dressing rooms it was.

I moved toward the rear, a nameless fear clawing at me.

Out front, the first of three mini-plays wound up. The theatergoers broke into a rousing applause. Cheers rose up. I heard the rustle of the crowd rising to its feet for a standing ovation. But when I looked back over my shoulder, in the dim recesses of the box seats I glimpsed dignitaries being ushered from their privileged places by shadowy guards.

Near me, a Secret Service agent with a sharp nose and roving eyes spoke hurriedly into the microphone at his wrist while his vigilant partner kept a watch on the back. I slid past them. The second man called after me but I ignored him.

A third shot rang out.

I broke into a run, my insides swamped with a rising dread, my black sneakers beating the backstage flooring. Five seconds later, footsteps pounded the path in my wake. One of the agents, I guessed.

The changing area turned out to be a perplexing maze of narrow halls and unpredictable turns. I'd heard about this. Temporary quarters had been erected for the flood of actors arriving from Tokyo.

No one was around, so I plunged into the network of plywood passageways. They were murky and ill-lit, the illumination from the small bulbs in the rafters overhead filtering down unevenly. A series of random turns brought me to a large communal area somewhere in the center of the makeshift paneled city, where I faced three routes, each winding away in a different direction.

A band of Japanese staffers fell silent when I appeared. These would be the wardrobe and makeup people charged with maintaining the props and helping the actors with their costume changes.

I took in the surroundings as I noted that footsteps no longer echoed in my wake. The space overflowed with racks of sumptuous Kabuki robes along one wall and spears and swords at another. On a long table against a third wall, the coiffed wigs of Japanese aristocrats, samurai, and courtesans bristled with topknots for the men and colorful lacquered hair ornaments for the women.

"Where is Tanaka's room?" I asked the group.

They stared back at me without comprehension. What was I thinking? Few, if any, would speak English. Fewer still would speak firearms. Gun control was fiercely enforced in Japan, the guttural crack of a handgun as alien to their ears as Swahili.

"The set designer, Tanaka-san," I said in Japanese. "Where can I find her?"

Heads bobbed, then one staffer pointed to an opening bathed in muddy hues of gray and brown. "Turn left at the end, then right at the second lane."

I nodded my thanks and sprinted into the dark hall. When I veered left at the junction, the shadows lengthened. Black cords bundled together with scarlet electrical tape ran like coral snakes along the bottom edges of the makeshift walls, then slithered underneath the plywood into individual quarters. Weak bands of light spilled from the gaps below doors.

I swung right in time to catch a light-skinned figure in a ball cap slipping from a room at the end of the corridor, tucking a gun into a shoulder holster under a coat. I registered size and shape and skin tone but couldn't grasp gender. Any long hair could be tucked under the hat.

"Hold it right there," I said loudly, not expecting him or her to listen.

Which proved to be the case.

Without looking back, the shooter picked up speed and disappeared around a corner.

I raced after the fleeing form. My shout caught the attention of actors readying for the next play, and doors creaked open. Heads appeared.

"What's happened?" one of them asked.

I didn't stop to answer. As I charged past the dressing room from which the suspect had emerged, I glanced in. The acrid smell of cordite rolled over me, then the tangy copper scent of blood.

There were two bodies in the unlit room.

Two.

No no no, I thought. *Not them. Don't let it be them.*

I dashed into the room and the forms clarified in the gloom. It *was* them. Mikey and Sharon were sprawled across the floor, dark crimson pools spreading out around them. I dropped to my knees.

This was bad. There was far too much blood.

Sharon had taken two shots in the chest. Mikey's wound was higher up, between the heart and the collarbone, as if he'd been in motion when the trigger was pulled. Sharon had no pulse, but I felt a faint beat at Mikey's neck.

I grabbed a towel off the dressing table and used it to stem his bleeding. Then I did the same for Sharon. Ghostlike, cast members crept forward from the muddy brown haze of the hall and crowded around the entrance.

In the back of my head, a clock was ticking. The retreating figure was twelve seconds gone.

I laid one hand over the other on Sharon's chest and began pumping. Rapid chest compressions from the CPR playbook. Three, four, five times. I stopped and passed a hand under her nose. Nothing. I hammered home a second series, glancing up at the gathering in the doorway as I worked.

Twenty-five seconds gone.

"Any of you know CPR?" I asked in Japanese.

"We do," a man at the back said. "I'm a doctor and my assistant is a nurse and physical therapist."

The medical personnel traveling with the troupe.

"Great," I said. "Can you take over? The man's got a pulse. The woman doesn't."

They jumped right in. The doctor dealt with the CPR; the nurse rushed to Mikey's side. I watched until I could verify the self-proclaimed medical staff knew what they were doing.

Thirty-five seconds gone.

"Anyone here speak English?" I asked, again in Japanese.

A young actor in the doorway said, "I do. I study UCLA two years."

"More than enough," I said, switching to English and enunciating clearly so he could catch the phrases he would need to use. I told him to run up front to the wings, ask for the first-aid station, and bring the defibrillator, the device that uses an electric shock to start the heart. At the same time he should have someone call 911, the emergency number in the U.S. After that, he needed to show a second person the location of the dressing room so the paramedics could be guided through the maze.

"Got all that?" I said.

"Yes."

"Good, then I'm off."

I bolted after the shooter, wondering if the fifty-five seconds I'd used to buy my friends a fighting chance had given the killer enough time to escape.

CHAPTER 3

FOLLOWED in the footsteps of the shooter, turning the same corner, then seconds later hit my first setback.

Twenty feet ahead the hall smacked into a T-junction. I peered down both legs. The left side circled back around toward the stage in a wide, lazy arc. The right leg drove deeper into the depths of the theater.

I hovered indecisively. Which way had the assassin gone? Was I too late?

Before I could decide, on the other side of an unvarnished plywood wall to my left, I heard an electric surge followed by a flat thud. *Buzz*-thud. A pressed button followed by a mechanical refusal. Or maybe it was a failure in the machine. The button was pushed again. First tentatively, then with more insistence. Repetitive jabs, each effort more forceful than the last. More demanding. In growing frustration. Once, twice, three times. And every time the mechanism jumped to life then died—*buzz*-thud, *buzz*-thud, *buzz*-thud.

Four or five yards away, someone was attempting to access a back way out. A cargo bay or an emergency exit. Someone unaware that major access points would be locked down with VIPs in the house. Or someone aware of procedure but trying to breach the system anyway.

Had to be the shooter.

No one else would be back here during show time. Not with the chance to catch a high-priced performance all the way from Japan for free.

I turned toward the sound. The hall before me banked left and looped back toward the front of the theater. Uninterrupted plywood paneling lined the outer edge of the corridor, while dressing room doors punctuated the inner wall.

Beyond the plywood barrier the killer hit the button twice more. *Buzz*-thud, *buzz*-thud. An angry muttering ensued as the door continued to resist. It was a foreign cadence, though not Japanese. The voice was too low to distinguish language but loud enough to supply hints: to *light-skinned* I added *male, lower register*, and *ragged cadence*.

I could think of only one reason why the assassin lingered near the rear exit, cursing. His escape plan had gone off script. He'd lost his way in the labyrinth, or his prearranged exit had been unexpectedly barricaded.

The attacker gave up on the door and moved off, still uttering expletives under his breath. This time I pegged the language as Spanish. Another fact to be tucked away.

I followed side by side along a parallel course, with only an eight-foot-high divider between us. *This is for Mikey and Sharon*, I told myself. *Wait for the cops and he'll be gone.*

I kept my breathing low, my footfalls silent. I could make out the spongy exhale of his sneakers. With each step, cushioned soles surrendered air to the cement flooring painted a Mediterranean blue.

Up ahead a rear entrance to the dressing area loomed. I eased up, alarmed. What if the gunman reentered the maze? The sane choice would be to plot a course along the walls of the theater until it led to another exit. But logic was no guarantee of action.

On the other side of the barrier I heard the shooter pause. He'd spotted the door. I pressed myself behind the curve of the wall and waited.

The next instant he started off again, his footsteps receding. I reached the door in three bounds and snagged the steel handle. I pulled. The portal swung wide. Somewhere inside the laminated timber, a poorly glued layer strained and creaked. The wood's protest echoed through the high-ceilinged chamber overhead.

I froze.

The retreating sound of compressed footwear ceased.

CHAPTER 4

THE killer stood motionless a good fifteen feet beyond the doorway, attuned to the disruption. Far enough away so that, with the curvature of the wall and the backstage gloom, a glance to the rear might not reveal the open door.

I held my breath.

He listened.

The silence was acute.

Five seconds passed.

Then ten.

Then he pushed on again.

I let him go, giving him a longer lead before easing through the door.

I shot a look to the rear, searching for the unyielding exit, and saw a freight entrance. There was a galvanized steel shutter and a forklift. Passage for oversize props, backdrops, and anything else of bulk. But not the assassin. Not now.

Up ahead I glimpsed the wing where Mikey and I had watched the kimonoed actor croon a lover's lament. As before, visitors and staffers hovered there. But in place of the two Secret Service agents, uniformed patrolmen had established a perimeter.

Law enforcement was in the process of sealing off the theater.

No one was getting in or out.

I clung to the shadows and scanned the crowd in the wings, wondering if the assassin had managed to infiltrate the group of observers. I'd seen him in profile. Most of the onlookers were from the Japanese crew. Of the remaining men, some had darker skin than the shooter. Others were too tall, or too short, or too wide.

My target wasn't among them.

Which meant he'd turned off earlier and I'd missed the turn.

I reviewed the layout from the freight entrance forward. There had been the maze of dressing rooms, a big lumpy circle of an affair. Then, fronting them, two rows of permanent dressing rooms, followed by three rows of industrial steel shelving six feet high and stocked with every kind of theatrical accoutrement. Next, perpendicular to the shelving, was a long row of freestanding painted sets, lined up like billboards, about five feet apart and propped in place by long, footed dowels of wood. And last, just before the drop curtain at the rear of the stage, was a ragged line of A-frame trolleys with Kabuki backdrops on each side of the A.

There were aisles between each grouping.

The killer must have turned down one of them.

From where I stood, I could look down the aisle between the A-frames and the freestanding backdrops. My target wasn't there. At the end of the row, beyond the line of painted sets, the muted green glow of an exit sign announced its presence.

That *had* to be his next destination.

There was no other outlet in sight.

I scrambled back the way I'd come, the theater wall to my left, the first of the thirty-foot-long painted backdrops to my right. I peered down the aisle between the backdrops and the first row of shelving. Halfway down, a figure retreated into the darkness.

Found you, you bastard.

The gunman was inching along with extreme caution. He wanted to avoid running into staff or security. Which told me he lacked a crew badge or a backstage pass to let him past the checkpoints in the wings and elsewhere without attracting attention.

I could still catch him.

I slipped off my black tennis shoes, hustled back toward the first aisle, then charged down it as fast as I could without making any noise. At the halfway point I lobbed both shoes high above my head, one after the other. Long, looping hook shots. The footwear rose above the tops of the sets, then clattered down between them. The disturbance would not draw the attention of the police in the wings but would give the attacker pause—and me the time I needed to push on ahead of him and circle back.

Shoeless, I sprinted to the end of the backdrops, paused, and took a flash-peek around the corner. The area was bathed in the pear-green aura of the exit sign, but I spied no trace of the gunman. Large red lettering on the door jumped out at me:

FOR EMERGENCIES ONLY.

ALARM WILL ACTIVATE.

I smiled. The killer's options were shrinking. He couldn't risk exiting this way. The alarm would alert any badges in the public corridors on the other side and they would rush his way to double-check his credentials.

I tore across the length of the backdrop and positioned myself at the far end, out of sight but between the shooter and the exit.

Then I cocked an ear to the silence and waited.

The stage set towered overhead, tall and imposing. Painted canvas was stretched across a framed crosshatch of two-by-fours. I stood alongside an ancient Roman patio with a colonnade. In the center was a marble table overflowing with roasted meats and wines and pyramids of fruit stacked on large silver platters. A feast scene. The brushwork was precise and convincing. In places where walls or buildings needed to look aged or crumbling, the detailing was impressive.

I heard the familiar compression of my target's footwear.

One step. A slight pause. Another step. Wary and guarded.

Three beats later a gun barrel with a suppressor poked its nose beyond the edge of the backdrop. A hand wrapped around the grip appeared next. I smothered the hand in both of mine and slammed the wrist against the sharp corner of the stage set. I heard a muffled cry. The shooter yanked his arm free and the firearm flew from his grasp and clattered away into the darkness.

I rounded the corner and advanced. The gunman backtracked with unexpected speed. I lunged. He shifted sideways and my momentum carried me past him. He unleashed a blistering blow to my kidney. An electric jolt launched up my spine.

Shaking off the pain, I turned—only to meet a looping right. I managed to deflect the incoming punch with my right forearm and lash out with a left fore-knuckle strike to the throat. But the impact of the blocked punch had knocked me off-center and my shot smacked ineffectually against his chest.

He dove and brought me down with an expert tackle. We both went sprawling across the floor, him on top. Rising and scissoring my ribs between his knees, he began swinging away. I jammed the heel of my left palm into the underside of his chin, then swung my right arm into the side of his torso with the force of a home-run batter taking his best swing. I heard his teeth crunch and the shooter toppled off me.

I rolled away and clambered to my feet. The assassin came up a moment later, favoring his side. As he rose, I aimed a strike at his solar plexus. A direct hit would immobilize him, but my shot crashed into the undamaged side of his rib cage, which did neither of us any good. However, the force of the blow flung him into a cluster of unclothed mannequins, which pitched over like jumbo bowling pins. He went with them.

He scrambled away on his knees, seemingly retreating in a panic. I lost sight of the upper half of his body in the gloom. I advanced. Then I heard metal scraping concrete. *Gun*metal.

He hadn't panicked or retreated.

He'd gone for the weapon.

CHAPTER 5

WITH no chance of reaching the gun ahead of him, or of preventing him from retrieving the firearm, I dove between the two closest stage sets.

I threaded my way through the narrow lane they formed, avoiding the long dowels that propped them in place. I needed to reach the far side and round the corner before the assassin could recover his piece, make it to the mouth of my Roman-style alleyway, and bury a bullet in my back.

Four yards had separated us at the edge of the passage. Sanctuary was ten yards ahead. I'd covered two and counting. Could I reach the end before he drew down on me?

Turned out it didn't matter: he had a better idea.

Gauging my pace, acceleration, and angle of retreat, he fired blind. A round punched through the scenery five inches behind me. A second bullet followed two feet on and an inch closer.

I kept running.

The deeper I penetrated, the less chance he had of a clean shot. He was blasting through maybe three backdrops to get to my "alleyway." The odds his bullets would hit crossbeams would rise as the distance between us increased. Clearly, he'd know that too. A third shot didn't follow. But I heard him scuttling toward the mouth of the passage. Stealth was no longer a priority.

He had four yards, maybe less. I had six. I was picking up speed but the odds weren't promising. Fifty-fifty, maybe less.

I glanced back. He wasn't there. My goal loomed five yards on, plus the turn.

Four . . . three . . . I snatched a second backward glance. I saw the silhouette of an approaching figure, gun arm rising. I flung myself to the floor. I heard a shot, then felt a trailing breeze as the round whipped by overhead. I slid across the floor on my belly, my momentum carrying me beyond the end of the lane. I rolled to the right, out of the line of fire, and bounded up and ran.

My breathing was loud and dissonant in my ears. I heard the assassin's feet pounding down the aisle on the other side of the stage sets. Our roles had been reversed. He was stalking me as I'd stalked him. I looked down the "spokes" of the lanes between sets and caught a glimpse of him. He was a step and a half behind. He fired between the upright backdrops, just inches behind me. Once, twice, three times in succession. Pop-pop-pop. The same partially muffled sound. Not fully suppressed, which was why the sound carried to the wings. He knowingly used a damaged silencer, no doubt preferring partial suppression to none at all.

I veered left, slipped behind an A-frame, dropped to the ground, and snaked under the large backstage curtain. To the left and right were racks of scenery ready to be whisked onstage. In the cavernous space overhead, I could make out the shadows of ropes and pulleys and catwalks weaving between girders.

Twenty yards away a commanding voice called for additional support: "New gunfire backstage. Where's our backup? Repeat, more shots fired backstage. We need backup now."

The salvo had triggered fresh alarm but no one was venturing into the dim backstage arena until more manpower arrived.

I was on my own.

I listened for the shooter but heard nothing.

I peered between the wheels of the closest A-frame and saw nothing.

After another moment I slipped from my hiding place and continued across the theater, using the string of A-frames as cover. Before I reached the police perimeter, I slid over to the other side of the A-frames, then crossed the aisle and ran silently back toward the front end of the row of standing scenery. I crouched down behind the end piece and tuned an ear to any sound.

More nothing.

The killer was still about. He hadn't risked the exit. He'd continue roaming about the backstage area, looking for another way out.

Which meant I might get another crack at him.

If I could find him before he found me.

The assassin's options were fast disappearing. More cops would be flooding into the Kennedy Center and its catacomb of corridors and byways. After the second round of shooting, they would be on even higher alert. All public escape routes were either sealed or in the process of being sealed.

Which made the killer more desperate and doubly dangerous.

I grew attentive to the whisper of his shoes—or any sound at all. I detected movement at the rear end of the backdrops, back near the emergency exit.

That couldn't be. It was suicidal for him to go out that way now.

Then a series of noises erupted. Loud and inexplicable. I heard the protesting creak of lumber, followed by what sounded like twigs cracking, then a loud slap. After a pause, the sequence repeated. A shade faster. Creak-crack-crack-crack-slap. There was another pause before the sequence began again.

It wasn't a man-made noise, and it wasn't the assassin coming for me.

The pattern replayed with increasing rapidity. It grew fuller and louder. The floor beneath my feet trembled. The din rose into the rafters. The sounds echoed. They were repeated and amplified and suddenly coming at me from every direction.

I felt the need to move but had no idea which way. I inched toward the center of the backdrop I sheltered behind. From the middle I could go either way. But which way was that?

From my crouching position, I pivoted quietly on my heels and scanned the area in front of me. I took in the shadowy forms of Roman costumes on racks against the wall. Took in a jumble of electrical equipment and wires on a table alongside the costumes. I shot long looks to the extreme left, then the extreme right. Nothing stirred. There was no sign of the killer. No cops approached from the wings.

Behind me, the clamor grew louder. The vibrations underfoot grew more energetic. I stood, hoping for a better view. The new perspective didn't help. The set towered fourteen feet above my head and an equal number of feet in each direction.

Which way to go? From which side might the shooter come? Left or right?

By the time I figured out the answer—neither—it was too late.

The oversize canvas behind me shuddered and groaned and tilted toward me. One of the three-foot dowels propping it up snapped like a twig. Another followed. *The cracking sound.* Others bent to their limit, then popped loose and somersaulted into the air.

I started to back away.

The backdrop, twisting and straining, broke free of its mooring and toppled forward.

In a flash I understood. The assassin had rocked the set on the far end back and forth, pressuring the moorings until they gave way. The first billboard-size backdrop broke free and fell against the next one in line with a loud slap. The scenery began to fall—ponderously at first, then faster—like giant dominos.

Now the last domino had capitulated and, with the combined weight of three or four of its closest brethren, threatened to crush me. At both sides, the space began to narrow. The 90-degree angle of the upright backdrop rapidly became 80, then 70 degrees.

I didn't wait. I turned and fled. Two steps later three hundred pounds of painted stage scenery slammed into me. My deltoids absorbed the brunt of the blow. The force dropped me to my knees and shoved me forward. I slid over the slick blue cement surface. The canvas slammed into me again.

The weight settled on my shoulders and pressed relentlessly down.

I pushed back. My momentum slowed, then stalled. The set creaked and moaned and forced me lower. The weight became cumbersome, then unbearable. I tried to inch forward but it was all I could do to hold my position.

My legs gave out and I found myself facedown, trapped under the insistent weight. My head and shoulders had escaped, but the rest of my body was pinned to the floor. My breathing grew labored. I took shallow breaths. Dizziness swooped in.

Then the power died and the backstage lighting went out. Shouts of confusion echoed through the darkness. I could feel the air being squeezed from my lungs. I tried to call out but only a ghostly rattle emerged.

A second before consciousness deserted me, the signature exhale of the assassin's footwear approached. A pair of shoes stopped inches from my face. The shooter reached down and plucked my backstage pass from around my neck. Helplessly, I watched the strap and plastic ID holder levitate and disappear into the blackness above.

The killer had found his exit strategy.

CHAPTER 6

A SHORT time later, the pressure eased.

    I opened my eyes.

I tried to speak but the words wouldn't come. My breathing was shallow, my air intake inadequate. When I tried to rise, I found myself still pinned to the floor. The pressure was heaviest against my calves. My left cheek rested on the cool blue cement. A vague throbbing pulsed across my upper back.

Oversize wheel stops had been wedged under the Roman-themed backdrops to lift some of the weight off me.

I'd come close to suffocating but breathed a little easier now. Images of Mikey and Sharon bleeding out in the back dressing room flooded my thoughts. What had happened in the short time I'd been out? Had the doctor and the paramedics been able to revive my friends? And what about the killer? Had they grabbed him?

My line of sight ran along the floor, about ankle height. Three pairs of footwear formed a neat semicircle five feet away: tactical boots, polished oxfords, pink canvas sneakers.

I craned my neck and matched the shoes to faces. But not before I found myself staring up into the barrels of two guns staring right back down. One rested in the palm of the sharp-nosed Secret Service agent. The owner of the oxfords. The other belonged to a local cop, who had a large squat face, two chins, and an upturned nose over the powder-blue shirt of the metropolitan police department. The owner of the boots.

"Your name?" the Secret Service agent said.

Raspy and low, a voice emerged this time. "Jim Brodie. Are the victims okay?"

"We'll get to that."

"Did anyone catch the shooter?"

"Looks to me like we nailed him just fine," the DC badge said.

The canvas shoes shuffled uneasily. They sheathed the feet of a blond-haired woman in beige cargo pants and a sleeveless gray sweatshirt. A stagehand. Maybe a manager. She tapped a clipboard lightly against her thigh. On hearing my name she raised the board and began flipping through a collection of papers. A leather tool belt with screwdrivers and pincers and clamps circled her hips.

I caught the Secret Service agent's attention. "You saw me in the wings. I was there when the shots were fired."

The local badge sneered. "Don't mean you ain't an accomplice."

"Don't mean you don't have spaghetti for brains either," I said.

The stagehand stopped flipping pages. "His name's on the list for backstage passes. Courtesy of Sharon Tanaka. Came in together with a Michael C. Dillman."

The metro cop's eyes gleamed. "Gotcha," he said.

"They're both friends," I said.

"Even better."

With the barrel of his gun trained on my head, he squatted down inches from my face, unhitched a pair of handcuffs from his belt with his free hand, and said, "Lookee, lookee. Your one-way ticket to hell."

———

Two members of the stage crew arrived with a long crowbar, a thick wooden block, and an abject apology.

"We're sorry," one of them said. "With all the extra backdrops for the Japanese plays, we ran short of A-frame racks for the Roman scenery of the next event. This isn't the first time the unsecured sets have toppled over, but the restraints have always been sturdy enough to prevent a chain reaction."

"Unless they were given some additional help," I said.

The Secret Service agent frowned. "What do you mean?"

"I chased the killer from the cargo bay. I caught up with him, then lost him. I was looking to jump him again but he outfoxed me the second time. He shoved the first couple of backdrops until they built up a natural momentum. Probably helped them along to keep them going."

"So where do you think he went?" the agent asked. "The whole complex is sealed off."

"If he's not here, he slipped out during the commotion. On a stolen pass."

"Whose?"

"Mine."

The local badge grinned up at the taller agent. "Just like I said. This guy's an accomplice."

"Can't rule him out," the Secret Service agent said.

One of the crew members slid the crowbar over the block and under the fallen sets and pried them up enough for me to crawl out.

At which point the DC cop planted a boot on my back and slapped on the cuffs.

"Is that really necessary?" I said.

"Yes," the two men said in unison.

The Secret Service agent holstered his gun, looped a hand under my left arm, and yanked me upright, then marched me over to a chair and dropped me into it.

"You sore?" he asked.

"Not much."

"Need medical attention?"

"No."

"Good. Stick around."

"What about Dillman and Tanaka? They okay?"

"All in due time." The agent walked away, calling over his shoulder, "Keep an eye on him, Hedges. Don't shoot him unless you absolutely have to."

_____

Law enforcement swamped the Kennedy Center.

The FBI, Homeland Security, and an assortment of others all made their presence felt. Washington has more law enforcement entities than an octopus has tentacles. The tentacles spread fast and latched onto everyone in sight.

Starting with me.

Hedges and another cop ushered me into a conference room, where some two dozen other backstage visitors waited. The metal wear around my wrists drew appraising stares.

"How about loosening the cuffs since the place is locked down," I said.

"No chance," said Hedges, waving over a young cop from his department before wandering off. "Watch this one. He's a live wire."

All the backstage personnel trailed in a minute later, then the interrogation process began.

Every agency had its crack at us. Off to the side, uniformed police officers rolled out a string of six-foot whiteboards on casters. As the interviews progressed, sightings of Mikey, Sharon, and the killer were logged. Witness accounts were cross-referenced. The boards slowly filled. I could read the headings but not the notations below. A timeline began to take shape. Then a second round of questioning commenced to confirm and expand on the emerging skeletal construction of events. Details were fleshed out.

I was a popular item. I retold my story maybe ten times, each time to a different badge. There was no way to circumvent the procedure. Or truncate it. For each interviewer, I laid out my tale from my arrival to my confrontation with the shooter. For each interviewer, I explained why I had a backstage pass. For each interviewer, when requested, I recited my contact information. They all requested it. At the end of the proceedings, Hedges removed the cuffs with great reluctance. Rings of chafed skin at my wrists brought him a measure of satisfaction he made no attempt to conceal.

Four long hours after the shooting, I exited the theater complex. A light breeze ruffled my hair. The white façade of the Kennedy Center with its majestic copper-colored pillars towered overhead. Beyond the edge of the courtyard, the Potomac River roared, robust with runoff from a recent storm. My deltoids throbbed and my wrists were inflamed.

But mental torment overshadowed any physical pain. I couldn't get an update on the condition of my friends. With each new sit-down, I'd asked about them. I was repaid for my cooperation with silence or shrugs. When I tried forcing an answer before an interrogation began, the interviewer took one look at the handcuffs and read me the riot act.

Now, since my Uber app was malfunctioning, I waited in line for a cab behind eight other "detainees." Theater patrons had long since vacated the playhouse. For the hundredth time I wondered about Mike and Sharon.

My plan was to take a taxi to the nearest hospital.

Then events took an unforeseen detour, and I never made it to a medical facility of any kind.

CHAPTER 7

S IR," a voice behind me said, "could you step from the line?"

I turned to find myself facing a woman in crisp navy suit, straight black hair, and distinctly masculine sunglasses.

"Why?"

"I'd like a word in private."

A blue oval pin trimmed in gold adorned her lapel. At its center was a gold star. At the end of each of the star's five arms was a small gold disc. I knew the insignia. Everyone who traveled through secure locations within DC knew the insignia. Plus, I'd had the distinct displeasure of seeing it all afternoon.

It belonged to the Secret Service.

"Your people have already interviewed me twice," I said. "And pointed a gun in my face. I've nothing more to say."

"If you wouldn't mind, I'd like one last word."

"I mind," I said. "I need to find my friends as soon as possible. So I'd like not to lose my place in line."

"If that's all it takes, we'd be happy to drop you anyplace in town after we talk."

She waved at a modified black Cadillac XT5 idling some twenty yards away. A man in a nearly identical outfit, with nearly identical shades, leaned against the front fender, his arms crossed.

"Thanks, but no thanks," I said. "Say what you have to say, then go. It's probably nothing I haven't heard at least a half a dozen times today. In fact, most of the people in this line have probably heard it."

Every ear and eye within range was tuned to our exchange.

"I would be happy to explain if you will step over to the rail for a moment."

"Seriously, there is absolutely nothing more I can add."

The woman glanced back over her shoulders and shook her head, then raised an eyebrow. What did he think? The other agent gave her an abbreviated nod, so she bent forward and whispered in my ear, "FLOTUS wishes a word."

The first lady of the United States.

Suspicion gripped me, then a flicker of fear. An over-the-top, ego-massaging compliment was the perfect ploy. Was this a confidential whisper meant to flatter and gain consent? Mentioning the president would be too outrageous, but using the first lady struck a nice balance. Problem was, I had no White House connections whatsoever. Direct or a few degrees removed.

The new rules of engagement between civilians and the greater law enforcement agencies made me wary. The playbook had changed—drastically. With the Secret Service now operating under the Homeland Security umbrella, agents could just as easily drive me away, throw me in a cell, and hold me without a lawyer in the name of national security. I'd already had two guns unjustifiably pointed in my direction. Why should I risk more? I wasn't sure the Secret Service could actually cart people away like Homeland and other agencies, but why take the chance? Thank you, Patriot Act.

There was another possibility. This could be a con job. My eyes shot to the lapel pin: the ornament looked real enough, but how hard could it be to fake? Or replicate? Or buy online?

"You have ID?" I asked.

Annoyed, the woman slipped a leather badge holder from her pocket and held it open at eye level. She allowed me ample time to inspect the contents—a badge and Secret Service card for one Bonnie Sternkart. I'd seen authentic federal ID before. Not Secret Service but CIA, FBI, and Homeland. I had an eye for detail. Developed from scrutinizing thousands of artworks, separating the dross from the gems, and both from fakes. The shield and identification were authentic.

"Okay, Ms. Sternkart, I'll give you that," I said, "but I think you have the wrong guy."

"Unlikely, sir."

"There were thousands in the theater today, and maybe two hundred backstage."

"You are Mr. Brodie, are you not?"

"The wrong Brodie, then."

Sternkart's jaw clamped down hard. She extracted a notepad from a jacket pocket, thumbed through a couple of pages, and began to read: "Age thirty-two, six-one, one hundred ninety pounds, black hair, blue eyes." She ran an unamused glance up and down my frame. "Seems to fit."

"Fits a lot of people here today." I looked around. "Could fit the guy at the head of the line."

She gave me an unyielding deadpan stare, then flicked over a page. Her eyes dropped like daggers to the bottom of the sheet. "Widower, one daughter, resident of San Francisco, born in Tokyo to Caucasian American parents. Japan expert, lived in Japan until the age of seventeen, art dealer and owner of Brodie Antiques on Lombard in San Francisco. Also half owner of an entity in Tokyo called Brodie Security. Japanese detective license through said agency. Involved in several high-profile cases in San Francisco and Japan."

"Ah," I said. "That guy. You're well-informed."

"Just doing my job. Would that be you, then?"

"It would," I said.

"Then would you be so kind?"

"I'll make you a deal," I said.

"We don't make deals."

"Too bad."

Sternkart frowned. "What do you want?"

"A status report on the two victims."

The woman's lips twisted. "That we can do."

"Good," I said.

"But in the car."

"Why? You think I might renege?"

"Our job is to ensure your arrival. Once you're inbound, we'll release the information. Agreed?"

"Agreed."

A well-turned hand rose and pointed toward the Cadillac.

I held back. "I need one last bit of proof that convinces me you're not going to haul me off to some black-ops site."

"We're Secret Service, not Homeland."

"Not enough."

"How about this?" She leaned forward again and whispered in my ear one more time. My eyes widened. I pulled away and stared into her eyes. They were open and reassuring. They held steady against my probing.

Stunned, I relinquished my place in line.

CHAPTER 8

THE Cadillac XT5 glided toward Washington Circle, then up Pennsylvania Avenue.

The black luxury sedan was practical rather than palatial. Elegant enough to transport visitors to the White House but small enough to navigate the capital's traffic with ease. The male agent piloted the machine with uncommon agility, weaving around lethargic vehicles with a silky smoothness. He drove with lights flashing but siren silent. From the passenger's seat, the woman spoke softly into a cell phone.

I sat alone in the spacious backseat, anxious to ask about Mikey and Sharon. The Caddie had a wood-trimmed interior, leather seating, extra foot room, and a stocked mini-bar. A transparent partition separating the front from the back was impressive if only because I heard not a word of what transpired in the forward compartment.

Sternkart finished her conversation, mumbled a few words to her partner, then turned and gazed at the passing scenery.

I tapped on the divider. "We had a deal," I said.

The woman hit a button on the center console and the panel retracted into the back of the seat.

"Ask away," she said.

Was it a one-way sound barrier or had a microphone been planted in the back?

"Were they able to revive Sharon Tanaka?"

She shook his head. "No."

Something in my chest tightened. Breathing became difficult. "How about the man? He was still alive."

The woman blinked once. "They worked on him for a while."

"And?"

"He a friend of yours?"

"Both of them are."

Frowning, she hesitated. "I'm sorry. He didn't make it either."

The blood drained from my face. No, no, no. I'd left them in good hands. Professional hands.

"Are you sure?"

She studied me for a moment, then the hard-edged mask dropped away. "Yes. I'm very sorry."

"In the ambulance? At the hospital?"

"A hospital never came into it," she said. "The killer was thorough."

My breathing grew raspy again, as if I were once more pinned beneath a massive weight. I slumped back against the cushioned upholstery. Again an image of Mikey during our college days surfaced. We'd hosted a moving-in party at our new apartment, and like many collegiate affairs it got out of hand.

Three times as many people showed up. We shrugged it off, figuring we'd make new friends. I stepped out for more supplies. When I returned, I found Mikey in a scrap in the courtyard with two oafish guys twice his size, and a gallery of gawkers doing nothing. Just as I turned a corner, they tackled him. I charged in, pulled both guys off my friend, and made short work of them. Turned out they'd come on to my then girlfriend and wouldn't back off. With me running an errand, the ever-shy but always loyal Mikey had stepped into the breach. He suffered a black eye and a broken arm, but from that day forward our friendship never wavered.

My chest collapsed in a dark hole of pain. Mikey and Sharon in one day? It made no sense. No sense whatsoever. Two gentler souls did not exist.

And I'd brought them together.

What had I done?

———

Five minutes later we rolled onto the White House grounds.

It required only a brief nod-and-wave at a sentry in a security booth for entry. The Cadillac eased to a stop near the East Wing. Having frisked me back at the Kennedy Center, Sternkart simply opened my door, nodded me out, then led the way, her partner swinging in behind us.

They guided me along a stone footpath, into the White House, then up a flight of broad, carpeted stairs. On the second-floor landing we stepped into a corridor wide enough to accommodate a marching band. The carpet was white and spotless. Ornate molding with raised scrollwork lined the upper edges of the walls.

From a door midway down the hall, a woman in a no-nonsense yellow power blouse and brown slacks emerged with a smile and her hand extended. She wore her black hair in a pageboy, side locks tucked behind her ears.

"Mr. Brodie, thank you for coming. I am Margaret Cutler, the first lady's chief of staff, and I will be your liaison in all further communications in the days ahead. Mrs. Slater will receive you immediately."

In the days ahead?

"The pleasure's all mine, Ms. Cutler," I said, wondering what the next few moments might bring.

"Margaret, please. Right this way, if you would."

The Secret Service agent stationed outside the door from which Cutler had issued opened it as we approached. Margaret stepped through first, followed by my lead escort, who plowed past her fellow agent like a sleek powerboat in overdrive.

I went next and found myself in a reception chamber where four staff members hovered anxiously. Margaret was already moving into the adjoining room with Sternkart on her heels. I glided forward in their wake, the male agent bringing up the rear.

Joan Slater, the first lady of the United States, rose from an overstuffed chair upholstered in a mauve-and-beige floral pattern. "Thank you, Bonnie, Jeff, for bringing Mr. Brodie to me."

"Ma'am," the agents said in unison before bowing and retreating from the inner sanctum.

The president's wife offered her hand. "Mr. Brodie, thank you very much for coming on such short notice. I can't tell you how much this means to me."

I shook her hand while two staffers swooped in under Margaret's watchful eye and began fussing over a tea caddie.

"Please take a seat," the first lady said, beckoning me toward a spot on a matching couch nearest her chair.

"Thank you, ma'am."

Once seated, we waited in silence for the tea to be served. Framed photographs of the presidential family hung over Joan Slater's desk behind her. Paintings by Paul Klee and Mark Rothko, no doubt on loan from the National Gallery of Art, found choice locations elsewhere in the room.

The staffers wrapped up and departed without a word. After casting a final approving look at the arrangement, Margaret shut us in.

"I hope my request wasn't too much of an inconvenience," my host said, her eyes finding mine. They were bright and warm and observant, with a shadow lingering at the back. "I hear you nearly turned down my emissaries."

On the walnut coffee table before us, wisps of steam rose from two cups of tea in fine china.

"Frankly, Madam First Lady, I didn't believe they had the right man."

"Joan, please. What changed your mind?"

Glossy shoulder-length black hair framed an intelligent face with fair skin and a candid smile. Vivid blue-gray eyes locked onto me with an intensity that implied I had become the center of her world. She was fully and deeply engaged. The effect was mesmerizing. A pastel green dress, cinched at the waist with a wide belt of silver leather, brought out the color of her eyes.

"Their extensive . . . shopping list."

Confusion crossed her face for an instant before understanding dawned. "Interesting way of putting what must have felt extremely intrusive. Please accept my apologies, Mr. Brodie. One cannot dictate the way the Secret Service operates."

I nodded agreeably. "I suppose not. And let's make that Jim. Though I don't know what you could possibly want of me."

"I have been informed that you were backstage when Sharon Tanaka was shot. I was also told you knew her."

Sorrow seeped into her voice as the stage designer's name left her lips. "You have good sources," I said.

Melancholy tinged Joan Slater's smile. "My husband's job comes with countless benefits, but 'good sources' is not one of which I ever expected to avail myself. Did you really know Sharon?"

"Yes. We ran in some of the same circles in Tokyo. Were you two close?"

The fact of their friendship, whispered in my ear by Sternkart, was what finally convinced me of the legitimacy of the agent's petition.

A girlish enthusiasm lit up her face. "Boy, did I. We attended Cornell together back in the day and were roommates in Manhattan for three years when she apprenticed at the theaters off and on Broadway. Her death is a shock. That it should happen on my doorstep is an unmitigated disgrace. There is going to be an official investigation, of course, but I also plan to do everything in my power to assure her killer is caught."

"I don't blame you," I said, the grief I'd tamped down welling up as she revealed her connection to Sharon. They had been roommates in Manhattan. Not unlike Mikey and myself.

Her expression sobered with my reply. "I would very much appreciate it if you could lend your talent to the endeavor."

I sat back, disconcerted. "Me?"

"Yes. I'm told you know Japan and Asia and that your overseas connections are superb. That was, after all, Sharon's territory."

"It was," I said.

My neutral response puzzled her. "I am also given to understand that you lost two friends today. Was Mr. Dillman an acquaintance of yours as well?"

Hearing Mikey's name spoken so openly jarred nerves still far too raw. The grief she'd sparked to life rekindled twice as hot, smothering any verbal response I might have summoned. I answered with a nod.

The first lady divined her misstep immediately. "I have been indelicate. Please accept my apologies."

I nodded a second time, knowing there was more to come.

"From what my people also mentioned . . . well . . . about you, Jim, I do not believe you are the type who will leave this matter untended."

My voice returned with a vengeance. "Never."

Which had always been true. Never had I let a serious slight, offense, or attack against friend or family go unanswered. Call it loyalty, justice, payback, or all of the above. I had the tools. I'd trained at Brodie Security, the Tokyo-based PI/security firm established by my ex-MP, ex-cop father. I'd studied martial arts in Tokyo with judo and karate masters and picked up some street moves along the way. Since I had the ability to act, I would. Period. It wasn't my preferred activity—dealing in art was—but when necessity called I stepped up. Even if I knew I might not come away unscathed.

"I thought not," the first lady said. "In which case, I would be very appreciative if you would allow me to hire you and your Tokyo people to assist me personally in my inquiries."

My reluctance surfaced immediately. I was in this for Mikey and Sharon. The last thing I needed was the White House looking over my shoulder.

Misreading my response, the president's wife said, "Let me assure you I will not abandon you. Margaret or I will be available to you any time of the day or night. You should not hesitate to call."

"That's very kind," I said, "but I prefer to work alone."

"You know, Jim, I am a public figure. There's little I can do openly. But today's . . . incident . . . is as personal to me as it is to you. You would be doing me a great service."

Penetrating blue-gray eyes pleaded the first lady's case with an ardor impossible to resist. Her look was silent yet deafening. But also deafening were the alarm bells blaring in my head. Joan Slater's request ran counter to a mantra vital to the survival of Brodie Security: Never accept high-level politicals as clients. They come with too many strings, most of them hidden and treacherous.

Our client list ran up the ladder from ordinary people to public figures of all kinds. From managing directors to movie stars to pop idols. From local Japanese politicians to minor European royalty to the occasional diplomat. But we never stepped onto the highest rungs. Brodie Security had done so once and was nearly destroyed. The White House occupied the highest rung of them all. I could already hear them screaming in Tokyo.

Sensing my unwillingness, the president's wife said, "Oh, before I forget, let me give you this."

She handed me her private card. Her name and phone number were embossed in silver on quality ivory-colored stock. The tone of the ink was subtle, not ostentatious. The card tendered no title, no official affiliation, no address, no White House emblem. The overall effect was one of unassuming and unadorned modesty.

The gesture itself, however, told a different story.

Joan Slater was advancing, not retreating.

"Will you work with me to find out who did this to our friends?" she asked.

I looked into her eyes. Their fervor had redoubled. I also saw intelligence, passion, and sincerity. I could not imagine her sandbagging me. She was not, herself, a politician.

"Maybe I can make an exception," I said.

CHAPTER 9

S PLENDID," the first lady said. "Now, with what information may I supply you?"

"To start, you could tell me more about you and Sharon Tanaka."

"Such as?"

"For example, did you have a chance to meet before the opening?"

Joan Slater bit her lower lip. "No. Our schedules were in conflict, so we planned to meet at the after-party tonight, then privately tomorrow . . . here."

"I'm guessing you were one of the people led out of the theater when the shots were fired . . ."

She raised a delicate hand to the hollow of her neck. "How did you . . . Never mind, yes. They told me there was gunfire but I never imagined Sharon would be . . . would be . . ."

Her eyelids began to flutter. Without warning, she rose and turned away. A lace-trimmed handkerchief appeared in her hand from a side pocket, and she dabbed at the corner of her eye. "Excuse me, Jim, I—"

"No, excuse *me*," I said.

Misgiving swept in whenever I stepped over the line. Not only the emotional one, but also the one that dragged me from my preferred occupation of art dealer to the one I'd inherited from my father. The artists and craftspeople I display in my shop dig deep. It's what inspires their work. It's what brings their pieces to life. Even anonymously crafted items glow under the influence of a gifted craftsperson's hand. In my father's world, I'm the one who must dig deep—but into other people's lives. Into their suffering. Into their most immediate pain. The answers I require are necessary but rarely extracted without eliciting heartache, which never fails to fill me with guilt and remorse and doubt about my second occupation.

Her back still turned, the first lady said, "I'll be all right in a moment. It's just that . . ."

Again the handkerchief rose. Joan Slater was a strong woman. She had always charted her own course, even as her husband's political star rose. Now her ship had been rocked by an unforeseen storm and was in danger of smashing against a treacherous shore. And she'd called me to help plot a course past the obstacles.

"Dealing with details in the aftermath is frustrating and torturous," I said. "But necessary. For both of us."

Her eyes glistening but steady, the president's wife reclaimed her seat. "Maddening for you, I expect. I so wish I could have done something to stop all this, but how could I have known? How could *anyone* have known?"

Someone knew, I thought. And I would find him or her or them.

"I am determined to get to the bottom of this," Joan Slater said, her agony transparent and crushing. "Please continue with your questions."

"If you're sure you're up to it."

"I need to be."

Steeling myself, I tiptoed back in. "Did Sharon mention any trouble in her life?"

"No."

"Did she offer any confidences?"

"No. Those would have come tomorrow morning."

"How did you arrange your meeting times?"

"A brief email exchange."

"Was there ever any sign of worry on her part? Any hint?"

"Good heavens, no."

I felt like a painter trying to mix together a last dab of color from a depleted palette. "Perhaps later you could email me a short description of how you met and a list of your social interactions over the years. I'll also need the names of friends in common and any other person who might be of help. All in confidence, of course."

"Of course. By the way, I plan to attend Sharon's funeral in Tokyo."

"I'll see you there, then."

"I do have one more minor request," Joan Slater said. "A Homeland Security agent by the name of Tom Swelley will be heading up the case for the government. I would like the two of you to share information. Working together might speed things along. Would you do that for me?"

Despite an attempt to suppress my consternation, my brow furrowed. How was it that sitting in the refined study of the first lady of the United States—among genteel furnishings, antique china, and the work of Rothko and Klee—I could be put down for the count by a sucker punch?

"Jim? Are you all right?"

I exhaled audibly. "I am afraid I spoke too soon, ma'am. With the whole of Homeland Security behind you, you have no need of my services."

Gingerly, I retrieved Joan Slater's name card from my shirt pocket, set it down on a side table, and rose to leave. From the way the first lady's eyes widened, I gathered people did not refuse her often, if ever. But a gracious smile soon supplanted her initial astonishment.

"Please, Mr. Brodie—Jim—don't rush off just yet. If I have been presumptuous, I apologize. Even if you choose not to extend your help in the end, I don't think our meeting should conclude on a discordant note, do you?"

The president had married no fool. Joan Slater was moving deftly to calm troubled waters even before she could fully divine what had stirred them.

"My refusal has nothing to do with you," I said from my standing position. The first lady remained seated. "I'm honored to have been considered, but with Homeland in the picture, I would only be in the way."

She clasped her hands together in relief. "Oh, I'm so glad I didn't offend you. Let me freshen your tea." She rang a small silver bell by her side before I could decline.

Immediately, the two staffers returned with a new pot and cups. The old china was whisked away while another round of tea was brewed and poured with presidential efficiency. Not ten seconds after the leaves had fully steeped, we were once more alone.

The president's wife looked up expectantly. Reluctantly, I retook my seat.

"The last tea cups were from Eleanor Roosevelt's china service," my host said. "She is one of my personal heroes. These are heirlooms from my great-great-grandmother."

Eyeing the setup, I said, "Nineteenth-century Meissen. In excellent condition."

Joan Slater's right eyebrow waffled. "Remarkable. My husband doesn't know that, even now."

"I'm a product of a mixed marriage," I said.

"Oh?"

"Curator and cop."

She laughed, delighted. "Yes, of course. But Meissen as well as Japanese antiques?"

My mother had worked as a museum curator before she went to Japan as a volunteer for the Red Cross, where she met my father. His entry into law enforcement began with a stint as an officer in the American army as an MP. Once he mustered out, he joined the LAPD but soon revolted against the command structure and returned to Tokyo, where he opened Brodie Security, parlaying his Japanese connections into the city's first successful Western-style detective/security agency. All of which Joan Slater would have learned from whatever report the Secret Service had scrounged up for her on short notice.

"I apprenticed with a generalist," I said. "He stocked antiques from nearly every continent."

"Remarkable," my host said again. An inquiring look crept into expression. "But the distaste on your face . . ." She paused, then brightened. "Your reluctance isn't because of Homeland but because of Tom Swelley, isn't it? You *know* him, don't you? That is the only explanation."

"I do," I said. "And to know him is to . . . wish you didn't."

She nodded. "Swelley is a piece of work."

"I voted for your husband," I said. "For what it's worth."

"This is not about politics, Jim."

"Not directly, but if you are friends with Swelley, I doubt you and I could work together."

Joan Slater gave a breezy laugh. "Actually, those very words confirm that we *could* work together. Unless you wish to take back your vote."

I chuckled in turn. "No, I'll stand by my vote, but Swelley is . . ." I shrugged. What I wished to say wouldn't do in polite company. To cover my embarrassment, I took a sip of tea.

Next to me, discerning eyes sparkled. "A dick?"

I came exceedingly close to spraying Earl Grey all over the first lady and her designer dress.

There was a light tap on the door, then Joseph B. Slater, the president of the United States of America, stuck his head in. "I'm not interrupting, am I?"

"No, dear."

I stood and we shook hands. The president was tall and slim, with a relaxed look as open and observant as his wife's, but honed with a shrewd glint from years in politics. No one made a fool of him. His full head of black hair, abundant and neatly parted, had a fringe of gray at the temples that had not been there when he first stepped into the White House.

"I have the Joint Chiefs waiting for me," he said, "but I wanted to stop by and see how Joan's enterprise was coming along."

He glanced toward his wife, whose expression was the perfect study of neutrality.

The president almost managed to work up a troubled face. "Ah," he said. "Trouble in paradise. Sharon was a family friend, Mr. Brodie. Whatever obstacle you might have encountered, I hope you'll find a way to circumvent it."

If he expected his words of encouragement to melt my resistance, a quick scan of my face assured him he was mistaken.

He turned to his wife. "A big hurdle then, is it, Joan?"

"Swelley" was all she said.

"Junior?"

"Yes."

"Ah." Her husband clasped his hands behind his back. "Mr. Brodie. Jim. Can I call you Jim?"

"Yes, of course."

"Well, Jim, in this household, as in many others throughout the capital, you have only to mention the name of Tom Swelley Jr. to find, shall we say, comrades in arms. I must say I cannot blame you one bit. Even without knowledge of what your complaint may be, I am certain I would side with you in a dispute. We have known the Swelley family for years. I attended the same college as Swelley's father. That would be Tom Swelley Sr. We pledged the same fraternity. While I cannot, in truth, say we are close, we keep in touch. When he and the missus asked us to find a place for their son in the early years of Homeland, I acquiesced with great reluctance. I was a congressman back then, and there were so many positions to be filled after the Twin Towers came down, I had little more to do than suggest his name. Junior was a deputy sheriff somewhere in small-town Pennsylvania, but that was not going well. However, I've heard he's risen quite rapidly in the DHS, perhaps in part because of my introduction, though I assure you I asked for no special dispensation. This is because Junior, like his father, is trouble, and I did not want my token gesture to come back to haunt me in any manner or form. Do you understand what I am trying to say?"

"I believe I do."

"Good. Your instincts about him are accurate, but please don't let that color your decision about accepting my wife's request."

I had been outflanked. Wedged between a presidential rock and a hard place.

"Knowing the full story," I said, "I may change my mind."

"I would appreciate it." The president looked at his watch. "I have to get back to the West Wing. I'm sure the Joint Chiefs are squirming. Hopefully, they haven't planned a war in my absence. I'll leave you two to finish your conversation. It's been nice meeting you, Jim."

"The same here, Mr. President."

"Joe. Call me Joe."

I nodded, he smiled—then he was gone. The door eased silently shut behind him before reopening a beat later. The president stuck his head back in.

"You helped Gary Hurwitz with his Pacific exchange program, didn't you?"

The mayor of San Francisco.

"Yes," I said.

"You see him, say hello for me."

"I will."

President Joseph B. Slater smiled warmly and disappeared a second time.

The rock had become a boulder, and the place a far tighter squeeze.

CHAPTER 10

DAY 2, MONDAY, 8:40 A.M.
NATIONAL MALL, WASHINGTON, DC

I SENSED their approach only a moment before the four men fell in alongside me, two on each flank. All of them were large. All of them clocked in far above the national average in height and girth. I glanced left, then right. They were flinty. Hard-edged. Trained. Their actions were coordinated.

I was strolling along the National Mall on the way to the Freer Gallery, to keep an appointment I'd made two weeks earlier. The museum wanted some new art for its collection and I'd signed on to supply them. The sun lapped at my shoulders, warm and welcoming. The sky was cloudless and blue and promising. The deaths of my friends had dominated my thoughts—until the newcomers showed up.

The men continued to replicate my stride step for step.

All of them exceeded my six-one height by a noticeable margin. The two closest ones carried shoulder holsters under lightweight jackets. I suspected the two on the perimeter were also armed.

This was the second breach of my "art day." The first had come earlier, when I'd fired off two email inquiries. One for a background check on Sharon Tanaka, to Brodie Security in Tokyo. Another for the same to an SFPD friend about Mikey.

The next moment Tom Swelley Jr. stepped from behind a tree. The Homeland agent wore civilian black with a slate-colored jacket. His silver hair was still cropped short. His feverish black eyes glowed with ill will.

"What happened to your other gorilla?" I asked.

Swelley snorted. "Guy that easy I don't keep around."

Last time I flew into the capital, Swelley had sicced a six-foot-six, 250-pound Homeland apeman on me in the terminal. I'd come out on top. This time Swelley had stacked the odds irretrievably in his favor.

"So you got new playmates. I'm happy for you, Swelley."

Calculating eyes glared at me from a well-tanned face of taut planes and surfaces. His crew sported the same baked look. Meaning the unit had recently returned from an assignment in toastier climes. They were in dark civilian clothing, like their leader. None of them wore any outer law enforcement markings. No protective vests with large acronyms on the back. No shoulder or chest patches. No lapel pins.

"I hear you talked to Joe and Joan," Swelley said. "Bet you're feeling superior."

There it was. I should have guessed. The Department of Homeland Security had been born in the post-9/11 scramble, and its power had expanded almost exponentially since then. It had sucked up a number of agencies, among them the Secret Service. Which meant the DHS had eyes in the White House.

"Actually, I'm not feeling anything except late for my appointment. Which I plan to keep."

I took a step forward and the biggest of the Homeland agents stepped in front of me. Another slipped behind me. In an instant I was boxed in on all four points of the compass, though Swelley's goons had been careful to take up positions just outside striking range. No doubt a takeaway from our previous airport run-in.

Swelley ambled over. "You'll go when I'm done with you, not before. In fact, from now on, you'll do exactly what I say, when I say. First order of the day is you report to me first. Not Joan. Not Joe. Not anyone in the White House. This is a national security matter."

"The first lady did say something about exchanging information."

"This is me exchanging."

"I'm all ears."

"You got it wrong, Brodie. I give orders, you listen."

"I think the first lady had something else in mind."

"I don't give an armadillo's ass what the little lady wants. We have bigger issues than Joan's college roomie. You need to back off. We're working on the case and don't want you in the way. So take it real slow, if you get my drift. You can follow up on her little assignment but you report to me. I'll decide how much you can pass on. We clear?"

"Sure thing," I said. "So what can you tell me?"

"You just got it. Everything else is classified."

I shook my head. "Of course it is. Always a pleasure doing business with you, Swelley."

"Comments like that remind me what I like about you, Brodie—nothing. Boys, give our new friend a memento of our powwow so he remembers his place. Nothing that'll show. He's got an 'appointment.'"

Of the four agents around me, I could see only three. I was moving before Swelley finished his grandstanding. On *memento*, I slammed the heel of my right foot into the kneecap of the agent in front of me. On *place*, after a split-second pivot, I thrust the hard bottom edge of my palm into the chin of the agent advancing from the left. Swelley strolled off as soon as he finished his lecture, confident his message would be delivered. Despite my preemptive attack.

My first victim toppled to the ground, clutching his knee. The second one staggered back, wagging his head to shake off the pain. The remaining pair of bullyboys backpedaled and circled. I did the same, alert for a tell.

I needn't have bothered. The younger of the two men left standing slanted his eyes at his partner, then charged.

The message I thought I'd sent with my first volley was *I'm not so easy, so let's call it a draw*, but the third man interpreted it differently. He rolled in on me with a combined judo–Krav Maga move. His right hand shot forward with a feint to my solar plexus while on the back end of the combination strike his left hand snaked in toward my throat. I slapped the feint away even as it faded, then blocked his stealth jab with a sweep of my forearm.

A textured follow-up, with layers of fakes and punches and support from the fourth man, might have been tough to fend off, but his hand-to-hand combat skills turned out to be basic security service issue. Like the weapon under his arm. In the field, it would suffice for an easy takedown of the minimally trained.

Which excluded me. Large and eager though he was, Swelley's young recruit had brought the wrong toys to the party.

My first victim was rocking on the ground in agony. The agent who had taken the blow to the chin had recovered and stepped forward to re-join his fellow agents. Had the trio charged immediately, they could have overwhelmed me. But they didn't. They continued to circle. I followed suit, now an unwelcome ringer in their rotating foursome.

I watched for a weak link but never found one. On the third rotation, when my first victim once more slipped momentarily into my blind spot, he rolled closer and stuck out a foot. Which I obligingly tripped over. His partners piled on. The blows rained down, mean and abundant and targeted with precision.

Orders were orders, so no one struck my face. No one swung at the ribs. But they pummeled everything else. Stomach, arms, legs, and groin. I curled up, knees to chest, hands clasped over the back of my neck, bent arms bracketing my head.

In the distance I heard a police whistle, then the pounding of boots on hard earth. Swelley's men leapt off me. I sat up. Everything throbbed. The scenery wavered.

Pulling out their badges, two of Swelley's puppet soldiers moved to head off the advancing policemen while a third protected the middle ground, throwing a jaded look my way.

His upper lip curled. "Stick around, Brodie."

"Not likely," I said, dragging myself up, flashes of white pain sparking behind my eyes.

"I'm warning you, Brodie."

"How's that chin?" I said.

He shot me a spiteful glance, but with the approaching uniforms he made no follow-up move. I brushed myself off, turned my back on Swelley's squad, and hobbled off to keep my appointment.

Tardiness is not a virtue, but sometimes just showing up can be.

CHAPTER 11

FOUND my way into the bowels of the Freer and Sackler. Past a marbled entrance. Past a lush arrangement of flowers and bushy clippings in an enormous vase set out on a waist-high table. In transit, bouts of dizziness brought me to halt more than once.

At the information desk a docent called ahead to announce me. "Dr. Kregg says for you to go right down. Do you know the way?"

"Know the way, the place, the collection."

The docent smiled. "And they're all good."

"No argument here," I said.

The Freer and Sackler Galleries were part of the extensive Smithsonian museum complex. At one time separate entities, the two had merged, combining staff, resources, and collections. So far it seemed a viable notion. Between them they covered the Asian art world from Japanese, Korean, and Chinese to Middle Eastern, Egyptian, Indian, and beyond.

I took the stairs to the basement, then pushed through an EMPLOYEES ONLY door. Sheathed in a creamy-beige skirt and a light-green blouse, Dr. Lisa Kregg watched my approach with the cultured repose of her Bostonian upbringing. She was tall and in her thirties, with incandescent silver-gray eyes and a delicate nose. A bloom of red hair cascaded over slim shoulders and silky pale features.

"Brodie, you nearly stood me up," Kregg called from the end of the hall.

"Never would," I called back.

Satisfied, she spun adroitly and dove into her book-lined lair. I followed. She trooped briskly around a large desk stacked high with art catalogs, a mild irritation riding her spine.

"Well?" she said, settling into a black-leather chair and giving me a piercing look.

"Sounds like I've been tried and convicted."

She tented her hands. "All but."

"The neglect was not intentional," I said.

Discerning eyes followed my efforts as I lowered myself into the visitor's chair. I tried not to favor the parts Swelley's thugs had worked over, and failed.

"What's wrong with you, Brodie?"

"Depends on which girlfriend you ask."

"Seriously."

"Can I plead a migraine?"

She raised two fingers, then pushed one down. "First, you're the wrong personality type for a migraine. And second, you're not favoring that part of your anatomy."

"Come to think of it, my girlfriends never complained all that much."

A faint smile crossed Kregg's lips. Behind her natural beauty lay a self-assured woman, two master's degrees, a PhD, and a spirited irreverence.

"You've come to us not so different from a suspect vase that crossed my desk a few days ago."

"Suspect how?"

"Wobbly. Damaged, perhaps, in unseen places."

"I had an eventful stroll across the Mall."

Her eyes dropped to my jeans. I followed the look. I'd missed a spot. Faint traces of Mall turf clung to the black denim at my left knee. I brushed it away.

Her eyes sparkled. "You are the most intriguing of my art dealer friends, Brodie. This wouldn't have anything to do with your visit to the White House yesterday, would it?"

A jolt of surprise electrified my every limb but I held my expression in check. "I don't suppose you'd believe me if I said I had no idea what you're talking about."

"Not a chance."

"Because?"

"This is my town."

"I'm beginning to think confidentiality in DC is an illusion."

"Our nation's capital has more security agencies than any other place on earth. Our country has over three thousand government and private-sector entities working on intelligence, counterterrorism, and security issues. There are eight hundred thousand people with top secret security clearances, many of them employed in the greater DC area, so the odds suggest some of them can be bribed or coerced or might just like to gossip. Even if they don't, the place leaks like a tire rolled through a nail factory." She leaned forward, a mischievous smile skirting across her lips. "When I say the White House, I use the term loosely. Care to divulge?"

The question was pitched with more charm than a Southern belle flirting with a potential suitor.

"You're hard to resist, but I'm afraid I must," I said.

"Disappointing, but a wise course. You may actually be as smart as I think you are. Moving on, how's Jenny? Is she tougher than her father yet?"

"Getting there."

"Still in pigtails?"

"Yes."

Kregg's smile surrendered its wry edge to a maternal softness. "You're safe until she outgrows them. Once that happens, the road gets hard."

"I'll keep that in mind."

I asked after her husband and two daughters, then my curator friend shifted to business. "So tell me about the robes you have lined up."

The museum had a new endowment for Japanese art, and with the Kabuki troupe playing the Kennedy Center, Kregg thought a traditional Japanese theatrical costume seemed a timely addition to the collection.

"I've tracked down two. They're hard to find."

"I know."

Kabuki robes were scarce for a reason. They get treated roughly. Abrupt movements on stage and quick changes between acts take their toll. Then there's the long storage between uses and the requisite cyclical airing, which on occasion gets neglected, leading to mold, mildew, and moths.

Unlike such traditional antiques as furniture, lacquerware, and ceramics, Kabuki garments don't grow richer with age. A patina does not emerge. When an outfit begins to fray, it is discarded, although sometimes a portion can be salvaged and reused. So, by definition, pristine Kabuki attire is nearly unobtainable.

I explained all this to Kregg, who said, "So museum-quality specimens are even tougher to find?"

"Extremely."

"Which makes them all the more desirable."

On my cell phone, I pulled up photographs of the two robes I'd managed to unearth and passed the device over to Kregg. Both were in good condition and from the late Edo period. About two hundred years old. One of them was an earlier version of a robe that appeared in last night's play.

She inclined her head. "After the shooting at the Kennedy, I suspect we should pass on the first one. The museum board would probably balk. What about the other?"

"An *omigoromo*."

Kregg sat up straighter. "A robe of the elite. Perfect."

We were discussing regal indoor leisure wear for a male samurai of rank. A prince, a shogun, a general, and the like. The garment I'd found was full-length and brocaded. The material's design was elegant and rich and classically Japanese. Gold clouds floated on a royal-blue field. A tall red pleated collar framed the head in a regal flourish.

Kregg flipped through the close-up shots on my phone as I filled in the details, then she said, "Delightful. A real crowd-pleaser."

"Glad you like it. I'll send you high-resolution images to show the board."

"Thank you. Allow the usual two to three weeks for a consensus, but in the meantime, if you come up with something better, please let me know."

"I do have feelers out."

My dealer friend in Kyoto was hunting around for Kabuki costumes. I'd expected him to bow out, but he surprised me by accepting my request, saying that although good robes were rare, his wife was active in traditional performing-arts circles.

"Then please pursue them. Now I have something for you. It's a token of appreciation, since you are always so thorough."

"Thank you, but it's really not necessary."

"Oh, but I think it is. I make it my business to keep abreast of what goes on in this town. Knowledge translates into donations for us."

I kept my face devoid of expression. "Why do I have the feeling you're circling back?"

"Because your instincts are impeccable, and you are a dear friend. DC has changed dramatically since the Twin Towers were flattened, Brodie. The town's had a major face-lift. You might say it now resembles a Picasso woman with three faces who is not aging well. Washington has become bigger, darker, meaner. National security has taken the helm of the military-industrial machinery. A lot of money is circulating. Do you see where I'm going with this?"

I knew the Beltway corridor was dotted with new clusters of secured sites. Where the GPS on your car's navigational system suddenly went fuzzy and the usual street signs were nowhere to be seen. Where posted sentries peered out from guard booths stationed behind tall chain-link fences capped with concertina wire. All post-9/11 changes.

I said, "The new growth industry."

"Not so new anymore but still growing. The town has been flooded with government funds for intelligence work. The salary level per capita is way up, which is good for those of us seeking donations but not for you. Or, to be more precise, not for your other job."

"How so?"

Her luminous eyes grew apprehensive. "These people are territorial. If you intrude on their turf, you threaten their golden goose. They won't hesitate to come down on you. So be careful. I am including government employees here because many of them have their eye on lucrative private-sector jobs once their pensions are secure."

We were back to talking about wobbly vases.

I leaned back in my chair. "I think you're off target this time."

Kregg protested with a shake of her head. Waves of red locks shifted. "Everything in the White House concerns the security-military-industrial complex these days. If not directly, then indirectly. If you've bumped into something that bumped back, you ran into them."

"I can't really talk about it, but to put your mind at ease, let me just say it was an East Wing matter."

She drew up short. "The first lady?"

"Keep it between us."

Kregg dropped into thought. She brooded. She brought clasped hands to her chin. She was stumped. Then a renewed look of determination suffused her features.

"Did the president put in an appearance?" she asked.

I felt a nerve in my arm twitch. "Yes."

Her look was triumphant. "I rest my case. Be careful, Brodie."

CHAPTER 12

THANKS for coming, Brodie," Mikey's older brother said as we shook hands.

"How could I not?"

Ian Dillman anchored the receiving line just inside three sets of Saint Mary's sculpted doors, thrown open for the funeral mass. He had his younger brother's auburn hair and bright-green eyes. But where Mikey was shy and retreating, Ian was hearty and outgoing. Eclipsing his smaller brother by six inches and forty pounds, Ian was a big lumberjack of a man, out of place in the black suit he'd stuffed himself into for the funeral.

"The first lady sent flowers for my baby brother," Ian said. "Called to talk to Ma and Pa all the way from Washington. Was that you're doing?"

I shook my head. "All hers."

Big Ian grunted. "Didn't vote for the husband but now I wish I did. That Joan Slater's a class act. Did my folks a world of good."

"Extremely glad to hear that," I said.

Mikey and Ian were seventh-generation San Franciscans. Their grandfather's grandfather's grandfather had arrived with the first wave of fortune seekers in the California gold rush of 1848. Rory Dillman dug and panned and battled the dust and the heat for a year and a half before striking a minor vein. Once the magic yellow glitter played out, he plowed his modest windfall into land and a steakhouse along what later became Market Street, in San Francisco.

Rory's place nurtured the City by the Bay through all her growing pains: from her pioneer shantytown days through the prosperous times fueled by the gold and silver finds in Northern California in the last half of the nineteenth century; through the growth spurts of the early 1900s and the Roaring Twenties; through the down decade of the Great Depression and the sacrifices of World War Two; through the postwar prosperity when America was flush with victory and optimism and big cars.

In the 1960s the fifth-generation Dillmans moved their family enterprise to the district rejuvenated by the newly built Ghirardelli Square. They recast their restaurant as an Irish eatery-and-bar combination to accommodate the new gold rush: tourism. Hearty meals, free-flowing beer, and a wicked Irish coffee drew visitors from around the world during the day. In the evenings and well into the night, the booths in the back rooms provided a late-night gathering place for Jack Kerouac and other legendary beatniks of the fifties, then luminaries such as Ken Kesey in the Haight-Ashbury sixties. After his graduation from San Francisco State, when it fell to Ian and Mikey to step into the family business, Mikey ceded his interest to his brother and took a position at Lucasfilm.

Ian lowered his voice before he said, "The first lady also said you nearly caught the guy. Too bad you didn't nail his ass."

"Give me time."

Ian nodded grimly. "She also let slip you're working on the murders for her. That true?"

Something hollow and raw opened up in my chest. As I gazed at the framed photograph on the casket across the nave, in my mind's eye Mikey stepped from the shadows, green eyes averted, inviting me over for Thanksgiving dinner. With my mother recently dead from cancer and my estranged father settled in Tokyo, Mikey knew I had no close family nearby. He brought me to his house and I met Ian and his parents. They couldn't have been more gracious, and by the end of the evening I felt, for the first time since I set foot in San Francisco after my mother's passing in Los Angeles, that I had, if not family, something close to it.

"She's a client, yes, but Mikey's and Sharon's interests come first."

Ian clamped a firm hand on my shoulder. "Government getting involved could help or it could send things sideways. You never know. But you won't be stopping, will you, Brodie?"

"Quitting's not in my playbook. You know that."

"I know you'll do right by Mikey." The hand on my shoulder tightened its grip, then Ian bent down and said, "You find the guy, me and the boys want a crack at the bastard before you hand him over."

"Nothing would make me happier. Don't know where this thing will lead, but if I can, I will."

Ian's eyes misted over and I glanced away.

What he didn't know, and I couldn't mention, was that the elephant backstage at the Kennedy Center had followed me out here and would have to be addressed. It trumpeted a simple but devastating fact: people are shot for a reason. Between Mikey and Sharon, one of them had a secret.

CHAPTER 13

LIEUTENANT Frank Renna of the SFPD and his wife, Miriam, were seated about ten rows from the front and had saved me a place.

Renna was a big and beefy man with a large square face and hard eyes. He wore a dark suit and tie for the funeral, but his occupation seeped through. Miriam was a tall, slender blonde with soft hazel-green eyes that quietly took in everything with a lawyer's thoroughness. The pair had met while she was an assistant district attorney for the city. As a friend, she'd let drop, on more than one occasion, that it was hard living with a cop. The workload dragged her husband down. I had no trouble understanding. Renna and I had been through some tough cases together, from the Japantown incident onward.

"Such a tragedy," Miriam said as I took my place.

"No rhyme, no reason," I said, just to say something.

"This kind of thing, there's always a reason," Renna said.

The elephant had reared.

"I was being rhetorical."

"Tells me you haven't gotten anywhere."

Miriam squeezed her husband's hand. "Honey . . ."

"I'm working on it," I said. "I've got people in Japan digging around and I'm flying there tomorrow. You'll cover this end, right?"

"Yeah. Already got some boys poking around."

The church interior was small but majestic and, in its soaring ceiling, otherworldly. Above us, the roof rose up with breathtaking swiftness, coming together at its tented pinnacle in a giant cross. From narrow windows, soft beams of light dappled pews and aisles. Shaded areas took on a rich chocolate hue.

"Good. I know something's out there."

The problem had to be faced. Only I planned to start tomorrow, thirty thousand feet above the Pacific, my seat cranked back, a scotch in hand. Until then, I hoped for a few more untroubled hours—make that less troubled—and some downtime with my seven-year-old daughter.

Miriam said, "Who's looking after Jenny while you're gone? Kerry Lou?"

"Yes."

Kerry Lou Meyers was the single mother upstairs whose daughter was Jenny's best friend. We exchanged babysitting favors, and I paid her to watch my daughter when I left town.

"Mention she's welcome to bring the girls over to play with Christine and Joey anytime. They all get along well. Jenny or both girls can even stay for a night or two if they wish."

"Thanks. I'll tell her."

A priest ascended the podium and spoke passionately about his long association with the Dillman family, then about Mikey, whom he had known since birth. He talked about a life tragically taken. About God's inscrutable ways. And about unmitigated violence in society.

From all sides, smothered sobs punctuated the priest's pauses. I didn't add to the muffled chorus, but I felt a sting at the corner of my eyes.

Renna poked me in the ribs. "Two o'clock. Asian on the far right. Seventh row on the aisle. Good suit. Just sat down. Eyeballed us, meaning you, I'd guess. Looked only once."

As far as I could recall, Renna had not turned his head in the direction he'd indicated and wasn't looking that way now.

"What's he doing?"

"Sitting, looking around the rest of the church casually . . . but not this way again . . . Wait . . . still looking around . . . Get ready . . . on my call . . . wait . . . wait . . . eyes shifting front . . . locked on the casket . . . priest . . . *now*."

I turned and smiled at Renna and his wife. I said something meaningless and Renna nodded. Miriam returned my smile. I focused on them, but out of the corner of my eye scanned the pews and counted rows.

At the end of the seventh row, I saw a thick thatch of well-groomed black hair hovering over the collar and shoulders of an expensive-looking, hand-tailored suit.

The sight sent a surge of adrenaline through me. Primal urges sprung up. I bristled with the desire to strike out.

"I don't believe it," I said.

"So you know him," Renna said, unsurprised.

"Do, and wish I didn't."

Renna grew interested. "Because?"

"He's one of the most dangerous men I've ever met."

CHAPTER 14

MIRIAM shifted nervously and her police lieutenant husband said, "He got a name?"

"Zhou."

Renna's eyes seemed to retreat as he flicked through the catalog of names in his head. "The spy out of Beijing?"

"Yeah, via Tokyo. The home invasion cases eight, nine months ago. Gave me background on Chinese gangs."

When an old Japanese World War Two veteran showed up unannounced at Brodie Security claiming Chinese triads were killing off his old war buddies in Tokyo, I'd eventually needed a knowledgeable source high within the Chinese embassy to guide me. Someone in a position to know secrets. Through a mutual friend, I'd been introduced to Zhou, who extracted blood before he delivered.

Miriam's eyes bounced from my face to her husband's and back. "What's he doing here?"

"No idea," I said.

Renna's cheeks puffed out, first one, then the next, as if rolling a clutch of marbles from one side of his mouth to the other while considering my reply. Eventually he said, "But nothing good?"

"Count on it."

In stages I felt my blood turn to sludge. A bleakness crept into my heart. Zhou and his ilk inhabited a slippery netherworld I had vowed to avoid after our first encounter. Not that I couldn't handle him. More that I didn't need the aggravation. I had a daughter and an antiques shop and friends in many walks of life around the world. Life was interesting. Rewarding. Zhou's world involved underhanded politics and manipulation and a constant undermining of friend and foe for an extra grain of power or position.

"Guy gave you a hard time, if I remember."

"He did."

"You also told me he was good."

"He's more than good. He's a genius at what he does. And he's a survivor. Which in his world makes him as devious as they come. He's also paranoid and more dangerous than a rattlesnake on steroids."

"The rattler's flexing in your backyard," Renna said.

"What's mine is yours," I said.

The last words of the closing prayer left the priest's lips. A subdued rumbling of amens rose to the ceiling, then a half dozen pallbearers ascended the podium. They formed a chain, passed the sprays of flowers adorning the casket to those in the front row, then lined up along either side of Mikey's coffin.

It pained me that I wasn't one of the men escorting Mikey to his final place of rest. Ian had put my name up for the honor, but other members of the Dillman clan had overruled him.

"By all rights you should be one of the pallbearers, Brodie," he'd told me by phone last night, "but others think his death is partly your fault. Not me. Not Ma and Pa, but others."

What others? I wanted to ask. Let them tell me to my face. I'd straighten them out. I already felt as guilty as hell. Every waking moment since Mikey's death, I wrestled with grief and self-reproach and a neverending list of *what-ifs*.

I cast a look over the heads of the congregation, wondering which of the Dillman family attendees had struck out my name. I wanted my day with them, but that wasn't going to happen and I would not burden Ian with my discontent. I gave him the "I understand" he needed to hear because it was Ian.

I had done nothing but arrange what had been for Mikey a dream meeting. And now, secretly, even as waves of remorse continued to wash over me, I found comfort in the thought that he and Sharon had had some minutes together before it happened.

The next instant the service was over. The congregation began to stir. The pallbearers hoisted the casket, descended the podium, and made their way up the central aisle.

"Originally I thought you should be up there," Renna said. "Now I'm thinking with Zhou around it's better this way."

In patches, people stood and followed in the coffin's wake.

Renna glanced across the room, then his bulk seemed to rise higher in its seat.

"He's on the move," my police lieutenant friend said.

CHAPTER 15

'M on it."

I rose while at the side of the podium the officiating priest was consoling Mikey's parents. He clasped Mrs. Dillman's hands in his as he spoke. Other mourners began to gather in groups at the entrance and outside on the elevated plaza.

I skirted past Renna and he said, "Miriam, we'll catch up with you at the cemetery."

"No reason for you to abandon your wife," I said. "I can handle this."

"The guy's slippery, right?"

"As they come."

"Then you need backup." He turned to his wife. "You'll be okay?"

Miriam's brow rippled. "I'll be fine. It's you two I'm worried about."

Renna squeezed her arm reassuringly, and we poured into the aisle with the rest of the guests. We were two lanes over and ten yards back. Zhou slipped easily through the departing crowd, adjusting the knot of his tie as he went. Then his head swiveled, lizardlike, toward me. Right at me. His eyes flicked once and he turned away.

Damn. He was playing us.

I expected him to exit out the front with the mourners, but he stepped into a stairwell at the back of the pews and headed down.

"You see that?" I asked.

"Saw the move and the look. Don't like this guy."

"Welcome to the club. What's down there?"

"Shop, restroom, offices. Which one do you think he needs?"

"Whatever's behind door number four."

We reached the stairwell. Like the rest of the church it was elegant and designed. Dark earth-toned tiles. Discreet lighting behind beveled rectangles. The spy was nowhere in sight.

I plunged downward with a stream of churchgoers. Renna stayed close on my heels. On the first landing, the stairs doubled back, dropping quickly to the basement level. The faint aroma of incense wafted up from below.

"The smell from the gift shop?" I asked.

Renna nodded. "Souvenirs."

At the bottom, the basement landing opened up into a hallway of gray linoleum and gray walls. All sense of the otherworldly vanished. There was still no sign of Zhou.

Renna shot glances left and right. "You see him?"

"No."

"Where to, then?"

The restrooms were to the right, a pair of arctic-gray metal doors to the left. Straight ahead, the gift shop display window offered hand-painted crosses and souvenir booklets about the cathedral. Two dozen people milled about. None of them was Zhou.

"Too public for a spy," I said. "You see any staffers?"

"No."

"Then I say we head into the back rooms."

Renna nodded. "Wish I'd brought my piece."

"That makes two of us."

On the other side of the arctic-gray entry a long hallway branching left and right confronted us. A paneled door brought the right-hand branch to a dead end. A few swift paces and a twist of a knob confirmed the route could take us no farther. Nor would it have accommodated our prey. We turned our attention in the opposite direction. The passage hobbled on for about ten yards before dropping into a short set of stairs and doglegging right.

"Only choice left," I said.

"Best of a bad lot. Really wish I had the gun."

We traversed the hall, stairs, and dogleg with caution, emerging on the far end of the turn into another long passage. No sign of Zhou. All the doors were locked. At the end of the passage we found ourselves peering through a pair of glass emergency doors.

"That's it, then," I said.

"Unless your rattlesnake slithered under."

"Not impossible."

The exit opened out onto an enclosed patio, which in turn led to a parking lot at the back of the church. The patio had painted cinder-block walls and a ground-to-ceiling wrought-iron gate to keep out riffraff. The gate probably did double duty as a back entrance for staff.

The glass doors were stickered with security system warnings. I jiggled the bar release on each door. Neither gave way, but the next instant Zhou stepped out from behind an exterior wall.

"Come back in and we can talk," I said loudly.

He grinned, swiveled on his heels, and sauntered off.

Scowling, Renna leaned a shoulder on the door and pressed down on the bar with the full weight of his six-foot-four frame. No go. He ran his fingers along the edges of the door, then under the handle.

"By law, this can't be locked. Your snake jammed it somehow."

"So what's his point then?"

In the same instant we both pivoted and looked back the way we had come. Our eyes raked floor tiles, walls, the ceiling. Renna dashed from my side. He drew up ten yards later.

"What?" I asked, not wanting to stray from the emergency exit in case Zhou reappeared.

"He's not coming back," Renna called.

"How can you tell?"

"The snake left you a love letter."

Renna stepped aside and pointed at what looked like an envelope tacked to the wall with a pushpin. I joined him. In our initial hunt for the spy, we'd charged right by it.

CHAPTER 16

THE eggshell white, garden-variety envelope bore my name. I lifted the flap. No note had been inserted but the underside of the triangular flap contained five words:

GARY DANKO.

AFTER THE FUNERAL.

Renna raised an eyebrow. "The restaurant?"

"The man likes good food."

Gary Danko had reigned as one of the city's premier dining destinations since it first opened its doors.

Renna scoffed. "And you know this how?"

"Took me to an expensive place in Ginza. That's an upscale district in central Tokyo. Japanese skewered delicacies, sashimi that melted in your mouth, and some brilliant saké. Everything was world-class. Cost the Party a fortune."

Renna shook his head. "And him an exemplary servant of the People's Republic of China."

THE FORT MASON AREA

After attending the burial service in Colma, just south of San Francisco, Renna and I raced back into town.

Now we stood outside Gary Danko, a few yards from the intersection of Hyde and North Point. In the tinted black windows of the chic restaurant we could make out our own reflections and those of the cars streaking by behind us, but none of the décor or diners inside. We still wore our funeral attire, which looked, if not stellar, at least presentable.

"How about that," I said. "We're dressed to dine."

"Better than your usual ratty jeans."

"Or that muddy blue thing you try to pass off as a suit."

We stared at our reflections some more. The wind snuck under our ties and waggled them about as if a pair of flirtatious women, invisible but frisky, stood by our sides. A short five blocks away, rough chop coming off the bay would be crashing against the pilings under Fisherman's Wharf.

"Ready to look at what's behind door number five?" I said.

"Getting tired of doors."

"It's his natural paranoia."

"Tough way to live."

I nodded. "Before a meet, there's always hoops."

"He came to us."

"Doesn't matter."

"Enough already," Renna said. "In we go."

He palmed the door, flashed his badge at a startled hostess in a long black dress with matching shawl hugging her shoulders, and—after a quick scrutiny of the bar and the seating to the immediate right—stomped into the more secluded dining quarters on our left flank, returning seconds later without a body in tow.

"Looks like you've been stood up, Brodie."

The young hostess's ears perked up. "Are you Mr. Jim Brodie?"

I looked into a pair of questioning pale-blue eyes. "Yes."

"We have a reservation for you and your friend."

"Do you, now."

"Yes," she said with a hesitant glance at Renna. "For both of you. At the bar. Right this way."

At the word *both* Renna's brow clouded over in a threatening manner and the tentative smile that had worked its way across the hostess's features lost its purchase.

"Don't worry," I said. "I promise to keep him on a leash."

With a weak smile, she led us to the last two open spots. The restaurant was bathed in warm wood tones and golden-orange lighting. We hoisted ourselves onto high barstools with low backs. Some of the guests at the bar sipped pre-dinner drinks and others partook of full-course meals. Two black place mats with folded black linen napkins had been laid out for our arrival, along with what looked like double shots of whisky straight up.

" 'Both,' " my SFPD friend muttered. "That shadow-hopping sleazebag's going into lock-up as soon as I catch him."

"In his own irritating way, Zhou's always been hospitable."

Renna's eyes turned flinty. "A rattlesnake with manners. So what?"

A valid stance from someone who knew the full story, which Renna did. Before Hiroshi "Tommy-gun" Tomita, a tenacious journalist friend in Tokyo, had introduced me to the upper-echelon Chinese operative at my request, he set out a chilling warning I remember to this day:

"With this guy you'll be stepping into an alternate universe."

"Don't go melodramatic on me, Tommy."

The newshound put his hands on the table and stared at them for an extended moment. "We've known each other for a long time, right?"

"Yes."

"I'd like to keep it that way. You're absolutely sure you have to talk to a Chinese spy?"

"It's vital."

"Okay, then I need your word on two things. First, no matter what happens, next time I call, you'll be ready for anything."

"What does that mean?"

"You see? You've got the wrong attitude. Can you be ready or not?"

"I'll be ready," I said. "And the second thing?"

"No matter what happens, we stay friends. I am your friend and you say you need this, but my advice would be to back down unless it's do-or-die mandatory. Is it?"

It had been.

"Like I said," I told Renna now, "Zhou's paranoid, and he's a survivor. Which makes him skittish. He tests you. He plays mind games. Nasty ones sometimes. You don't make it into a trusted position in the Chinese regime otherwise."

Frowning, Renna eyed the drinks unhappily. "Guy like this, better he's in your debt than the other way around."

"Wish it were so."

"He know you like whisky?"

I thought back to our first encounter in Tokyo. The evening had started with a stunning saké from a Kyoto brewery and ended, memorably, with two pints of beer I was required to finish before leaving the restaurant. They had been Zhou's idea of a time clock so he could retreat unhampered by any attempt I might make to follow. Failure to finish the brews would get me shot by his sniper on the roof across the street. Plenty of alcohol had laced the evening's events, but not one ounce of whisky.

"He didn't get it from me," I said.

We both stared down at the amber liquid before us with renewed suspicion.

Renna's frown deepened. "I really don't like this guy. You want to do the honors or should I?"

"This is going to get embarrassing."

"Got to be done."

The bartender came over. "Welcome, gentlemen."

"I see you anticipated our arrival," I said, casting a significant look at the drinks.

"Mr. Zhou called ahead with the order and said you'd appreciate having your drinks at the ready."

"He wasn't wrong," I said, glancing at the man's name tag. "Did you lay out the drinks yourself, Kevin?"

"Yes, sir."

I nodded agreeably. "What am I looking at?"

"Hibiki, a twenty-one-year-old blended whisky from Japan. It has an oak and fruity nose, with dark cherry, caramel, and light spices on the palate."

"Hard to resist."

"A popular one, sir, because of all the awards. And scarce now."

"Kevin, would you mind bringing me three clean glasses?"

A worried pair of eyes dropped to the two place settings. "Is something wrong, sir?"

Napkins and place mats were perfectly aligned. The crystal tumblers of Hibiki were spotless.

"Not a thing. I'll explain in a minute."

Relieved, the bartender was back in thirty seconds with a trio of new glasses. I distributed the two drinks equally among the three fresh tumblers.

"I don't wish to impose on Mr. Zhou any further," I said, "but I'd be remiss if I didn't ask you to join us. In place of our host."

I nodded toward the fresh pours.

"That really isn't necessary, sir."

"I insist."

I handed him a tumbler, we all raised our drinks, and I said, "Best of health."

The three of us touched glasses and drank. Or rather Kevin drank and Renna and I faked it.

Kevin gave us a smile of satisfaction. "Thank you, sirs. It is a rare day I can sample a Hibiki of any vintage. I'm most appreciative."

"As are we," I said.

Catching a gesture at the end of the bar, Kevin excused himself with reluctance.

"You feel as bad about that as I do?" I asked.

Renna shrugged. "Day in the life for me. A snake's a snake."

Renna squinted at the bartender, and we both watched Kevin for several long minutes before Renna said, "Guess the drink's safe. He's still standing."

"So we're in the clear unless there was something on the glasses?"

Renna shook off the idea. "Too tricky in a place like this."

"Good. Hate to waste a good whisky."

We touched rims a second time and swallowed in earnest. I'd had the twelve- and seventeen-year-old Hibiki but not this one. Suntory's star blend was smooth, subtle, and silky. Everything Kevin mentioned and more passed over my palate. I had no complaints.

Renna sighed. "The bastard knows his whisky but that doesn't buy him a pass. Give me Zhou's full name and I'll run him through the system."

"Can't," I said, thinking back to my first meeting with the Chinese diplomat-cum-spy.

"You have a name?" I'd asked the stranger who had claimed the seat across from me.

"Ten of them. Take your pick."

"Any of them real?"

"As real as anything else in this world. How does 'Zhou' sound?"

A spy and a philosopher. Tommy could pick them.

Settling down his drink, Renna's eyes narrowed. "Why not?"

"Zhou is not his real name."

"Got a photo?"

I shook my head. "Nope."

"This is new territory for me, Brodie. Exactly what the hell are we dealing with?"

"You sure you want to know?"

Renna's eyes burrowed into mine. "What kind of question is that?"

"More than one person I know has come to regret what I'm about to tell you, *if* you give the go-ahead."

CHAPTER 17

RENNA leaned back in his stool. The low backrest strained under the pressure of the police lieutenant's overpowering frame. His expression darkened.

We'd been through a lot together. The Japantown incident for starters, in which Renna had nearly died from an exotic poison in an unimaginable way. So he took any warning out of my mouth seriously. But he also had two decades of police enforcement under his belt, so there was pride and a justifiable self-confidence.

"You think you need to pamper me?" he said.

"Been trying to spare you."

"You mean news worse than Mikey and the Tanaka woman getting axed?"

"Yeah."

Renna scowled. "Least you waited until Miriam wasn't around. Let's hear it."

I took another sip of the Hibiki. "Zhou's gone to China Rules."

Renna ran his fingers through his hair. "Okay, that doesn't sound good, whatever it is."

"It's as bad as it gets."

"I need more."

"China Rules can be boiled down to a single axiom: 'If you want to live a long life, trust no one or no thing. Not Party, country, friend, or sky.'"

"I'm going to need a translation. Start with the 'sky' bit."

"In China, the sky can fall without warning. Attacks can come from unexpected directions. You hit a trip wire and spoil some VIP's money-making scheme, it falls. In going about your job as usual, if you unknowingly become an obstacle to the ambitions of a powerful businessman, politician, or influential Party member, it falls. Someone in your clique butts heads with a stronger clique and loses, it falls. Or, worst of all, someone within your own circle sells you out. If any of those happen, you end up in a dark cell. Possibly in a place off the books where your relatives or associates or your lawyer will never find you."

"How does that relate to the snake?"

"Zhou's steeped in the paranoia of his trade. On top of that, he has all the headaches of climbing the Party ladder at home, where deception and treachery is a way of life, especially with runaway corruption. *Guanxi*, the traditional mutual system of support, is crumbling in places."

"How so?"

I filled Renna in with short, bold strokes. For centuries the Chinese have relied on guanxi—circles of personal influence among relatives, friends, and business associates. These are carefully nurtured relationships built over time with a balanced give-and-take on both sides to establish trust and loyalty. These networks of contacts act as both springboard and safety net.

Chinese society has been rife with turmoil and uncertainty for hundreds of years. From the early feudal dynasties to the rise of the communists and Mao to today, there have been never-ending waves of warring factions, revolving-door politics, and new regimes that have left the everyman with nowhere to turn, so guanxi circles sprung up. Prudently established bonds allowed people to find others of like mind they could depend on. Those who survived and thrived developed an "extended guanxi family."

The arrow, sword, and musket of the warring years of old have been supplanted by today's battles on the political and business fronts. Corruption influences minds and destinies. The weapons are different but the danger is larger than ever.

"So why is guanxi losing ground?"

"In a word, money. Greed. The new affluence. Loyalty has become a commodity. It can be bought and sold. New money is breaking the old bonds. Not always, but enough of the time. And the large supply of cash is shifting alliances more swiftly than ever before."

"Okay, I get that. But how does that play out in my backyard? We're on the other side of the Pacific, for Christ's sake."

"Chinese money is spreading its influence around the world. Zhou is going to presume it has reached the States and bought some influence in some spheres—until he can see it hasn't. Which is on a case-by-case basis, by the way."

"And today you're the 'case'?"

"Yep."

Renna paused, marbles rolling. "So it's like he's standing on a solid patch of ground in the middle of a quicksand swamp and looking for the next safe place to step?"

"Yeah, just like that. He's got to test every step before he commits."

"So he doesn't trust you even though you've played it straight with him before?"

"Not *doesn't*. Can't. From his point of view, he has no way of knowing if I haven't been corrupted since we last met."

"That's not going to happen."

"You know that and I know that, but in his world he sees quicksand in every direction."

"Which means he's armed and dangerous."

"Fangs at the ready."

"We still need to reel him in."

"I'm working on it."

"Work harder."

Then Kevin the bartender walked over and placed a shallow white porcelain bowl in front of each of us. Something neither Renna nor I had ordered.

We eyed the new offering with suspicion.

CHAPTER 18

I SAID, "What have we here, Kevin?"

"This, gentleman, is a house specialty," our server said with evident pride. "Glazed oysters with Osetra caviar. It's Mr. Zhou's favorite."

We stared into the bowls. Tender oysters swam in a pool of cream sauce laced with dashes of bright green pureed lettuce and beads of zucchini. Islands of black caviar nudged each oyster. Kevin gave a slight bow, said "Enjoy," and departed.

"Well?" I said.

Renna's eyes turned glassy with desire and mistrust. Like those of a man crawling in off a desert might if a bottle of vintage wine were thrust into his hands. Was this unexpected nectar from the heavens going to soothe or, in his distressed, dehydrated state, rip his insides apart?

"Can't pull the 'new glasses' move with this," he said eventually.

"Nope."

"I think we can risk it."

I nodded. "There are worse ways to go."

The dish turned out to be Danko's home-run swing. The oysters were plump and delicate. The caviar provided a potent and contrasting texture. Tying the seafood together was a rich buttery cream sauce lightly accented with a zesty white wine and subtle flavorings.

Had the dish been poisoned, we would have died happy deaths.

"Man, that was good." Renna hauled his bulk out of his seat. "Going to make a pit stop. Back soon."

He lumbered past the cheese bar and disappeared around a corner. A moment later Danko's front door whipped open and a stiff wind brushed the back of my neck. I turned in time to see a thuggish Chinese gangbanger strut up to the reservations desk. His almond-brown face was gaunt but young. His black hair was streaked with tawny highlights, long on top, and cropped to a buzz on the sides. A black leather jacket hung open to reveal a T-shirt decorated with a gang slogan in stylized gold Chinese characters.

The hostess forced a smile. "May I—"

"Sure, bitch. Which one's Brodie?"

"I'm afraid—"

"Screw you, woman. I'll do it myself." He cupped his hands around his mouth. "Brodie, I know you're in here. We need to talk. Catch me outside. But make it quick."

Scanning the crowd, he backed up toward the door. Every diner watched his retreat. His glance alighted on me and a cruel smile crossed his lips. He pointed a gloved finger my way, mouthed "You," then he edged out into the cold and was gone.

I rose and headed for the exit in his wake.

The disturbance brought the manager from the neighboring dining room. "Sir, you do not have to go out there. I can have the police here in five minutes."

"He'll smash your windows in two," I said.

"Do you know the gentleman?"

"Not yet."

"Then I would strongly suggest that—"

I waved him off. "Just have my friend join me as soon as he gets back."

Outside, the gangbanger had zipped up his jacket against the brutal evening bluster. The zip-down in the restaurant had been for show. Now his hands were jammed in his jacket pockets, the bulge at the right fuller.

I said, "What have you got for me?"

"Trouble, white man."

Chilly winds off the bay slapped my face and mussed my hair. This was no fledgling spring breeze. The city had them, just not tonight. Which seemed fitting on the day of Mikey's funeral. His death had stirred things up inside me, and one way or the other I was going to stir things up where they needed to be stirred.

Starting with this Chinese punk in front of me, if I had to.

Two look-alikes in matching black leather lounged on the hood of an old, wide-bodied Lincoln Continental nudging the curb ten feet away. They looked fifteen but were probably nineteen or twenty.

"Make sure your friends keep their distance," I said.

"You behave, won't be a problem."

"What do you have for me?"

"How you know I got anything?"

"I know."

"Maybe I got nothin'."

"Then we're done before we started, which doesn't make sense, does it."

"You're not running this meet, white face."

A sudden gust flicked my hair back.

"Keep pushing, you'll learn different real quick."

With one eye on the bangers, I swept the area and found what I expected a half block down. A helmeted rider sat on a bike partially tucked away behind a corner liquor store. His face was hidden under a dome of hardened black plastic.

"You better get some respect," the banger said.

I wondered if he and his friends were from the Jackson Street Boys, the Wah Ching, or one of the newer gangs. None of the three displayed their gang affiliation. Which showed some smarts.

"He speak to you in English or Chinese?"

"Who?"

"The Mainland guy who sent you."

The skin between his eyebrows bunched. "How'd you know that?"

"I know a lot of things. All you are is a messenger."

A scowl rolled across his lips. "You better watch your tongue."

"That's a two-way street."

"How you know about the Chinese guy?"

I nodded at the biker down the street. The gangbanger looked and the corners of his mouth drooped. He hadn't expected to be under parental supervision.

"They're watching," I said. "Guess you didn't impress them as much as you thought."

"You're gonna be dead, white boy, you sass me again."

When they wanted to sound tough, Chinese hoodlums in town adopted the phrasing of black gangbangers or some mixture thereof. The dusty stylings of old-school Triad gangs out of Mainland China lacked a contemporary flare.

"You don't sound to me like you can speak Chinese," I said.

"I got the hearing. You think you can do better?'

"No."

"That's right, you won't be doin' better. *Ev*-er."

He slathered a truckload of scorn onto the back of his words, but I let it slide. "You called me out here for a reason. Let's hear it."

With a disdainful flourish he pulled out an envelope and waved it at me. It was a brother to the one at the church.

I stuck out my hand and he said, "Cost you two C-notes. Guy said you'd cough it up."

I scoffed at him. "No, he didn't. Everything these guys do is prepaid. You got your fee up front."

"Pay with green or pay with blood."

The fist in his right pocket began to move. The wrist appeared. Then whatever he had bunched in his hand snagged on the corners of the pocket. His hand went into contortions as he tried to wrench the load free.

I caught a glimpse of metal, which is all I needed. I moved in from the opposite side, slamming the heel of my right hand into his chin. His head snapped back. His fist popped loose with a folding knife in tow. I swatted the arm away and the sheathed blade flew from his grasp and skittered away across the pavement with the staccato tap-tap-tap of a dancer on speed.

His backup came off the hood of the Lincoln fast, a pair of switchblades springing open. Shiny steel glittered in the orange light of the Danko signage.

The lead gangbanger rubbed his jaw. "Now you gotta pay. A pair of Cs or we puncture you bad, man."

"Not going to happen," I said.

"Then you're mine, Brodie. There's three of us."

From the shadows of the doorway behind me came a soft two-note whistle that said, *Over here, boys.* Renna had his gun pointed at the young thug's chest.

"You got a cop backing you? Man, what kind of shit is that?"

"At the moment the best kind."

He shrugged, waved off his partners, and held up the envelope again. "Got to be worth a C-note, man."

"You don't want to deliver it," I said, "keep it."

Down the street, the helmeted sentry maintained his surveillance.

"This sucks."

He thrust the envelope at me, shoved his hands in his pockets, and strutted away, his shoulders rocking from side to side. The trio slid into the old Lincoln and peeled away from the curb with attitude.

"Glad you didn't leave the piece in the car this time," I said.

"Wasn't going to happen with the invite we got."

This time there was a note. I extracted it from its envelope, read it, and said to Renna, "You may be the one with the firepower but you've been snubbed anyway."

Extending his thick paw, Renna stepped from the shadows. I passed the message over.

Mr. Pollo on Mission and 24th.
7:45 sitting.
Come alone, without your friend. Don't be late.

Renna said, "A restaurant called Mr. Chicken? What the hell is that?"

"A good restaurant in a sometimes dicey part of town."

I glanced at the time. We had forty-five minutes yet. I rang Karen Stokely, a freelance photojournalist I knew. She answered on the first ring and I said, "You in town?"

"Yes."

"You anywhere near Mission and Twenty-Fourth?"

"Fifteen minutes by car."

"Get over to a place called Mr. Pollo now. It's a restaurant. Snap a photo of everyone going in and out as soon as you arrive."

"Until . . ."

"Eight ought to do it. Be discreet."

"How discreet?"

"The guy doesn't like to be photographed."

"A celeb?"

"A Chinese spy."

"They still have those? Thought everything was cybertheft with them."

"Far from it," I said. "And this guy will bite, Karen. Don't let him see you. He may have a watcher or two hanging around outside. Can you handle that?"

"Been doing it for years. I'll want hazard pay."

"You get what I need, I'll add something on top of the usual fee."

"Is there a story in this?"

"Could be down the line. But the main thing is to stay out of sight. These are not nice people."

"Have you seen the men I've been dating lately?"

We signed off and I strolled back into Gary Danko with my wallet out.

The hostess held out her palms. "Mr. Zhou has already taken care of the bill and the tip."

"Very generous of him."

"He usually is."

"You mind a question?"

"Of course not."

"When did Zhou make the reservation?"

"That would be last night, when he dined with us."

"Originally for one?"

She looked surprised. "Yes, until it became a plus-one a few hours ago."

Cautious, calculating, and five steps ahead.

Trust no one and no thing.

China Rules.

CHAPTER 19

THE MISSION DISTRICT

WE drove to Mr. Pollo in an unmarked SFPD car.

"Cop who knows the beat told me there's one way in and out," Renna said, having just finished up a phone conversation with a buddy back at HQ. "Seen the layout. Deliveries come in through the front door. Doesn't sound like a place your snake would go."

"Your friend's wrong."

"Oh?"

"Zhou would never let himself be boxed in, so there's a back way out of some kind. Maybe just a window, I don't know."

Renna chewed on the comment. "My guy's never seen one but he did say there could be a jerry-rigged exit. He said the storefronts are even along the street but the sides are sometimes pieced together like a jigsaw puzzle because of the way the land was divided in the old days. Streetcar tracks and narrow lanes cut through neighborhoods at odd angles, so some lots were trapezoidal, which gives you odd lots and rooms with diagonal walls. And because rear access was difficult, some basements are connected."

"Meaning Zhou could exit through a neighboring basement if necessary?"

"If he's the type to scout things like that out in advance, yeah."

"So he has all the breathing room he needs."

Renna scanned the rearview mirror for a tail. "It's the kind of warren people can pop out of too. You be careful."

"Always am."

"I'll make myself scarce but won't be far. You still have me on speed dial?"

"Yep."

Renna eased the cruiser to the curb two blocks short of the restaurant. I undid my tie and slipped out of my jacket. I tossed them in the backseat, hopped out, and covered the remaining yardage on foot. Mission Street was alive with pedestrian and vehicular traffic. People were going out for a bite or an after-work drink. A steady stream of weary workers on their way home headed into the Twenty-Fourth Street BART station.

Mr. Pollo occupied a modest storefront three doors down from the southwest corner of Mission and Twenty-Fourth. Dark curtains in the display windows cloaked the interior from view. A quick glance around revealed neither my photographer nor any of Zhou's watchers.

But they were out there.

Mine and his.

I entered, pushed aside another black curtain on the other side of the door, and was confronted with a single wedged-shaped room. Just like Renna's friend had said. It was pleasant and clean and divided on a diagonal by a counter with two stools facing a grill and a chef's workstation. A short glass partition running along the edge of the counter marked the dining area from the kitchen, which was open and part of the experience. Local art, some signage, and a framed movie poster decorated the walls.

"Glad you could make it, Brodie," Zhou called out in English. "I hope my messenger didn't inconvenience you."

The elusive spy was playing with my head. He was camped at one of only four small tables on the dining side of the divider, tucked against a wall, where he could watch the door.

"No problem at all," I said. "Considerate of you to send an escort."

The helmeted biker had followed in our wake, at a distance.

Zhou looked unhappy. "He's a loaner. Sounds like I need to trade him in."

Oops. I'd given my Chinese adversary more information than I should have. Next time his man would be harder to spot.

Zhou waved me to a seat and watched my approach with alert dark-brown eyes. They raked over me, probing, I knew, for any clue about my inner state of mind.

I slid in opposite him. "Some coincidence seeing you at the funeral."

"Not at all. My people know I know you."

The dapper spy had changed into a tan suit fashioned from quality summer linen and paired with a pale-yellow shirt and light-brown tie. Despite his epicurean leanings, he was as slim as a knife blade, and the suit fit him like a sheath. His abundant black hair was neatly parted, and its fullness clashed with his sharp features: narrow eyes, angular nose, and sunken cheeks.

"So you were sent?"

"I don't know what you are talking about."

Here we go, I thought. Zhou came with an operating manual. Tommy Tomita had filled me in:

"First, only when he says no does it mean no. Everything else is up in the air."

"Diplomatic tendencies?"

"Officially, that's what he is, yeah."

"How do you get a yes out of him?"

"He'll say, 'I don't know what you're talking about.' Deniability in case of electronic ears. Everything else will depend on context."

"You do know some characters, Tommy."

"Meeting Zhou is a window onto a world I don't think anyone should ever have to look through," Tommy had told me at the outset. "But if you've got no choice, then step in knowingly. Because it's going to be like nothing you've ever encountered."

He'd been right. But it was too late then, and it was too late now.

CHAPTER 20

ZHOU waved the server over and introduced him in impeccable English. "This is Will McGuire, one of the proprietors. The other is the chef, Jonny Becklund."

On the far side of the counter, Becklund was busily preparing asparagus for a salad, arranging the pieces on four rows of three plates—a full seating at Mr. Pollo, but only one of three nightly sessions.

Hearing his name, Becklund raised his head from the compact yet efficient workstation, nodded in our direction, then returned to the evening's meal. In keeping with the casual, earthy atmosphere of the place, he wore a ball cap backward in place of a chef's hat and was dressed in a clean white T-shirt and an apron with cowboy art. Tattoos ran up his arms and peeked out around his neck. Letters inked across his knuckles spelled *foie gras*.

"There is no printed menu," Zhou said. "They work up a four-course meal every day based on what they find at the local farmer's market."

Will was a tall man with a reddish beard. He wore a black T-shirt with white dropout letters from a saké brewery up in Oregon. Zhou asked after the saké, liked what he heard, and ordered a small carafe for starters. To be followed by a bottle of pricey Napa red. Once again I was about to dine grandly on the People's money.

As soon as Will turned away to procure the saké, Zhou's eyes locked onto mine and without missing a beat he said, "Let's continue in Japanese so we can talk freely, if that's acceptable."

Zhou was a man of many talents. He was smart, devious, and strategic. He spoke at least three languages—English, Chinese, and Japanese. His Japanese was accomplished, subtle, and far too smooth for a non-native speaker. The same could be said for his English. His country had invested heavily in him. He was the wrong kind of million-dollar man.

"I see no problem with that," I said.

"Good. I'm told your lieutenant friend is close."

Before I could rein in my surprise, the shift of my eyes confirmed the spy's suspicion. Renna intended to ditch our tail then circle back, and probably had.

But Zhou was a master. He'd played a hunch, his statement abrupt yet matter-of-fact. The chameleon had sandbagged me, starting with a cordial introduction to the owners, then transitioning into a polite request to switch languages before slipping in a languid observation about Renna's whereabouts and skimming off my reaction before I could raise my guard. I'd forgotten how good he was. I'd have to up my game or Zhou would suck everything out of me and leave me a dry husk, with nothing to show for the encounter. And I needed something—for Mikey and Sharon.

The damage done, I swung into recovery mode. "After I gave him your résumé, he insisted on tagging along."

"'Alone' means alone, Brodie."

Aside from the proprietor-waiter, no one paid us the least attention. The other diners chatted happily over wine or saké or imported beer. Chef Becklund was seasoning the salad. Pots simmered on the stove beside him.

I shrugged. "Ever try to stop a determined policeman?"

Zhou's voice dropped to a lower register. "Many times."

Considering the talent present, the question was badly phrased. I changed tracks. "I did you a favor, coming here."

"You came to satisfy your curiosity and because you need information about your friends' deaths. But the fact is my line of work has prerequisites. You are aware of those."

China Rules again. The attrition rate of Chinese diplomats and spies was high in the People's Republic. Aside from the predictable perils of the spy trade in general, and the type of fall from grace I'd outlined for Renna, infighting on the home front was also fierce. Infamously so. Losers found themselves demoted, discarded, or disposed of in one of several unappetizing ways. They might be arrested. They might be tortured. They might disappear altogether. Sometimes all three.

In short, the quicksand might swallow them whole.

"True," I said. "But we have history and a mutual friend."

"Tommy Tomita is only a start."

"Fair enough. You've taken your precautions, I took mine. How many guys do you have backing you up this trip?"

"That's my business."

I scanned the room. Last time we'd met, aside from the sniper zeroed in on my window seat, there had been Chinese watchers in the restaurant. Mr. Pollo was far too small for embedded confederates. Further, with Renna floating around the edges, Zhou would not risk summoning a shooter. His sentries would be outside, in close proximity. And possibly one or two in the basement passages.

"My police friend's down the street. You behave, we'll have no problem."

Before my host could reply, the first course arrived, shaved asparagus with a lemon vinaigrette and creamy burrata cheese. The first bite released a bouquet of flavors and textures. Tart, creamy, and mellow layered over a tender yet crisp vegetable and a soft, multilayered cheese with a creamy center. After the first bite, I knew the stellar reports I'd heard about Mr. Pollo were no exaggeration. They also claimed the place was a treasured hideaway foodies held extremely close. I could see that too.

Once the waiter drifted away, Zhou's look turned somber. "So the question becomes, have you done anything else to expose me?"

"Don't take this the wrong way, but when I sit down with you, insurance seems a wise move."

"Is that a threat?"

"No."

"Sounds like one to me."

I lifted another serving of asparagus and cheese to my mouth, thinking that paranoia takes many forms. In China, when you wake up to find your neighbor gone, you wonder if he scampered away on his own or was grabbed by the authorities. Was he snatched at his office? Off the street? From his home, at night? You may have no more than a passing acquaintance with the person or persons next door or in the next office, but speculation inevitably starts.

It haunts you.

Is he—or she—being interrogated for something he did, or are the powers that be pumping your neighbor or office mate for information about you? Are you next on the list? The paranoia is endless. It is a way of life. And with China's expansion, overseas territories no longer offered the brief reprieve they once did. Money talked. It bought influence and eyes-on, and China spread funds around—liberally.

"I'm smarter than that."

"It is reassuring to hear you say such a thing, Brodie. I would hate to have to report your death to our mutual friend."

"After our first meeting, taking precautions is a logical move."

Zhou's eyes blazed, his anger unmistakable. He leaned forward, cracked the curtain maybe half an inch, and said, "Precautions like that?"

I peered through the slim opening out onto the darkening street. In the shadowed doorway of a shuttered taqueria across the road, Karen stood in an unnaturally rigid pose. She wore Levi's, a light blue linen shirt, and a utility vest for the odds and ends of her trade. Looking far too much like the photojournalist she was.

I sighed. So much for discreet.

The only inspired touch was tucking her long blond hair under a sapphire-blue panama hat. When I took a closer look, I saw her eyes were skittish with worry. A Chinese man stood behind her, half-hidden in the layered gloom of the shop inlet. One hand hung by his side; the other would have a weapon jammed in her back. Firepower or a blade. Dread crawled up the back of my neck.

"I should advise you," Zhou said, "to stay out of the spy business."

A genius at what he does. I ought to heed my own assessments.

"Like I said, I only wanted insurance. You'll get the memory chip from the camera. Let her go."

"I would also advise you to stay out of the insurance business."

"Let her walk, Zhou."

"It's not a wish I'm willing to grant you just yet."

"Unless?"

"I hear something I like."

CHAPTER 21

THE next course arrived.

"We do an arepa," Will said, setting down a chicken arepa in front of each of us, "as a nod to the original Mr. Pollo, which was a Colombian fast-food place before the tasting menu."

My Chinese host ate with gusto. Juicy chicken laced with cheese and a light tomato sauce was sandwiched between hot grilled bread made of white-corn flour. Highlights of cumin and a cilantro garlic aioli blend added nice accents.

"Let her go," I said, my thoughts on Karen but straying unavoidably to the second course, which proved equally impressive.

Engrossed in the food, Zhou's expression moved from satisfaction to displeasure. "Had you honored my request to come alone, we could have enjoyed our meal in peace and perhaps enlightened each other."

"Uh-huh. What are you doing in San Francisco, Zhou? At Mikey's funeral, of all places?"

Ignoring my questions, he plowed on with his reprimand. "Had you honored my request, your pretty friend would not be my hostage."

The word *hostage* clued me in to how far he was willing to go. Even though Karen stood on a public street, Zhou could do plenty of damage before either Renna or I could reach her. But it turned out I'd underestimated the master spy. He had a far worse scenario in mind.

"You need to release her," I said.

"I don't *need* to do anything."

Stalemate.

"What are you doing in my town, Zhou?"

His glance had shifted upward, to a movie poster of *Big Trouble in Little China*. It looked to be an original.

Zhou's gaze lingered on the Hollywood handbill. "Maybe I'm visiting my people. The city's got one of the best Chinatowns around."

"Try again," I said.

Dark eyes dropped suddenly. "What was the connection between Dillman and Sharon Tanaka?"

I studied him for a moment. "They both designed stage or movie sets."

"Is that all?"

"As far as I know."

"You and Dillman went to school together. You were at the Kennedy Center. The Tanaka woman was at the Kennedy Center. You knew both victims."

"It's not a crime."

"But it's suspicious. What was going on there?"

"What can you tell me about why you're in town?"

We glared at each other. During our first meeting, Zhou had tried to buy me off with a substantial piece of San Francisco real estate if I would finger a longtime Chinese dissident hiding in Tokyo. His government had been hunting the man for decades. I had just met the activist, knew his associates, and could make an educated guess about where he lived, but I didn't bite. So this time Zhou had found stronger leverage.

The eternally paranoid spy pushed his advantage. "You are in no position to dictate terms, Brodie, since you've been kind enough to gift me your friend."

I had slipped up worse than I thought. Zhou had come looking for a more persuasive bargaining chip and I had unwittingly supplied him a game changer.

"You're not going to hurt her."

"Actually, I am seriously considering it. One of the things I dislike most in this world is having my picture taken, so I am not inclined to extend any favors to your photographer friend. Unless you have something of value for me."

"If you touch her I'll—"

We grew silent as the main course, fresh braised lamb and sautéed summer squash, arrived at the table. It smelled wonderful and looked as delicious as its predecessors.

Neither of us touched it.

Since we'd polished off the saké, Will poured us each a glass from a decanting bottle of Napa cabernet. Neither of us touched the wine either.

Once we were alone again, Zhou said, "Do you know how many bones there are in the human hand, Brodie?"

I stiffened but said nothing.

"Between twenty-seven and twenty-nine," he told me. "Curiously, the number varies."

"If you—"

"Do you know which hand Ms. Stokely uses to take her photographs?"

"I'm warning you, Zhou."

He waved a finger at me. "Shame on you. Your friend is left-handed. I have done my homework. I am prepared, while, quite apparently, you are not. So this is how it will go. You will tell me what I want to know or my men will escort Ms. Stokely to a quiet place where they will give her a local anesthetic and pulverize every bone in her left hand. I can assure you we are not without heart. The 'operation' will be quite painless. Not even a whimper will pass Ms. Stokely's lips. This I can promise you."

"I don't believe that for an instant."

Zhou shrugged. "It's true, at least until the medication wears off. By that time we are gone and it is out of our hands, so to speak. The process is extraordinary. It involves a small grape press and a ball-peen hammer. The bones are pressed in stages. Gently. The hand is passed through a large gap in the press, which is set to ever-narrower gaps. A fraction of a millimeter at a time. The bones will be—"

"Zhou, if one hair on her—"

He dismissed my protest. "—pulverized to the granular level in a way that leaves the muscle and veins functional. They, unlike the bones, are elastic. The hammer comes in at the end only if the pressing is uneven. It is a delicate procedure, which my men have nearly perfected. The genius is in the end result. The hand will not need amputation. It will just flop around like a distended water balloon. The skin of the hand acts like a sack for the powdered bone. She will be disfigured, of course. And her career will be over. But she will be alive and an ever-present reminder to you of your trespass."

He set his cell phone on the tabletop. "One call . . ."

I slid my phone across the surface until it nudged his. "One call," I said, "and my cop friend grabs your men."

"He can't get them all."

"I just need one."

He shook his head sadly. "You play badly, my friend. Diplomatic immunity."

"You, yes, but not all your men, I bet."

"You don't know that."

"I'm willing to take the chance."

Zhou's expression gave away nothing.

"But either way," I said, "it doesn't matter whether whoever we catch is eventually released, because your man will be charged with attempted kidnapping. If he lacks immunity, he will go away for a long time. You'll try to hush it up but I'll make sure some of my journalistic connections in the Bay Area have enough ammunition to run a very convincing story. The SFPD will be heroes, having caught the right-hand man to a master spy. Which will lead to another round of stories and most likely an escalation in the news media. In all the stories, your name will be prominent, with the phrase 'alleged spy' attached. Your protégé will become the poster boy for the Chinese menace skulking around on American soil. The scandal will play from Washington to Beijing. Who knows what they might do to you back home? Everything I know about the People's Republic tells me you won't return to a hero's welcome. And we both know it will give your enemies an irresistible window of opportunity. I imagine they will happily absorb your territory. China Rules."

"I take it back. You play well."

I offered no reply.

"Maybe there is more to you than I can see."

"Not along the lines you're thinking."

"Maybe you are an operative for someone after all."

"I'm not. I'm an art dealer."

"So you always claim."

"I happened to have inherited a stake in my father's PI/security firm in Tokyo, and I've picked up some tricks about the family business. That's all. But what I do there is secondary to the art. We've been through this before, Zhou."

His eyes glittered. "An exchange, then?"

"Information and people?" I said.

"Done."

"Your word. My cop friend leaves your people alone. Karen walks away unharmed."

"On the life of our mutual friend."

I consented with a nod. With a temporary truce agreed to, we dug into the lamb with relish. It was superb—succulent and lightly flavored with curry and coconut. The Napa red complemented it to perfection.

After we finished, the dessert arrived, a pastry spilling over with passion fruit and fresh whipped pineapple cream, the filling garnished with toasted macadamia nuts.

We ate and, between bites, exchanged information, all as I wondered how much Zhou valued the life of our mutual friend—or the life of anyone, for that matter.

CHAPTER 22

"I LOST, Daddy," Jenny said, stomping into the apartment.

"Sorry to hear that, kid. Did you do everything the sensei said?"

Renna and I planned to meet at his office in ninety minutes for a wrap-up session, but as I was flying to Japan tomorrow I wanted to squeeze in as much time with my daughter as I could. Guilt always trickled in whenever I had to leave her behind for an overseas job.

Jenny yawned. "Sorta, but everyone's bigger than me, even the girls."

She crawled into my lap, rubbed her face against my chest like she was settling in for the night, and closed her eyes. My seven-year-old had long black hair, quick brown eyes, and a pert nose exactly like her mother had had.

"Hey," I said, "don't doze off on me."

"What am I going to do, Daddy?"

Jenny was in pre-tournament mode, and struggling. My policy consisted of offering encouragement in the form of paternal pep talks but leaving the technical side to her sensei. Clearly this time my daughter needed more.

"We can work on it early tomorrow morning before I head off to Japan. Would you like that?"

She twisted her head around. "Yes, Daddy, yes. I have to beat Donna. I almost did today, but she's bigger and really really mean."

A Tokyo policewoman by the name of Rie Hoshino had inspired Jenny to take up judo. The two met while Rie and I worked a case in Japan's capital involving a Japanese war veteran. The same case brought me Zhou. Fortunately, Rie's entry into my life far outweighed the conniving loose cannon that was Zhou. Rie and I were in the middle of a long-distance romance that was due to pick up again once I hit Japanese shores.

"Then it's settled," I said. "A special coaching session tomorrow morning, early. Now let's get you into your pajamas and your teeth brushed."

She jumped off my lap and landed lightly on her feet, assuming a judo pose. "Okay, but show me one thing first."

I held firm. "Shower, pajamas, and teeth."

"Then one thing?"

In the way that only children can manage, her brown eyes sparkled and seemed to grow larger.

I caved. "Okay, one."

She washed, slipped into her red cotton sleepwear with the plump Japanese cartoon character Totoro scattered all over them, then grabbed her toothbrush and began brushing furiously, baring her teeth in the bathroom mirror.

"Slow down there, Jen," I said. "You'll tear up your gums."

With a mouthful of foam, she shook her head. "The sooner I finish, the more time we have for judo."

Specks of white foam flecked the mirror.

She wrapped up, we trooped into the sitting room, and Jenny showed me several of her starting positions. I corrected each stance. Jenny listened and asked questions. I soon found myself tweaking her throwing technique and demonstrating how she could better leverage her smaller size for the takedown. Before I knew it "one thing" became more. I pretended not to notice, and as the session progressed I felt the guilt over my leaving begin to ease.

Twenty minutes later I said, "We can review everything again tomorrow before I take off for the airport, but now it's upstairs to bed."

"Piggyback!" Jenny began jumping up and down, reaching out for me.

I acquiesced, she clambered onto my back, and I carted her off to her best friend's place one floor above ours. Flinging open the door as we approached, Lisa Meyers said, "Totoro pajamas!"

Jenny slid down from her perch. "Oh, yeah, Daddy, I forgot. Lisa loves Totoro too. Can you bring her back some pajamas like mine?"

Lisa smiled up at me expectantly. She was an Iowa blonde, like her mother, with a sprinkling of freckles across the bridge of her nose.

"Sure," I said.

"You're the best daddy ever," my daughter said, wrapping her arms around my waist and pressing her cheek into my stomach. "Especially when you're here."

The guilt trickled back in.

THE SoMa DISTRICT

San Francisco Homicide was in the Hall of Justice.

The HOJ was a formidable, if dated, ferroconcrete building south of Market Street at Bryant and Seventh Streets. As I'd driven by I'd taken a moment to appreciate the twenty-five-foot bronze jungle gym of a sculpture by the late great Bay Area artist Peter Voulkos gracing one corner of the lot.

Now Renna and I sat facing each other across his battered metal desk, behind his closed office door. Two tumblers had appeared on the desktop.

"No dust on those glasses," I said.

"I keep a clean house."

"That's not what I meant."

Renna's admission arrived with a shrug. "They might see more use than Miriam would like."

After the standoff in the Mission, we wanted a drink to unwind, but neither of us felt like heading to a bar, so we settled for the Jack Daniel's stashed in his bottom drawer. Which showed up next.

"These lips are sealed. Looks like a new bottle."

"We can probably remedy that."

"When duty calls."

He poured, we drank, Renna dispensed refills. In the outer office, a large Irish flag reigned benignly, while we batted around ideas, sorting threads and trying to match ends. Most of them didn't line up.

"Full-body armor," Renna said eventually.

"What?"

"Forget it. Just thinking out loud. Glad the woman photographer got away unharmed."

"It was close."

"Zhou is a vindictive prick. How much is the damaged camera equipment going to set you back?"

"Five thou."

Renna shot me a sympathic look. My Chinese adversary had kept his word about releasing Karen but slipped in a costly slap-down so I wouldn't think him a pushover.

"Expense it to your client."

"FLOTUS?"

"Yeah."

"Only if Sharon turns out to be the focus of all of this."

"Doubt this came from Mikey's end."

In some ways San Francisco's a small town. Renna had attended high school with Ian and Mikey but only knew them in passing.

"I don't know," I said. "He had his secrets, and Zhou grilled me about him."

Secrets I'd sensed over the years but knew nothing about. Shy soul that he was, Mikey kept his own counsel. He'd been an usher at my wedding. On the day of the ceremony, he'd stood proudly in the groom's party. His ruddy Irish-American face had beamed at me throughout the festivities. Later that night, after too much champagne, Mikey had embraced me. "This is one of the best days of my life, Brodie."

"That's supposed to be my line," I said.

He gave me a sloppy, inebriated grin. "To see you so happy makes me happier than you could know."

And his expression backed up every syllable of his drunken proclamation—until a phone call later in the evening sent him rushing out the door with the deepest of apologies.

Mikey had had his secrets.

I downed the rest of my whisky. Renna tipped in some more of the amber liquid, then asked, "You think Mikey was hiding something? My boys haven't found anything."

"I know he was. Just don't know what. Wasn't my business back then."

"Think it got him killed?"

"Might have. If it did, I plan to put it straight."

Renna nodded, his SFPD face securely in place. "I'll look into it. There are other avenues. What about Zhou?"

"What do you mean?"

Renna scowled. "I don't like Asian bullyboys messing up my town. I don't answer this, who knows what he and his buddies will try next. You mind?"

"No. Save me the trouble. If you can find them."

"I set up a tag team while you were being wined and dined. My boys trailed them back to the Chinese consulate."

"You get photos?"

"Of the pair outside, yes. Zhou, no. His boys pulled up curbside at Mr. Pollo's and Zhou slipped into the car, chin to his chest and wearing one of those ugly floppy hats seniors hide under to ward off the sun. There was no shutter chance. My men got a license plate, though. I move on him, you want your name on it?"

"No need. He'll assume."

Renna nodded, his eyes drifting toward the ceiling. The silence lengthened, and I thought once more about how close I'd come to getting one of my friends crippled for life. I'd drawn Karen into the game I'd inherited from my father. I stepped consciously into the world of Brodie Security. It was my skin on the line and I could watch out for myself. But this time I'd put Karen in harm's way. She'd worked war zones, so I figured she could handle herself, but she'd been a mouse before Zhou's snake.

Renna's gaze drifted back down, an inquisitive gleam in his eye. "Isn't all this above your pay grade?"

"What do you mean?"

"Spooksville."

I inhaled deeply. "You have a point."

"You told me about the shooting in DC, the first lady's interest, and Homeland Security. Am I missing anything?"

"No."

"Think Zhou's appearance has something to do with White House involvement?"

"I don't know. But he's a big gun."

"Do you have any idea as to why he's here?"

"Not a clue. Even after his story."

Marbles rolled. Renna's cheeks inflated in turn. "Then you're missing something."

"Can you do better?"

"As a matter of fact, I can. But you won't like it."

CHAPTER 23

THIRTY minutes into our session, we'd made admirable progress with the Jack Daniel's but little headway elsewhere.

After Zhou and I had come to an uneasy agreement, the spy across the table asked about Mikey and Sharon. I gave him everything I had, except FLOTUS, and he divulged some scraps of his own.

According to the master spy, Sharon Tanaka had been hired to design theater sets for a Chinese-Japanese coproduction scheduled to debut in Beijing in three months. A niece of the Chinese president played one of the leads. After Sharon's death, Zhou's boss dispatched him to determine if the Kabuki killings could be a threat to the niece or the president. Zhou had been selected because of the Japanese aspect of the inquiry—Sayuri "Sharon" Tanaka and me.

"Is there another connection between the Chinese play and the Kabuki in DC?" I'd asked.

"No. Only Sharon Tanaka."

"So how is this a threat to the president?"

"It's too close to home."

It turned out that once the Beijing run wrapped up, the show would tour Asia and Europe. The president's daughter and his niece were more like sisters than cousins, and if the niece were kidnapped, she could be used as leverage to get to the president. Low-level leverage, admittedly, but leverage nonetheless. With high-profile kidnappings on the rise worldwide, the precaution made sense, especially considering the level of paranoia that percolated around the edges of the People's Party.

Though we skirted any discussion of what Zhou would do if he uncovered a connection, it was clear he'd been assigned the task of eliminating any potential threat beforehand. He would be judge, jury, and executioner.

"You believe him?" Renna asked once I finished my detailed recital.

"Could be true or a lie."

"So check it out. You're the Asian pro."

"Oh, I will, but I already know what I'll find. The basics will be true. The niece will be in the play. Sharon Tanaka will have done the set design. But there's a lot of wiggle room between the facts, so who knows? It's China."

"Well, stay sharp. I'm not the one with a one-way ticket to Spooksville."

"One way?"

He webbed his fingers over a taut stomach. "Yeah. If we take the worst case and figure Zhou is lying, we're left with a big old hairy why. As in, why does a slick high-level spook show up here after two people at the Kennedy Center end up dead? Which leads to a second question: Did the China connection bring out Homeland, or did Homeland's involvement draw the Chinese?"

"Or did whatever's behind the curtain attract them both?"

Renna reached for his drink. "All questions of the hour."

We each sipped some more Jack and silently sorted through the new bundle of threads for a while.

Finally, Renna threw up his hands. "This thing's too messy. Too many parties. Plus with Homeland and Zhou involved, it's got a pair of wild cards right out of the gate. Give me a good old double murder without complications anytime."

He downed the rest of his drink, poured another inch into both glasses, and said, "Well, at least this Swelley character didn't show up today."

I shook my head. "He was at Saint Mary's."

"You're yanking me, right?"

"Well, not him personally. A proxy. One of the men who braced me in DC was in a back pew. Watched us chase after Zhou."

"He try to hide?"

"No. Gave me a smirk and a two-finger salute."

Renna's eyebrows rose. "He wasn't surprised about Zhou?"

"Didn't look it."

"And he's from Homeland?"

"Far as I know."

"So we have the Kennedy Center play and another one in Beijing. We have Mikey and Sharon Tanaka dead. We have a Chinese spy on a job for the Chinese president. And as an added bonus we have Homeland prowling around the edges, watching and waiting and maybe readying to pounce."

"I'd say that sums it up about right."

"And the spy is so paranoid, he's rolled out a no-trust, no-holds-barred thing called China Rules. Any of that tell you anything?"

"Nothing." I rubbed my eyes. "How about you? You did say you had something."

Renna's nod was grave. "What I have is full-body armor. That's what you'll be needing on this one if you're looking to get a round-trip ticket back to these shores and your daughter."

CHAPTER 24

**DAY 4, WEDNESDAY, EARLY AFTERNOON
NARITA AIRPORT, NEAR TOKYO**

AN unexpected welcoming committee greeted me at Narita Airport seconds after the plane hit the tarmac and began the long slog to the gate. A petite ANA flight attendant approached and asked me to accompany her to the front of the plane.

"We need to deboard you immediately, Mr. Brodie."

A chill crawled up the back of my neck.

"What's this is about?" I asked, snatching my duffel bag from the overhead bin and following in her wake.

"The pilot received a request via the control tower."

"So it's an official summons?"

"It appears so."

"Immigration services? Security police?"

She glanced back. "No information was supplied, but on the rare occasion when this happens, it is usually one of those."

Both of which I took seriously. Together they monitored arrivals into Japan. Immigration ran passport inspection. They fingerprinted and photographed visitors and certified entry. They could also revoke visas or shove passengers right back onto an outward-bound plane. The security police stood right behind them.

Had Homeland or Swelley poisoned the well, or was this another's doing?

My friends were legion in Japan, but after taking up the position left me by my father at Brodie Security I'd made enemies—some in the underworld, others in positions of power in the ministries and political sphere. Occasionally, rumors of ill will reached Brodie Security. If the Immigration authorities rescinded my right to entry, my shop in San Francisco would suffer. Perhaps fatally.

But the stakes were much higher than losing access to Japanese art and antiques. Barred from Japan, I would lose a part of myself. The country was a touchstone. It was vital in ways I couldn't always explain but felt to my core. As an American born of Caucasian American parents who'd been serving in Japan at the time, I'd spent the first seventeen years of my life in Tokyo. I attended neighborhood schools, which was how I absorbed the language and the culture and made so many friends. I was American by nationality and inclination, but the country and its people had seeped into my life's blood. The place was something of a second home, the people like an extended family. To be denied access would be devastating.

As the aircraft eased to a stop, I braced myself. I stood in front of the cabin door with the flight attendant at my side. She gave me a faint smile.

We heard the weighty rumblings of the jetway being slotted into place. We heard scuffling. I queried my guide with a glance and she mumbled something about additional security measures. Inwardly, I cringed. After a long wait, she received the go-ahead signal and unsealed the hatch. Teeth gritted, I followed her out the door.

"Mr. Brodie?" asked a young American in an expensive-looking gray suit and a red power tie. "My name is Gerald Thornton-Cummings."

He possessed clear, untroubled blue eyes under blond hair and a confident handshake. His bearing suggested privilege. *Diplomatic corps, fast-track,* I thought. *From a well-connected family.*

"American embassy?" I asked.

He blinked, his lips growing momentarily slack. "Yes, a junior attaché. How did you know?"

"Lucky guess. Has something happened?"

He treated me to an indulgent smile. "I am here merely to expedite the matter at hand."

"Which is?"

"I am not at liberty to say. Would you be so kind as to come this way?"

Behind him stood a pair of security police.

"Do I have a choice?"

His indulgence redoubled. "I want to say yes because, technically, you have rights, but in reality your choices are limited."

I trailed after him, the security police swinging in behind me. We moved briskly off the end of the jetway, into the terminal, then down a long glass-walled passage.

Thornton-Cummings stopped at a door marked PRIVATE. "This is the back way out."

"Because?"

His expression turned enigmatic. We entered a brightly lit room with thin office carpet the color of limpid seawater. A pair of booths identical to those at Passport Control stood against the far wall, with a stone-faced official ensconced in each.

I understood in an instant. This was a VIP immigration portal. For movie stars, royalty, and others who shared the spotlight. Which meant this was *not* a Tom Swelley move. Was this the first lady reaching out?

"May I have your passport?" my escort said, sticking out a pink, fleshy palm.

I passed over the blue booklet and he tendered it to one of the officials, who dutifully flipped through the pages, compared my portrait to the actual item, and stamped an unmarked page before returning the document to me.

I stood still for a digital snapshot and a fingerprint scan, then Thornton-Cummings showed me into an adjoining room. Inside, a sharp-nosed American woman in a white blouse and a knee-length navy skirt whispered into a satellite cell phone with a row of blinking green lights running down its side. She relinquished the device to my escort.

State-of-the-art mobile . . . green security lights . . . yep, FLOTUS.

I heard a click. Thornton-Cummings said, "Six-two-G-X-seven out of Narita, Japan." More clicks. Then: "He's beside me now. Yes, of course."

The fresh-faced diplomat handed me the phone.

In my ear a distant click signaled a new party arriving on the line. I jumped right in.

"Hello, Madam First Lady?"

"Guess again, Jim."

My heart did a stutter step. "Mr. President."

"Joe," he said.

CHAPTER 25

"YOU have to start calling me Joe," the president said. "Sorry to drag you off the plane, but it is getting late here."

Three p.m. in Tokyo meant two in the morning in the American capital.

"'Getting'?" I said.

"What they don't tell you about this job is that you put in a lot of overtime."

I laughed. "I'll bet. Is everything okay on your end?"

"No, and that's why I'm calling. I'm afraid Joan won't be attending Sharon's funeral after all."

A minor illness would not stop the first lady. Nor a minor obstacle. The woman I had met in the East Wing was the kind of person who would muscle through lesser impediments.

So what had derailed her plans?

The White House played on a loftier field than Brodie Security, but trouble followed patterns. It was repetitious and predictable. Like waves breaking on a shoreline, only the height and intensity varied.

I could come up with three reasons the first lady might miss her friend's funeral: a major illness, a schedule conflict, or a security issue, the last of which could range from an unsafe travel warning to terrorist activity in the region to a death threat.

"Sorry to hear that. Security issue?"

The president paused. "Was that a lucky guess, or have you uncovered something?"

"I chose the most likely scenario, that's all. Is there any more you can tell me? New information might be helpful."

"I received an advisory saying travel for Joan was ill-advised at this time."

"Because?"

" 'There is movement among foreign entities in Japan.' "

Aside from Thornton-Cummings, *everything* from here on in was likely to be a foreign entity.

"Sounds awful vague."

"Welcome to the big leagues, Jim."

"Could it be a move to keep your wife away from the situation here, sir?"

"Joe."

"Joe."

"Yes, the possibility occurred to me, but I can't take the chance. Not much help, is it?"

"No."

"Speaking of less than helpful," Joe Slater said, "how have you and Swelley been getting along?"

"Haven't."

My answer elicited a sigh. From the president of the United States.

I covered the receiver and asked my two minders to give me a moment. With undisguised disappointment, they trudged from the room. Once alone, I filled in the president on my encounter with Swelley and his men on the National Mall.

"Regrettable but not unexpected," he said. "Tom's always been aggressive. I'll have my chief of staff call Homeland. With some tigers, I want to rip off their stripes. But let's not poke the cat just yet. If Swelley gives you any trouble you can't handle, let me know."

"I can push back as well as the next guy. May even see what I can do about those stripes."

"You have my blessing."

"Do you happen to know where Swelley is at the moment?"

"He's managing our Japanese resources."

I felt the blood drain from my face. "Tell me you're joking."

"No. Homeland put him in the driver's seat over there. That's why I'm calling instead of Joan."

Damn. Swelley was no longer a cog in the machine. He *was* the machine.

The tiger had grown sharper claws.

CHAPTER 26

SHIBUYA, CENTRAL TOKYO

WHEN I pushed through the doors of Brodie Security an hour and twenty minutes later, an unexpected hail of hellos greeted me. All of the women crowded around, jostling for position. A couple of the younger men stood among them. The rest of the staff looked on, some in amusement, some with aversion.

"What's going on?" I asked.

"It's totally awesome," said Mari Kawasaki, the office tech whiz and my right hand when I came to Tokyo.

"What's awesome?"

Mari grinned at me. She wore a black pants-skirt and a peach-colored blouse with images of Raggedy Ann and Andy as vampires. Ruby-red hair extensions threading through her jet-black locks played off the peach color. Mari's genius with computers and her links to Japan's youth counterculture earned her license to dress as she pleased.

"You're like pretending, right? We all want her autograph. She's wonderful."

The reason for the unforeseen flurry became apparent. " 'She' being Joan Slater?"

"Yes, of course."

"What happened to client confidentiality?"

Information on a case normally didn't extend beyond those running it, and maybe one or two support staff. At least initially.

"We haven't told anyone," Mari said, unfazed. "The first lady's *so* cool. Glamorous and dignified and her own person. She's not hanging around the White House to, like, just boost her husband's image. You *have* to get us her autograph."

A dozen eager faces gazed at me in expectation.

"How about a trade? If everyone promises to keep the secret, I'll ask her when the case is over. If it leaks, no deal."

Everyone agreed without hesitation, then returned to their seats, satisfied.

I turned to Mari. "Is Noda around?"

Kunio Noda was Brodie Security's head detective. He was a compact bundle of power: barrel chest, thick waist, and a broad, flat face with shrewd eyes on an unstoppable five-foot-seven-inch frame. He was also brusque, ill-mannered, and the best investigator in the outfit. A fact that had brought him his share of run-ins, the most famous of which left him with a scar buried in a severed eyebrow that flared when his anger surged.

"He's out on an embezzlement case in Otemachi." The financial district.

I nodded. "Could you leave him a note about not missing the Tanaka funeral tomorrow, just in case?"

"Sure," Mari said.

I shut myself in my office, dropped my duffel bag in a corner, slipped behind the desk that once belonged to my father, and pondered the appeal of Joan Slater's star power. What the gathering out front demonstrated was that celebrity attracted notice from unexpected directions.

What other unwanted attention would White House involvement bring?

———

It was nearly four in the afternoon in Tokyo, which made it close to midnight in San Francisco, but I still rang my daughter. Kerry Lou picked up on the first ring.

"Hi," I said. "What are the girls up to?"

"Celebrating that I let them stay up for your call. They're watching a Disney double feature."

"So Jenny's judo went well?"

"She's right here, yanking on my arm, as usual. Always an ear peeled for the phone, this one. Here she is."

Panting into the receiver, Jenny told me she'd won her matches and her age group. "I beat Donna too. What you said worked, Daddy."

"That's great, Jen. Did you get a new belt?"

"Yep-yep. A big shiny trophy too."

"Wonderful."

As promised, I'd practiced with her again the next morning, reviewing the throwing and takedown techniques of the previous evening. Then I showed her how to up the wattage on her pre-fight stare for a psychological edge.

Jenny said, "Tell Rie, okay? You are going to see her, aren't you?"

"Definitely."

"Say it first thing, before you do the other stuff."

" 'Other stuff '?"

"*You* know."

I did. But what did Jenny know?

I tried to probe a little deeper, but my daughter begged off, eager to return to the Disney flick. Once we signed off, I leaned back in my chair and wondered what my seven-year-old could possibly know, and how. The guilt burrowed deeper. As a father, I should know. If I were absent less often, I *would* know. I'd promised myself to limit the time the detective work kept me from Jenny, but to date I'd been only partially successful in keeping the promise.

Getting nowhere with that line of speculation, I rang Renna, who had left a message to call anytime before one.

"I found it," my SFPD friend said.

"Found what?"

"Mikey's secret. You're not going to believe it. I'm holding it in my hand and *I* still don't. Officially *sealed* records."

That didn't sound good. "Sealed why?"

"Mikey's got a sheet."

"Our modest, mild-mannered, shier-than-shy, salt-of-the-earth friend? I'm not buying it."

"Yeah, well, he was underage, but technically he does."

Turned out, back in high school, Mikey and his friend Billy Cantor had caught a ride home with a guy called Jared Trooger. Trooger looked older than his eighteen years and always bragged about scoring some cold ones whenever he wanted, even though the drinking age in California was twenty-one. Did they want in? They were fifteen and said sure, why not? It was Friday afternoon.

Trooger drove to a 7-Eleven over on Clement Street. They waited in the car a half a block away while Trooger went for the suds. The clerk carded him, so Trooger shot the guy and grabbed the beer, two bags of Lay's potato chips, and a handful of bills from the register. All of which was caught on camera.

The police nailed Trooger the following day, and Mikey and Billy the day after. The high schoolers had no idea Trooger had killed the clerk and robbed the place, but he fingered them as accomplices. He was tried as an adult and received fifteen years. The two kids spent five months in juvie and were on juvie parole until their eighteenth birthdays.

I was incredulous. "You went to school with Mikey and his brother and never heard about this?"

"The department was pretty careful about minors even in those days, and there was no gossip at school. But I remember both brothers going away to the East Coast for a semester and staying with relatives."

"That would be it," I said.

Mari tapped on my door, stuck her head in, and signaled that Noda, the head detective, was on another line. I held up a pair of fingers. *There in two.*

Renna said, "I talked to a couple of old-timers and they told me the assistant DA saw an easy way to boost his win count."

"I don't even know where to start with that. 'Despicable' would be too polite. Did you know Billy Cantor?"

"Yeah. He went off the rails. Spent a lot of time on the couches of a lot of different shrinks. Mikey just got quieter."

I hated to hear this sort of stuff. Their lives were upended due to the raw stupidity of the likes of Jared Trooger.

Through gritted teeth, I said, "Was Trooger still locked up when Mikey was shot?"

"Released six months ago on good behavior."

"Whoa. That's a coincidence I don't like."

"I'm already on it."

"Better you than me. I get my hands on the guy, he won't be standing for long."

Once I hung up, Mari patched through Noda.

As I reached for the phone, my eyes fell on a portrait of my daughter. Luminous liquid-brown eyes beamed at the camera with uninhibited trust and love. Mikey and Billy Cantor would have had exhibited some of the same trust and naiveté as they waited for the walking, talking disaster-waiting-to-happen that was Trooger to come back with a six-pack.

Into the phone I said, "Thanks for checking in. Going to see you this afternoon?"

The bulldog detective was my go-to guy for any complex case. He was also less talkative than a tree stump.

"Not till the funeral."

"So you have something?"

Noda never made social calls. He kept to himself and barely managed polite, Japanese though he was. Prying loose more than a truncated version of any event from the head detective was always trying. To normal Japanese, he was an impertinent mutt. But he was loyal and got the job done.

"Bad news. Old PSIA friend called."

An unseen hand wrapped itself around my heart and squeezed. Spooksville again. PSIA stood for the Public Security Intelligence Agency. It handled counterespionage activities on Japanese soil and any threats against the country's security. A sort of hybrid of the FBI and CIA with inward-looking tendencies, it has ties to major intelligence agencies around the world.

"Your friend offering to help?"

"Told me to back off."

"The Kennedy Center case?"

"Yeah."

"You happen to mention that I knew both victims personally?"

"He already knew. Made it worse."

I bit my lip. "Because?"

"*Because* you're the only one who knew both victims."

Homeland, Zhou, and now the PSIA. "They were my friends."

Noda snorted. "He didn't see it that way."

"How did he see it?"

"One coincidence too many."

"Where'd they get their intel?"

"Homeland."

I opened my mouth to speak, then closed it. I knew hopeless when I heard it. But far worse was the bald truth behind Noda's words: the PSIA and Swelley had opened a line of communication.

How long would it be before one or both of them came for me?

CHAPTER 27

I RODE the elevator down from Brodie Security's fifth-floor office to street level. During my last visit to Tokyo, I'd bedded down in a local hotel. Tonight's lodging would be different. It had once been my childhood home.

Where I'd spent the first seventeen years of my life.

Where I'd also left every weekday morning for the local Japanese school my parents insisted I attend. Where I'd been the only Caucasian. Where I'd learned to appreciate Japan. It had all just clicked with me.

Despite living in the middle of the Japanese capital, my parents had found a balance between East and West. Tucked away in the warm confines of our small Tokyo home, I was in America. We spoke English. We watched satellite TV. My mother served American-style food.

I glanced around for a taxi, a cool May breeze brushing my face, balmy and carrying the promise of an early summer. Tokyo has more cabs than the central fish market has shellfish, but none trolled the backstreets tonight or cruised the main avenue, so I decided to hoof it, an excursion I once made four or five times a week.

From the age of thirteen, after school let out, I would head down the main avenue to Brodie Security, where I'd hang out. My father put me to work, sorting through office minutiae. But the real training came from being a teenage fly on the wall, soaking up the detectives' discussions about their cases, which ran from blackmail, corporate malfeasance, and kidnapping to con games and murder.

The conversations were gritty and complex and pockmarked by life. I mingled freely with the detectives, who, with my father's blessing, took me under their collective wing and out on cases.

And all of that clicked for me too.

Then one day my mother invited me into the bowels of the Tokyo National Museum, where she was consulting on an upcoming exhibition. She showed me centuries-old screens with glittering gold-leaf backgrounds. She showed me Zen ink paintings by famous Buddhist monks, then swords and ceramics and the robes of princes and shoguns of old that echoed the dramatic flourishes of the Kabuki robes the Freer Gallery in Washington sought. A third click.

Which is how it happens for all of us, I don't care who you are. A farmer or a factory worker or a tech junkie or a dentist. In our lives, we find one or more things that click for us. And when they do, we should pay attention.

Which is what I did instinctively back then.

As easily as I devoured the rough-and-scrabble work of my father's world, I took in the muted elegance of my mother's. I was young and fascinated and I absorbed it all like a sponge.

Then upheaval shook my world.

My parent's marriage crumbled and divorce followed. My mother and I landed in an affordable but dicey area on the edge of South Central Los Angeles; we both worked to make ends meet; I learned to hold my own on the street; my mother struggled to find a curator's job while holding down a minimum-wage position as a drugstore cashier; I graduated high school, then enrolled in college; a couple of years later my mother died suddenly of intestinal cancer; I deserted Los Angeles for San Francisco, a city that had always beckoned.

Then, for a short spell, the roller-coaster ride ran straight and even.

At twenty-one, I rented a walk-up in the Mission, yet another dubious neighborhood. I found a job at a local garage as a grease monkey, since, for some reason, tinkering under the hood of a car came naturally. One day, looking for something to hang on my wall, I wandered into an antiques shop and sifted through a stack of neglected Japanese woodblock prints tossed on top of a dusty nineteenth-century American dresser.

I carried my choice up to the front to pay. Instead of taking my money, the owner grilled me about my upbringing. When I started to protest, he offered to *give* me the woodblock print—if I'd answer a few questions. I agreed. He soon nosed out my exposure to art in Tokyo under my mother's tutelage. Next he pointed to a trio of European vases across the room and asked me to pick out the best piece. Without hesitation, I chose the one that danced before my eyes. On the spot, he offered me a job as his apprentice. Why? Because aside from selecting the correct vase, I'd brought him the best Japanese print from the stack.

I embraced the chance to get the grease out from under my fingernails. I also enrolled at SF State, where I polished my art chops and met Mikey. By then I was twenty-two, three years older than him—and became his big brother away from home.

Later, Mieko, a Japanese woman whom I'd helped out in Los Angeles several years earlier, tracked me down in San Francisco to express her condolences over my mother. We got to talking, dating, and soon after I turned twenty-five we were married. Jenny was born some fifteen months later, and I opened my own antiques shop out on the long stretch of Lombard in the Marina District.

A few more good years followed, then the roller coaster plunged down again. I became a widower, with a child, after Mieko died in a midnight fire in her parents' home. Three years later, my father was killed in a car accident in Tokyo and I came into half of Brodie Security—and what my mother labeled "the other life; the dangerous one."

I'd never expected to set foot in Brodie Security again, but when I did I found that some of the people of my teen years still worked there. I bowed to their request to continue as the American head to what they called "my father's legacy."

The legacy ran on a shoestring. Once expenses and salaries were met, what remained gave me little more than a stipend most times, but combined with the up-and-down income from my art endeavors, I paid the rent on my apartment and shop in San Francisco, put food on the table, and during a good month stashed away a few bucks in Jenny's college fund.

Adding a further twist, my father had attached the deed to our old family home to Brodie Security, so in theory I'd inherited half of it with my half of the company.

My father had prepared well.

But, at times, preparation alone is insufficient. I had the uneasy premonition that Mikey's and Sharon's deaths would be one of those times. Especially with Homeland Security, a Chinese spy, and the PSIA lurking at the edges.

And as if in confirmation, I unlocked the door to my old family home—and sensed in the next instant that I was not alone.

CHAPTER 28

SLIPPED inside, ignoring the light switch.

Another pace and I stepped out of my shoes and up onto the raised floor, also disregarding a set of indoor slippers. As with every house in the land, street grime intruded no farther than the entryway. None of the dust or soil on the roadways would be tracked over carpet, wooden floors, or linoleum. As long as it didn't cost me, I did not have to bypass the finer points. Without a sound, I unburdened myself of my duffel bag. I was doubtful I'd entered without alerting the intruder. I had only a single advantage. He was unaware I knew of his presence.

I turned left into the main body of the house, which was dark and still.

Too still.

My body tensed.

Nerve endings buzzed.

My South Central warning system kicked up a notch. I could feel the intruder's presence. As I often did when a hostile third party was in the vicinity. Six years in dangerous neighborhoods gave you skills.

The shadows near the kitchen doorway shifted. My night vision was good but the interior darkness was complete, ambient light nonexistent. Still, the vague outline of a human form took shape before me. The intruder was short. Clothes tight against the body. The left hand rose. Empty. Without weapon. *But rising.* I was on the point of launching an attack when the uninvited intruder spoke.

"Trick or treat."

A woman's voice. Soft, gentle, bemused. And one I recognized.

A light flickered on.

Rie Hoshino stood before me in her Tokyo Metropolitan Police uniform. Navy-blue jacket and pants, sky-blue blouse, thin navy tie. Each item was crisp and creased and as fresh as the first time I'd laid eyes on her in the outfit. The brass buttons running down the middle of the jacket picked up the soft light.

"It's May," I said.

Without a word, she raised an eyebrow over mesmerizing cocoa-brown eyes, spread her arms, and twirled around once in a complete three-sixty. Her pinkish beige skin glowed.

"Treat," I said. "Definitely treat."

Smiling, she stepped forward to meet me. "Wise choice."

"Maybe we should make preemptive celebrations a habit." I wrapped my arms around her waist and pulled her close. "How'd you find me? More to the point, how'd you get in here?"

"Do I need to remind you yet again that I am a third-generation cop?"

"I've heard rumors the talent runs in the family, but proof has been lacking."

"I just put you off your question with a question."

"Touché."

She pressed in closer, raised her head, and our lips touched. Beneath the uniform her body was warm and pliant. The kiss was long and lingering, then passionate and heated.

It was our first kiss in three months and worth the wait.

Our embrace soon escalated to a higher plane. Wrinkles were introduced into Rie's perfectly pressed uniform, but she voiced no complaints.

———

Later, in an upstairs bedroom, we sat back against the headboard.

From the first floor, Rie had brought a bottle of champagne and two tall crystal glasses. We now sipped the sparkling beverage with considerable contentment. The bedsheet was pulled over her breasts and tucked in at the sides. A faint smile played on her lips.

"What are we celebrating besides the early arrival of Halloween?" I asked, wondering if I'd missed a key date. A three-month marker? A six-month one?

We had met less than a year ago, but—as in most relationships where the parties lived in distant places—the timeline was convoluted. Three months separated our first date in the quaint Japanese beachside town of Kamakura from our next, at an upscale Tokyo *izakaya*, a kind of Japanese gastro pub. The second get-together ended abruptly when I was forced to rush off to Kyoto after a client's son went AWOL. We almost did not survive the third date at a *fugu* restaurant, the poisonous blowfish being only one of several hazards that night.

Interruptions were the norm for us, so anniversary calculations were subjective at best. Serious computations would be speculative, algebraic, complex. For the romantically inclined, possibilities existed, I supposed. On the other hand, I was dating a soft-on-the-outside, tough-on-the-inside Japanese policewoman. Or was that the other way around?

"Just us," Rie said. "It is a miracle we have made it this far."

An unexpected answer. And touching. "I could drink to that."

"You had better."

Maybe tough all around.

We drank. Twice. Which led to an encore engagement. After which Rie refilled our glasses, saying, "I know you would much rather have a beer, whisky, or saké than anything bubbly."

"True."

"But I think it is sweet you are willing to suffer for me."

"I've been through worse," I said, and when she smiled added, "but not by much."

The remark earned me a poke in the ribs before she took another sip from her fluted glass.

We were in the master bedroom. Mercifully, the staff at Brodie Security had hauled away the old furniture and changed the color scheme. Over fading beige tones, they lathered on a fresh coat of mint-green paint, unfurled a pearl-white carpet, and installed a new dark-wood bedroom set in a masculine mode. Any lingering ghosts floated off to more familiar quarters.

Even with the face-lift, the place still felt like my old home. Upstairs, the two bedrooms, storage area, and half bath received touch-ups or complete makeovers. Downstairs, the two-story Tokyo cottage retained its original charm. The old refrigerator and other dated appliances were swapped out for newer models, but the sitting room, my father's fully stocked wet bar, and the traditional Japanese woven-tatami-mat room remained untouched.

Although Jenny's "other stuff" had slipped in ahead of schedule, I did my duty and reported on my daughter's martial arts accomplishments. Rie was delighted, and gave me a special message to pass on. Then she turned serious.

"How's the case coming?"

"It isn't," I said, "aside from an unsettling sit-down with Zhou."

She didn't know any more than she'd read in the papers, so I filled her in, after which she said, "You chased him through the church?"

"Yes."

Her brown eyes grew still. "And the threat to cripple your friend, do you think he was serious?"

"Without a doubt."

She shuddered. "Homeland Security *and* a Chinese spy. This is a horrible case."

I added Noda's warning about the PSIA.

Rie closed her eyes and a darkness crept into her manner. "Brodie, this is bad. Hand the job over to someone else in your office, please. Someone who has experience dealing with *those* kinds of people."

"This is about Mikey and Sharon, so that's not going to happen."

She blinked and her tone softened. "I'm sorry for your loss. I never met him."

"If you had, you would understand."

"I understand now. He was a dear friend. But this is very dangerous. I worry about you."

"Maybe you can help. Do you know anyone over at the PSIA? I could use an in."

She looked down, hesitating. "I do, yes. The son of my father's best friend. But he . . . those kind . . . are best avoided unless really needed."

Again the darkness intruded.

I wrapped an arm around her shoulder and pulled her to me. "I can do without more spies for now. Besides, PSIA's reputation for secrecy precedes it. If you told me more, you'd probably have to kill me."

Her expression brightened at the thought. "Actually, I believe we've *already* crossed that line. Say good-bye."

She pounced with a giggle, pinning me to the sheets with a move suspiciously reminiscent of a modified judo hold. The crystal in my hand went flying and shattered against the wall.

Neither of us paid the broken glassware the least attention, but when I stole a glimpse, above her closed eyes her forehead was knotted with the wrong kind of tension.

CHAPTER 29

BACK-TO-BACK funerals were no one's idea of a good time, but I trundled over to the Buddhist temple where Sharon Tanaka's send-off was scheduled.

I had trouble wrapping my mind around the idea of a world without her. We'd met at a Tokyo exhibition for Shiro Tsujimura, a Japanese ceramic artist whose pieces I showed in San Francisco. Sharon claimed to be a fan and owned half a dozen of Tsujimura's pieces. When we compared notes about the talented artist's work, we found we had similar tastes in Japanese art. Our common interests led to lunches when I was in town, and I came to appreciate her advice about raising Jenny, especially in regard to the Japanese side of things. Sharon Tanaka's absence in my life left an irreparable hole.

But our closeness did nothing to gain Brodie Security access to her family.

Approaches by the tenacious Noda and our more diplomatic staff were rebuffed. No one gained access to the grieving family. At the funeral they were, of course, untouchable.

Not unexpectedly, Zhou turned up with a man who was clearly a senior Chinese official. Eyes straight ahead, the two of them marched down the left aisle and took seats four rows in front of us. Ensconced near the back from the start, Noda and I monitored all arrivals and did not miss their entrance.

From the outset we also kept a lookout for Swelley's agents. Though he would send eyes, we could not predict what form they would take. Homeland Security operated more than seventy overseas offices since, as they are fond of saying, national security does not start and stop at American borders. But as all of the agents I'd bumped up against in DC had been large Caucasians, their presence in this crowd was a nonstarter. Swelley would most likely dispatch a local from the Japan office who would attempt to melt into the crowd, which could complicate things for us.

But we needn't have worried.

Noda said, "Left side, three rows in front of the spy."

The funeral hall filled swiftly. There were thirty rows of folding chairs, ten on either side of a central aisle, with additional aisles running along the sides for easy access. Six hundred in total.

"You pegged him too?"

"Yeah."

I nodded. "Japanese-American trying to pass. Trying even harder not to look around too much."

Noda grunted. "Another behind the family."

"Entered first," I said. The agent in question was infected with the roving eye and met everyone's gaze, another un-Japanese trait. "What about the guy who nodded at us on the way in? He your PSIA friend?"

"Yeah."

I'd clocked a man with a hard face and sharp eyes. His requisite black suit might have been new once upon a time but now looked decidedly secondhand.

"Frown could have cracked a mirror."

Noda grunted again. "Trouble ahead, we get any more involved."

Which we would.

His so-called friend had stood in a discreet corner of the temple grounds, just inside the gate, cataloging all entrants. Openly displeased with our arrival, he'd shot Noda a reluctant nod.

"He a warning beacon?"

"Yep."

Noda hooked a finger inside his shirt collar and tugged. Stuffed into a black suit snug at the neck and waist, the chief detective's stout frame looked like a poorly wrapped oak barrel with legs. I wore a black suit and tie procured for my father's funeral nearly two years earlier.

"It's not just for us, then."

"Nope. We already got walking papers."

"Then who else?"

Noda shrugged.

The parade began ten minutes before the scheduled start of services. Sharon moved in celebrity circles, and now the famous began to arrive. Or more accurately, emerged from the greenroom. Movie stars, singers, and other luminaries from Japan's film, television, and theater industries entered and took reserved places at the front. Each new appearance whipped up a flurry of whispers.

Noda studied every entrant. "Turning into a talent show."

"On any other day autograph hounds would have a field day."

A moment later a Buddhist monk in a black robe stepped up to a stagelike altar at the front of the hall. The crowd grew quiet. All eyes lingered on a large framed photograph of the deceased embedded in an ocean of flowers. Somewhere underneath the tsunami of blooms rested the casket.

A trio of chest-high incense stands stood just in front of the altar. Incense was lit. The monk bowed and began a lengthy recitation of sutras.

Listening to the low, comforting hum of the monk's chant, I felt a tingling sensation in my limbs. It spread like a contagion through me. My body grew lighter. I seemed to be floating. My vision brightened as I thought of Mikey and Sharon in better times. Then my thoughts returned to the present, and darkened. My friends were gone forever. For what possible reason? For what possible gain? Their deaths seemed senseless to me. As I returned my attention to the monk's chants, the appalling senselessness of the act struck me with renewed force.

But the double homicide made sense to someone somewhere.

———

At the appropriate time, the first row of mourners stood and filed down the center aisle.

Lines formed behind each of the three incense stands.

Mourners bowed to the deceased, then the grieving family, then the immediate relatives. They added a pinch of new incense to the smoldering pile, offered their prayers, and bowed to each party once more before edging up the side aisles and returning to their seats.

I watched as people paid their final respects. Some offered short prayers. Others bent their heads for longer moments, clearly grieving. Many had handkerchiefs ready in their hands.

Japanese funerals are open affairs. The mourners come from all walks of the deceased's life. As long as attendees bring the required condolence money in the proper envelope, no one questions a person's presence. Which explained why Zhou, Noda's PSIA friend, and Swelley's people could slip in unnoticed. Who would question them? Who was to say they *hadn't* known Sharon Tanaka at one time or another during her long and varied career?

Now Zhou and his colleague offered their prayers. The Chinese official returned to his seat but Zhou walked somberly, up the aisle, heading to the restroom. He paused in front of my row, lowered his head chastely, and whispered in my ear, "I want to talk."

"Thought you might."

He retrieved an envelope from his suit pocket. "Seven p.m. Alone. No photographers this time." He glanced sideways at Noda. "No police either, but you can bring your man if you wish. Keep him at another table."

The master spy straightened and slipped out the door.

A grimace flickered across Noda's features. "Welcome to the club."

"Which one is that?"

"The How-many-peckerheads-do-I-know Club."

"And a fine club it is."

Zhou returned, retook his seat, and whispered a few words in his seatmate's ear.

A beat later, they struck.

Like a well-planned invasion.

CHAPTER 30

THEY were an army of thirteen.

They arrived unannounced and advanced with purpose and precision, marching into the hall in a loose but practiced configuration. When one of the ushers stepped into their path to shoo them away, a two-foot billy club connected with his right cheek and he folded up with a low moan. The sharp crack of cheekbone shattering forestalled any further protests.

Two men broke off from the rear of the thirteen, slammed the back doors of the temple hall shut, then stationed themselves in front of the barricade, feet spread and menacing clubs in gloved hands.

The remaining men tramped onward, the pounding of their heavy boots echoing through the hall. They detoured around the fallen usher. A splinter group of three peeled off and headed down the closest aisle. Three more streamed down the broad center walkway. A final trio filed down the far-right side.

The last two men surveyed the scene impassively from the back of the room as the troops deployed. The rear man of each trio took up a post at the end of his respective aisle. They each faced the altar. They planted their feet, then raised their truncheons and rested the working ends of the weapons on the palms of their free hands. The second man—and they were all men—peeled off at the halfway point. The three front-runners stormed all the way to the tops of their respective lanes, stopping just short of the altar. They turned and faced the crowd. Not with the synchronized timing of a crack military unit but with the casual arrogance of a gang following a plan.

None of them spoke, but each one gripped the handle of his bludgeon in a manner that could not be ignored. Some tapped the business end against the heel of the other hand.

It wasn't an invasion so much as a staking out of territory.

And not a small army so much as a gang on a mission.

They wore tight black pants and clinging black shirts with long sleeves. Their hands were sheathed in thin black gloves. A black ski mask cloaked the face of each intruder, exposing only the eyes. There was no opening for the mouth. The total effect of the black clothing made them look sleek and larval-like.

Skin of various hues along a spectrum from buttery yellow to a roasted almond peeked through at the neck and around the eyes. All within the Japanese color scheme. And much of the Asian palette, for that matter.

But that was the extent of their footprint.

They would expose no faces. Leave no telltale impressions. A clean, controlled in-and-out was planned. But why? From our seats, Noda and I searched for even a hint of what we were facing but gleaned nothing.

A tide of murmurs welled up. The front man in the center aisle said, "Everyone calm down unless you want to end up like the usher." To punctuate his point, he tipped over the incense stands and sent the funerary paraphernalia bouncing across the hardwood floor. "Now all of you sit down."

Those who had been waiting to pay their last respects scurried back to their places. When the aisles were cleared of mourners, the last two men filed down the far right side of the seating area. The guards flattened themselves against the wall to let them pass. The pair strode to the front. The shorter of the two scanned the four rows of relatives, then whispered in the ear of his partner with unmistakable deference.

He had unintentionally pinpointed the leader, who was short and solid and meaty.

"You," the boss said, jabbing an angry finger at an elderly man in the middle of the second row with thick glasses, gray hair, and a rumpled suit. "Get over here."

From where I sat, I saw an old man's head jerk up, startled. But he remained seated.

Sharon Tanaka's brother—the gatekeeper who guarded the family during its grieving period—rose from the first row, hands clasped in supplication. "Please, sir, this is my sister's funeral. I would request—"

The leader backhanded Sharon's brother with a club. A second bone-splitting crack echoed through the hall. The blow flung the brother against the wall before he folded up like a puppet with severed strings.

"Anyone else?" the gang leader asked, flat eyes sweeping the crowd.

I started to come out of my seat.

"Don't," Noda growled under his breath. "Watch now, strike later."

I glanced over at my partner. He sat as still as a stone. Waiting. Our time might come, or not. But, in either case, it was not now. We were outnumbered and outmuscled. With effort I brought my impulse under control. My blood boiled.

My movement drew the attention of the nearest guard. Raising his rod, he took a step in my direction. The sleeve of his black shirt slid lower and revealed a barbed-wire tattoo at his wrist. No, that wasn't right. A row of three Xs with a line through them.

The leader repeated his command, but the old man simply shook his head. The tattooed guard lost interest in me and turned to watch the confrontation across the hall.

The boss mumbled something, and the shorter man edged down the row of seats and yanked the recalcitrant man from his chair. The old man's glasses flew off—as did his hair.

The long black mane of a Japanese woman cascaded down from under the hairpiece. I inspected the unmasked face, envisioning it without the aging effects of the makeup, and the image of a woman in her late twenties came into focus.

One, I realized with a chill, I recognized—Akemi "Anna" Tanaka, Sharon's daughter.

What was going on?

The men grabbed her arms and hustled her up the aisle and out the door.

"*Hikiageru zo!*" the man at the front of the center column shouted. *We're leaving.*

That set the remaining troops in motion. In each aisle the guards began a ragged retreat. Walking backward and tapping truncheons lightly against their palms, they called on the mourners to stay seated until they were gone.

Then they were.

CHAPTER 31

THE police arrived in waves.

The first incursion rolled in all blue—blue caps and blue uniforms. Within ninety seconds, they had sealed the exits.

No one was leaving.

Mourners stood in small clusters, murmuring in hushed tones. A spokesman asked them to retake their seats.

A second inflow of uniforms arrived on the heels of the first and commenced counting heads and recording names. The third and final surge brought plainclothes detectives, and the real threat—the interrogations—began.

The Japanese phrase used to announce the proceedings was neutral in tone and could be translated as "information-gathering interviews." It reassured many of the anxious attendees, but Noda and I weren't fooled. The police would be gathering eyewitness accounts as well as attempting to ferret out coconspirators among the detained.

The detectives secured a pair of rooms at the back of the temple complex and the questioning commenced. The immediate family entered first, one at a time.

The rest of the bereaved were ushered into the adjoining room, where sushi, appetizers, and a range of free-flowing alcoholic beverages awaited. Sharon's designated public wake served an unintended secondary purpose of loosening tongues before face-to-face confrontations with the Tokyo PD. More than a few mourners angled into the interview room in finely inebriated form.

Noda and I waited our turn, partaking in moderation. Zhou's companion played the diplomacy card. The pair met with the detectives soon after the family, then waltzed out unscathed. Of like mind, Mr. PSIA sauntered into the back room uninvited, emerging a minute later followed by a scowling detective who gave a head nod to the badges at the door to grant passage to the clearly uncooperative agent.

Noda's friend ignored everyone in the room, including Noda. Zhou, however, had caught my eye on his way out and tapped his watch.

Despite the delay, our meet was still on.

10 P.M.
CENTRAL TOKYO

It was time to put the first lady to the test.

Stretched out in a taxi taking me across town to meet Zhou, I dialed Joan Slater's private number. Noda and I had escaped detainment. Following his friend's example, the chief detective had slung some of his own weight around. He had friends on the force. After the police noted Brodie Security's involvement and reserved the right to interview us at a later date, they sent us on our way with the same disgruntled scowl.

"Good morning, Mr. Brodie," said Margaret Cutler, Slater's chief of staff.

"Morning, Margaret. Could you put me through?"

"I'm so sorry. She's speaking to three hundred leaders of Red Cross chapters from around the country for another half hour, then there's a Q and A and post-event chitchat."

So much for instant twenty-four-hour access.

"I'm up against a wall here. I need to talk to her."

"How soon do you need her?"

"Sharon Tanaka's daughter has been kidnapped."

"You can*not* be serious."

"Wish I weren't."

The police were grilling each of the mourners without giving away the identity of the woman under the wig, but the truth circulated like the winning number of the year-end lottery.

"Oh, dear lord, that's horrible. How can we help?"

"Get FLOTUS on the phone."

"I can't pull her out of the meeting but I can take her a message."

I considered. "I need to talk to Sharon Tanaka's family ASAP. There are layers of people running interference for them, and none of us can get through."

"But you're a friend."

"There's a blanket 'no access' sign out."

"I can have an attaché from the embassy contact them."

"Won't work."

"Hold on." I heard her tap her phone screen. "Rats. Our ambassador to Japan is at a conference in Kuala Lumpur until tomorrow, so he's out. Can you wait until Mrs. Slater is finished?"

"Not a problem."

She tapped some more. "The earliest I can spring her is ninety minutes from now. That will be eleven thirty at night in Tokyo."

"That works."

"Okay, I'll see what I can do."

"Not good enough, Margaret. The first lady told me access twenty-four/seven and this isn't it."

"You got *me* right away."

"Which is great, but I need the rest of the package. I need Joan to call the Tanakas the minute she's free."

"There's a problem. Mrs. Slater is a stickler for courtesy. It is a big part of her job. Quite likely she will want to call the family in the morning their time, even if it is late for her."

"Too late. I guarantee that tonight the Tanakas won't be going to sleep anytime soon."

"I don't know . . ."

"It's got to be now, Margaret. We're dealing with a gang of hired kidnappers. They were efficient and focused. They won't waste time passing her along."

"To whom?"

"I have no idea, but the answer won't be good."

"Oh my god, this is unbelievable."

"Believe it. The clock is ticking."

CHAPTER 32

ZHOU had selected an oyster bar called Ostrea in Tokyo's Akasaka quarter, a place with history.

When the samurai-run shogun government fell in 1868, the newly installed leaders began to frequent the dining streets of Akasaka to unwind. A more affordable geisha district sprang up to accommodate them, competing with the established one in Shimbashi a few miles down the road. Today, office workers unchained from their desks stroll down brick-lined lanes past rows of enticing eateries and Japanese-style gastro pubs.

Ostrea was one of them. The dining spot had recessed lighting, discreet seating, and petite French etchings on cream-colored walls. Fresh oysters from all across Japan were coddled in a glittering nest of ice at the front, visible to passersby.

As soon as I entered, waitstaff in black coats guided me to Zhou. The master spy's secluded perch at the back shielded him from passing pedestrians. He'd posted two men at a table halfway into the restaurant, his first line of defense against an unwelcome intrusion.

"You come alone?" he asked when I'd drawn within earshot.

"Yeah," I said, dropping into the chair opposite him. "But don't get any ideas. My people know I'm with you."

And I hadn't arrived blind. From the funeral hall, I'd sent staff from Brodie Security to scout the meeting place. They'd learned Ostrea had sixteen tables and seated fifty, inclusive of the eight seats at the L-shaped bar at the front. Zhou's escape route—or mine, if it came to that—would be through the kitchen, which was long and narrow and funneled into a pantry lined with steel refrigeration units, then out into a service area and a connecting passage bleeding into the next street. In an emergency, freedom was a thirty-yard sprint, with two turns.

Zhou considered me with narrowed eyes. "No photographers or police?"

"None."

"Good, then let's get started."

The spy raised a warm carafe of saké as a peace offering. He filled my cup, then his, then we drank. Deeply. Sharon's funeral and her daughter's kidnapping had depressed my spirits, and Zhou too seemed pensive.

"Another?" he asked.

"Keep 'em coming."

While my host ordered a large platter of his favorite oysters, my thoughts drifted toward the kidnapping. Maybe the master spy could offer an explanation. He'd known enough to show up, so he knew something.

Zhou rubbed his hands together. "You'll like what is coming."

"Does nothing discourage your appetite?"

He shrugged. "Oysters are the cure, and saké is a Band-Aid. A superb one."

I couldn't argue. The brewer had engineered a full-bodied drink that floated on the tongue with a soft mellow feel and offered a faint hint of citrus as refreshing as I imagined the oysters would be.

I drank some saké. "You have an opinion on the kidnapping?"

"Looks bad for the daughter."

Which said nothing and gave me even less. I watched for a tell but found none. On the other hand, a void can provide nuance. Zhou had spoken softly. Too softly for him. Proactive change-up was his game— badger and boast, coddle then prod, console and jab. A modest Zhou was an evasive Zhou.

"You anticipated it," I said.

An eyebrow twitched but offered nothing.

It's going to be that way, I thought. *Okay.*

The first round of oysters arrived. A tiny placard embedded in the ice told us the Noto spring oysters hailed from Nanao, on the Noto Peninsula, which was along Japan's northern shore. A place of cold, pure water.

Promising. My first bite elicited a hint of honey from a plump, sea-fresh body, followed by a sweet finish.

"Good choice," I said, then nodded at his pair of watchdogs across the room. "My guess is you had men stationed at the temple too."

Zhou pushed out his lower lip, irritated. "It is a shame you were not born Chinese. Or refuse to work for me. Perhaps you would like to reconsider. You could eat like this every day."

"Maybe in the next life."

He frowned, his eyes roaming over my features, soaking up every modulation in expression, body language, and voice. But unlike the last time we'd met, I'd steeled myself in advance. He'd find nothing other than a firm resistance to his probing.

"Your answer is disappointing, though I am not surprised."

"What did your lookout see?"

"Who said I had one?"

Zhou lifted a half shell to his lips and let the oyster slide into his mouth, chewing with obvious contentment.

"You always have one, if not more."

He looked bored. "And what if I did?"

"Tell me what he saw."

"Would you really like to know?"

"Dying to."

Zhou shot me a suspicious look I couldn't interpret, then shook off the thought and opened a photo app on his mobile phone, selected an image, and flipped the screen around. The image rattled me. Zhou's dejection stemmed from reasons other than the Tanaka family's misfortune.

"He dead?"

"I don't know what you're talking about." *Yes.*

"I see."

Sprawled in a distant corner of the temple was a Chinese man. An oblong patch of blood the size of a beach ball had collected around his head.

The light in Zhou's eyes dimmed. "Casualties of war."

"Is that what you call it?"

"What else?"

I stared at him. His expression was grim but I saw no sorrow behind the mask. I wondered again how much Zhou valued the life of our mutual acquaintance—my buffer when dealing with the volatile master spy. I recalled a fragment of conversation from our first meeting:

"The world needs people like you and Tommy," Zhou had said. "To protect it from people like me." A disarming comment. Followed by the return of his thousand-watt smile. "May I be frank?"

"Refreshing idea."

He gave an icy chuckle. "You'd make a fine asset if I could turn you, but we're on opposite sides."

"Meaning?"

"Meaning we'll never be friends. But an enemy well regarded is better than a friend you doubt."

In his own inimitable way Zhou followed a code. The circles he trolled abroad were treacherous, but he navigated even darker territory back home. In the troubled, churning waters he habitually traversed, I was an island of stability.

"Integrity is a valuable commodity," I said now, taking a sip of saké.

"But is it enough?"

I considered the tightly wrapped bundle of paranoia before me. Outside China, the master spy was functional, formidable, and moved about with relative freedom. Back home, he lived in a shark tank. He was a medium-size predator maneuvering endlessly among larger, more duplicitous Party sharks while fending off countless smaller ones gaining girth and strength with each passing day. With me at least there was no pretense—which, however, didn't make Zhou's teeth any less sharp.

"We have Tommy," I said. "One of the good ones."

"What we have," the spy across the table said, "is excellent liquor, oysters from around the world, and the remainder of the evening."

He signaled the waiter for another flask of saké.

CHAPTER 33

ZHOU had exchanged his black funerary wear for a high-end Italian suit in a light-gray summer cotton-and-silk weave and a crisp tailored white dress shirt open at the collar to allow the blue and yellow vertical stripes running around the inside to peek through.

"You didn't have to dress just for me," I said.

"I have another engagement afterward."

And I knew what it was.

All the tailored elegance in the world could not disguise the retirement plan wrapped around his wrist: a Richard Mille chronometer with a pair of green dragons winding around the open watch works. Diamonds were embedded along the edges in the wide gold frame. The piece was worth three-quarters of a million dollars, minimum. I knew this because I never forget a person, piece of art, or wristwatch with notable craftsmanship.

I glanced at the encased dragons. "Will you have the watch by the end of the evening?"

The spy's jaw tightened. "You are too observant, Brodie. It is why I want you as an asset. But a piece of advice: keep such thoughts to yourself. Under the wrong circumstances your talent will get you killed."

I nodded, his retort sobering. But my less-than-discreet comment had a purpose. Pushing Zhou off balance when the rare opportunity arose should not be overlooked.

"It *pays* to be a civil servant in the Party," I said. "But it also requires an insurance policy."

He rattled the watch. "This and its cousins are the only insurance I have. When our enemy comes, he will be merciless. Our arrests will happen late one night. My wife and child will never know where I have been taken. Then, on a busy news day, when the whole country is looking elsewhere, we will be blindfolded, marched out into a dusty courtyard, stood up against a forty-foot wall, and shot."

"And for no other reason than your boss lost a tug-of-war."

He nodded, his gaze drifting wistfully toward the white-hatted chef shucking oysters. "It will happen with little or no warning. To survive, my underlings will turn their face to my replacement. Only my wife and child will be sad. And perhaps you and Tommy."

For centuries, shifting winds had been a way of life and death in China. The motivation remained unchanged through the years and regimes—power, money, and, on occasion, love. The tricks grew dirtier, the traps more inventive, and the excuses more complex, but the pattern remained the same.

"I wouldn't want your worries," I said, then shifted back to business. "Except where they overlap mine. You showed up at both funerals."

"Just doing my homework."

My eyelids dropped to half-mast.

Zhou sighed. "Okay, you're not a pushover. What do you have to trade?"

"Nothing."

"That's not how this works, Brodie."

My phone buzzed with an incoming call from Noda. "I've got to take this. You mind?"

"No."

"What's up?" I said.

"Can you talk?"

"Hold on."

To Zhou, I made a motion about stepping outside so as not to disturb the other diners, then cruised toward the front of the restaurant, past his guards, and out into the concourse, where a flood of pedestrians filled the lane, searching for a last drink or heading home on a late train.

"You ready?" Noda asked.

"Give it another a second."

On the edge of my peripheral vision, I saw a man step from the shadows of a doorway, look around in confusion, and consult his cell phone as if searching a map for a nearby shop. He paused within earshot and began to swipe screens.

I turned my back to him and lowered my voice. "Okay, I'm listening."

"But still can't talk?"

"You got it."

Noda grunted. "Tattoo belongs to a yakuza splinter group known for working with the Chongryon."

I felt my eyes widen. Bad news. "You got a name?"

"Sasa-gumi."

Gumi meant group and was a common suffix attached to many yakuza gang names, aka the Japanese mafia. The Chongryon was a long-established pro–North Korea association in Japan that funneled money and supplies to the feisty dictatorship. The Chongryon was an old-school political anachronism. With North Korea's ongoing antics and the early promise of a "utopian socialist society" now in shambles, the Chongryon was composed of die-hard elder loyalists. Young Koreans were no longer drawn to the cause, but the group carried on. It still had bite, if not relevance.

"What else?"

"Sasa-gumi's a splinter group."

I exhaled in frustration. "The combination complicates things."

Noda grimaced. "A high-level complication."

A reference to Brodie Security's aversion to dealing with clients like FLOTUS because of just such a thorny political mix.

"I gave my word," I said, "and I'm going to keep at it. You don't want to come along, don't."

"Didn't say that."

"I can take a hint."

"It wasn't a hint."

"I'm giving you an out if you want it."

"I want it, you'll know."

Loyalty had never been an issue with Brodie Security's chief detective.

"Good. Thoughts?"

"We need to talk to the Tanakas."

"I'm working on it."

"I'm not seeing it," he said, and disconnected.

Loyalty with a short fuse.

I rubbed my eyes, sympathizing with Noda's discontent. This case was heading in all the wrong directions. Spies, yakuza splinter groups, and the Chongryon. Distasteful and dangerous backdoor North Korean politics.

I strolled back into Ostrea. I saw Zhou hurriedly shut down his cell phone and set it on the table. How could a shooting at the Kennedy Center in DC possibly be tied to a Tokyo gang with links to North Korea's underground funding routes? And why was a Chinese spy poking around the edges? Any one of the three would singe eyebrows if you drew too close. Together they were just the sort of inflammatory cocktail the Brodie Security staff avoided with a passion.

Retaking my seat, I snatched up my saké cup and drained it. "Sorry for the interruption. Where were we?"

Zhou refilled my glass. "You were going to tell me what you could trade."

"Asked and answered."

The master spy leaned back in his chair, his eyes gleeful in the soft light. "We both know that has changed."

I glanced at Zhou's phone and he grinned. "My man outside heard enough."

"He heard nothing."

The grin widened. "Fragments, body language. Inferences were made."

Noda's unexpected find had knocked me off my game and the master spy swooped in without mercy.

"Okay," I said. "You're no pushover either."

"So talk."

"You first," I said. "Or you can take your oysters and go home."

CHAPTER 34

BEFORE he could open his mouth, the second round of oysters arrived.

Zhou's eyes lit up. "This is the jewel of the menu." He turned to the waiter. "After we finish these, bring us the oyster risotto to finish."

"Certainly, sir," the waiter said in Japanese, with a slight bow, then retreated.

"You were saying?" I asked when the waiter was out of earshot.

The spy shrugged. "You already know Sharon Tanaka was selected as the set designer for the joint Chinese-Japanese production. What you do not know is she was championed by the president himself."

That was a surprise. "Celebrity politics?"

Zhou reddened slightly. "No, simpler."

"Enlighten me."

"Anna Tanaka went to Harvard with the president's daughter. They are friends. It was our president's daughter who pushed for using Sharon Tanaka."

The Tanakas seemed to have a talent for latching onto high-powered people. Must be something in the family gene pool.

"Label me shocked," I said, polishing off the rest of my drink. "How close are they?"

The spymaster filled his glass and mine. "Close enough so what I told you before applies. Anna Tanaka's kidnapping offers low-level leverage. The president dotes on his daughter and she will ask him to help as soon as she learns of the kidnapping."

"You're saying the president might bend Chinese policy over this kidnapping? To please his daughter? I still find that hard to believe."

"It is very simple. If the Tanaka girl dies because of inaction on the president's part, he alienates his daughter. She's spoiled and stubborn and famous for it. She won't forget for a long time. Our analysts predict the kidnappers' demands would not put the president in a position where he could *not* act. They would be minor but somehow significant to the kidnappers, or whoever hired them."

"It's a slick move, if true."

Zhou nodded. "Extremely clever. Except for one thing. We would give them what they want to avoid headlines. But eventually we would find them and, well, they would never be a threat again."

Without missing a beat, Zhou reached for one of the newly arrived oysters. This time I was looking at Sakoshi oysters from Ako, in Hyogo Prefecture, on Japan's southern coast, tucked away on the edge of the Inland Sea. Home of the famed Forty-Seven Ronin.

Zhou swallowed one oyster, then another. He hummed in pleasure.

Mulling over all the implications of my tablemate's answer, I tapped a few drops of red vinegar on an oyster, then slid it into my mouth. The first bite drew a sweet fleshy burst, with a creamy flavor up front and a soft milky wholeness on the follow. A jewel of texture and creaminess. Just the right balance. Which was more than I could say for Zhou's explanation.

"Something is missing from your story," I said. "Why not just kidnap the Tanaka daughter without killing the mother?"

"Because the girl was receiving treatment for depression at an undisclosed location."

"So?"

"Killing the mother flushed out the daughter."

"Isn't that a bit extreme?"

Zhou spread his hands. "*Extreme* is a willingness to go as far as it takes. These guys have it."

I considered the boldness of the kidnapping and found the statement hard to refute. "So the niece you mentioned when we were in San Francisco was a lie?"

He shrugged. "She was the official reason for my presence, and my little tale turned out to be close to the truth. Just substitute Anna Tanaka for the niece and you have the real story. Your turn."

"Does the niece even exist?"

"A distant relative who's in the play. Your turn."

I fell back in my chair and stared at my dinner companion. I'd caught him in a lie and yet he expected an answer.

With casual disregard, he popped the last oyster in his mouth.

I gazed at the master spy for a long moment. What if the new explanation was also a lie? *Only my wife and child will be sad. And perhaps you and Tommy.* In the paranoid world in which he operated, Zhou had extended an olive branch when he opened up about his fear. On the other hand, his revised story was a tainted offering. Giving him what he wanted was risky. But sometimes you had to jump the chasm. Time was short. I gave him Noda's find.

His reaction was immediate—and as startling as Noda's original information.

The master spy sat up straighter. Something at the back of his eyes rippled in understanding. I asked him if the tattoo meant anything to him. He said no.

"What is it, then?" I said.

"I am not sure."

"*What* are you unsure of?"

Rising, Zhou shook his head. "I need to check my sources."

He dropped a handful of bills on the table and shot past me, past his minders, and out the door.

So much for sharing. I'd risked and lost.

Or, as Noda put it soon after, "*Suzume no nami da.*"

Zhou had left me only a sparrow's tear.

CHAPTER 35

11:30 P.M.

I FOUND myself gnashing my teeth in frustration as I stepped out into the warm May evening. Spooksville was not a place I cared to frequent, but events seemed determined to drag me there.

When I filled Noda in on my last moments with Zhou, the crusty chief detective ran the "sparrow's tear" slight up the flagpole and I couldn't argue. I'd given the spy gold and received a pittance in return.

But Zhou's reaction allowed me to connect some dots.

When the Soviet Union collapsed in 1991 and their last morsels of monetary sustenance for North Korea dried up, the satellite rogue nation began to flounder. Over time, China slipped into the role of senior ally, then found itself playing the exasperated foster parent to an ungrateful enfant terrible.

The North walked hand in hand with no nation. Its contrarian leadership continued its tantrum-throwing, saber-rattling ways. The theatrics are, in fact, well-honed performance pieces designed to jack up regional tensions and bring allies or enemies—Seoul, Washington, Beijing, even Moscow—to the bargaining table for an eventual payoff.

In distilled form it goes like this: stage outburst, make unreasonable demands, extract money for promises of better behavior. Renege, repeat, and fleece again.

In short order, China grew disgusted with North Korea's antics and devised a plan of its own. It assumed the role of an aloof uncle rather than attentive parent—and settled for the status quo.

The People's Republic preferred an erratic neighbor to a collapsing one, which would see a flood of refugees and half-baked nuclear material crossing the border and entering the black market. It preferred a divided Korea to one unified under Seoul's leadership, with the inevitable leaning toward the United States, even if the stance led to the North's eventual nuclear armament.

For its part, the Kim dynasty favored keeping a cushioned distance as well, aware of its more powerful neighbor's desire to dominate. The two countries remain close, even if the love-hate relationship is one of wary cooperation seasoned with a hefty measure of distrust.

China was the North's closest ally, and yet my revelation had rattled the master spy.

Which meant the tattoo told him something he *didn't* know.

Which is the same as saying China *didn't* know—but wanted to.

I'd given him the end of a thread he could pull.

Out on Sotobori Avenue, I slid into the backseat of a cab. I reeled off my home address, closed my eyes, and began pulling on threads of my own.

China and North Korea . . . the tattoo . . . Zhou's swift exit . . .

What did the master spy know? He had attended both funerals—but why? Best guess: the enfant terrible was acting up again and Zhou and his masters were waiting or watching for something.

And?

I had nothing.

Next thread. Anna's kidnapping shifted some of the focus away from Mikey and onto the Tanaka family. But only some. What if the Kennedy Center murders and Anna's abduction were unrelated? What if they were two separate events? It was possible. Was Sharon collateral damage for something of Mikey's making?

Seemed like a long shot but it needed checking. I dashed off a text message to Renna, asking him to find out if the beer-stealing, clerk-shooting Trooger spoke Spanish. The shooter had.

Back to my food-loving tablemate. He'd been sniffing around as far back as Mikey's funeral. Which argued for a connection, unless I was missing something. Not that I had gathered up enough to miss.

Was Zhou looking for a North Korean component even then? Could have been. If that was the case, the replacement story he'd just spun about Anna being used as leverage was also a ruse. So I was looking at a double feint.

But why?

The kidnapping had forced him to change his story. What was it about Anna's abduction?

On this point I had two threads to tease out. First, why had the gang risked a public grab for Sharon's daughter? I was in a holding pattern on this one until the first lady came through with access to the Tanaka family. Second, how sure was I the kidnapping actually constituted a North Korean–backed enterprise? Chongryon's affiliation with the yakuza gang suggested it, but a solid connection was still lacking.

But *if* the North was involved, what did that mean?

Was North Korea back in the kidnapping business? Possibly. Old habits die hard. Or maybe it wasn't an old habit. Rumor of the occasional abduction still surfaced. Back in the day the targets had been young people, snatched to help teach North Korean spies the language and culture of the victim's homeland, whether it was China, Japan, Thailand, Singapore, France, Italy, Romania, or Holland. Then the program shifted to breeding. Marry off the abductees, raise an "organic" batch of children loyal to North Korea, and educate them in the fine art of spying.

But Anna's case was different. Her kidnapping had been an in-your-face affair. Why? And what on earth was the disguise all about? We needed to get to the Tanaka family to untangle that one.

Too early to tell for both of those. Next thread—and the most urgent.

Once kidnap victims were smuggled into North Korea, they rarely resurfaced. Which meant that until I knew otherwise, I had to assume the worst. Which meant I needed to act fast. Which is why I'd pushed Margaret to push the first lady to act tonight. It also meant I needed a good source to guide me through the intricacies of the Korean underground in Japan.

Which was where my momentum was in danger of dying.

Ask me about Korean ceramics, folk paintings, or traditional furniture and I could talk about how soulful and underappreciated the artwork was. I could even hold my own on the finer points of North Korean policy and its tentacles in Japan. But my knowledge of the North's down-and-dirty moves had more holes than some of the moth-eaten Kabuki costumes I'd viewed in the early rounds of my search. The main problem was that Brodie Security's tentacles did not extend to the Korean community here in Japan. The topic was too specialized.

Then it hit me.

I knew a guy who was plugged in. I'd run across him ten months ago: Jiro Jo, a famous ethnic Korean bodyguard based in Tokyo. He worked for one of Brodie Security's rivals and served the rich and threatened. He was the best private bodyguard in the land and his combined knowledge of the Japanese *and* Korean underworlds rivaled none. If you felt threatened by the above combination, you dished out money for Jiro Jo. He could help me connect more dots.

Problem solved, except for a few minor details.

One, he worked for our main competitor. Two, when we'd first met, I'd knocked him unconscious in the back room of my antiques shop, and the Tokyo grapevine was abuzz with his desire for revenge.

With bright brown eyes and a brighter smile, Rie cracked open the front door of my father's house and stepped out onto the stoop. She was a welcome sight. My policewoman girlfriend was in her civilian clothes tonight but held something behind her back.

"Treat," I called out the window of the cab as I paid the fare.

"Perhaps," she said, the smile fading as she scanned my face. "Unless you've brought tricks."

"By the bagful. But not willingly."

Her gaze softened. She reached for my hand, led me inside, then stood on tiptoe, kissed me, and revealed what she had been hiding: takeout from my favorite neighborhood sushi shop.

"A midnight snack," Rie said. "After Tanaka's funeral and another sit-down with Zhou, I figured you would need a pick-me-up. Was I wrong?"

Alcohol and oysters had fueled Zhou's meal, which was heavy on the first and light on the second. I *was* still hungry.

"No, right on the money."

She smiled. "You should bathe, then we can eat and you can catch me up on the case." Her glistening skin told me she had gone before me.

The Japanese bath is genius in liquid form. It offers clean water, continual heat, and a deep tub in which you can relax. The Japanese had perfected the experience. While you luxuriate in a miniature hot spring–like pool in the privacy of your own home, the warmth of the water penetrates to the core, "massaging" muscles, drawing off the workday stress, and miraculously whisking away any and all weariness. The simple nightly ritual rejuvenates *on a daily basis*. How rare is that? I'm convinced its restorative powers contribute to Japan's position at the top of the life-expectancy charts.

"One cure-all coming up," Rie said when I emerged.

From the couch, she waved at the spread on the coffee table. The sushi was elegantly displayed on a square ceramic platter with an emerald-green glaze and faint apricot-white clay. An Iga-style piece. The fish ran the color spectrum from flesh tones to pink, orange, and red, with the pristine white rice underneath the unifying factor. Garnished with sprigs of Japanese greens and a mound of mint-colored wasabi horseradish, the whole offered a startling fresh composition pleasing to eye and palate.

"It's already working," I said.

"Good. One thing first. Your dealer friend in Kyoto called while you were cleaning up."

"This late?"

"He'd planned to leave a message but I picked up. Says you are one lucky guy. Through a connection of his wife's, he's found a one-in-a-million Kabuki robe."

"That *is* lucky," I said.

" 'But I'm luckier in love' is what you mean to say."

"That too. By far."

"Much better."

I took a minute to review the email material. He'd found a stunning robe with an equally stunning history. A couple of bidders were already panting after the piece. I passed the photos on to Lisa Kregg at the Freer to see if there was any interest, then turned back to the feast Rie had so thoughtfully laid out.

We sampled a line of delicacies: *uni, anago, ikura,* and *toro*—sea urchin, saltwater eel, salmon roe, and rich fatty tuna. Rie glanced my way and smiled. I smiled back. We ate and drank in a comfortable silence, then she asked about the latest developments on the case.

"Fair warning," I said. "You're not going to like any of it."

Concern flickered across her features. "Tell me anyway."

"I may have to go see Jiro Jo."

Rie turned pale. "Is that really necessary?"

I said yes and told her why. By the time I wound up my recital, Rie was frowning big-time. "But he's so violent."

"You mean he strikes out when he has to. So do I."

"He's on our watch list."

"*I'm* probably on your watch list."

Frustration rippled across her forehead.

I said, "Getting on the list can be a backhanded compliment. Jo takes calculated risks. We all do. It's what makes us good."

Rie did not respond favorably. "Be that as it may, meeting him is still dangerous."

"I have no choice. Brodie Security doesn't have the right connections. Jiro Jo might. Unless you have a strong in with the local Korean community, that's the direction I'm going."

"I don't. But aren't you two feuding?"

"It's all on his side."

"Then he will refuse to see you."

"I'll persuade him. He's my best bet."

"He's your best bet to get your throat slit."

CHAPTER 36

DAY 6, FRIDAY

A GIANT hornet swooped down on me for the third time.

The insect's persistence forced me to seek shelter in a cluster of shrubs. With each pass, its buzzing grew louder and more threatening. I marveled at the hornet's size and the mesmerizing pattern of red and yellow stripes ringing its abdomen. My attacker circled overhead, then dove again.

When I finally dragged myself back to consciousness, the drone's fevered hum morphed into the angry vibration of my smartphone turning circles on my bedside table.

I looked at the clock. Two twenty-seven in the morning. Next to me, Rie rubbed her eyes. "You were tossing around. A bad dream?"

"A strange one."

Red and yellow stripes? The colors of the Chinese flag. Zhou had gotten inside my head.

Rie put a hand on my shoulder. "Maybe you should answer the phone."

Since the caller ID was blocked, I countered with a flat hello.

"Mr. Brodie? Margaret Cutler. Did I wake you?"

Finally. "Don't worry, I'll live."

"I should hope so. Otherwise, you won't be of much use to the first lady or the president. I have Mrs. Slater on the line, if you're ready. This was the only time I could—"

"It's fine, Margaret, really. Is she right there?"

"Actually, she's in her private quarters, changing for her next appointment. She's anxious to speak with you."

"The feeling's mutual."

"Transferring you now."

A soft click and a new background sound hummed in my ear. "Jim, is that you?"

"Yes, ma'am."

"It's Joan, remember? I've called the Tanakas as you requested. They seemed aware I was a friend of Sharon's. They aren't seeing anyone outside the police. I offered to help, they accepted, then I told them you *were* that help. They will receive anytime you are ready."

"Thank you."

"Thank *you*. This is all just terrible, Jim. Do you have any idea what is going on yet?"

"Not yet, but we're working on it nonstop."

The first lady sighed. "I know these things take time, but I wish you had some answers. I'm told you were at the funeral when Anna was taken. Was it as bad as it sounds?"

"It wasn't pretty."

"Tell me about it. I wanted to ask the Tanakas but I didn't have the heart, the poor things."

I revisited the abduction for her sake but stopped short of mentioning the tattoo, an exclusive bit of intel I did not want circulating.

"One more thing, Jim: why is it Anna arrived at her mother's funeral in disguise?"

"That, ma'am . . . Joan . . . is the first question in a long list I have for the family."

"For which we'll find an unpleasant answer, I imagine. The poor, poor things. Be *very, very* careful over there, Jim. I mean in Japan. Not at the Tanakas'. Do *not* put yourself in harm's way for me. I couldn't bear it."

"Understood," I said.

But not possible.

With everything in play, I saw no way around doing just that.

Setting down the phone, I turned to Rie. Her eyes had widened beyond a point I would have considered physically possible.

"Were you just talking to the first lady of the United States of America?"

"You make it sound so grand."

"It *is* grand if it's true. Is it?"

Propped up against the headboard, Rie had listened to both ends of the conversation. She spoke no English, but, like most Japanese, she had a passive knowledge of the language because she had studied the grammar for six years from junior high school on. Phrases stuck. Were reinforced when they appeared in movies and TV and ad campaigns. Or in the phone conversations of your boyfriend.

"Yes," I said without enthusiasm.

"And you called her *Joan*."

Maybe the observational thing was more elementary than I thought. I shrugged. "At her insistence."

"I don't recall you mentioning *Joan* previously."

"Her involvement is confidential."

Storm clouds gathered. "Oh, really?"

"Can I claim 'need to know'?"

"Don't you dare. How did it happen?"

"The first lady and Sharon Tanaka were at college together."

Rie folded her arms. "And?"

I sighed. Dating a TPD officer was harder than it should be. "Stays between the two of us?"

"Of course it does."

"And if your superior should question you?"

"I will keep your secret."

"As I am trying to do right now."

"But I do not have a relationship with my boss. I have one with you."

"I'm not sure that qualifies as a—"

"It does."

Short and abrupt and allowing no argument. Rie *had* earned insider's rights, I suppose. She'd found pivotal clues in my last two cases, one involving a ninety-six-year-old World War Two veteran in Tokyo, the other an elusive killer working both sides of the Pacific. Had we spent more time together since my arrival in Japan, it would have spilled out naturally—with a confidentiality clause attached.

"All right," I said. "But you cannot tell *anyone*. Brothers, father, uncle—"

"Of course not."

"—cop buddies. Men, women, Martians."

"I wouldn't think of it."

"Okay, fine," I said and brought her fully into the loop.

Once I filled in the gaps, Rie dropped into thought. I could see her engaged with the facts. Ordering and reordering them. Slotting them into one place then another. I watched a range of emotions roll across her face like cloud shadow passing over a field.

Eventually her eyes swung up to find mine. "Don't take this the wrong way, but, considering all that has happened, you don't have much, do you?"

I nodded unhappily. "Crumbs. But under them is a secret."

"With Homeland Security, Chinese spies, and the PSIA involved, it must be a big one."

"I'm coming around to that opinion too."

"Secret agencies are stingy with their facts by habit, so scraps are all any of us get. Even the Tokyo PD."

Her comment gave me an idea. "What if we make an end run around the first two?"

"What do you mean?"

"A back door."

Rie pulled the sheet tighter around her. "Go on."

"Noda's bumping heads with his PSIA friend, as I told you. But it's a big organization. Think your PSIA guy would talk to us? As a personal favor? We might get a jump on what Swelley is up to. He's leading the charge."

Rie's eyes hollowed out. "Covert badges are tricky."

"Can you try?"

Rie chewed on her lower lip. "For you, I'll ask. But it'll be a personal back door, not professional, so I can't go with you. If I arrange a meeting, promise you'll take Noda . . . for protection."

What was that about? I wanted to ask, but since I'd all but dragged her this far, I held back.

"Fair enough," I said.

"Unless there's another way . . ."

"I can't think of one."

Rie nodded. An uneasy reluctance sullied the air between us, and only later would I recall it.

CHAPTER 37

JIRO Jo and I first clashed in my antiques shop in San Francisco, during the Japantown case.

The Korean had a dark, round meaty face with flaring cheekbones and short black hair. His eyes glistened with intelligence. His shoulders were broad, his muscles were firm, and his overall demeanor spoke of speed and strength. At six-four and with 240 pounds hanging on long, thick bones, he was a great wall of a man. In fact, "Great Wall" became my nickname for him. Other than his size, there was nothing excessive about him, which signaled trouble. There was not even an inflated ego to use against him.

He had accompanied a Japanese billionaire businessman named Katsuyuki Hara, who was weighing the idea of hiring me for a job. It turned out Jiro Jo was an integral part of the interview process . . .

The billionaire had moved his chin maybe a half a millimeter, and the Great Wall charged.

Anticipating the move, I preempted his attack, brushing his rising hands away with a forearm sweep and plowing the heel of my other hand into his nose but pulling back enough to keep the breathing apparatus from turning to pulp. Anything less and he would have trampled me. The Wall staggered sideways and grabbed for his face. I connected with a knee kick to the stomach, eschewing the more damaging targets above and below. He went down.

Hara stared at the immobile form at his feet.

I said, "A little less bulk, he'd make a nice doormat."

The businessman raised his eyes to mine, his expression empty of mirth, anger, or any other emotion. "The Sony people recommended your firm. Highly. I guess it hasn't slipped any."

"Guess not."

Our second encounter started the ball rolling downhill.

Jo had said, "I underestimated you the first time."

"I know."

"An art dealer. Dropped my guard."

"By a fraction."

"Won't happen again."

"I know that too."

We'd both been ignorant of the other. Turned out Jo topped the list of bodyguards in Japan. I'd outfoxed him once but a repeat performance was unlikely without absorbing a tall measure of pain. We left it at an uneasy standoff to be settled another time.

It looked like the time had arrived.

———

First thing in the morning, Noda and I ambled into the offices of Tokyo VIP Security, Jiro Jo's employer, and informed the receptionist we had come to visit the big man, then looped around her desk without waiting for a reply.

Noda threaded his way through islands of desks. I followed in his wake. Behind us, I heard the receptionist scramble for her phone to announce our arrival. In places, the walls were plastered with wanted posters and large colorful recruitment notices for the Tokyo PD, a display meant to curry favor with the neighborhood badges. I wondered if such an obvious ploy actually worked.

"Nice place," I said. "The décor's thematic."

Noda grunted without interest.

As we advanced, the room—quiet to start—grew deathly still. Heads swiveled. Recognition crossed the faces of many. We were, after all, the competition, and had made headlines several times. Some of the employees were women. Most of them were men. They all looked like they could handle themselves. Their body language, while not openly hostile, was far from welcoming.

Exiting the firm might not be as easy as entering it.

Jiro Jo's office was next to the president's. Noda tapped once on a frosted glass door with Jiro Jo's name on it and entered without waiting for a response.

Jo had just returned the phone's receiver to its cradle.

"Noda, Brodie," he said flatly.

Noda grunted. I nodded.

A cold smile stretched the bodyguard's lips. "This ain't a social call, I see. Otherwise, Brodie and I got business."

"Otherwise," I said.

"One day it needs settling."

"I know."

The Great Wall sat behind an expansive desk, which his bulk still managed to dwarf. "When that day comes, I plan to crack your head open like a coconut. Or maybe I'll just gut you."

"Ambition's a fine thing."

Jiro Jo didn't sneer or smirk or taunt. "Lightning don't strike twice" was all he said. Then: "What you doing here?"

Since he didn't wave us to seats, we stood. Which, in close quarters, with someone of Jo's caliber, was the safer bet.

"Got a question," I said.

"Can't say I care much."

"You might once you hear it."

Jo's eyes flickered across my features, wondering about my direction. Our rivalry had complications. Not long after his defeat, I'd revealed his billionaire client's duplicity. The deception had put my life in danger and most likely sent Jo's friend and colleague to his death.

Jo cracked large, rock-hard knuckles. "Since you've come this far, let's hear it. Then I'll decide whether you two are gonna leave here undamaged or not."

"You heard of a splinter yakuza group called the Sasa-gumi?"

"Of course."

"I need whatever you can tell me about them."

Jo's glance strayed toward Noda. "You need it too?"

The chief detective nodded once. Jo paused to consider. While Tokyo VIP Security's prime bodyguard sat atop the list of Japan's best bodyguards, Noda's position in the upper ranks of Japan's private detectives put them on equal footing. Which was why there was a clear and mutual respect between them.

"This is business, then," Jo said. "Today."

Noda acknowledged the gesture with a nod. Which satisfied Jo.

Leaning back in his chair, the Korean wove thick fingers behind his head. His dark walnut eyes grew darker. "Answer's simple. They're scum. Stay away from them."

"Can't," Noda said.

"Actually," I said, "we need their leader's name."

"Bigger scum. Stay clear of him too."

I shook my head. "Wish we could, but his men just kidnapped a woman."

Fingers still cradling his oversize cranium, Jo closed his eyes and raised his face to the ceiling. He breathing slowed. We waited. Jo opened his eyes and met Noda's gaze. "Kidnapped girl, front page, this morning?"

"Yeah," Noda said.

"You're looking for a guy called Tadao 'Habu' Nakagawa."

I blanched. "Habu as in the snake?"

With a measure of dry amusement, Jo nodded. "There's a resemblance."

"How so?" I asked.

The *habu* was a poisonous pit viper found in the Okinawa Islands to the south. Averaging four to five feet in length, it has a large diamond-shaped head and is a mild brown or olive, with a row of distinctive darker patches of green or black or brown on top. On a warm day it is easy to stumble on one sunning itself on a roadway or rocky surface. They are aggressive when threatened, and their bite can be deadly if not treated immediately. A high number of its human victims suffer from permanent disabilities.

"He's Okinawan, his head's kind of pointy, and he strikes fast."

As the bodyguard counted off Habu's traits, he'd rocked forward in his chair, raised his hand, and bent down a finger for each of Habu's three attributes.

"Lucky for us you still have two fingers up," I said.

The Great Wall folded the fourth digit. "And he's deadly when he wants to be."

Noda asked, "He have a weapon of choice?"

"Carries a double-edged fixed blade. Prides himself on one cut. Across the throat. But he'll slice open your belly just as happily. He's quick and hits his mark. Best not to irritate him."

By definition, that was the least of what we intended to do.

Jo's fifth finger was wavering.

"And the last item?" I asked.

The thumb went down. "Rumor mill says he's turned his basement into a viper pit, filled with his namesakes. Enemies get tossed in, so don't let him grab you."

Noda glared at the big man, the scar slicing across his eyebrow darkening. "All that true?"

A knife fight with a yazuka pimp had left Noda with a bisected eyebrow, but the pimp fared far worse. The scar acted like a barometer, changing color when the head detective's inner pressure rose.

"Yeah."

The chief detective thought the bad blood between Jo and myself might cause the bodyguard to embellish the story.

"No games?"

"None."

"Forewarned is forearmed," I said.

Jo stared at me. "Most people hear that list, they drop any idea of approaching the guy. You're not. Why not?"

"I got a client." *And I lost two friends.*

Jo shook his head. "Got to be a lot more."

"What makes you think that?"

"Because you risked coming here and Noda *let* you."

The Great Wall had a point. We weren't going to fool him, and with the clock ticking we needed his cooperation. So I told him about Mikey and Sharon, then mentioned the spy agencies but left the presidential couple out of the picture. Jo listened stone-faced. A nerve on his left cheek flickered when I mentioned the PSIA and Swelley's Homeland Security boys.

Once more Jo threaded his fingers behind his head. "Losing two friends is hard."

I nodded.

"Lost one in the Japantown case. You dug out the truth."

There was nothing to say to that, so I stayed pat.

Jo's brow clouded and a question hung in the air for a beat. "You sure he was there? Short, broad. Broken nose. Scar at the corner of his right eye, running down the cheek."

"Where'd the scar come from?"

"Me."

"Doesn't seem to have slowed him down."

Jo nodded. "Made him meaner. Was he there?"

"Don't know. They wore masks."

"Then how'd you ID him?"

I told him about the tattoo.

Jo's nod carried an edge I couldn't decipher. "That's his group. But he don't do that kind of work unless he's hired, so the woman's hot property. Stunt like that is going stir up the badges bad, so he woulda gone to ground last night. The exchange'll be tonight after dark. Once he's got the cash in his grubby mitts, you'll find him in Ni-chome celebrating."

"Did you say Ni-chome?" I asked.

"Yeah."

I rocked back on my heels, confused. In the Tokyo address system, *chome* designated a cluster of city blocks. *Ni* meant two, so *Ni-chome* was shorthand for a second grouping of blocks in some district. But in this case it was also shorthand for a section of the Shinjuku area known fully as Shinjuku Ni-chome. Which as any Tokyo resident will tell you is the city's most prominent gay quarter.

"He gay?"

Jo snorted. "He's a womanizer and a partier. Can't stay away from the nightclubs. Especially after a mammoth payday."

"Who hired him?"

"Got no idea."

"Any idea about who it *might* be?"

Jo shook his head. "He went in big, so it'll *be* big. Big client, big pay-off, big endgame. Only one other group in Tokyo can do what Habu's group did, but their leader's in Indonesia this week. Habu can be as thick as a whale, but when he smells money, he's fast as a whip."

"He an alkie?"

"No, just likes clubbing. Izakaya, hostess bars, all of 'em."

"Why Ni-chome?"

The bodyguard's eyes flared. "Not obvious?"

I looked at Noda. He shrugged. I looked back at Jo. "Enlighten us."

"Winds up a big job? Lady's man? Can't stop partying? Think on it."

I did. Then I knew. "Ni-chome is the last place the cops will look for him."

"You got it. He brings his own ladies."

"You have names?"

"Yeah."

Jo rattled off three places.

"Thanks," Noda said. "We owe you."

"*You* owe me," Jo said. "Not the dead man standing next to you."

I fired a final question at the elite bodyguard: "Why you being so cooperative?"

"Purely selfish motives." The Great Wall swiped a finger across his windpipe. "I need you breathing so I can kick your carcass across town and back. Most people who make Habu mad don't come back alive."

CHAPTER 38

THREE surprises followed on the heels of our confrontation with Jiro Jo. One came from Frank Renna out of San Francisco, the second from Lisa Kregg at the Freer Gallery in DC, and the last from Rie.

Noda and I were hunkered down at a local café for a few cups of Dutch summer-drip ice coffee some Japanese barista in Kyoto had perfected back in the day. Stoking up on caffeine for our upcoming night moves.

Renna had tracked down Jared Trooger, the braggart who, as an eighteen-year-old, had shot the convenience store clerk and fingered Mikey and his friend. Trooger was serving out his parole in Springfield, Virginia, his hometown.

My face grew hot. "Son of a bitch."

"Yeah. Less than fifteen miles from where Mikey was popped." Renna's tone echoed my disgust. "Guy could have driven over to the Kennedy Center on his lunch break."

"You pass it on?"

"Hardly had time to finish the conversation before the head investigator was out the door."

"So we're waiting on Springfield PD?"

"Yeah. I'll keep you in the loop. Why do you want to know if he speaks Spanish?"

I filled him in on Anna's abduction, then told him about the fork in the road: whether the kidnapping and the DC killings could be linked or not. The shooter at the Kennedy spoke Spanish. If Trooger spoke the language, we might have a link. If not, we'd need to look elsewhere. Before I wound up, my call waiting began its insistent bleating and a message popped up on my screen: incoming from the Freer.

"An eliminator," Renna said. "Got it. I'll pass it on."

I said thanks, we disconnected, and I switched over. "Hi, Lisa. You looked at the Kabuki costume?"

Kregg's voice was crystal clear. "It's brilliant, Brodie. I need you to grab me that robe. I showed it to two board members. They practically did cartwheels and they're both in their eighties. Did you *see* the design and stitching? Wasn't it great?"

"Superb."

The elegant woman's ceremonial robe had bowled me over. A pine-and-wisteria pattern in lime green and orange stretched across a dramatic black background, with fallen maple leaves in a yellowish tone scattered in the open areas. All three motifs were done in an intricate hand stitching.

"This is the best costume I've seen in years. Maybe ever. What's your take?"

"The same. A once-in-a-lifetime find."

"If it holds up in person, snatch it for us, okay? Whatever it takes."

"Be happy to. But know there's other bidders."

"We'll roll over them."

"That's all I need to hear. There's a story too."

"Give me."

Mitsue Bando, one of the rare nineteenth-century *female* Kabuki actors, had worn the costume. While women were forbidden to take the public stage, *only* women could perform for the wives and daughters of the ruling shogun and daimyo lords, not to mention the official concubines. Since the wife and concubines lived in the same area of the palace under guard, the all-female cast went to them. No man other than the lord was allowed to visit the women in their quarters. The robe had seen use in a play most likely produced in the early 1800s for the harem of the eleventh shogun in Edo Castle, Edo being the previous name for Tokyo.

"Incredible," Kregg said. "The piece is a true rarity. Don't forget us."

"I won't. Got to go."

During my talk with Kregg, Rie had texted me with an urgent message about meeting her PSIA contact. It was a go but with strings attached. Ibata would see me provided I showed up within the next ninety minutes because he was leaving tonight for "vacation," most likely a euphemism for a covert assignment. In a postscript, Rie reminded me about taking Noda.

I passed my phone to the chief detective. He scowled at the message. "Can't go."

"Why not?"

"My PSIA guy hears, he'll skewer me. Take Mari."

"She can't cover my back."

"She's a second pair of eyes. That's all you need today."

"Meaning if they come after us, it won't be on their territory?"

Noda grunted in assent, then stood without warning, his bulldog frame tense. "Time for you to take the 'Kasumigaseki stroll.' "

Tokyo's Kasumigaseki district plays home to a cluster of Japan's all-powerful ministries, the true seats of power.

Which is why, back in the nineties, the radical religious group Aum Shinrikyo targeted the area with its poisonous sarin gas attacks.

I met Mari in front of the old Ministry of Justice building, a stately redbrick edifice erected in the 1890s as Japan was shedding its feudal past. Colonnades fronted the two main entrances, and rows of pictur-esque white-framed windows ran the full length of its elegant block-long façade. Leaning against the short wall encircling the site, I watched Mari hop from an Uber cab and dash the last fifty feet.

"Hi, Brodie," she said, breathless, her face flushed with the sprint. "Thanks for thinking of me."

"Sorry about the short notice."

"I feel so stupid. I'm, like, what is the PSIA?"

Brodie Security's latest detective-in-training arrived in a navy-blue pantsuit. No vampire decorations. No colored extensions in her hair.

"Not your fault. Most Japanese have never heard of the PSIA, and I'm guessing that's the way the agency likes it."

Mari nodded. "I dug into some online ghost files. The agency keeps a low profile. Creepy low."

I pointed to the new Ministry of Justice tower coming into full view as we circled the block. "They're buried in there somewhere, along with the MOJ and Japan's public prosecutors' office."

The ministry had relocated to a double-winged ferroconcrete-and-glass tower directly behind the redbrick original, which now housed a training institute, library, and museum.

"I know, right? Did you notice that the text message from this Ibata-san just said 'Government Building 6A'? What kind of address is that?" As she spoke, a shiver overtook her.

We turned the final corner and headed toward the tower. A pair of signs warned arrivals against riding a bicycle and wielding a camera beyond this point. *On a public street.*

Mari took it all in. "Do you notice how shushy it is around here?"

"I think people avoid this street if they can."

There were cameras nestled high overhead on utility poles, in the trees, and on the walls of the building.

Mari glanced around uneasily. "At least the planners put in some nice landscaping."

"If you can call siege architecture disguised as contemporary urban planning 'nice.'"

"What are you talking about?"

"Look again. The landscaping you like is camouflaged security."

She did. To our left, decorative waist-high posts studded the curb at three-foot intervals. At the right was a double tier of stone planters. Tall shrubbery filled them. Narrow, short stacks of stairs allowed passage at carefully controlled intervals, with gates and guards.

Mari said, "I don't see anything."

"There's three layers of defense. The decorative stone posts are the first and only obvious line."

"You mean, like, maybe, to stop a suicide bomber in a car?"

"Just like that. Or any angry protester wanting to ram the building."

"We don't have either of those in Japan."

"But you *could*. You do have domestic protests."

"You said three. There's the watchmen, so that's two."

"I didn't count them. Any serious attack would plow right through them."

Mari looked startled. "Really?"

"Really. Half of them are in their fifties and sixties."

"Then what else?"

"Two sets of stone steps no more than four feet wide, separated by a landing, is about crowd control. Funneling people through narrow passages. The tiered levels retard attacks. The two rows of large granite planters with the tall bushes keep out prying eyes and give the watchers inside more time to gauge a potential threat. They'll also stop buses or large trucks."

"But it all looks so ordinary."

"How about that."

"So, like, none of this is normal?"

"Not even close."

After a uniformed guard handed us a pair of color-coded badges, we followed a tight-lipped blue-suited agent into an elevator, exiting sixty seconds later into a long hallway with oyster-gray walls and a row of unmarked doors on each side.

There was no directory on the wall. No signs or arrows.

We turned right.

New corridors branched off to both sides with more doors, all of them identical. None were numbered or labeled or supported descriptive plaques alongside. It was a modern version of the old samurai castle approach with a maze of passages invaders could not navigate before alerted troops took them down with a swarm of arrows from above.

Another turn. More doors. A third turn. We entered a room. Lidded porcelain cups of the obligatory green tea awaited our arrival and dictated our positions at a conference table for eight.

Our guide motioned us to sit and disappeared through a second door, which reopened a moment later to silently emit another blue-suited PSIA agent. He was polished, proper, and perfect. We exchanged bows and names, all in Japanese. Ibata didn't offer his card or a full name. Unusual but not unexpected. This was, after all, the PSIA.

"Please sit," he said.

Ibata had sculpted cheekbones, dimples, and wide, Western-style eyes that could have come down through the family gene pool, though my money was on the knowing flick of a surgeon's scalpel. Plus a few extra swipes to upgrade the dimples and nose, both of which verged on movie-star perfect. His suit and haircut towered leagues above the norm, meaning family money, not a PSIA salary. As Ibata displayed these last two perks openly, in complete disregard for the jealousy they would engender in his colleagues, I assumed he had unassailable backing higher up the line.

"I have heard about you, Brodie-san, and been wanting to meet you."

"Have you?"

There was a lot of oil in his hair.

"Yes." Hooded eyes glided over my face and person, then raked over Mari in open admiration. "I have heard less about your attractive companion, though." He turned to Mari. "At a more opportune time I would enjoy hearing about how *you* contribute to Brodie Security, Kawasaki-san. The PSIA is always looking for new talent."

He gave Mari a slick smile suggestive of a job far removed from PSIA's standard assignments. Her eyes dove into her lap.

"She's a valued colleague," I said.

The slickness slid my way. "I *bet* she is. Your activities in Japan are well-known to us, Brodie. Like your father's before you."

His voice had turned dismissive. I bristled at the tone until a vision of Zhou brought me to my senses. Could this be more spycraft? The manipulative measures of his kind? Draw a reaction and see what rises to the surface? Only one way to find out.

"Our work does make headlines from time to time," I said, shifting into neutral.

His eyes became small black beads. "And how do you know Rie Hoshino?"

"We worked on a case together involving the Tokyo home invasion murders a few months back. She was assigned to a senior detective by the name of Kato."

He nodded. "Shin'ichi Kato. Promoted sideways and considered deadweight."

"Actually, he's one of the best detectives the Tokyo PD has. Just doesn't play the political game well."

What little light remained in the black beads dissolved inward. "How would *you* know that?"

"Because the powers that be keep him close. Otherwise he'd be finishing out his days in some backwater."

Ibata sucked in his lower lip. "So what can we do for you, Mr. Brodie?"

The royal *we* had surfaced. The meeting was spiraling downward at a bewildering rate.

"Well, as we're all in law enforcement, I was hoping we could exchange information about the Sharon Tanaka case."

Since Rie would have informed him of my needs, I kept my reply open-ended, allowing him several avenues he could explore without compromising himself or the agency. He chose one I hadn't considered.

"And this is because Ms. Hoshino's father and my father both served in law enforcement together?"

The back door was closing.

"That's one way to put it. Of course, we would reciprocate."

His eyebrows arched. "How very kind of you to think of us. Do you and your companion have something to offer?"

"Not at the moment, but I expect we will."

Ibata tapped his lips with the index finger of his right hand. "Hoshino-san comes from a highly respected law enforcement family, and she did request I assist you. But she may have taken a wrong turn by recommending you to us."

I felt my face freeze. More tactics or something else? "Maybe she's expanding her horizons. Brodie Security deals domestically and internationally."

Ibata's surgically enhanced features hardened. "I understand you two are dating."

The meeting had veered officially off the rails.

"Did she tell you that?"

I knew she hadn't, and wouldn't.

"I follow her career."

"I see. I'm not sure her personal life is part of—"

His palm shot up abruptly. "Hoshino-san wondered if we might not be able to help you. Unfortunately, the way I see it, there *is* no helping you. We're done here."

He rose with a stiff formality and swept from the room without another word, leaving us alone with two steaming cups of untouched green tea, a host of new questions, and not a single answer.

CHAPTER 39

WAS that a threat?" Mari asked once we were well away from Government Building 6A and any ears it might have.

"Yes. Veiled, with deniability."

"Super-creepy."

I nodded. "Couldn't have put it better myself."

"If he wasn't going to help, why did he agree to a meeting?"

"Two reasons, I'd guess."

"He totally has a thing for your lady friend. What's the other one?"

"He wanted a good look at us."

Mari cleared her throat. "Um, you're, like, being polite by including me, aren't you? What you really mean is *you*, right?"

"Yes, to both questions," I said.

———

It was time to visit the Tanakas.

This was the hardest part of my father's calling: interviewing members of a victim's family, who are usually devastated and suffering from unimaginable shock. This time they faced murder, kidnapping, and a brutal beating.

Noda, Mari, and I headed west to the upscale Setagaya enclave of Sakura, west of central Tokyo. The area had once been the wooded hunting ground of the shogun, where he practiced falconry, a popular status-affirming sport of the ruling samurai class. Animals roamed the forest. Birds glided in for a rest on the waterways. From the gloved arm of an elite samurai, a trained hawk would soar high into the sky, then sharp claws would swoop down on an unsuspecting duck or goose or swan.

Not unlike the way the gang had swooped down on Anna Tanaka.

———

The home was firmly upper-middle-class: tasteful beige tiling across the façade, a wrought iron fence around the property, and entry through an iron gate with sculptured peach blossoms.

Soon after we rang the bell, Sharon's husband opened the door. He hadn't shaved. His hair was uncombed. Worst of all, the gentle brown eyes I'd remembered from our one brief meeting were muddy and unfocused.

"Welcome," he said. "Please come in."

He led us into a Western-style sitting room with a long couch, overstuffed chairs, and a central table set down between them. In an adjoining tatami room I caught sight of a scroll painting, a short-legged table, and an L-shaped legless chair. A ninety-year-old woman dozed in the chair. She shared Sharon's facial structure. *Her mother.* I couldn't begin to imagine what the matriarch of the Tanaka clan must be going through as she watched her family being assailed from all sides.

"Who else will be joining us?" I asked.

"My apologies," Mr. Tanaka said, waving us to the couch. "I'm on my own today, so please give me a minute."

Translation: we would not be interviewing the entire family.

Joan Slater had parted the gate, but not by much.

Tanaka shuffled off into the back of the house, returning a long moment later with a pot of steeping green tea. Sliding into one of the facing chairs, he poured a cup for each of us, then beckoned us to drink.

"Joan Slater says I should talk to you," he said, pausing to sip his tea, "so I will, out of respect for her. But I think this is a hopeless exercise. I've told the authorities everything I know two dozen times. So the sooner we can get this over with, the better. My family prefers its privacy. I hope you understand."

"More than you know."

Tanaka's hand trembled as he set down his cup. Swollen half-moons underscored eyes brimming over with exhaustion.

I said, "Would you mind bringing us up to date?" I kept my voice low and gentle. "Have you received any ransom demands?"

"Not yet."

"Any contact at all?"

"None. What do you think that means? The authorities would not share their thoughts."

"I'm not sure. The kidnappers may want money or they may want leverage. Or it could be something else altogether."

"Leverage?"

"Your family seems to know a lot of highly placed people. If Anna or someone else in your family is, say, close to an elite government figure or a VIP, like your wife was to the first lady, the kidnappers might be able to use your daughter's abduction to extract a favor."

I was playing a long shot from Zhou's dubious playbook.

"No, no. That was Sayuri's territory."

Sharon's Japanese name.

"What does Anna's husband do?"

"Oh, there's nothing there either. He's a professor. He frequents dusty libraries, not halls of power."

"Teaching what?"

"Folklore. That's how they met. Our Anna loves folklore."

I queried Noda and Mari with a look. They had nothing, so I took the leap.

"Mr. Tanaka, why did your daughter come to the funeral in disguise?"

His eyes darted away. "Let me get you some more tea."

He swept up the teapot with one brisk move—suddenly and inexplicably energized—then vanished down the hall to the kitchen before I could stop him.

CHAPTER 40

MR. Tanaka refreshed our cups, then retook his seat. "I'm sorry. I needed time to think. Do you mind if I ask *you* a question?"

"Not at all."

"The first lady, she's, uh, cleared for top secret stuff, right?"

"I'm sure she has a security clearance. Not as high as the president's, though, or others working for him. Why do you ask?"

"How about you?"

"*Me?*"

"Yes."

A puzzling turn. There were dots to be connected. But which ones?

"This has to do with your daughter?"

"I don't want to get her in trouble." His eyes skipped away again.

The first lady's security clearance . . . mine . . . I had it. "You're protecting Anna. No, not *her*. Her job. Right? She's got some sort of job with a security clearance?"

He didn't answer, which I took as a yes.

I said, "Maybe a secure status you don't want to compromise?"

"I am her father," he said, which served as another yes.

"Fair enough," I said. "I do not have any official government security clearance but I *am* working for the *White House*. And whoever took Anna is working for the other guys. Isn't that enough?"

Tanaka frowned. He dropped folded hands into his lap, his gaze settling on the nest of intertwined fingers.

"Listen," I said. "We are on your side. You lost your wife and I lost two friends. The first lady herself asked me to look into this over and above Homeland and the DC police because I'm one of the few people who knows both the U.S. and Japan. And mostly because she really cares about Sharon and knows I do too."

He shifted uneasily in his chair, confused.

In a softer voice I said, "I know this must be unbearable for you, but Anna is still out there. She is in hostile hands but she's *alive*. Yes, the Japanese police and other authorities are working on it, but why not let Brodie Security help too? We've been around for forty years. Joan Slater wants us involved. I want to be involved. Other than the first lady, no one else has a personal stake in this."

That brought his head up fast. "You hardly know my daughter."

His tone was accusatory and the comment hurt, but I swallowed the offense without judging him. Tanaka was in pain and, justified or not, was lashing out at the closest target.

"That's true. I only met her that once in passing, when I ran into the three of you in Nihonbashi. But I knew your wife well, and I was there at the Kennedy Center when she and Mike Dillman were shot. I feel responsible because I was the one who brought them together. What's worse, I saw the killer and couldn't catch him. Those things are tearing me apart. If anyone can understand my pain, you can. And if anyone outside your family can understand *your* pain, I can. If that's not enough, I give up. Say the word and I'll walk out of your life and never bother you again. I'll drop the first lady's commission and go after the killer on my own, without your help. But, either way, I'm not stopping."

He stared at me through eyes still muddy and bloodshot but now tearing up. A frail clarity clawed at the cloud of confusion hovering over him. "Maybe you're right. I don't know. I can't think anymore. This may kill me. I might not live to see my daughter's return, assuming she is alive, as you say."

"She is," I said.

The corners of his mouth sunk. "How can you possibly know that when even the Japanese police don't know such a thing?"

"Because there's been no ransom note."

He blinked. "If that's true, why didn't the police tell me that?"

"Because you only just gave me the other piece of the answer a moment ago."

He blinked again. "Me? I don't understand."

"No ransom note and no leverage. If they don't want your money and there's no reason to use Anna for blackmail, that leaves only one thing."

"What?"

"They want something from Anna herself."

"What's that?"

"I don't know yet. But if you'll work with us, I promise I'll do my best to find out."

His eyes rolled around in their watery sockets like an unmoored oyster in a half shell. I'd pushed him too far. Then his gaze refocused and found mine with feverish intent.

"Of all the agencies and officials and policemen who have tramped through this house, no one has put it that way." The haze of hurt and confusion parted some more. "What do you need from me?"

"I need everything you know *and* everything you know but don't know you know."

He began to nod and kept nodding. At first in acknowledgment to my answer, but next to an inner voice. Then, without warning, he rose on unsteady feet, saying, "Let me bring more tea," and headed off once more to the rear of the house.

Mari's eyes spilled over with worry. "Is he coming back?"

"I don't know."

The teapot remained untouched on the table in front of us.

My phone buzzed with an incoming message from Renna, back in San Francisco. It was a follow-up about Jared Trooger and the murder-robbery that earned Mikey a sealed juvie record.

Trooger is out. Springfield PD jumped on him first thing in the morning. Doesn't speak Spanish. Accounting office where he works has him punched in at the time of the Kennedy Center murders. SPD will cross-check alibi with boss and employees, but accounting head said Trooger operates a machine on an assembly line for vacuum cleaners. Any absence would have stalled the whole line until they found a replacement. Nothing else on Mikey in SF has led anywhere. Ball's in your court.

So Trooger wasn't the Spanish-speaking killer I'd heard backstage at the Kennedy Center, and none of Mikey's skeletons were going to get me the why behind the murders. If we didn't find the answer here, in the Tanakas' living room, my inquiry into my friends' deaths would stall out. Some ball.

———

Relief swept over us when Tanaka finally reappeared.

Another minute and we'd planned to dive into the back rooms after him.

Sharon's husband had used the time to wash his face and comb his hair. Perhaps for the first time that day. He'd also shaved.

"Forgot this," he said with a sheepish grin. He picked up the bamboo-handled teapot and headed off again, reappearing a moment later and pouring fresh tea all around before reclaiming his seat. "Let's bring my daughter home," he said.

For the first time since our arrival, there was a glimmer of hope in his eyes. In my peripheral vision I saw Mari perk up. Noda's eyebrows rose, then resettled.

"Let's," I said. "We can start with your daughter's job. What exactly does she do?"

"I don't know."

"She didn't tell you?"

"No."

"She never talked about her work?"

"No."

"Did you ask?"

"Of course. I'm her father. It's just that . . . that . . . Akemi—Anna to you—made me promise not to mention her security clearance, which is the only thing I know about her work. And only because some people from the American embassy came to interview me."

"How about the name of the company?"

"No."

"Do you know if it was a company or, say, a government agency?"

"No."

"Did she ever mention any of her colleagues by name?"

"No."

"Or introduce you to any of them?"

"No."

"Is there anything more you *do* know?"

"No."

I'd slammed into a wall of *no*'s erected by the very woman we were trying to rescue.

Mari spoke up for the first time. "Brodie, would you mind if I asked Mr. Tanaka some questions?"

"Please," I said.

Our detective-in-training smiled at Tanaka. "Aside from folklore, did your daughter have any other interests?"

"Of course. Volleyball and computers."

Mari's eyes sparkled. "Did she, like, maybe go online sometimes?"

"Constantly. Why?"

This was no coincidence. Mari had found some hint of Anna's online activities.

"Because from the age of eight I was that way too," Mari was saying.

"My Anna started at six," Tanaka said with a measure of pride.

Mari grinned as if she'd found a soul mate. "Did she have a handle?"

"A what?"

"A screen name she used when she was online."

"Oh, yes, although she stopped all that nonsense once she graduated college. Online she was Spiker13. She always dreamed of playing on the women's Olympic volleyball team, so she made herself the thirteenth member."

"No way," Mari said. "*Your* daughter is Spiker13?"

"Yes. Why?"

"Spiker13 was my idol. She was a white-hat hacker and *the* top female computer talent in Japan for four years running until she graduated college and was headhunted by SoftBank."

"I don't know what a 'white-hat hacker' is but the rest of it's correct. How do you know all that?"

SoftBank is one of Japan's premier tech companies. Its founder, Masayoshi Son, was one of the first people in Japan to ride the Internet wave to riches. He went into broadband, software, and Internet properties, then cell phones, banking, and beyond.

"Are you kidding? In my circle, your daughter is a rock star." Mari fired an impassioned look my way. "Brodie, Anna Tanaka is a software genius. She was lured away from SoftBank by Google, where she stayed only two years before being poached by a company on the East Coast."

"Who?" I asked.

"No one knows. My hacker friends and I plowed the trenches to find out, but couldn't."

"Is all that true?" I asked Tanaka.

"Your partner knows as much as I do."

I cleared my throat. "That's a good start, but we're going to need more. You need to tell us why your daughter came to her mother's funeral in disguise."

Tanaka's gaze bounced between Mari and me, then he shrugged. "You seemed to have guessed so much already. It's because of her security clearance. Her employers didn't want her to come at all. The disguise was a compromise Anna herself suggested. We enlisted one of her mother's friends to do the makeup."

I sat back, stunned. "That's some plan. And you have absolutely no idea who she works for?"

"No."

"Or even a hint of what she does?"

"No."

"Can you give us anything new at all? It could make a difference."

His brow furrowed. "Well, I did see an email of hers once by mistake, but I doubt it's important. I read it and I shouldn't have. I've always taught my children to respect the privacy of others, so you can understand my embarrassment. My lapse is unforgivable, so please keep this between us. All of it was too technical for me except for one thing. Akemi worked at a place called Fort Meade."

His answer electrified me. "Are you sure that was the name?"

" 'Stationed at Fort Meade' was the phrase I saw. Do you think it's important?"

"It changes the whole ball game," I said.

ACK out on the street, Mari turned immediately to me. "What's at Fort Meade?"

"The NSA," I said.

Mari shook her head. "I know the name but I don't follow that stuff. Do you, Noda-san?" He said no, so Mari said, "You need to fill us in, Brodie."

Which I did.

Aside from a handful of military installations, Fort Meade housed the headquarters of the National Security Agency. The NSA collected and analyzed the emails, phone calls, Internet movements, and any other form of digital activity of Americans and foreigners around the world. Tens of thousands of people worked directly for the NSA or its contractors. It was all part of the buildup of the security-military-industrial complex in Washington that Dr. Kregg had mentioned at the museum—as a new source of donations for her, and as a warning to me. And just the kind of place that could find endless uses for someone with Anna's talent.

Mari could not contain her agitation. "You've got to find her, Brodie."

"*We've* got to find her. We're a team. You did well in there."

She blushed and looked away. In Japan, a nonverbal sign of approval was the traditional route.

I said, "But first I need to know if Anna Tanaka is really as good as you claim, or were you just being nice to her father?"

"Spiker13 is awesome. She's a top Japanese talent."

That clinched it.

This wasn't about Anna herself or someone she might know.

This was about what was in her head.

11 P.M.
THE SHINJUKU NI-CHOME DISTRICT, TOKYO

Habu will post guards front and back, the Korean bodyguard Jiro Jo had told us. *You want him, you'll have to get past his men.*

Noda and I arrived at the edge of Tokyo's gay quarter. A light shower earlier in the evening had swept away the dust. Streets and storefronts glistened. Bright neon signage cast rainbow streaks across rain-slicked sidewalks.

Barhopping men cruised the narrow lanes. They strolled by alone and in pairs. Splashy clothes and plumage were rare on the street. Shy to a fault, most Japanese preferred to unwind behind closed doors. To that end, colorful attire was cloaked under a light spring jumper or carried in a shoulder bag. More ambitious souls dragged small carry-on luggage with wheels in their wake. Tourists from the countryside flicked sly glances at the native exotica. A few outright gawkers rocketed through the streets, laughing and talking in loud speculative voices.

Further intel from Jo gave us a handle on Habu's movements. The yakuza boss would keep it low-key until the police let up. Low-key for him meant a woman on each arm, two of his best men roaming the room, and guards posted outside his chosen club to screen for unfriendlies.

"Habu is sly," the bodyguard had said. "He uses Ni-chome as another layer of defense. You two won't pass."

Our arrival would trigger an immediate alert, we were informed.

"What about the club proprietors?" I asked.

"Habu spreads a lot of money around up front. You'll be in hostile territory from all sides."

We hit the first two clubs with negative results and were beginning to doubt Jo's street creds. Ni-chome housed three hundred bars of all sizes. Most were select, clubby affairs catering to special segments of the community, with seating of fifteen to twenty, sometimes less. Habu frequented large nightclubs where the crowd stretched to several hundred.

Noda and I strolled through Habu's first two hangouts to flesh out our target's preferences: he liked loud, noisy, dark, and cavernous. On a Friday night, the clubs were busy and chaotic. Habu could hide in plain sight. Both of the first two spots confined the dancing to one corner of the club, which worked to the gang leader's advantage. Dancing created too much random movement and made it harder to detect an approaching attack.

Dragon Skin was the last name on the list. As with the first two haunts, we planned to circle around the front and back, an eye peeled for Habu's watchmen. We needn't have worried. From a block away, we spotted two soldiers leaning against the wall of the building, four lots from the corner.

"Sign says third floor," I said. "The green and yellow one."

"Might be men in the stairwells too," Noda said.

There was nothing buff or bear or butch about the pair of thugs hovering around the entrance. They made no pretense about blending in. They would note the same of us, so before we hit their radar, we took the next turn and swung around to the rear. On the back side of the block, a narrow lane four yards wide was lined with a string of Japanese-style "snack" bars offering karaoke, drinks, and "hostesses" of the male persuasion.

I glanced down the alley.

"Two more men," I said.

"Makes a good blind. Gonna call in the boys."

Noda hit redial on his cell phone, laid out the location, said "Ten minutes," disconnected, and turned to me with: "That enough time?"

"It'll have to be."

We walked on.

CHAPTER 42

THREE minutes later we looped back.

A jumble of music peppered the night air. Buoyant notes from *The Phantom of the Opera* trickled through the parted window of a third-floor club, and the heavy base beat of dance mixes reached our ears two doors down.

Side by side, Noda and I turned into the slim passageway. Despite attempts to deflate our natural bulk, we filled the opening. Five yards in, the pair of watchers spotted us. Suspicious eyes swung our way—and stayed.

Our gait was loose-limbed and lubricated. We walked a crooked line, weaving about like drunks pretending they could hold their liquor. Just a couple of guys who maybe wandered down the wrong alley in the wrong section of town.

"The welcoming committee's spotted us," I mumbled. "They don't seem to be buying."

It was an impressive committee. Both were muscular and bulked out. They leaned side by side against the back wall of the building housing Dragon Skin. One had a leg cocked and bent, foot planted flat against wall. The other turned to face us, then let a shoulder fall back against the brick.

Noda stumbled and fell into me.

I pushed him away, saying with undisguised disgust, "Drunk already?"

"Ain't drunk, you stupid *gaijin*." Stupid foreigner.

That earned a laugh from our audience.

Noda took a sloppy swing at me. I sidestepped the attack, and the momentum of his ill-aimed punch dragged him sideways. He stumbled and nearly fell.

One of the guards snorted and looked away. *No threat there.* The other, not yet convinced, continued to monitor our progress.

"Get a grip, you idiot," I said. "Night's still young."

Noda connected with a long, loping roundhouse to my ribs and I said "Hey!" and stumbled back against a wall, knocking over a knee-high trash bin.

Snickers from the onlookers reached our ears. The second one finally lost interest.

We wove on. Maybe five microbars lined each side of the lane, and more of the same were stacked six or seven stories above them. We passed narrow staircases leading upward to the off-street establishments. Distant snatches of music and chatter swept down the stairwells.

Behind us came a screech of wheels and then a tap of a car horn. Not a rude blast of an irritated driver but a tolerant, prodding, nudge-the-drunks-to-the-side sort of beep.

We turned in time to see the driver of a large restaurant supply van thrust his head out the window. "Need you to give us some room, gentlemen. We have a delivery to make."

Gentlemen. No road rage here.

Noda and I veered out of the vehicle's path. I slipped in behind the chief detective. The delivery van advanced at a glacial pace, afraid we'd lurch back into its path in a drunken misstep. The wheels made a sucking sound on the wet pavement. I laid my hands on Noda's shoulders to steady myself. Noda tripped and stumbled into the path of the truck before weaving back the other way. The driver hit the brakes. Tires screeched on the slick pavement.

Noda and I trekked on single file. The truck inched forward, not daring to pass us.

"Take your arms off," Noda said, his voice carrying down the passage.

"Not till the damn truck goes by. You can't hardly walk. *Know* I can't see straight."

I glanced around. The truck consumed most of the alleyway's girth.

The head yakuza shot us a disgusted look, but despite our world-class acting job he and his partner tensed as we drew near. I released my grip on Noda. Without his steadying presence, my legs drifted sideways and buckled. I slumped against the wall and slid to the ground, groaning.

"Maybe I'll rest here a minute," I said.

Noda walked on, heedless. He passed by the sentries without a glance and they relaxed.

"Hey," I said, "wait up."

Noda waved a hand above his head in dismissal without looking back.

I picked myself up and staggered after him.

The van stopped in front of the guards.

"Keep moving," the lead sentry said, stepping forward.

The driver jerked a thumb at the Boy's Room across the way. "Just be a second, gentlemen. Got a bundle of towels to deliver to that bar and I'll be gone."

The yakuza curled his upper lip. "You ain't stopping here. Take it to the end of the—"

Behind him, Noda pivoted and charged. The man closest to me noticed the sudden movement and shouted a warning. I launched off my back foot. Catching my advance out of the corner of his eye, the yaki soldier turned toward me as I plowed a fist into his stomach. Noda wrapped the second man in a bear hug, pinning his arms.

As my prey doubled up, I brought clasped hands down on his neck and he collapsed to the pavement. A favorite go-to move.

The side panel of the supply van slid aside. Two men leapt out, lifted my conquest from the ground, and flung him into the van. He sailed across the empty compartment and slammed into the far panel, collapsing with a groan. A third man waiting inside jumped on his back, pinning his arms, while a fourth wound a spool of duct tape around the man's ankles three times, slapped a strip across his mouth, then secured the target's arms behind his back with three more rotations of tape.

Twenty seconds had elapsed.

I turned toward Noda. His captive struggled to break loose. I was two feet away, staring into eyes bulging with fury.

"Be good and we'll avoid the rough stuff," I said.

His cheeks puckered. I slammed my fist into his nose before he could spit at me.

"That was a short-term, nonnegotiable offer," I said. "Throw him in."

The second guard followed the first and seconds later he too was secured.

"Wrapped, packed, and stacked," the driver said. "You still wanna do the guys out front?"

That had been the original plan.

"Yeah," I said. "Be two less coming down on us if things heat up inside."

So we circled around the front, waited for a lull in the foot traffic, and gave an encore performance. With the two guards sharing a bottle of Nikka whisky, we corralled them without much resistance.

"Now that the hard work's done," the driver said, "are you good or do you need us inside as well?"

Noda snorted, and I said, "We're good. Just keep those four under wraps."

"Not a problem," the driver said, and drove off.

I headed toward the stairs.

Noda grabbed my shoulder.

I flung a glance at the chief detective. "What?"

"Careful on this one."

I cocked my head at him. Being careful went with the territory.

"You know something else besides what Jo told us?" I said.

The chief detective's look turned feral. "Rats get bold in the dark. Scurry away from the light. This one runs *toward* the light."

"Agreed. It's unusual."

Noda shook his head. "No. Abnormal. The most dangerous of all."

CHAPTER 43

DRAGON Skin was a cavern of darkness.

The door opened inward into a serpentine room that slithered forward with the ropey grace of a dragon's tail. Then the tail split in two, with secluded alcoves and booths that faded into ever-deepening shadows. Black walls, black tables, and curving tufted black leather booths sucked every ray of available light into a vacuum.

Dim recessed ceiling lights silhouetted clusters of gay men gathered in the booths and standing on the floor and up against a long bar farther on into the club. Designer cocktails were plentiful. Heterosexual couples, though in the minority, mingled. Dragon Skin put out a distinctly Ni-chome feel, and yet it looked to be an equal opportunity party place. Habu could slip in without ruffling feathers.

Hoisting trays of drinks, black-tuxedoed waiters in matching skintight short pants slipped in and around groups. Thin pink laser beams pulsed through the blackness at indiscriminate angles, slashing across bodies and faces, then just as suddenly disappearing.

A lithe Japanese maître d' in a green tuxedo and short pants glided up to us. Silver threads in his getup shimmered in the dim light, giving his approach a magical lizardlike quality.

Dragon skin.

His smile was wide and welcoming. Maybe too welcoming. Under the tux, he wore a green bow tie with a crisp white shirt and a green cummerbund. On the left wing of the tie was a winking eye. The pants squeezed the tops of his thighs.

"Hi, boys! I'm Donnie. Welcome to Dragon Skin."

Naturally he winked. Perfect Ni-chome. Camp and corn rolled into one. Jo was right: this was the absolute last place the police would hunt for Habu. *If* they even knew to hunt for him.

"Thanks," I said. "We're looking for a friend."

Donnie raised a tapered finger to his chin and looked doe-eyed at Noda. "*I* could be that friend."

Noda growled and the maître d' rose up on his toes. "Oooh, feisty. I *like* it." His eyes slid up and down Noda's body. Subtlety was not the order of the day at Dragon Skin.

The chief detective's growl grew louder, and I stepped between them. "Don't lead the poor boy on, Noda. It'll only encourage him."

Donnie slapped my shoulder. "You're so fresh." His fingertips glided down my arm to my biceps. "Oooh. Aren't you the burly one. But your friend is more my type. I like a little trouble with my spice."

"Hear that, Noda? You're set if you ever decide to dump me."

Donnie said, "I would offer to guide you, but I'm sure you two brutes can find your way just fine."

"That we can," I said.

"Then let me give you the little Dragon speech. You can order drinks from the booths or go to the bar. Tonight is Dance-Free Friday, which we have once a month because it gets *so* hot and crowded at times and not everyone likes up close and clammy. Tonight you can mix and chat and flirt till you drop, but it's no-dance casual. So let down your hair, boys, and go grab 'em. And you, stud muffin"—he pointed a finger at Noda and rotated it slowly—"come find me if you want anything special. Anything at all."

A white card appeared as if by magic in Donnie's hand. The glib maître d' stepped around me and tucked it in Noda's shirt pocket.

"You live dangerously," I said.

Donnie's face lit up. "One must, sweetie. One must."

Then he scooted off into the darkness, silver threads twinkling in his wake.

I turned to Noda. "Well, stud muffin, do you have time to look for Habu or should I leave you and Donnie to—"

"Don't."

Donnie's flirtation had put the chief detective in a sour mood.

I shrugged. "You see Habu anywhere?"

"No."

"More soldiers?"

"No."

"Anyone who might be a contender?"

"No."

"Same here on all counts."

We moved farther into the gloom to where the room forked. We could make out no faces beyond the five-yard range, except when a pink laser spiked the darkness.

"Split up?" I asked.

"Yeah. Stand out less."

"Not going to happen. We blend in like German shepherds in a kennel of whippets."

Noda muttered under his breath in reluctant admiration. "Smart move, this place."

Reports placed weekend attendance of the club at two to three hundred, with a loyal base of die-hard regulars. Clearly, new blood was welcomed but immediately noted. Donnie had recited the club rules without even inquiring if it was our first time. He knew. Which was bad news if Habu had lookouts clocking fresh faces.

Noda rumbled down the left fork and I veered to the right, drawing lingering looks of appraisal from clusters of regulars. I imagined my bulldog partner attracted an equal measure of unwanted attention.

The club was fragrant with flowery scents and colognes. Lively chatter, club music, but nothing outwardly untoward.

I was two-thirds through my section when I sensed an approach from behind. Before I could turn, the point of a knife sliced through my shirt and nicked my spine. Blood trickled from the cut.

"Start walking," a voice leavened with menace and saké snarled in my ear, "or next time the knife goes deeper."

I began to raise my hands but he slapped the left one away with a rough, thick-fingered paw. "Keep 'em down. Don't want any glamour boys eyeing us."

I wondered from what crevice he'd emerged. No one who looked anything like his voice sounded had been lingering in the shadows I'd passed.

I let my hands drop and my knife-wielding captor said, "What are you doing here?"

Rumor mill says Habu's turned his basement into a viper pit. Enemies get tossed in, so don't let him grab you.

"What do you mean?"

He flicked his blade again and a second nick opened up next to the first. "You ain't gay. Why you here?"

"There's hundreds of people here. Why you bothering with me?"

"'Cause you ain't one of *them* but you been to the funeral today."

"You're mistaken," I said.

"I don't make mistakes. But you just made the biggest of your life."

CHAPTER 44

MY captor led me deeper into the dark nightclub, past knots of mostly gay men drinking cocktails or wine or the occasional pint. Regardless of dress or costume, all of the men were well groomed. All of the cocktails were ornate in color or plumage or both.

I kept an eye peeled for Habu or any of his men. I spotted the gang leader from five yards out, his image solidifying in the gloom as we drew closer. He sat at a booth in the farthest corner, happily sandwiched between two professional bits of arm candy in clinging summer knit dresses with swooping necklines. A pink beam flashing over the table revealed that the women wore vivid spring colors ripe for the picking: a cool strawberry pink and a papaya yellow. He had one arm slung over Papaya's shoulder and the other snaked around Pink's waist, his hand fondling Pink's left breast with evident appreciation. A magnum of champagne rested in a red-lacquer ice bucket at a cocky tilt. A bottle of premium Yamazaki single malt whisky stood upright a few inches away.

"You're gonna be a nice present for the boss," the yakuza soldier at my back said.

Habu was decked out in upscale gangster gaudy: a black dress shirt and a lemon-yellow tie. Against the black leather of the high-backed booth, his head bobbed like a balloon on a yellow string.

"He like surprises?"

"From the skirts, yeah. You, no. He'll likely wanna slice you up some to impress the girls."

He's deadly when he wants to be, Jiro Jo had told us. *Carries a double-edged fixed blade.*

"Lucky me."

"Don't worry. You won't see it coming."

Habu's radar zeroed in on us the instant we drew near. Mean eyes and a big diamond-shaped head swiveled in my direction. Along the right side of his face, the shiny surface of the scar Jo mentioned picked up what little light there was.

"What you bring me, Sai?" the gang leader said.

"A gift."

"Name?"

Sai pressed the tip of his blade harder against my spine, then with his free hand withdrew my wallet from my back pocket. I heard him flipping through my cards.

"California driver's license says 'Jim Brodie.' Three credit cards got the same name."

"Name don't mean nothing to me." A husky whisky rasp hung on to the edge of his words.

"He was at the Tanaka funeral."

Habu's lascivious grin fell victim to a tight-lipped frown. Giving Pink's breast a last affectionate squeeze, he whispered in her ear and she scooted, giggling, from the booth. In an instant Habu clambered out after her and straightened to his full girth: five-seven and approaching two hundred pounds. He was blocky and broad and quick on his feet. His head, narrow at the front, flared out the sides, then tapered off severely again behind the ears.

"Don't know what you're doing here, gaijin, but you just found trouble like you ain't never seen."

The lingering whisky vapors followed the lascivious smile into oblivion. Sai's revelation had sobered his boss.

"Don't want trouble, just a talk," I said.

"Get down on your knees like my women and Habu will accommodate you."

The women twittered.

"Not going to happen," I said.

The knife at my spine urged me forward. I planted my feet. I felt a sharp prick, then a third trickle of blood. I didn't budge.

Habu flicked his wrist, and from a hidden spring-loaded holster up his sleeve a glittering shaft of steel shot into his palm. His personal admiration society admitted gasps of delight. The entertainment portion of the evening was about to begin.

The rest of Jiro Jo's warning came to mind: *Prides himself on one cut. Across the throat. But he'll slice open your belly just as happily. He's quick and hits his mark. Best not to irritate him.*

"You want his ID?" Sai said.

"Yeah."

The henchman lobbed my wallet to Habu, who caught it with his free hand. He cradled it in his palm, stood it on edge, and thumbed through the contents.

"San Francisco address. That where you live?"

"Yep."

"Ever take a boat under the Golden Gate?"

"Many times."

"Got to get me there one day. Bad news is you ain't gonna make it back."

He snapped the wallet shut and tossed it at the bartender. "Hold that for me, Masu-kun. The gaijin won't be needing it."

"I'll keep it right here, boss."

The weapon at my back faded away. Habu rolled his blade around his thick knuckles a couple of times. Pink and Papaya applauded in a flutter of dainty air claps. The yakuza boss's chest inflated.

I took the opportunity to edge back half a foot. The movement refocused Habu's attention on me. His eyes flickered over my abdomen, throat, and eyes. All potential targets, I realized with a chill. Then he gave the left side of my head special attention. I inched back another six inches.

The yaki leader sneered. "You afraid of Habu, gaijin?"

"The knife deserves respect."

"*Habu* deserves respect."

"Naturally," I said. "Look, all I want is a quiet chat."

I angled my head to catch a glimpse of my escort. Sai had cinnamon-colored skin and a large flat face dominated by a broad, flat nose. He leaned back against the bar, elbows resting on the slick black countertop, a smirk on his lips, a flask of warm saké nearby. His hands were empty.

Behind Sai, the bartender cranked up the music.

Auditory camouflage.

Confrontation was not a new scenario at Dragon Skin.

Noda and I had walked into a trap.

"Habu don't answer to strangers. And barging in without an invite is gonna cost you a souvenir for the ladies."

I let him babble while I looked for an exit strategy from a nearly impossible situation. In close quarters, I had the knife-wielding gang boss in front and his henchman behind. Sensible people had exited to other parts of the club. Maybe fifteen customers remained. None of them were yakuza. None of them would intercede on my behalf.

". . . either a finger or an ear . . ."

I'd stumbled into Habu's private house of horrors, peopled with his women, his soldiers, bought-and-paid-for bar staff, and what I now understood to be a core group of admirers-slash-gawkers. The devotees stared in rabid fascination, their eyes dancing, their expressions expectant.

". . . got a finger last week, so maybe an ear this time . . ."

I scanned the crowd of groupies. Not a sympathetic face among them. And no Noda. Had the Sasa-gumi gang taken him down? I didn't know, but waiting for him would only get me flayed.

So I didn't.

CHAPTER 45

THE next time the cocky thug cast a boastful glance at the ladies, I swept inward, hoping to catch him off his game.

But Jiro Jo's assessment had been spot-on: the guy was faster than fast. Even partially inebriated. The knife rose like steel lightning.

Habu lashed out, his free hand hovering at his hip for balance. I dove to my right, away from his strike, but the gang leader had come alarmingly close.

And yet he didn't chase me. Instead, he tethered himself to his table, where his female admirers would have a clear view as he took me apart. Penned in, I couldn't range far. He could wait me out. Meanwhile, in anticipation, the groupies crowded closer together. The whites of their eyes glistened.

"Running scared, gaijin?"

I flashed a look at Sai, but the henchman hadn't budged. He too was content to watch the action unfold. I wondered how many had gone down before me—either here or at one of the other clubs.

In a showman's flourish, Habu slashed the air between us. "You ain't leaving here unless I get an ear. Or your life. Maybe both."

"Why'd you take the woman?"

Habu grinned. "I *like* women. I take 'em any way I can."

"The Tanaka girl."

His look grew shifty. "How you know about that?"

He didn't like his private business spread around in public.

"Like your man said, I was at the funeral."

"We wore masks."

"Maybe I'm psychic."

"Maybe you're dead."

I nodded at his wrist. "Gang tattoo."

"Gonna take out both your eyes too."

On the last syllable, he pounced. Excited whispers from the gallery fluttered under the pulsing beat of the music. Habu's thick bulk hopped forward with surprising agility. A rangy muskiness rolled off him.

I backpedaled in haste. He followed this time. His body was a surging mass of muscle. I looped around, feinting a move toward a hall that offered a convenient escape route. When he shifted to cut me off, I changed direction, swinging back toward Papaya and Pink. Habu could not have been more pleased.

He grinned.

Showtime.

I paused in front of the women. Habu stopped across from me, within striking distance. Up came his free hand for balance. The weapon followed, rising like the head of a cobra, weaving and bobbing. Habu licked his lips. A buzz rippled through the crowd.

He lunged again. I backed off. He lingered in front of the women.

I was beginning to decipher the gang leader's blade work. He had speed but no formal training. No martial knife techniques. No full-on assault with an unfolding series of moves. Rather, he relied on staccato lunges and slashes, each independent and distinct.

Habu didn't dance either. He planted his forward foot, then the knife arm followed in one swift, flowing thrust, the trailing foot coming to the fore as he swept in. Even with his natural agility, the combo gave me an extra second of warning. I'd uncovered an advantage, but with his phenomenal speed it was only a slight one.

The yakuza leader's glance glided from my torso to the side of my head. He wanted the ear. He rotated the blade until the cutting edge faced the ceiling. He was going for a single fluid uppercut along the side of my head. Running the steel up my cheek like a barber might field a straight razor. Only he would continue upward to lop off his trophy.

From some hidden reserve, a new acceleration kicked in. The extra momentum propelled him forward and he came within a half an inch of taking the ear.

I angled away, stunned and wary.

Habu's grin was sly. He'd been holding back. The oldest play in the book. I cursed my gullibility. So much for my slight advantage. I retreated into the gloom, and Sai edged from his perch, ready to block my retreat.

I circled back and Habu pursued me. He sensed victory. His pace quickened. I loped away at a faster clip. His knife arm began to undulate to a private rhythm. The free hand came up again, ballast for his bulk—and a tell I could rely on, I decided. The light in his eyes grew brighter. We'd drifted away from his preferred arena. The women couldn't make out the details of our scrimmage.

He'd changed strategies. Why? His eyes were glued to the left side of my head. I got it. His two female devotees didn't need to see the strike if he brought home the prize.

I snatched a high-end designer coat off an empty barstool as I passed, ignoring a protest from the occupant of the neighboring stool. A beat later Habu stormed in. I flung the garment in the air between us, my fingers curled around the collar, weaving the stylish vestment between us in a horizontal figure eight pattern. The yaki's blade got tangled in the flailing cloth. I swooped in for two quick jabs to the nose with a panther strike—a hard fore-knuckle punch. Hand rigid, fingertips bent under, knuckles tense.

Many fighters this close would choose a closed-fisted boxer's punch or an opened-handed jab. The panther strike gave me a vital two inches of additional reach over the closed fist, and yet the fingers were tucked under, a protective move that would save them from being lopped off should the steel sweep up unexpectedly.

Habu staggered sideways, ripping the garment and freeing the weapon. I doubled back toward his booth. Blood trickled from the left side of the yaki's nose. He wiped the liquid away with his free hand, then the next instant the bloodied appendage bobbed at his hip. Glittering steel followed, and he charged in again. I flung the jacket at him. The cloth spread open in flight like a cape. Habu was ready with a counter the second time, as I knew he would be. He waited a beat for the fluttering threads to fully expand, then brushed the nuisance aside and roared in.

But the airborne garment had served its purpose—Habu had missed the beginning of my next play. Having scooped up a champagne glass from his table, I pitched it at him, then dodged away. The fluted vessel bounced off his disfigured cheek, the tart bubbly liquid flooding his vision. He rubbed at his eyes with his free hand.

As he tried to clear his vision, I barreled in with a third jab. Again targeting the nose. This time with a boxer's punch. Full-fisted, no holds barred, rock solid. The blow staggered his compact hulk. I pressed forward. I peppered him with a flurry of jabs, weaving in and out, still wary of his weapon. He howled and tried to bring up the blade, but each time I stepped out of range. By his third upward thrust, his speed had noticeably diminished. I moved inside, knocked the knife arm aside with ease, then connected with my knockout punch. I needed Habu down for the count. But he hit the ground still conscious. He was stunned, brow furrowed, teeth grinding, engine still revving.

The man had staying power.

Which is why Sai hadn't jumped in earlier.

But now the soldier came off the bar, a whirlwind of movement. At my feet Habu groaned, tongue flopping out the side of his mouth. He teetered on the edge of consciousness but had yet to pass over. An eye on the downed leader, I pivoted to face Sai, who advanced with a wicked grin and knife poised to attack.

Wielding a wine bottle like a club, Noda bolted from behind a cluster of groupies. With a decisive thump, thick glass collided with Sai's thicker skull. I dodged Sai's body as it fell forward at my feet and lay still.

New movement stirred in the shadows behind Noda. An indistinct form charged. I yelled a warning to the chief detective as I raced past him. Having swung around the far end of the lengthy counter, the bartender advanced with a baseball bat raised. I snatched up a barstool and slammed it into his ribs as his club connected with a tempered steel leg of the stool, leaving a sizable dent. The dull ring of wood on metal was echoed a beat later by soft flesh against steel. And cracking ribs.

The momentum of my blow slung the bartender against the bar. The weapon fell from his grip. His fingers grappled for his rib cage, a moan escaping his lips. Before he could regroup, I kicked his legs out from under him. His feet flew up, then his whole body plunged downward, his head smacking against the brass foot rail with a moist thud. The loyal Dragon Skin employee lay in a heap, unmoving, and I expected he would stay that way until medical assistance arrived.

I returned my attention to his master. Habu's nose would need extensive reconstructive surgery but the rest of him was fine, if malfunctioning. His eyes bounced around wildly, unable to focus. I pinned the wrist of his knife hand with my foot, then extracted the blade from his grasp, pocketed it, and stepped back.

Eyes crazed and bulging, the yaki rolled over onto his stomach, dragged himself to his knees, then staggered to his feet. Brute animal strength powered his upward movement. It was an impressive feat. His manner was bestial. His eyes roamed the room, seeking me. I stood five feet away, but in the disconnect he was experiencing, I was one among many. What I saw in his unfocused gaze was the slow-witted wakefulness of an ox.

Saliva spilled freely from the corners of his mouth. His eyes locked onto my form, lingered in uncertainty, then lit up as recognition registered. His arms rose. His fingers spread and curled, clawlike, grasping at the air. His chest wheezed and huffed like a bellows.

"Brodie . . ."

His body was in distress but a sort of loutish stubbornness propelled him onward. He took a tortured step toward me, his movements leaden. I backed away, fists ready at my side. It was like watching a wounded man struggle through a vat of molasses. Behind a great savage determination was pain admirably suppressed. I felt guilty even though, moments before, Habu's goal had been to separate my ear from its perch. I'd hoped for a swift mercy, but my KO punch had idled his motor without shutting it down. I might have to hit him again, something I was loath to do.

He shifted his back foot to the fore. The strain sent ripples of effort across his face. I raised my fists, and in a mirroring move he raised his. His chest heaved and fell as it sucked in the massive quantities of air needed to sustain his equilibrium. He took a third step and steadied himself. A slight swaying started, as if an anchoring rope had come loose. Then his whole frame shuddered, his eyes rolled up in his head, and he toppled forward face-first as easily as a hollowed-out tree touched by a breeze.

CHAPTER 46

WE kidnapped the kidnapper.

I threw the unconscious gang leader over my shoulder and hauled him downstairs, then dumped him unceremoniously into the back of the supply van. His five-foot-seven, two-hundred-pound bulk was compact and manageable.

The Brodie Security men bound his hands and feet, then slapped a strip of duct tape over his mouth. I wondered if our actions were illegal or a public service. Personally, I leaned toward the latter, but the authorities would see it differently. Possibly even Rie would disapprove. But the Tokyo police moved at the speed of an intravenous drip. With Anna in hostile hands, we needed what Habu knew immediately if not sooner.

"Wake him up," I said.

The driver slapped Habu sharply, right cheek and then left. Groggy with drink and the beating, the gang leader was slow to regain consciousness. We'd relocated to a deserted back alley a few blocks removed from Ni-chome.

"You've done this before," I said.

The driver grinned. "On occasion. When they deserve it. Wait for the good part."

Habu's eyes opened, closed, reopened. They focused, then sparked with anger. The yaki boss released a string of profanity, conveniently muffled behind the gag.

"There it is," the driver said.

While the beast had slept, Brodie Security minders had wiped away the dried blood that had pooled around Habu's shattered nose, and scabbing had done the rest. Now the driver tore off the glue-backed strip.

The granular echo accompanying the action told me stubble had been uprooted in the process. Habu howled.

"Nice touch," I said.

"You're dead, gaijin," the gang leader said.

"Yeah, yeah, fine," I said. "Until then, we need to know who you gave the girl to and where they're taking her."

"Habu ain't tellin'."

The driver gave me a puzzled look. "Isn't his name Habu?"

"Yeah. He talks like that."

"Another puffed-up yaki."

"And that's only for starters." I turned to our captive. "You are going to tell us about the girl or we're going to beat it out of you."

"You already tried that."

He had a point.

"Got an easier way," Noda said.

The chief detective stalked off and I trailed after him. Once out of earshot, Noda slipped his phone from his pocket, stabbed at the screen, hit the speaker function, and waited for pickup.

The phone rang twice.

When Jo's voice came on the line, Noda said, "We need to talk."

"So talk. I'm working."

"Face-to-face."

"Why?"

"We have cargo."

"Bad idea, but your funeral."

————

Noda's text message to Jo had been succinct: *Arriving 3 minutes.*

The elite Korean bodyguard slid out the back door of the Hotel New Otani thirty seconds after we pulled the van around to the delivery entrance. He was draped in a classic tuxedo and bathed in a distinctive cologne.

"Had to see this for myself," Jo said.

I nodded at the van. "Look all you want."

Cold eyes slid my way. "See you managed to hold on to all your body parts."

"Yeah. Old habits die hard."

"Don't get used it." The Great Wall turned to Noda. "What do you want? I'm working here."

Noda slanted his head at the delivery van. "Need answers."

"From the garbage," I said.

Strolling over to the van, Jo flicked the side panel aside with a two-fingered swipe, peered in, then let out a snort of contempt. "Disposable as it comes. Habu, you made the wrong guys mad."

At the sound of Jo's voice, Habu's eyes bolted open. The bound-and-bundled yaki threw himself against the wall of the van in some sort of self-flagellating protest. He kicked his legs, still secured at the ankles, and cold-cocked one of his own guards tied up at the rear.

I eyed Jo curiously. "That's some reaction. What's between you two?"

Invigorated, Habu was bobbing his head at Jo. We'd gagged him again for the ride but clearly he wanted to talk. I nodded, and two of our men subdued the thrashing gang leader, then the driver once more ripped off the fresh strip of duct tape.

Habu howled again. "That's twice, puke face. Payback's coming."

Jo said, "Focus, Habu. You got something you wanna tell me, make it quick."

Habu shot the Korean a pleading look. "*Onii-san*, get me out of this."

Beside me, Noda stiffened.

The term *onii-san* translates as "older brother." Honorific in nature, it was a common form of polite address among unknown parties but could also imply a close relationship, either one of friendship or family ties.

"What's going on?" I said.

Jo sighed. "He married one of my sisters. The dumb one."

Pieces began slotting into place. "Where does the scar come in?"

"I cut him after he beat her the second time. The first warning lasted only a week."

"Short-term memory problem?"

"Long-term idiot problem."

"Can't choose your in-laws."

"We're blood," Habu said. "Stomp these guys."

Noda and I exchanged a glance. If the Great Wall turned on us, we were going to have a tough fight on our hands. Maybe an uncontainable one.

Jo glared at the gang leader. "We're *not* blood. Won't ever be. I got more in common with these two than I'll ever have with you."

"That ain't right, Older Brother. You and Habu—"

Jo raised a hand for silence. "Don't ever call me that again. You got a jumbo target on your back, you wasabi-for-brains nitwit. Nothing's worth that."

Habu squinted at his brother-in-law. "You're jealous is what it is. 'Cause we've struck gold."

"You got two *governments* after you, boy."

"That ain't true. I snatched the girl clean."

Jo's voice dropped to a low bass whisper. "*Shut up*, Habu. Shut. The. Hell. Up. You say another word, I'm going to put you out of your misery with my own hands. You're nearly brain-dead already."

"But—"

"*Not—another—word,*" Jo hissed.

Habu shut his trap.

"Good. Now think about it for once in your worthless life. These guys rolled you up the day after you kidnapped the girl. What you think the PSIA is going to do?"

Or Homeland Security, I added silently.

The gang leader's brow grew shifty. "I didn't do nothing to them."

From nowhere, a knife appeared in Jo's hand. He stepped forward and pressed the sharp edge of the blade against Habu's unscarred cheek, his voice dropping to a low rumble. "One more word, you dung beetle, and I do the other side of your face. You have no damn idea what you stepped into, do you? Do *not* make a sound. Just move your head."

Deflating before our eyes, Jo's brother-in-law shook his head.

The Great Wall's eyes had become dark tunnels. Pre–fight mode. "Now I'm going to let you talk. But the *only* things I want to hear are who paid you to kidnap the girl and where they are taking her and why. That's it. No begging. No bragging. No nothing. One word more and I slice you up. Nod if you got it."

Bloodshot eyes straining toward the sharp steel resting against his cheek, Habu moved his head up and down once, with care.

"Good, then let's hear it."

Habu spilled.

And what Jo excavated sent the case into the stratosphere.

CHAPTER 47

DAY 7, SATURDAY, 1:18 A.M.

STEPPING away from the van, I slipped my cell phone from my pocket, and made a call I could never have anticipated. Noda moved off in the opposite direction, on an equally pressing mission.

The pickup on the other end was tentative, the voice sheathed in a drowsy politeness. "Hello?"

"You told me to contact you if I ever need anything," I said.

Unexpected calls, if not the norm, should have been a semi-regular occurrence for him.

"Mr. Brodie?" The drowsiness yielded to an immediate alertness.

"Yes. Does your offer still stand?"

"Absolutely," said Gerald Thornton-Cummings, the young deputy attaché who had pulled me off the airplane out at Narita. "But I envisioned a more common hour. It's after midnight. So it's urgent. What's up?"

"I need to get to Ambassador Tattersill. Quickly but quietly. Can you make that happen?"

An outrageous request under normal circumstances, but Gerald had been in the room when I'd spoken to the president, the elephant in the current conversation I hoped to leverage.

"At this hour?"

"Yes."

"The ambassador hates to be woken in the middle of the night. He's a bit . . . proper."

Tattersill was hardly proper. Swinging into full diplomatic mode, Gerald was hoisting a warning flag for the unaware. I was not among them. An appointee from the previous presidential administration whom Slater had kept on for reasons that puzzled observers, Ambassador Stewart Lester "Inflexible Lex" Tattersill was a tall, photogenic man with a mellifluous voice, dimpled chin, and a full head of well-coiffed blond hair. On the public stage he oozed charm and posed for the cameras with great aplomb, which played well in the media. But in diplomatic dealings he'd proved inflexible and unimaginative, and thus highly unpopular in Japan and the United States. Hence the nickname.

"Point taken. We'll have to work with what we have."

Gerald hesitated. "Has POTUS cleared you with the ambassador?"

"I don't know. But he sent you out to Narita, right?"

"Actually, that came through embassy channels."

"Well, wing it, Gerald. Make the connection for me."

"And this is about what, business for FLOTUS?"

I frowned. We hadn't discussed the first lady. Gerald had gone on an information-gathering spree since we'd met. The guy had moves—and had just succeeded in pushing me into a corner.

"This started with the Kennedy Center killings and FLOTUS, but it's expanded since then."

Gerald pondered the problem. "Assuming I can get around the ambassador's usual reluctance, is this going to help or hurt me?"

"In the long run, help. Short-term, it may irritate a few people."

"The safest way forward would be to table this until tomorrow."

"It can't wait."

Gerald sighed. "Fine. Then let me warn you in advance that I will not get past the ambassador's wife without something more concrete. She guards him like a hawk since his heart attack two years ago."

"Fair enough. Here's what I have, but it's for the ambassador's ears only, plus whatever tidbit you need to feed his wife to get him on the phone."

Then I laid out Habu's confession . . .

With Jo holding the knife edge to the gang leader's one unblemished cheek, Habu opened up: "There weren't no names but the guys came through the Chongryon."

Which confirmed the gang's association with the old-school underground group in Japan sympathetic to the North Korean regime.

Jo put some pressure on the knife. "What else?"

"They're flying the girl to Niigata, then shoving her on a fishing boat to North Korea. They smack into the Japanese Coast Guard or military boats, they'll scoot over to the South Korean coast, then find a ride up to Seoul. There's a tunnel goes under the DMZ."

Unscrambled, plan A was a flight to Japan's northern coast and a boat to North Korea. If the sea route was blocked, they had a built-in plan B. A tunnel in the demilitarized zone to take them under the border between Koreas and into the North.

"Dump it all," Jo said, waving the knife in front of Habu's eyes.

"Tunnel's an old one the South ain't found yet. It's burned once they use it, so they've been saving it for something big."

What on earth, I wondered, did Anna know that got her the wrong kind of VIP treatment?

"Tunnels are always dicey," I said. "They have a backup plan?"

"Course," Habu said. "They ain't idiots. The tunnel don't work, they go across the river."

Plan C.

Jo clicked his tongue. "The river between North and South is blockaded, you moron."

True, but defectors seeking asylum routinely fled across the Yalu River, a waterway that ran along the other border. The one North Korea shared with China. Escapees swam or boated across in small rubber dinghies most of the year, or walked across when the river froze over.

"You're talking about the Chinese border, right?" I asked.

Habu scowled. "Yeah. The DMZ don't work, they fly to China. Meeting up at a place called the Dandong Noodle Shop in Changbai. Hope you choke on it, gaijin."

"You left out two things," I said. "Where along the DMZ? It's one hundred and fifty miles long."

"They didn't say."

"What do you think, Jo?"

"I'm thinking I'm gonna send lots of small pieces back to my sister."

Habu flinched. "Okay. About one and a half kilometers from Dora's. Don't know what the hell that is and don't care. Makes no sense to me."

But it did to me.

"Sounds like a woman's house," Habu said with a smirk. "Knew where it was, I'd pay her a visit."

"It's not a 'her,'" I said. "It's a place."

A place deep inside the heavily guarded demilitarized zone on the South Korean side, but within walking distance of the border—if you could get past the military installations and the guards and the minefields.

Apparently, Anna's kidnappers could.

CHAPTER 48

To Gerald, I relayed the gist of the kidnappers' plans, minus many of the specifics. No DMZ, no Dora, no plan C to China. Every word out of my mouth would pass from Gerald to the ambassador and to places and people beyond, which might include Homeland and Swelley. Equally important, with each detail divulged, I lost leverage—and I needed leverage to stay in the game.

While I talked to Gerald, Noda reached out to a connection at the Japanese police agency, which would contact the Japanese Coast Guard about a blockade. Anna Tanaka's kidnappers weren't taking the seaways north.

"Jesus," Gerald said when I'd wound up my recital. "North Korean agents? Are you quite sure?"

"Looks that way."

"So the Hermit Kingdom is directly involved?"

One of North Korea's nicknames.

"Yep."

"No one ever comes back from there. The poor girl doesn't have a chance."

"Unless we give her one," I said. "Which is why you must get past the wife."

"Logic and common decency dictate I should be able to get you an audience, but you're facing a double hurdle. She's tough but he's the real wild card. Between you and me, he's earned his nickname ten times over since I've been here."

Despite the obstacles, we banged out a plan to circumvent Inflexible Lex's defenses. Gerald would call ahead, then we'd meet outside the ambassador's mansion, a luxurious guarded estate inside the greater American embassy complex surrounded by twenty-foot whitewashed walls.

"Work some magic," I said. "I'll be there in fifteen minutes. And, Gerald?"

"Yes?"

"Be discreet."

"Of course," he said.

But he wasn't.

1:35 A.M.
AMERICAN EMBASSY COMPOUND, TOKYO

Noda and I girded ourselves. At best, our late-night arrival would irritate. At worst, hornets would descend.

Near the entrance to the ambassador's residence, a policeman signaled for our taxi to pull over to the curb. His uniform was clean and pressed, his hat properly squared. Even this late.

"Think the TPD will give us trouble?" I asked Noda.

"Only if things sour."

The cop was point man for an extensive protective detail stationed around the clock on all sides of the compound. I spotted four more TPD uniforms, including one in the guard booth talking to Gerald and another on the other side of an imposing twelve-foot-high wrought iron gate.

Noda and I stepped from the vehicle, wallets flopped open to our picture IDs.

"You're the gentlemen Thornton-Cummings–san is expecting?" the policeman asked in Japanese.

"That's right."

Gerald turned and waved. An open, friendly gesture. So far, so good.

The badge moved aside and we covered the last ten yards at a brisk pace. Gerald wore a lightweight windbreaker zipped to his chin. His fleshy face was pale and unshaven.

"Thanks for getting over here so quick," I said as we walked up to the guard booth.

He nodded, his blue eyes restless and red around the rims. "All part of the job. Not my favorite part."

"Sorry about that."

Gerald shrugged, then gave a go-ahead nod to a U.S. Marine in the booth. The Marine punched the screen of a secure phone similar to the one Gerald had used at Narita Airport, then handed the device to me.

As the ringtone sounded in my ear, I let my gaze drift back toward the first Japanese policeman. He stared back boldly, alert eyes locked onto our every move.

"Hello, Ambassador Tattersill? Sorry to wake you at such an hour."

"It comes with the office, son. We just need to confirm that your situation falls within our bailiwick. Can you give me a rundown?"

Tattersill's voice was soft and coaxing and suggestive of instant camaraderie. And yet the word *son* hinted at a budding condescension.

I let a hint of exasperation surface. "Is that really necessary? I'm sure Gerald briefed you. Nothing has changed since I talked to him fifteen minutes ago."

Noda frowned. I'd left enough of a gap between ear and phone so he and Gerald could eavesdrop.

"I make it a point to get the story straight from the horse's mouth."

A sour feeling pinged the lining of my stomach. "There is some urgency here, sir."

"Always is, son. Always is."

With an inward sigh, I repeated Habu's story at a fast clip, again bypassing the details I wished to keep to myself.

"I wonder what result we might expect of the coast guard?" the ambassador asked.

I relayed the consensus opinion that Noda had received through his backdoor channel. The sea chase would boil down to a nautical game of cat and mouse. The Japanese Coast Guard and navy would move to block the northern passage. They would also be calling on their South Korean counterparts. A defensive line would be strung across the Sea of

Japan between the two countries. With radar guidance they could track all approaching vessels. Anna's kidnappers, no doubt equipped with their own radar, would hide among the numerous fishing and commercial craft on the water at night. Once they saw there was no sure way through the blockade, they would opt for the South Korean coast, not wanting to risk being captured.

"Interesting," Tattersill said. "Perhaps we should wait until we hear the results of the joint maneuvers."

"We need to get ahead of them," I said, "which means making the two-hour hop to South Korea now."

Tattersill sounded a different note. "If the kidnappers land on the South Korean coast, I think we can leave the sweeping up to our brethren over there, don't you?"

"That's not what the White House wants."

"I do not believe you can equate Joan Slater's desires with those of the president. I have also been informed Homeland is working this."

The sour feeling in my stomach mushroomed into full-fledged nausea. "They are working one end and I'm working the other," I said carefully. "That was the Slaters' original intention. So could we get on with the transportation?"

"When it comes to wielding government assets, one does not simply wave a wand, Mr. Brodie."

I blinked. Inflexible Lex had surfaced. For him, that's exactly how simple it was. He gave an order and people jumped.

I pushed harder. "Again, this is urgent, sir. Once Anna's kidnappers get her to the Japan coast, a high-speed boat can cross the Sea of Japan to South Korea in three or four hours. We need to get there ASAP. A quick trip by helicopter to the closest base, then a plane to Seoul ought to do it."

"You presume quite a bit."

Pursing my lips, I fell silent. The ball was in his court. I glanced over at the gated entrance to the ambassador's residence. Front and center on the gate was the Great Seal of the United States: an American bald eagle clutching an olive branch in one claw, arrows in the other, signifying peace and power. In ominous contrast, a black windowless police van parked across the street signaled another kind of power.

Tattersill cleared his throat. "Well, this is highly unusual, but I'm going to make the arrangements. Everyone should be happy then, don't you think?"

"Yes. Thank you, Mr. Ambassador."

"I'll be down in a few minutes," he said, and disconnected a little too abruptly for my taste. But whatever got us across the water.

Budging the ambassador had not proved the herculean task Gerald had made it out to be. I cast a sideways glance at the attaché. His features had a pinched aspect, as if they were being drawn toward an invisible vortex at the center of his face.

Something wasn't right.

A little too abruptly . . .

Eyeing the junior diplomat's expression, Noda emitted a deep rumble.

In Japanese I said, "You don't like it either?"

"No."

"Gerald, anything you want to tell me?"

He shook his head, then darted a look at the Marine.

I turned back to Noda. "Tattersill should have pressed me for more detail. I wouldn't have given him any but he should have asked. Anyone would."

"People like him don't come to people like us."

A chill edged up my arms. Noda had pinpointed the gremlin in the shadows.

We'd been set up.

CHAPTER 49

I'LL *be down in a few minutes.*

The ambassador wouldn't come down to the guardhouse to meet us. Not only was the gesture out of character, but security protocol would forbid it. If anything, we'd be led inside, either to the residence itself or to an interim staging area safely inside the grounds.

I fired a look over my shoulder at the first police officer. Two more uniforms had joined him. I cast a look at Gerald. His expression was one of studied indifference.

I scowled. "What have you done?"

"Just what you asked."

His reply came too fast. And, worse, it trailed off with a trace of defiance.

With habitual rapidity, Noda and I scanned faces. The policemen's, Gerald's, the Marine's. The chief detective shot an inquiring look toward the cops, a Japanese-on-Japanese communiqué suggesting that they step away from this American-on-American confrontation. An effective ploy most times.

But not this time.

I grabbed the young diplomat by the neck and squeezed. "Who else did you call?"

His blue eyes widened in fear and disbelief. "No one."

"You're lying. Who?"

He wrapped both of his hands around my arm and tried to break my grip. He couldn't. I applied more pressure. His breathing became difficult.

"Swelley," he wheezed. "I was under orders."

"And Tattersill knew?"

"Of course."

"How soon?" I said.

"Soon."

I let my arm fall. Gerald doubled over, sucking up air in large gulps.

"Why'd you do it?" I said. "Homeland doesn't run the embassy."

He held up a hand, signaling for a moment to catch his breath. "These days . . . security trumps all . . . You don't cooperate . . . demoted . . . or worse."

We were lost. The Homeland agent had dropped out of sight on this side of the Pacific. So much so that while I hadn't forgotten him, I'd discounted him. But I should have known better. I did know better. Swelley was the gremlin in the shadows. Plotting. Maneuvering. Setting traps and trip wires. My reaching out to Gerald had sprung one of them.

More damned spycraft.

I closed my eyes and exhaled audibly, angry with myself. I didn't need this aggravation. I could be home playing with my daughter, working in my antiques shop. Talking art. Placing meaningful pieces in the homes of appreciative clients. Pieces that could add a spark of inspiration to someone's life. Except I did need to find out who killed Mikey and Sharon. And more than anything, I wanted to get Anna back.

Alive.

Because bringing her home was something I would never be able to do for my two friends. Her return was the only token I could offer up to them—and to myself to assuage the illogical guilt that plagued me.

I opened my eyes to seek Noda's opinion but never got the chance.

On the street, forces were amassing. A fourth uniform now stood with the other three. Behind them, a fifth officer unfolded a collapsible steel barrier. It expanded, accordion-like, into a series of linked waist-high steel Xs with sharpened ends. The bottom leg of every third X was elongated and slotted into a hole in the pavement. Probably into steel tubes embedded in the blacktop. In minutes the assembled barrier was locked into place and blocked the road. It would not only stop a charging vehicle but would also keep us penned in.

I looked in the opposite direction. Thirty yards down the road another barrier was being erected while a trio of officers stood by, focused on us.

To my right, the Marine's hand inched toward his holstered weapon.

The world had changed.

Irretrievably.

I'd only closed my eyes for a few seconds but that had been enough.

I jumped the Marine. I slammed him against the exterior wall of the guardhouse and rammed my knee into his stomach. He doubled over, both hands grabbing for his injured midsection. Then head down, he charged. With less than a foot between us, he gained no momentum. Realizing his mistake, he wrapped his arms around my waist and heaved.

I held my ground and planted the palms of my hands on the top of his skull. My thumbs crossed, my fingers spread. His hand snaked back toward his weapon.

"Don't go there," I said. "I'll snap your neck."

The hand dropped. He attempted to raise his head.

I growled. "Don't do that either. Relax and we'll be okay."

"I get mobile, you'll be feeling the pain."

Pinned between the guardhouse wall and my body, he was going nowhere. Still he resisted.

"Another inch and my knee comes up," I said. "You know what that means."

He stopped struggling. The threat of turning the nose to pulp would be a potent deterrent for most people. Especially since an inch either way on a second strike could pulverize teeth, cheekbone, or jaw. But a highly trained Marine was not most people.

I said, "I need to know you understand me."

More silence. Which signaled ongoing resistance.

In a flash, I brought my knee to within an inch of his nose, then allowed my foot to resettle on the blacktop.

"Next time it's real," I said.

He unwound. The tension in his muscles dissolved.

"Good. Now shove your hands into your pockets, straighten slowly, and show me your back."

As soon as he faced away, I planted a palm between his shoulder blades and slapped him against the guardhouse wall. With my free hand, I unsnapped the cover on his holster and extracted the weapon.

Then everything fell apart.

CHAPTER 50

NODA yelled, "Move, move, *now!*"

Before I could respond, short, muscular bursts at the small of our backs shoved both the Marine and myself into the guardhouse. The chief detective charged in behind, pressing us forward, then slamming the door shut and twisting the lock home.

When I turned to peer through the window, I saw the Japanese police less than three feet away, disappointment on their faces. They'd been ordered to sweep us up but Noda had been faster. The three of us were sealed in the booth. The police settled for a containment maneuver. Time was on their side.

The ambassador was nowhere in sight.

I frowned at Noda. "We're going to pay for this later, aren't we?"

His scar flaring, the head detective grunted.

Too late I recalled my first impression of Gerald Thornton-Cummings at the airport. Young, eager, well connected, prep school polish, diplomatic fast track. Soft skin. Manicured hands. A desk man. No field savvy.

And I remember also thinking he could get a person killed.

It might still happen.

—————

The Marine took a stool in the corner, teeth clamped, jawline tight. From five feet away, Noda trained the gun on our captive. The name tag pinned above the soldier's shirt pocket said J. PEREZ.

"Sorry about this, Perez," I said. "We've just screwed you, haven't we?"

Hard gray-green eyes spewed hatred. He balanced on the edge of the stool, ready to launch a counterattack if he spied an opening. Even with the captured weapon pointed at his chest from an impossible distance.

"Don't do anything stupid," I said.

My comment did not dim his desire for a counterstrike. There was pride in the rigidity of his spine. Perez just might take the risk.

"Is that on?" I asked with a nod over my shoulder at the camera in an upper corner of the booth behind me.

His nod was reluctant.

"So they can see us up at the house?" I asked.

"Yeah." His face reddened.

"Sound?"

"No, but don't matter no more."

"Had to be done. Sorry."

"Enemies shouldn't apologize."

"Enemies we're not."

"You're mistaken only in number, sir. You just made an enemy of me and every single Marine in the country."

I considered him for a minute. He had no accent, so he was at least second-generation Latino. His features suggested Central Mexico. Intelligence lay lightly on his brow. His eyes were alert. They still sought a way out of his predicament. I saw all kinds of smarts. Street, survival, and fighting smarts. He was also a thinker. A planner. Not just an enraged bullheaded fighter. An impressive skill set—and a potentially volatile combination unless . . .

"You plan to take on more than guard duty when you muster out, Perez?" I said.

He shot me a spiteful look. "Until tonight, yeah. I was going to re-enlist on the officer track."

"Good to hear," I said. "You wait this out, you still might."

Perez rolled his eyes. "That bridge is burned."

His glance returned to his lost weapon. I followed it, then added in a low, menacing tone he could not misinterpret, "Whatever you do, don't rile my ornery friend here. He *will* shoot you."

———

I called the White House and the first lady's assistant, Margaret Cutler, picked up before the initial ring died down.

"Hi, Brodie. Do you have news for Joan?"

"What I have is trouble."

"You got that right," Perez said. "There's only two ways out of this for you guys. Painful and more painful."

Noda snapped at him in Japanese. *"Urusai!"* Shut up!

Whether Perez understood the language or not, the tone left no doubt as to the translation.

"Who was that?" Margaret asked.

"Don't worry about it. I need to talk to Joan."

"I can't go in empty-handed."

"I've got a line on the daughter," I said.

"Oh my god. Even Homeland doesn't have that yet. Is she still alive? Have you talked to her? Did you—"

"Keep it together, Margaret. I believe she's still alive. For now. Get the first lady out of whatever she's in. Every second counts."

At the words *first lady* Perez sat up a little straighter.

"You always call at the wrong time, Brodie. She's at a—"

I glanced at the police guard outside. "I don't care if she's in with an entire contingent of angels. No offense. It's do-or-die time, Margaret. I need her. Or, better yet, get the president if you can. He's the endgame."

"I can't get anywhere near the president."

"Well, get someone now. They're coming for us."

"Who? What? Never mind. I believe you. I'll do what I can."

I heard the rattling of a receiver snatched from the cradle of a desk phone. "Samantha? Margaret. Put me through to Joan . . . No, no, put me through now . . . I know, I know, but I got Brodie from Tokyo and he's— What? . . . Well, I'm sorry, drag her out. Make apologies . . . What do you mean you can't? You must—What? No, seriously? . . . Oh, crap. Cupcakes. Crap, crap, crap."

Even filtered through the gentile swearing of the East Wing, I could tell the problem was unusual. Bordering on insurmountable.

Margaret came back on the line, frustrated. "Brodie, could you stall whoever you're dealing with over there? Maybe forty-five minutes? An hour tops?"

I surveyed the roadway. The number of policemen had risen to ten. They'd unhooked their truncheons from their duty belts. For the moment their guns remained holstered. Their leader squinted down the road, as if expecting more men or a new arrival with orders in hand. Or maybe equipment. The glass in the booth was bulletproof.

"Not workable, Margaret. I have minutes, if not seconds, before they cart us away in handcuffs."

"What have you done?"

"Only what needed doing. You've got to get her. Now. Or the president."

"He's impossible. She's signaled no interruptions. The only time she restricts access is when she's entertaining international visitors of the highest order. I have nothing on my calendar, so it's a sudden appointment, probably at the behest of the president. My guess is that she's in with her husband and the president of France and his wife. There must be a break from the ongoing work session about the latest Middle East crisis. I'll have to run across to the West Wing to get to her. I need to ask again, in the context I just outlined—Is what you're involved in that vital?"

Outside, the lead officer barked an order. The rank and file unholstered their firearms and held them unobtrusively at their sides.

"Yes," I said.

"Okay, stay with me, then."

I'm not going anywhere, I thought, *except into a dark cell if this falls apart.*

I heard her slam down the desk phone. Then something clattered to the floor. "It's off with the heels. I've got to make a mad dash to the West Wing. This is going to cost me a pair of high-priced nylons."

I sucked in a deep breath. "Margaret, there are ten armed policemen directly outside the shoe box I'm holed up in, and Homeland is on the way. None of them are on my side. You get the first lady, I'll spring for a dozen pair."

"Oh, crap. Cupcakes. You weren't joking about the do-or-die. Everyone in DC exaggerates, you know, to get their way. I thought—"

"Just hurry, Margaret."

"Sorry, I babble when I get nervous, but I'm on my way. I'll talk and run. I'm switching to stealth conference mode, so you can listen in, but don't say a word unless I signal you, okay?"

"Got it."

"We're off."

I heard a series of beeps on the line, then Margaret shouted, "I'm heading to you, Samantha. You're going to let me in."

"Impossible," Samantha said.

Margaret flung the office door open with extreme violence. It bounced off a wall or doorstop with a loud crack. Next I heard panting sounds.

"Samantha," Margaret said to the beat of nylon-sheathed heels pounding over carpeting, then an unpadded surface. "Can you get her a message . . . No? . . . Oh, come on, Samantha, work with me. This is urgent. Top priority for Joan. . . . What? . . . Oh, shit . . . I mean crap . . . cupcakes . . ."

Another door slammed.

In the distance I heard Margaret say, "Sorry! Sorry! I'll explain later," then her voice was loud in my ear again, breathing heavily: "Hold on, Brodie. I'm almost there. I'll get to Samantha if it kills me. I knew I should have gone on that diet last month. I'm carrying too much weight. I'm here! Just through that door and . . ."

I heard a large rattling sound.

"Crapola. It's locked. Somebody open this friggin' door."

I heard a fist banging on wood.

At the foot of the road, a slick black sedan with tinted windows rolled up with an unearthly silence. On top, flashing blue lights spewed blinding barbs of light in all directions. Swelley stepped from the back.

An agent hiding behind a massive wall of the compound stepped into the open and nodded at Swelley. The two went into a huddle. When had the watchdog arrived? The unnamed agent was no doubt bringing Swelley up to date. As Swelley continued to listen, his head jerked up once from the street-side conference and swiveled in my direction until he found me behind the bulletproof glass of the guard booth.

Time was up.

CHAPTER 51

PEREZ had absorbed it all.

He'd listened to my ongoing conversation with Margaret with skepticism, given me an odd look when I mentioned the president, then—as soon as he saw the black sedan pull up—smiled, knowing the cavalry had arrived. Now, with Swelley set to breach the guardhouse, the Marine was looking smug.

"You're toast, man," he said. "I've seen these face-offs plenty of times. They never turn out well. Why don't you restore me my weapon and I'll ask them to go easy on you?"

"I'll pass," I said.

He raised his palms. "I'm cool with it, man. I got big dreams too but no way am I delusional. You pretending to call the White House while playing terrorist is over-the-top, man. If they don't shoot you dead in the next couple of minutes, an insanity plea is a no-brainer. You got a good witness in me."

Noda told him to shut up again. This time in English.

"Brodie? You still there?"

It was Margaret, her breath blasting from my phone in ragged, irregular bursts. Without effort, I could imagine her in stocking feet, her black pageboy in disarray, bangs bouncing, face flushed.

"I'm here, Margaret. Is the news good or bad?"

"I've got FLOTUS. Or nearly have her. She should be here any second." Loud panting powered through the speaker. Margaret could squeeze out no more than four or five syllables before the need for air halted her speech.

A cold grin spread across Perez's face as a black, discreetly armored SUV pulled up. Four doors opened simultaneously and the DC crew that had braced me on the National Mall stepped out as one.

"The sooner the better, Margaret," I said.

"I'm doing the best I can."

"Above and beyond, if your sound bites are anything to go by."

"You are such a sweetie. Oh, here she is! It's Brodie. He's got news and he's in trouble."

I heard some fumbling as the phone exchanged hands, then FLOTUS was on the line. "I'm here, Jim. What do you have for me?"

"We've got a line on Anna Tanaka, Joan," I said.

I mentioned the first lady's given name for Perez's benefit. His skepticism remained unchanged. The Marine was a hard sell.

"Thank god," she said. "Is Anna okay?"

"We don't have her yet, but we know where she's going to be in about twelve hours, give or take."

"Where?"

I told her and Joan Slater gasped. Perez listened with growing interest. When I wound up, the president's wife said, "Oh my god. If they spirit her away to North Korea, she's gone forever. We can't allow that."

"My thoughts as well."

"What do you need?"

"I need you to bring Stewart Tattersill around to our way of thinking. I'm outside the residence now."

The number of Japanese officers had reached an uncountable level, but my eyes fixated on Swelley and his crew. Overwhelming numbers of Japanese police was standard operating procedure. When in doubt, the authorities smother the scene with roving uniforms. What worried me more was the rising head count among the Homeland Security agents. Most of them wore black. Swelley, his head bobbing agreeably, listened to a briefing from a senior Japanese police official. Possibly the Tokyo PD suggesting a course of action.

"In front of Tattersill's place? Isn't he helping you?"

"He refused."

"Stewart turned you down? He was advised of the situation beforehand. Someone must have got to him."

"If you need a clue, let me know. He's amassing an army outside as we speak."

"Swelley?"

"Yep. And he's getting set to move. We could use the president right about now."

Joan Slater sighed loudly. "Oh, Brodie, Joe's locked away with the French president. Something about a new attack, or the drone policy. I don't know. Can you get the ambassador back on the line?"

I'd seen Perez do it once. I picked up the secure phone and hit redial. I heard it ringing. Redial was not an ideal function for a so-called secure line, but who was I to argue?

The ambassador picked up immediately. "Perez, is the situation under control yet?"

"It always has been," I said.

"Brodie, you need to surrender before you get hurt or . . . worse."

"Thanks for the advice, Tattersill, but I'm going to try a different tact. There's a call for you and I suggest you take it." I flipped my cell phone around so the two could hear and speak to each other. "Joan, he's ready."

"Stu? Joan Slater. How are you?"

I was rewarded with a long pause before the ambassador said, "Uh, fine, Joan. Just fine. How's Joe?"

"Doing well, Stu, but juggling enough for a dozen people, as usual. Which is why I am calling. I need you to get Mr. Brodie to Seoul as fast as our resources allow. Mr. Brodie and anyone else he deems necessary to accompany him."

"With all due respect, Joan, you are not part of the chain of command. We have all been informed of the kidnapping. I understand Sharon Tanaka was a college friend and am sorry for your loss. Your concern for her daughter is also quite natural, but when all is said and done, she is a Japanese national."

"Her name is Anna Tanaka, Stu, and she's married to an American citizen, has American citizenship, is a highly placed software expert with a top secret security clearance, and is working on an NSA-funded project out of Fort Meade. So much so, she and her husband have been required to live on the base for the past two years, under the tightest security, until her project is complete. She goes off base only with bodyguards."

My heart nearly jumped from my chest.

There it was. The missing link.

Living on base and traveling outside with protection. Those two facts spoke as loudly as the kidnapping itself. We were another step closer to what was inside Anna Tanaka's head. Something computer related and top secret and important enough for the all-powerful National Security Agency to assign her bodyguards when she went out in public. Something apparently the North Korean regime coveted, as did the Chinese. What was it Zhou had said? Killing the mother flushed out the daughter.

Another lie camouflaged in a half-truth. Anna wasn't "receiving treatment for depression," as the master spy had claimed. She was sequestered behind a sky-high fence and razor wire surrounding one of the most secure places on the planet.

Which is what must have triggered the whole series of events.

The North Koreans killed Sharon Tanaka to draw Anna out from behind the wall and the mandatory security detail. To get their hands on the NSA stash. And Mikey had been an unlucky bystander in the operation. My anger surged at the realization. Then all over again I was shamed at having arranged the meeting. No matter what it took, the North Koreans were not going to walk off with Anna Tanaka. Not on my watch. Not after this.

It was all coming together. It hadn't occurred to me to ask the first lady about any of the details regarding Anna's work, because, like Tattersill, I assumed she didn't have clearance for such matters. If what Joan said was true—and I had no reason to doubt it—then she'd only just learned of it from her husband, probably after the kidnapping the night before. What's more, the NSA would not have allowed Anna out of their sight. They had probably put her on the plane and had people meet her at the other end. Someone had probably watched her back while she was in Japan, and we knew Homeland had sent two men to the funeral.

"I do not mean to be disrespectful, Joan, but you just confirmed what I have been saying. This is a matter of national security, and you are not cleared for that level of operation. And, worse, your personal . . . representative . . . has been nothing but disruptive."

"He's been briefed by the president and myself . . ."

"Careful, Joan. Are you telling me Brodie is acting under direct orders from the president? Because if you are, and that turns out to be inaccurate, well, we will be in uncharted territory. It could be problematic for the president when it comes time for reelection. And if Brodie is acting under a presidential mandate, that creates a whole new set of problems and protocol to deal with. For one—"

"He's acting on my behalf, Stu, and you damn well know it. And if you ever threaten me or the president again—"

"I did not threaten either of you, Joan. I merely took the opportunity to—"

"Stu, I may not be an elected official but I know a threat when I hear one."

"There's no need to get huffy, Joan."

"I'll get huffy if I want to, Stu, and I can get a damn sight worse."

"Joan, listen to me. I am truly, truly sorry, but you are not cleared for the reports I have seen and I am afraid I have no choice. Homeland is on standby at the gate. Brodie and his friend have taken a hostage, so they leave me no choice."

"Stu, don't you dare order an attack."

"Not an attack, Joan. I am ordering Homeland in. Snipers will be in place shortly to protect our men, but this is an unstable situation. In consideration of your role, I will hold them off as long as possible. I suggest you advise your man to stand down. If we do not receive cooperation soon, I cannot guarantee the situation will not escalate. Further, if—"

"Stu, you better listen to me and listen good. If you don't, I swear I will—"

"It's out of my hands, Joan. I'm sorry."

The ambassador hung up.

On FLOTUS.

We were dead in the water.

CHAPTER 52

PEREZ shook his head. "Listen to the ambassador, Brodie. Give it up before the sharpshooters put some holes in you."

Joan said, "Was that the 'hostage' Stu was on about?"

"You got it."

I watched Swelley walking resolutely toward me. He was talking on his mobile. Thirty seconds later he disconnected. He wore camouflage pants and a black T-shirt that flattered his muscled, V-shaped bulk, and unlike his personal team he had forgone a Kevlar chest covering. His men flanked him. Two oversize Homeland agents to the left. Two to the right.

"Joan, stay on the line," I said.

There was a chance they wouldn't shoot as long as the connection remained active. By now the ambassador would have informed Swelley of the first lady's interest. They would know she could hear everything I could. But they would be working on a way to jam the signal.

Which wouldn't be too hard.

Or take too long, once the right equipment became available.

"You bet I will," Joan said. "Is there anything I can do?"

"I'm working on it."

I stared at our captive.

Resentment no longer suffused his features. The gleam in his eye had swung to anticipation at the upcoming takedown. There had never been any outright fear. Just an ever-present tension and a readiness to spring into action if the opportunity presented itself. And disappointment as he realized neither Noda nor I were dumb enough to allow it.

I put my hand over the phone's mouthpiece, turned to the soldier, and nodded at his nametag. "The *J* is for what? Juan, Jose, Jesus, what?"

"Jacobo."

Turning my back on the camera in the corner, I returned to the first lady. "Joan, I need you to put in a commendation for a Marine corporal by the name of Jacobo Perez. He's going to take me and my partner into custody in a moment and then use good judgment of officer caliber and hold off handing me over to Swelley and his Homeland mob until he hears from his superior."

With a deep frown, Perez shook his head in a way that implied that was the last thing he would do if he regained control of the situation.

"Although," I said, "he does seem a tad resistant to the idea."

Perez's upper lip curled. "A tad? First off, it's an insane plan. Second, I'm going to smack you down so hard when I'm back in control, pygmies will be looking down at you."

"Nice turn of phrase," Joan Slater said. "Pass him the phone."

I did, and though her voice was faint, I could make out the first lady's words.

"Corporal Perez, this is Joan Slater."

Despite his resistance, Perez straightened involuntarily. As if someone had just rammed rebar up the back of his shirt. "I recognize your voice, ma'am."

"Do you see the man standing in front of you?"

"Yes, ma'am."

"As a personal favor to me, I want you to take very good care of him. If you do that, I will not forget it."

Perez's face worked furiously as he sorted through this new wrinkle. He'd listened to my exchange with the first lady, so he understood the new framework I'd just proposed, which landed him in the kettle with us. I'm sure he also understood the plan made a hundred-to-one long shot for the Japan Cup out at Tokyo Racecourse seem like money banked. His job was to protect the ambassador. FLOTUS was not part of the chain of command Perez had taken an oath to obey, but she was the first lady of the United States of America and married to the commander in chief. And she was on the phone with him.

"I'm not sure I can do that, ma'am."

"Did you hear my conversation with Stewart Tattersill?"

"Yes, ma'am."

"Let me assure you the president will be on board with this, Mr. Perez. Despite 'Inflexible Lex's' protestations, the ambassador will reverse himself."

Perez grinned at the nickname in spite of himself. "He *is* a diplomat."

"Precisely. You want to be on the right side when the dust settles, Corporal Perez."

He hesitated. "Yes, ma'am."

"Can I count on your support?"

The Marine's eyes bounced from me to Noda to his captured weapon to the rescue team beyond the glass of the booth.

Decision time.

Time to see what Perez was made of.

Many people joined the Marines to bring order to their personal lives. Lives that were otherwise chaotic and unfocused and often without proper parental role models. The Corps gave them a set of rules and regulations to follow. Gave them a necessary boost up to adulthood. But once you absorbed the rules and regulations, you needed also to be able to apply them to the real world outside the framework of military situations, and the real world had a way of not playing by the rules at times.

This was one of those times.

Could Perez make the leap from the blind obedience drilled into him by the Corps to one of applying the rules in an unprecedented situation? Would he march forward like an automaton, or jump the hurdle?

"Can I?" I heard Joan Slater ask again.

If it were possible, Perez's body grew more rigid. "Ma'am, yes, ma'am."

"I like your enthusiasm, Corporal. The president and I will not forget your decision. I know it is a tough one. Now shake your head like you're disagreeing with everything I'm saying; then, if you wouldn't mind, please pass the phone back to Mr. Brodie."

"Yes, ma'am."

Perez cast a look of disgust at the phone, then thrust the device back at me.

I held it up to my ear. "I'm here."

"That should help."

"We'll see soon enough," I said, casting a curious glance at Perez. "Not to offend, but any sign of the president?"

"No, sorry."

Any window of opportunity Noda and I might have had on this side of the Pacific had been slammed shut by Swelley and his crew. They were fanning out. Swelley's lead man held a crowbar in case they got a chance to pop out the windowpane in our booth.

The barrel of a sniper's rifle poked over the ledge of a second-story window across the street, and two more muzzles rested on windowsills on the next floor up.

There was no reason to be coy. They were coming and our chosen cover offered no more than temporary protection. There would be steel plates in the guardhouse walls, but the sharpshooters would have selected ammo that would plow through the metal like a truck through a haystack.

No one would activate the snipers with FLOTUS on the line, but Swelley's men might tear the booth apart. That would give them a chance to extract a measure of revenge before carting me off. Perez was not a viable hostage. They figured, rightly, that we wouldn't shoot him. Swelley held his phone up two inches from his ear. He neither spoke nor listened. He was waiting for the final go-ahead call. With FLOTUS in the loop, that would be pretty high up the chain. Higher than Tattersill.

"Not to seem selfish," I said, "but Homeland is getting ready to pounce."

"I understand," Joan Slater said in a tone that told me this was not the first time she'd been up against it.

We hung up. Salvation rested on a return call from halfway around the world. There was nothing to do but wait until the first lady could pry her husband loose from the Situation Room. I shoved my phone into the front pocket of my jeans, bowed my head in case someone outside or on the other end of the visual feed could read lips, and told Perez to look down. He complied.

"We good?" I asked.

"Yes, sir."

"Glad to hear it. Going forward, probably best to ditch the 'sir.'"

"I can do that."

I asked him if he understood Japanese. When he replied in the negative, I said, "Okay, I'm going to give some instructions to my colleague here in Japanese. When you see your opportunity, take it. You understand what I mean?"

"Yes."

"Then we'll get along just fine. Until we don't."

I looked up. Hope had returned to his eyes.

CHAPTER 53

A MOMENT later I mumbled a few words to Noda without moving my lips. The chief detective glanced at the growing forces mobilizing on the street. The overwhelming display of manpower seemed to distract him. His gun hand drooped. Perez sprang forward, snatched the firearm, then pointed the weapon at my chest and ordered us both toward the back end of the guard booth, then down on our knees with our fingers laced behind our heads.

We complied.

From five yards away, Swelley raised his hands and began a slow, exaggerated clapping in appreciation of Perez's takedown. The rest of his team joined in. The Japanese cops looked on without expression.

Squaring his shoulders, Swelley approached the booth with a big grin. The silver-gray bristles on his tan scalp glistened under the streetlight.

"Well done, son," he called through the glass barrier. "You make all of us proud. If you'll open up, we'll take it from here."

"I'm still waiting for final orders, sir."

"Well, I'm high man on-site, so you can hand off to me."

"Excuse me for asking, sir, but who exactly are you?"

Swelley whipped out a badge holder from his back pocket and spread it open with one hand, a silver DHS badge on the right, a picture ID at the left.

"Tom Swelley, Homeland Security. I'll take your prisoners."

"Can't do that, sir. Chain of command. I need to hear from my direct superior or the ambassador."

"You're a hero, son. We all saw that. I'm asking you to kindly stand down, in the name of national security."

"Sorry, sir."

"I'm asking nicely now, Corporal, but I can get mean. I want your captives and I want them yesterday. They are enemies of the US of A."

Perez glanced over at us, down at the phone in my pocket, then back at Swelley. "I can guarantee neither of these two will be making my Christmas list, sir, but I cannot release them into your custody without—"

"Enough!" Swelley shouted. "Not another goddamned word, Marine. You are only a corporal. Low on the totem pole. I am in command here and I won't tolerate disobedience. Either you release those prisoners into my custody this very minute or I will personally see you court-martialed, your military career destroyed, and your family sent back to whatever shithouse American-hating country south of the border they came from. No one will be able to help you. I get real mad, you might not be coming up for air for a long, long time. Am I making myself clear, Marine?"

From the first derogatory *Marine*, Perez's features had begun to petrify. Now his jawline protruded and his eyes shot daggers. I knew the look. Swelley had adopted the wrong course.

"Sir, you can insult me all you want, but I am a Marine. While I am on duty I will not leave my post. However, sir, as soon as I am off-duty, I request permission to kick your ass all the way down this street and back again. Sir. In the meantime, I must ask you to step away from the booth. You are not—I repeat, *not*—part of my chain of command. I answer only to my direct military superior, or the ambassador."

Now's a good time to bring on your husband, Joan.

"Then we'll call the ambassador. After that, your ass is mine, and I'm shoving it down a black hole."

Pulling out his personal cell phone, Swelley backed up, dark eyes locked on Perez, clearly measuring him for one of the more exotic appliances in a Homeland dungeon.

Perez turned his back on the cluster of agents, undeterred. One of them drew a gun and snapped back the slide.

Stiffening, Perez slanted eyes in my direction. "Did one of those half-wit goons just draw down on me?"

"Yes," I said.

"At my back?"

"Center mass."

"Dumb."

"You'd think they would know bulletproof glass when they saw it."

"Dumb on that count too."

———

It took Swelley two minutes to raise the ambassador. Noda, Perez, and I listened intently for a ringtone from the secure phone inside the booth. Several times Perez glanced at my mobile.

Swelley waved his phone at Perez.

We were out of time.

Perez started to unlatch the door.

"I wouldn't advise that," I said. "They'll rush you as soon as you open it."

Perez looked out and saw the agents behind Swelley had risen up on the balls of their feet.

"Son of a bitch," the Marine said under his breath. "This is the trash they hire to protect our nation. Long view, we're on the same damn side. Man, I may have to find another line of work."

"Or get in there yourself and upgrade the talent pool," I said.

Pointing at the secure phone, Perez shouted to Swelley, "Ask the ambassador to call me on that line."

"Mine is secure, Corporal."

"And so's the door. House line or nothing, sir."

Swelley swore at the Marine, then spoke a few words into his phone and disconnected. "Tattersill's calling now."

The console buzzed and a miniature red dome lit up. Perez punched the button below it and lifted the receiver from its cradle. "Sir?"

"Perez, you're back in control now, are you?"

"Yes, sir."

"I want you to—"

Just then my cell phone rang.

"What was that, Perez? It sounded like an alarm."

"No, just incoming."

"Are you in danger or in control?"

"I'll let you know in a minute, Mr. Ambassador."

Perez waved the gun for me to answer, which I did.

CHAPTER 54

M R. Brodie?" an assured male voice asked.

"Yes?"

"Hold for POTUS. He's calling from the Oval Office and asked me to inform you that both the secretary of state and the secretary of Homeland Security are in attendance. Stand by, sir."

The buzz on the line softened then I heard a click.

"Jim?"

"Hi, Mr. President . . . uh, Joe."

I heard a smile in his voice. "You're learning." Then the good cheer dissipated. "My people tell me we have a situation."

At *we*, relief swept over me. "We do."

His gun still trained on us, Perez pressed the phone receiver to his chest, blocking the sound. "Is that him? Really him?"

"Yes."

Perez grinned. It was his first smile of the night. "Oorah! Then let's kick some ass."

"Brodie, what's going on?" the president said. "Is that the Marine?"

"It is indeed," I said.

He chuckled. "I'm looping you in as a silent third party. Listen but don't talk. Under any circumstances."

"Got it," I said. "The guard's got Tattersill on another line."

"No problem. I'll light a fire under the bastard's ass. Now stay quiet, hear?

"Will do."

I heard a click, then Joe Slater said, "Jonathan, patch me through."

Covering the mouthpiece, I said to Perez, "You want in on this?"

"Hell, yeah."

"You sure? It means blowing your cover with Homeland outside and the guards at the house watching the camera."

"I know." He raised the receiver to the console phone. "Sir, something critical's come up. I have to put you on hold for a minute."

"Perez, do not—"

The Marine cut him off, rushed over, and leaned in. I put my finger to my lips. He nodded.

We heard a click, then a dead silence, a second click, and the ambassador's voice.

"Mr. President, to what do I owe the honor?"

"To the emergency unfolding on your doorstep, Stu."

"Sir, I can explain."

"There's no time, but I would be grateful if you would give Brodie whatever he asks for."

"Sir, I don't think that's advisable. In fact, I would argue for—"

"There's to be no more arguing, Stu."

"But, Mr. President—Joe—I think it very unwise to—"

"This is not a political issue, even though we are on opposite sides of the aisle. I've kept you on in your position because—"

"I assure you, sir, that politics plays no role in my—"

"Stu, no need to say more. I believe you. My people have caught me up. By 'my people' I mean the secretary of Homeland Security and the secretary of state. Carl, say hello to Stu over there in Tokyo."

Carl Jordenson, the secretary of Homeland Security, headed all branches of the agency. Helen Mitchell, the secretary of state, oversaw foreign policy and the diplomatic corps, for starters. The first was Swelley's overlord, the second Tattersill's. Joe Slater took no chances.

"Hi, Stu," the secretary of Homeland Security said. "It's been a while."

"Yes, Carl, it has."

"I want you to know we are the active lead in this operation and the DoD secretary has been looped in since the NSA is also involved."

The National Security Agency operated under the umbrella of the Department of Defense.

"Helen?" Joe Slater said.

"Hi, Stu. We're so sorry to get you up at such an ungodly hour."

"Terrors of the job, Helen. As we all know. We have a live situation unfolding here and first lady wasn't on-site. If you will just give me a few more minutes, I can sort it out and you won't have to bother."

Even outnumbered, Inflexible Lex trooped on.

"Stu, the president has brought me up to date on his end. We all agree you should cooperate with Mr. Brodie."

"Yes, of course, Helen. I just thought this is something best handled by our people."

Agreement followed by a slick reversal so smooth, you could miss it if you weren't at the top of your game. But all three people on the other end of the line were, and wouldn't.

The president stepped into the breach. "By 'our people,' do you mean Homeland?"

"Yes, I do. They're the professionals. But now that you've conferred with Carl, my services are no longer needed. I will gladly step aside."

"Thank you, Stu. I appreciate that. Carl tells me Homeland has not come up with anything on the location of Anna Tanaka. Were you aware of that?"

The ambassador cleared his throat. "Yes, sir."

"Were you also aware they had two agents undercover assigned to protect her?"

"This is the first I am hearing of it."

"Let's examine that for a moment, shall we? Are you in the loop over there, Stu? Since, as you say, you are on-site?"

The ambassador hesitated. "Basically."

"You should be in or out. Not in the foggy land of 'basically.' Has Tom Swelley been in touch? He's running things over there for this."

"Yes. In fact, he's outside the residence now and—"

"I'm sure he is. What do you know of Homeland's progress in your backyard?"

"Nothing much, sir."

"Neither do I, Stu. Neither do I. And I am one unhappy camper. I have told Secretary Jordenson this."

"Of course, sir."

"Further, I informed him that Brodie has a lead on the daughter's whereabouts. Do you know what Carl said, Stu?"

"I imagine he thought it extraordinary, sir."

"That is the precise word he used, which is good. Puts us all on the same page. Because of his long association with Japan, Mr. Brodie has his own set of unique sources. Get him what he needs."

"I should think—"

"Are you about to second-guess me, Stu?"

"No, Mr. President."

"Good. You get Brodie over to Seoul, you hear me? Give him everything he requires and don't let me hear you've dragged your feet."

"Yes, sir."

"And keep Swelley and his goons off Brodie's back. In fact, keep them out of the loop until I give the word. Have you got that? Anything further, you are to work through Helen or Carl. Do you understand?"

"Yes, sir."

"Good-bye, Stu."

"Good-bye, sir."

With a note of relief in his voice, the ambassador dropped off the line without another syllable.

Perez broke into a wide grin. Swelley stood frozen on the other side of the glass. He had not been privy to the president's conversation but he could decipher the Marine's expression. A string of expletives filtered through the glass.

"You still there, Jim?" Joe Slater asked.

"Yes. Just enjoying the scenery."

"The weather's changed, has it?"

"For the moment."

Tellingly, the president's response gave a whole new meaning to the word *farsighted*. "Rest assured, neither Joan or I are fooled by Swelley's childish maneuvers."

"Good to know."

"And there's more. My esteemed colleagues and I have something for your ears only."

CHAPTER 55

"Y ES, Mr. President, I'm listening," I said into the phone as I stepped
from the safety of the guard booth.

"I presume that was for your audience," Joe Slater said.

"You got it."

"Are things moving?"

Unattended, the tall gate emblazoned with the Great Seal of the
United States parted with measured dignity. From inside the estate, a
Marine beckoned us to enter.

"Yes, in all senses of the word."

"Excellent. Listen, I've talked this over with Carl and we've agreed to
bring you into the loop, but we need you to stay close-lipped regarding
what I'm about to tell you. Can you do that?"

"That's a yes for myself and my partner."

"Would that be"—a rustle of papers—"Mr. Noda?"

"Yes."

"Excuse us for just a minute." I was put on hold. A minute later the
president returned. "Okay, inclusive of Mr. Noda but no further. He's got
the seal of approval."

"From?"

"The CIA. This level, that's how things work."

I considered the implications and decided it was a battle for another
time.

"Jim, we okay?"

"Yes."

"Then I'm passing you over. Carl?"

They were on speakerphone in the Oval, so the "passing" was figurative.

"Hello, Mr. Brodie," the Homeland secretary said. "What's your personal opinion of the NSA?"

Or maybe a battle for now. "Do they have information on me, my daughter, and my friends?"

Noda and I strolled into the ambassadorial compound and the gate slowly reversed course, shutting us in.

"I imagine they do."

"Despite the restrictions to the Patriot Act?"

"There are many ways to intercept data."

Not the best answer but an honest one.

"Then I hate it. I want my private life to remain private."

"Can you separate your personal opinion from the issue at hand?"

"In this case, yeah."

"Fine, then we're in business. First up, you're to be accompanied to Seoul by a Marine recon team of four men."

"Don't want them."

"Jim," the president said, "these boys know the terrain and are some of our best men in the Far East. They are military, not NSA or Homeland. I'm afraid I must insist on this. But they are to follow your orders."

"That a guarantee?"

"Yes."

"No Homeland? No embedded spies?"

"None."

"Don't like the idea but I can work with it."

"Good. Thank you. Here's Carl again."

The nose of what I presumed was Tattersill's official car, an elongated maroon Lincoln Continental with glazed black windows, rolled around the bend in the drive and eased to a silent stop alongside us.

"Mr. Brodie, I want to assure you—"

"Sorry to interrupt, but the ambassador's car just turned up. Do you want him in the loop?"

"Mr. President?" the secretary asked.

"I think not. Jim, top priority is to get you to your plane. I have work I can juggle for the next three hours, so get back to us when you are alone and we'll continue your briefing. Carl will stick around. Is that workable?"

"Absolutely," I said.

A chauffeur hopped out with brisk efficiency and opened a rear door for us. Noda and I slid onto the seat facing Tattersill. The ambassador sat in the far corner of the backseat, pointedly ignoring us. He'd dressed in haste. His clothes and his signature wavy blond locks had the ruffled look of a startled pigeon.

The chauffeur climbed back behind the wheel, the gate eased open, and the nose of the vehicle crawled forward. The crowd of badges edged aside. From the entrance of the guard booth, Perez saluted. The officers of the Tokyo Metropolitan Police formed a respectful line along the drive, while Swelley's crew gave way with undisguised defiance.

"I suppose you want to hold on to that phone for a while longer," Tattersill said, his tone peevish.

One wing of his shirt collar flopped over the lapel of his topcoat.

"Yes, our talk is ongoing. I'll see that it's returned."

"Didn't think you could tap into the Oval too," he said.

Too. That one word told me everything. Behind Slater's back, Swelley had also played the presidential card.

But days earlier.

Laying out his traps and trip wires.

From which Noda and I had only just escaped.

In stilted English, the chauffeur informed us we would be heading to an alternate helipad ten minutes away, since the Roppongi site normally used was under construction.

Noda and I sunk into the padded leather comfort of the Lincoln. I felt my nerves settle. Each passing second whisked us farther away from Swelley's troops and the police. The Tokyo PD wouldn't follow, but Swelley's people would. Not immediately, but soon enough.

At my side, Noda read my concern. "No time for that now. Get your passport here." He reached for his own phone.

I nodded as the Lincoln, with its sleek rounded corners and a wide regal grill, glided through the Tokyo night. My personal phone vibrated with an incoming call from Jenny. I answered and she jumped right in: "Hello, Daddy. I just wanted to say hi before I rush off for soccer—so hi!"

I laughed. "Hi back. I miss you."

My daughter sounded effusive. She'd made a whole new set of friends playing soccer, and her spirits and her health had benefited.

"I miss you too. When are you coming home?"

I winced. "As soon as I can. I'm helping out some friends."

"That's okay, Daddy, just don't forget me."

The barb pierced deeper than anything Habu could have thrown my way. His blade work drew only blood.

"Not possible, Jen, and you know that."

"Did you tell Rie about my judo wins?"

"I did. She gave me a special message to deliver in person."

"Tell me now."

"I can't. I made a promise."

"You can tell. I won't say anything."

"Sorry, kid. A promise is a promise."

"Fudge. It's so hard to wait."

From the next seat, Noda growled at me.

"Listen, Jen, I have the message memorized, so I'll tell you first thing. Got to go. Love you, kid."

"Same here, Daddy. Bye-bye. Oh, and don't forget the Totoro pajamas for Lisa."

"I won't."

We disconnected and I called Rie. She picked up on the fifth ring, sounding groggy and unlike her usual self. "Where are you? Are you okay?"

"Sorry. Had my hands full. I have to go away for a few days, so I won't be able to make it tonight, but I need a favor."

"What's happened?" Her voice was strained.

"I found out where they're taking Anna."

"That's good, but are *you* okay?"

Something wasn't right. "Yes, of course. Is everything okay there?"

"I'm . . . just worried. Tell me what you need."

I explained where I'd stashed my passports, then asked her to hand over both to the Brodie Security op Noda had asked to swing by the house.

"Two passports?"

"Yes."

"Where are you going?" I told her and she said, "I'll bring them myself," hanging up before I could protest.

"Trouble in paradise?" Tattersill asked with a snarky grin.

As much as I wanted to ignore him, Inflexible Lex might be right this time. Rie had sounded odd.

We arrived without any further interruption at a midtown office building of white concrete and black windows. It was boilerplate commercial architecture and instantly forgettable, which may have been the point. Private security processed us through the gate at the rear, which guarded a passage to a subbasement parking lot, where a Marine sentry waited.

"ETA for the bird is five minutes, Mr. Ambassador," he said as we stepped from the vehicle.

"Very good."

"Will you be accompanying the gentlemen, sir?"

"No. Five minutes and they will be the military's headache."

Noda and I traded a look. I wanted to punch the disgruntled diplomat. Inflexible Lex led us to a pair of locked double glass doors, where a second Marine pulled out a key ring anchored to his service belt and let us in.

"Third elevator from the left has been activated, sir," he said as he swung the door aside.

"I know the way."

"Sorry I can't light her up for you, sir. New security requirements."

Tattersill gave a curt nod and we followed him down a dimly lit hallway, then into the elevator and up to a roof, where a helipad stood lit and waiting. Embedded roof-lights the color of turquoise encircled the landing site. They cast a discreet ring of light bright enough to direct the pilot without attracting attention from tenants in the neighboring buildings.

Two minutes later a Black Hawk with the signature humpbacked dome and long rotors set down in a flurry of wind and dust. A pilot dropped from the cockpit, scrambled over in the half-bend run they all use, and saluted the ambassador, saying, "Ready for boarding anytime you are, sir."

With a cavalier wave, Tattersill said, "They're all yours. Up, up, and away."

"I need an extra minute or two," I said. "I'm waiting on a delivery."

"Two deliveries," said Noda, who had hung back and informed the driver of our incoming messengers.

The first delivery arrived six minutes later: five Brodie Security ops in black with clubs, Tasers, and radios on equipment belts at their waists.

The ambassador turned indignant. "What are you up to, Brodie? You said a 'delivery.'"

The lead man handed over Noda's passport and some documents, including a map I'd requested.

"There you go," I said.

"It doesn't take five men to deliver a sheaf of papers."

"They'll be riding with us."

"Unacceptable."

"'Get him what he needs.' Word for word from the Oval. Have you forgotten already?"

Tattersill's eyebrows formed a near perfect V of scorn. "You're out of control."

Again I felt the urge to smack him. If the pilot hadn't been present, I would have. But I restrained myself because I knew the game Tattersill was playing. He was laying groundwork for a counterattack in case the expedition blew up in our faces. He wanted the flyboy to be able to recall the exchange, anecdotal though it was.

I turned to the pilot. "How many people will this bird hold?"

He cast an uncertain look Tattersill's way. "This site can handle size, so we brought a big bird. Up to eleven combat-equipped troops. Twenty with light loads."

"Good to hear," I said, casting an *Anything-else-on-your-mind?* look at Inflexible Lex. He fumed and showed me his back.

The next minute my delivery arrived—with unforeseen extras.

CHAPTER 56

'M downstairs," Rie said when I answered her call.

"See you in a minute."

I headed to the ground floor, still puzzled by her earlier tone. The elevator doors slid open to reveal Rie alone in the unlit passage. A band of pale-yellow light slanted across her face, the rest of her nothing more than a silhouette. Panic consumed her look.

"What's wrong?" I asked, a mild anxiety seizing me.

Moist tracks glistened on the high plains of Rie's cheeks. She could not have passed the outer checkpoint in this state, nor the inner one. Neither Marine would have permitted a tearful woman to enter without alerting the ambassador. So she'd disguised her distress before entering. Which meant her tears were fresh.

"I had an awful nightmare before you called. I don't cry and I don't have nightmares, but tonight I saw myself crying over you. You were in a dark place, and dying. I don't know where or why, but wherever you're going, please don't. It's too dangerous."

A tear rolled down her cheek and plunged into the darkness between us. I pulled her into my arms. I could feel the fullness of her form. Where her face buried itself into my shirt, a dampness spread.

"I don't cry, Brodie," she said again, her head buried in my shirt and her fists coming up and pounding my chest.

"I know, I know."

After a long moment she raised her head and we kissed. It was long and deep and desperate. When she pulled away she said, "Can't someone else go in your place?"

"It's Seoul. I've been there a dozen times."

"But it's not going to end there, is it? Where else? The DMZ?"

Rie knew Seoul was too easy.

"Yes, but Noda will be with me."

"In my dream he wasn't there."

"There's a Marine recon team accompanying us."

"They weren't there either. This is different."

"They're all different."

She shook her head. "Not like this. This is China Rules. You're dealing with spies and covert ops. It's their world, not ours. None of those people can be trusted. Let them deal with each other. Give it to Homeland or the CIA or the PSIA. Or even the South Koreans."

"I can't do that."

"Do it for me."

"You know I would if I could. But none of those people care about Anna as much as I do. None of them have the history with this case that I have."

Once more I saw Mikey's face at the Kennedy Center. Attentive to every nuance playing out on stage. Eager to meet his idol. Then I saw the blood and the bodies and my chase through the maze of dressing rooms and painted backdrops. I saw the killer's ticket to freedom—my backstage pass—floating away into the darkness. And then there was Sharon Tanaka's husband, resurrected in front of me when I told him why I believed his daughter was still alive.

Fear pooled in Rie's eyes. "You can't go, Brodie. Something bad is coming."

"I have to."

Her head slumped against my chest. She clung tighter. My throat went dry.

"I brought both passports," she said into my shirt.

"Thank you."

"One of them in a different name."

"I know."

"Which one do you need?"

"The alternate."

I felt her stiffen. "Brodie, in my dream—"

Behind us, the elevator chimed and the doors parted. Noda, stout and still and stone-faced, stood in the interior. He nodded at Rie and she nodded back.

"It's time," he said.

Rie released me with reluctance, shooting me a last pleading look.

"It'll be fine," I said, the cliché ringing false the moment it left my lips.

"You don't even know what *it* is," Rie said, a justifiable rebuke to everything shallow and inadequate in my attempt to comfort her.

And, as no one could have foreseen, entirely true.

CHAPTER 57

3:10 A.M.
YOKOTA AIR BASE, TOKYO PREFECTURE

RETURNING to the roof, my mind still on Rie's parting look, I boarded the Black Hawk. The roar of the rotors whipped up an ever-faster syncopated beat and the powerful machine lifted into the night.

Below, the city slept, dark and still and laced with strings of lemon-yellow streetlights twisting and turning with the scramble of boulevards and backstreets.

A few minutes later my personal phone came alive, vibrating to signal an incoming text message. The source was cloaked but I hit OPEN anyway.

> B, we're your rear guard. We'll have your back as soon as you
> land. This has come straight from the top. Your line is not
> secure so do not reply. Just know J sent us.
> —KC

Straight from the top. The president and his team, with the first lady riding shotgun. Or maybe Joan whipping the horsemen forward behind the scenes.

My phone quivered a second time, though not with its signature tremor. Something lighter. Feathery and foreign. No notification appeared on my screen. No window popped up. As I sat in ten tons of throbbing machinery, I watched as the text rose and fell in waves. Letters stretched upward like taffy toward the crest of each wave before dropping back in place and returning to form.

This was new.

I planted my elbows on my knees and clasped the phone in both hands, holding the instrument steady, isolating it from the Black Hawk's pulsating core. The phone continued to quiver. The waves continued to ripple through the text. The distortion originated from a source other than the helicopter's pumping pulsations.

Your line is not secure.

Then the quivering ceased and the text clarified.

Someone had reached inside my phone.

———

The Brodie Security ops team hit the tarmac first. The men bent low, hustled to a point beyond the rotor, then spread out in a protective circle behind the Black Hawk.

Noda and I exited next and stepped into the circle.

Since then, seven minutes had passed and KC's team had yet to show.

We stood in the middle of the tarmac for general activities, alert, on edge, and exposed. At our backs was the taxiway paralleling the main airstrip. In front of us stood a line of humpbacked hangars, each with its own oversize shutter.

"Can't hardly see my hands," Yasuhiro "Shooter" Watanabe muttered under his breath. The wiry leader of the Brodie Security team was a sharp-eyed former member of the Japan Self-Defense Forces. Military from head to toe, and Brodie Security's one armed-forces asset.

"I can engage the navigation lights," the pilot said from the cockpit. "Port or tail?"

"Keep her dark."

"Roger that."

No sense in pinpointing our location, even if we were supposed to be on friendly turf. The ambassador's residence should have been friendly turf.

The pilot, who knew KC, had no luck raising him. My men grew increasingly nervous. The rotor blades had long ago wound down to a standstill.

"How many times have you tried?" I asked.

"Auto-calling every sixty seconds."

"Any pickup at all?"

"Nothing. It's like a graveyard out there."

The row of hangars ran in both directions into the night. They were shuttered and unlit except for number 26-B. Behind us, the taxiway and primary runaway stretched into the unseeable distance, dim blue pinpoint lights flickering at their edges. Aside from the airstrip illumination, our surroundings were steeped in total darkness.

"Code beacon for approaching aircraft is operating," the pilot said, "but the tower isn't answering. Somebody could have taken it out or it's shut for the night."

"Which do you think?"

He shrugged. "Hard to tell."

Eight minutes.

The only sign of human activity had occurred before our arrival. The plane scheduled to take us to Seoul had been rolled out of hangar 26-B.

Now it sat alone and unattended, without pilots or ground crew.

Our helicopter had set down on the designated helipad. On the only vacant landing site in a row of silent Black Hawks with long drooping blades, menacing and ghostly in the shadows.

Nine minutes.

"Don't like this," Shooter said.

"Nothing to like," I said. "Special forces guys roll out of their bunks ready."

Shooter's eyes slid over the outskirts of the landing area. "We've been here too long with no cover other than the Hawk."

"It's all open ground. And the hangars are a no-go."

Shooter nodded. "Anyone gaming us would expect us to head that way. Damned if I will. Silver lining is they won't want us dead, just out of commission until the Korean leg is over."

I said, "You're talking about putting us on ice like we've done to Habu and his men?"

"If there's unfriendlies out there, that's got to be their plan."

"We're not that easy."

"Thing is, we've got sticks and electric juice guns. Everyone on base starts with semiautomatics and ramps up from there."

Summation: we had no safe cover, no firepower, no options.

"Which way is base headquarters?" I asked.

One of the men pointed into the darkness. "About eight hundred meters in that direction."

"Anything in between?"

"No."

Shooter walked over to the cockpit. "You have any signal at all?"

"None."

My private phone began buzzing. I answered and a deep bass voice on the other end asked for me by name. Confident, precise, clipped syllables.

"KC?" I said.

"Yes, sir."

"Let's drop the 'sir.' Trouble on your end?"

"Turbulence, sir . . . Brodie."

"Homeland?"

The soldier let out a low whistle. "Good call."

"Traps and trip wires."

"If you say so."

"I do."

Standing on the tarmac, I'd considered all potential enemies: Swelley, the PSIA, Tattersill, Gerald Thornton-Cummings, a double cross at the White House, or a rogue in the chain of command. I even considered Zhou. Then I chose the closest and most brazen.

KC said, "Someone makes a call like you just did, I want to be on their team. Certainly don't want to be on the other side."

"Glad to hear it. What happened?"

"Spooks have their place and job, but neither of them better be in my face. You may not agree, but that's this military man's SOP, sir."

"We're going to get along just fine, KC. Assuming you can get here in one piece."

"Roger that. Transportation is rolling up as we speak. An armored brown Humvee."

"Too much too late."

"I hear that. Also heard you have your own team out there. That true?"

"You're well-informed."

"Always. Brown Humvee. Don't let 'em shoot at us," he said, and signed off.

Swelley's reach was impressive. With no high-speed cross-city transport available, he'd changed tactics, intercepting KC's text message, then attempting to hamstring the recon unit.

What was Swelley up to? If the president's intervention could not deter him, nothing would.

CHAPTER 58

THE Humvee roared up three minutes later and a large Marine in green-and-brown camouflage fatigues leapt from the passenger side and advanced with a sure step. He stood six-two and had short-cropped blond hair, a weathered and penetrating look, and bulging thighs.

I met him halfway and we shook hands.

He said, "Brodie, I presume."

"For better or for worse."

He grinned. "We're here to make it better."

"Good to know."

"As soon as we load our gear, we can get airborne."

His men were already hauling equipment lockers, gear belts, and rifles from the Humvee. One of them shouted over about the lack of crew and pilots.

KC shook his head. "Same guys probably sent them across base to get them out of the way. I'd better chase them down."

"Good deal," I said. "Got to make one quick call."

"Anyone I know?"

"You do, whether you voted for him or not."

The secure phone rang three times before someone picked up. I identified myself and was told there'd been orders to patch me through immediately. Three rings later, the Homeland secretary picked up.

"Hello again, Jim. This is Carl. Joe will be right here."

"Okay. Do you mind a question from my end?

Over by the open hangar, KC was on his radio, trying to track down the errant pilots and prep crew. His men stacked their supplies and weapons by the locked aircraft.

"Go right ahead."

"You must have others working on this."

"We do."

"Including Swelley?"

"Including but not limited to him, by any means."

"And no one else has found any trace of Anna Tanaka or her kidnappers?"

"Currently, only you've found the trailhead. You dug out the proverbial needle in the espionage haystack."

I sensed an incipient excuse for a congressional committee in the making.

"I got lucky," I said.

Carl's chuckle was bitter. "Send some of that luck our way, would you?"

"Are you in on the day-to-day?"

"No, of course not. Why?"

"Nothing."

I couldn't throw Swelley's latest at him without knowing more, and wanted to avoid slinging mud with the president nearby if I could.

Joe Slater came on, saying, "I assume everything's gone smoothly since we last talked."

"We're moving forward," I said.

The president was no fool. He hesitated for a second before resuming. "Okay, but you yell if you need my help. One reason I'm insisting on bringing you aboard is because you've demonstrated an impressive ability on two fronts. Not only did you identify the kidnappers but you also defused the scene at Tattersill's."

"Thank you. But, really, I only want to get Anna Tanaka back alive."

"The Tattersill incident could have blown up in any number of ways. Inflexible Lex would not have been unhappy to see this White House take some flack. You heard me mention Homeland had two men undercover at the funeral and we still lost Ms. Tanaka?"

"Yes. I saw them."

"Wait. Did they identify themselves to you?"

"No."

"So how . . . ?"

"They weren't passing as smoothly as they believed."

The president was startled. "You hear that, Carl?"

KC called one of his men over, gave some orders, and the Marine jumped into the Humvee and roared off.

"I did and I'm not liking it."

"Neither am I," Slater said. "Brodie, you've done great work, and I mean that sincerely."

"Just doing my job," I said, finding something on my side to dislike. An abundance of compliments usually came with baggage.

The president plowed on. "You understand the gravity of the current situation?"

"Yes, of course."

"Then we need the landing site on the South Korean coastline and their destination inside the DMZ."

There it was. The president didn't need the locations. Probably hadn't even thought about them. This was the Homeland secretary pushing, or maybe someone at the Department of Defense.

"Let me stop you right there, Mr. President. While I understand the desire, I am not supplying anyone with any new information just yet. I've come too far and it means too much."

"Joe," the secretary said, "let me take this. Jim, this is national security we're talking about, and it's vital we have that information. You agreed to join the team."

"No," I said. "I agreed to allow a team to accompany me to Seoul. There's a difference."

Carl snorted. "I'm not going to argue semantics with you."

The Humvee roared up with the pilots and ground staff.

"It's not semantics and you know it. I won't let my work be sabotaged anymore."

"If you're talking about Tattersill's little temper tantrum—"

The secretary had shown his hand. Time to lay down mine.

"No, Carl, I'm talking about a steady stream of run-ins and attempted sabotage by Homeland agents. First, in the National Mall they warned me off the case and talking to the White House. Next, your people pushed Tattersill's buttons, not me. And finally, just minutes ago, the recon team sent to accompany me was attacked by Homeland men here on the base."

So much for saving the secretary's face. I'd just made a powerful enemy.

After a long silence in the Oval, the president said, "Is all of this true, Jim? You're not exaggerating?"

"Yes to the first, no to the second."

"Carl?"

"Brodie must be mistaken. Or it is a case of a mistaken interpretation of an order."

KC flashed me the okay sign. His men hopped aboard and the plane's engine started up.

"Any way you look at it, they couldn't all be mistakes," I said. "I don't have time for this nonsense right now. Anna doesn't have time. And, again, she is all I care about. There were four witnesses to tonight's so-called mistake and I'll be happy to produce them after Anna is back safely. But right now I have a plane to catch and a woman to find. I won't allow the information I have to be compromised. So if there's nothing further, I'd like to be on my way."

"Actually, there is," the secretary said. "At the president's request, I need to brief you."

No apology. No conciliatory comment.

"And I want to hear it, but I need to get airborne, so it'll have to wait," I said, and disconnected.

KC crouched in the open doorway of the plane ten yards off. "You ready?" he yelled over the roar of the engine.

Tattersill had hung up on the first lady, and I'd hung up on the secretary of homeland security—in the presence of the president.

Must be something in the air.

I said, "Let's get going before I shoot somebody."

"Roger that."

CHAPTER 59

OVER THE SEA OF JAPAN

"**E**XPERTS agree it's one of the most dangerous spots on the planet," said Kevin Wilson-Yun.

Wilson-Yun, the information officer on the Marine recon team, was talking about the DMZ, the demilitarized zone. The flight was two hours and fifty-four minutes from Yokota Air Base on the outskirts of Tokyo to the K-16 Air Base in Seongnam, Korea, twelve miles southeast of Seoul. From there we'd make two short hops—a second helicopter ride to our landing spot in the DMZ, then ground transportation to our final destination within the Zone. For security purposes, I planned to phone in the first location thirty minutes before landing and reveal the second after we alighted from the final helo ride. With luck, my scheme would discourage any outside interference.

"So I've heard," I said.

"Have you been there?"

"Yes."

"To the Zone?" he asked suspiciously. "Or just South Korea?"

We sat facing each other in a stripped-down military plane meant for the transport of special fighting units. The six of us occupied thinly padded metal seats against a bare-bones fuselage, three to a side. Blackout curtains covered the windows, and red shoulder harnesses hung from the walls. Everyone ignored them. Overhead were metal lockers and an array of first-aid kits and dressings for battle operations. The loud, rumbling whine of the engine made hearing hard unless passengers leaned forward. Which all six of us did.

I said, "South Korea a dozen times, the DMZ once."

"But how much do you know?"

Wilson-Yun was a beefy, thick-limbed second-generation Korean-American from Torrance, California, I learned soon enough. Both sides of his heritage were reflected in his hybrid last name.

"More than most, less than some."

"You know your DMZ from your CCZ?"

"Now you're showing off."

He grinned. "Got to pass the time." Then the grin vanished. "So *do* you?"

"Yes."

The DMZ is a restricted area on either side of the border between the two Koreas. It hugs the Korean Peninsula like a tightly cinched belt, measuring two and a half miles top to bottom and 155 miles coast to coast. Every square inch is marked and mapped. Everything not built on or patrolled is mined. Collectively, two million soldiers on rotation are said to guard the border, and on the southern half of the DMZ 1.2 million land mines defend the interior. No one knows how many are on the northern side.

South Korea has a secondary buffer called the CCZ, or the civilian control zone, which runs below the DMZ. Also controlled by the military, it provides an additional measure of protection against any invasion attempt, of which there have been several. One of the most dangerous occurred in 1968. A team of thirty-one special commandos from North Korea crossed the DMZ to assassinate the South Korean president. Point men came within one hundred yards of the presidential residence.

In the sweep-up that followed the failed coup, twenty-nine North Korean special-ops soldiers were killed. One was captured; another found his way back across the DMZ. Even in retreat, the special-ops force inflicted heavy casualties, killing twenty-nine soldiers and police and injuring sixty-six others, among them four American personnel and two dozen civilians. It was lost on no one that the elite squad had, even in defeat, meted out a kill ratio of greater than three to one.

"You don't get the lay of the land dead right, you'll be dead, period," Wilson-Yun said, stern eyes shooting up from under a no-nonsense brow, his earlier humor nowhere in sight. "We're talking armaments on top of armaments, not to mention snipers, bunkers, tanks, missiles, gun embankments, and minefields. Plus all that and more in the CCZ."

"The Cold War is alive and well in Korea," I said.

"Affirmative. Hostilities are ongoing. And toxic if you drop your guard."

Wilson-Yun's spin on the real-world danger at Seoul's doorstep caused me to reconsider Rie's dream in a new light. Could it be some sort of premonition? I hoped not.

With another barbed look, Wilson-Yun all but pinned me to the fuselage. "If you know your geopolitics, then why don't you give us your intel now?"

I replied with an equally unyielding look. "Contrary to what everyone thinks, I don't know where they'll come ashore on the South Korean coast."

"Okay, give us the DMZ incursion point, then. The mission's on. This is go day. It'll make it safer for all of us."

The rest of the team listened intently.

I remained defiant. "We're talking about a group of two to four people. Anna Tanaka and one to three minders. Not knowing now won't make it any safer or any more dangerous for us."

"Three people total," Noda said, speaking for the first time.

I nodded. "That's the most likely scenario. One handler is not enough; three will draw more attention than desirable."

"So let's have it," Wilson-Yun said.

"On my schedule."

He frowned. "We need to set up over there. An advance party could get things rolling."

"Or create enough of a disturbance to alert any early watchers. At this rate, we'll arrive well ahead of them. It's South Korean territory. The six of us will do nicely."

"What games are you playing, Brodie?"

"Only one: to get the hostage out alive. There's been interference along the way, and I don't want any more of that at this stage. Your team ran into Homeland and nearly didn't make it. I've run up against them twice and seen them watching twice. The longer I hold on to the location, the better the chance no outside party will intrude."

Wilson-Yun's tone turned accusatory. "You don't trust us."

"I want to, but I don't know you, do I? I certainly don't trust your handlers or anyone insisting on advance information."

"So you leave us in the dark?"

"Tell me you have control over how those above you will handle the information, and I'll pass it to you now."

The intelligence officer stared at me. "Who the hell are you? They told me you were an art dealer."

"Not tonight."

"Bastards."

"You're catching on."

He'd been underbriefed. His team had fended off one threat and we'd uncovered another. What else waited for us?

CHAPTER 60

THIRTY minutes before our scheduled landing, I called in the first location. The White House had paved the way well. We encountered no red tape. No questions. No resistance of any kind.

On arrival, we found a Bell helicopter waiting to fly us to our next destination, the Joint Security Area within the DMZ. The JSA was a high-risk, tightly controlled territory overseen by the United Nations Command that straddles both sides of the border. In a classic Cold War style, there were armed guards on the ground and in watchtowers. More than six decades on, the area remains on high alert around the clock, every day of the year, with no end in sight.

A South Korean army liaison with a name tag stepped up and saluted KC. "At ease, Kim," KC said, returning the salute.

"This is Jim Brodie, the civilian heading this mission."

"Sir," Kim said, saluting me in turn.

"Call him Brodie," KC said.

"And you can call me Robert, sir, if you choose."

KC nodded. "Robert it is, soldier. How much do you know about the DMZ?"

"Everything there is to know, sir. I grew up in Daeseong-dong."

An alarm went off in my head. Wilson-Yun, who had been observing an operation unfolding across the field, swiveled around and focused his full attention on the South Korean. KC allowed his hand to drift toward his weapon, casually surveying the immediate area, suddenly on guard against another attack.

Daeseong-dong village was the problem, and the three of us knew it. Located within the DMZ extremely close to the border, the village had been given special dispensation. Everyone knew the story. Inhabitants had insisted on returning to their ancestral land after the war, so arrangements were made, but at a price. Residents had to bed down in their own homes most nights of the year, and could leave the village for only a finite number of days every twelve months. They also had a curfew. Soldiers came around to count heads to make sure no one had been spirited away to the North. In return for accepting these hardships, the government offered concessions, among them exemption from the draft.

"So you lived in the village?" I said.

He looked surprised. "Do you know it?"

"It's famous."

He flushed. "It's just a village, sir."

"It's so famous, it's common knowledge that villagers get paid top dollar for their crops, don't pay taxes, and don't have to serve in the military."

"That's all true," he said, his embarrassment deepening. "I enlisted. My friends called me crazy."

"Why would you do that?"

"It's a family tradition. My father joined. My grandfather served alongside US Navy commander Robert M. Ballinger."

Wilson-Yun's face lit up. "Your grandfather worked with Commander Ballinger?"

"Yes. You know him?"

"Every American soldier working the region knows the name." Wilson-Yun looked my way. "The commander was killed in an explosion during an examination of the first North Korean tunnel. He's a local hero."

I turned back to the liaison officer. "Which is where 'Robert' came from?"

"Yes, sir."

I relaxed. KC's hand drifted away from his weapon.

"In that case, we're honored to have you aboard."

"Thank you, sir—Brodie—but the honor's all mine. I hear this mission is important."

"Very."

KC caught my eye. "We'll be right back, Brodie. We need to change out of our fatigues into civvies."

"Because?"

"Snipers are less likely to take potshots at us that way."

———

After changing, the Marines humped their gear from the plane to the Bell in record time.

As Noda watched KC's team transfer the last of the equipment, he switched on his phone and it lit up with a voice mail notification. The Bell helicopter powered up. The chief detective stepped away from the noise of the rotors. I had to call him back after the rest of us had boarded.

"Anything useful?" I asked, raising my voice as we lifted into the air in a swirl of dust and heavy winds.

"Yeah. Two messages."

The aircraft changed bearings, turning north by northwest and picking up speed.

"So spill."

"Best you hear for yourself."

He pressed playback and a NO SIGNAL box popped open on his screen. The chief detective tapped the CANCEL button and tried again.

While Noda continued to fiddle with his mobile, I looked out the port window. We were coming up on central Seoul. Ahead was the wide band of the Han River, winding its way through the heart of the city like a mammoth snake. It had dark-blue segments and light-aqua ones and was divided at irregular intervals by its bridges.

Noda shrugged, and shoved the phone into his pocket.

"Anything important?" I asked.

"Yes."

"And?"

"Best you hear for yourself."

CHAPTER 61

I T is one of the ironies of the Koreas that the combined CCZ and DMZ security areas represent the best-preserved nature site on the Korean Peninsula.

Only here has mankind's touch been restrained.

Step away from the military installations, permanent base camps, and watchtowers—all of which leave a small collective footprint in the swatch of land that stretches from coast to coast—and the region is close to pristine. Asian black bear, Korean water deer, Amur leopard, and Eurasian otter roam the fields and woodlands. Herons, golden eagles, black swans, kingfishers, and cranes glide in for a migratory rest. The human touch is light yet firm: a string of rusting border signs, an electric fence, and the one-million-plus land mines, which are obstacles but not eyesores.

Nature reigns in peace. Stillness dominates. But it is different than the uneasy calm of the silent human sentries on both sides, who are mute but tense, on permanent high alert, and fall victim to an above-average number of ulcers.

In this unsettling middle ground I listened to Noda's messages, both in Japanese. The first one came from the police connection he'd used to alert the Japanese Coast Guard. The joint coast guard–military operation had held a firm line—no crafts, large or small, had crossed over—so Anna's abductors were headed our way.

The second message, left by Jiro Jo, came through in the Korean bodyguard's deep, sonorous rumble:

"Was thinking about my lowlife brother-in-law. He's got the IQ of a bowl of udon, but he's as slippery as seaweed. So I had your boys pass on a message he wouldn't be released until he coughed up two more items.

This morning he gave up this: 'The tunnel the gaijin's looking for is hidden under a known tunnel.'"

"Jo's good," I said. "Except he promised to release Habu."

Noda raised an eyebrow. "You're still underestimating him."

"How so?"

"He said two. Means he figured Habu was holding back one."

Time to bite the bullet.

I sure as hell didn't want to, but I needed to hear the rest of the Homeland secretary's briefing.

I rang the same number as before and the same voice in the White House answered. He informed me that the president was no longer available, but the secretary had left standing instructions to forward my call regardless of the time. Which, of course, was a show not of Carl Jordenson's goodwill but of the president's. Joe Slater had not abandoned me after I hung up on his man.

I met Jordenson halfway. "Let's try this one more time," I said when he answered.

"Excellent idea. I'd like to get right to it if that's okay with you."

"Always has been."

"Yes, well, for details, I'm looping in Hank over at the NSA."

"He have a last name?"

"Not today."

"Not an answer to build trust."

"The agency's comment was that one kidnapping's enough."

"Okay," I said, thinking, it works for me as long as I get the information I need.

I heard some juggling on the line, then Carl said, "Hank, you there?"

"Yes."

Carl performed the preliminary introductions, then handed the briefing over to the partially identified NSA official:

"Well, then we're off. The Tanaka woman has a special talent. Genius-level, and of the kind the NSA usually can't afford. Even if we could, most people of her caliber won't work for us. Ms. Tanaka did because she'd only recently become an American citizen and wanted to assist her adopted country."

"Sounds like the kind of story I'm going to like."

Hank agreed. "Made a lot of people happy over here, believe me. She has an immense gift and she was . . . is . . . quite nice, so she's all-around popular. Her coming over to the NSA and DoD was unselfish and patriotic. Once she passed her security clearance, we put her right to work."

"On what?"

"A lot of different projects. She excelled on all of them and raised the bar of every operation she touched."

Spiker13's rep was ongoing. Mari would be proud.

"And recently?"

"A complex universal back door linking up select servers with high-priority information."

"In normal English, what would that be?"

"She was building hallways between systems so those with top-tier security clearance could more easily navigate our various operations in a secure environment."

"Thank you. What kind of high-priority information?"

"I can't tell you that. But I can tell you about cyberdefense and cyberlooting."

"Okay."

"Everyone's been saying the cybersphere is the new battleground, and it's true. But what they don't tell you is how it manifests. It's all virtual. Meaning you can't see it. Things happen that no one knows about, or we find out after the fact. Sometimes long after the fact. Russia, China, and others are on the attack. North Korea has its moments too. Not the Hollywood nonsense—serious cyberattacks. You know about the DarkSeoul malware, right?"

"Only the name."

"It was a North Korean software termite and did tremendous damage. Shut down South Korean banks and ATMs and caused seven hundred million dollars' worth of damage. DarkSeoul's been used to steal upward of a hundred and fifty thousand South Korean military files, some of them containing information we shared. With what Ms. Tanaka knows, North Korea could do a hundred times more damage—against the United States. Do you see where I'm going with this?"

"Yes. Can you change your security?"

"Oh, we've shuttered our servers. Problem is, she's got a lot of coding in her head. With what she knows, not to mention her talent, she can write programs to penetrate our systems and set implants."

"Implants?"

"Spyware. Malware. In layman's terms, she is capable of making keys to our system. This is as bad as it gets."

"Is it fair to say the North Koreans found a glaring gap in our national security?"

"Let's call it a loophole."

"Something smaller?"

"Yes."

"So while your people were protecting digital assets like hardware and software, they made off with a human asset?"

"That is correct."

"One who can roam anywhere in the system?"

"Yes."

"And the NSA data banks might have information about what?"

"I can't tell you. That's classified."

"About my daughter?"

"Okay, well, yes."

"Could they, say, access all her homework assignments on her computer, all the searches she does online, all her judo tournament results on the website of her judo club, all her phone calls to her friends and to me?"

"They can capture her digital footprints over all lines and services."

"And, naturally, there just might be some more data in those NSA data banks on a few of my daughter's friends?"

"Yes."

"Maybe all of them?"

"Yes."

"And the data could be collated and cross-referenced?"

"If desired, yes."

"Is there anything the NSA might not have intercepted about my daughter?"

"If it's digital or cellular, no."

"Then do you know what my daughter might say about that?"

He hesitated. "I'm not sure I do."

"She'd say a loophole is a small thing, like a loop. But what you have is not a loophole."

"She'd say that?"

"Using nearly those exact words."

"What would she call it, then?"

"She'd say, with a little coaching from me, that North Korea is hours away from getting the keys to America's biggest stash of data ever. Maybe the world's biggest stash. Much bigger than a loophole. Maybe a treasure trove."

"Smart daughter you've got there."

"Yes," I said. "In fact, she is."

CHAPTER 62

THE North Koreans' move was pure genius.

They'd gone in search of the pot of golden data at the end of the rainbow and nabbed it.

With one hand they shoved their growing nuclear prowess in the face of the world's most powerful nations while with the other they reached in where no one expected them. An impressive sleight of hand.

The NSA's explanation clarified everything. All the events slotted into place. The bold abduction at the funeral, the plan to smuggle Anna out of Japan and into North Korea. All of it. What was in Anna's head was priceless. She could provide a back door to the NSA's darkest data banks. Whoever controlled her could reach into the heart and mind of any American they chose. They could blackmail politicians, generals, spies, journalists, CEOs, or any American with his or her hand on a financial, technological, industrial, or military secret.

They could infiltrate the secure facility of their choice. Everyone from our top leaders down to the night security guard could be pressured or threatened. North Korea could sift through all the domestic data netted by NSA's software and make any of us dance.

————————

By the time I finished up with the phone call, KC's men had loaded their gear into two jeeps.

"Where to?" the Marine said.

I spread a map out on the hood of his jeeps. "Give me a minute. I just received an update."

About one and a half kilometers from Dora's, Habu had said in the van. *Don't know what the hell that is and don't care. Makes no sense to me.*

Dora was Dora Observatory. The surveillance post offered an overlook onto a large swatch of North Korea. With the observatory at the center, I marked off a point one and a half kilometers—roughly a mile—in four directions of the compass, then drew a circle to connect the points. Somewhere inside the circle should be the hidden entrance to the as-yet-undiscovered tunnel.

With Jiro Jo's latest message, we had a hidden tunnel under a known tunnel, which narrowed the area we needed to watch. Officially, only a single tunnel fell within the circle: the infamous Tunnel Number Three, meant to have been a precursor to an invasion from the North.

The problem was the qualifier, officially. Publicly, there were four recognized tunnels, but off the record there were said to be more than twenty tunnels in existence. Details were kept from the public. In part, to confuse the North Koreans about what the South knew or didn't know. In part, to avoid disheartening South Koreans. With heightened nuclear and missile testing, they lived with enough cross-border tensions.

I waved Robert Kim over. "Quick question. See this circle?"

He peered at the map. "Yes."

"What other tunnels are inside the circle besides Tunnel Number Three?"

"None. The other three are elsewhere."

His flicker of hesitation had been slight, but enough.

"I'm talking about the undisclosed tunnels."

"I don't know what you mean."

"I've heard there are at least twenty."

Robert's jaw clenched.

Wilson-Yun jacked up the pressure. "Numbers that have come my way run from fifteen to twenty-five."

Robert stiffened. Petrifaction Korean-style was winning out.

KC joined the fray. "Hell, Robert, the news channels were talking about a new tunnel last month."

"Maybe, but I'm not sure I can help."

"Thought that's what you were here for."

"This was not . . . mentioned to me by my superiors." He lifted his head and began looking around for help.

KC punctured Robert's indecision fast. "You were assigned to us. We need to know, soldier. Now."

The military tone did the trick. "Okay, there are other tunnels, but none of them pass through your quadrant there."

I studied the young army enlistee. "You sure?"

"Yes."

KC said, "A wrong answer compromises the mission."

"There are none. I am certain."

"Okay, good then," I said. "We should get in position as soon as we can, so here's what we need," and I told him. KC and Wilson-Yun put in some requests of their own.

When I finished, Robert asked, "Do you want me to make arrangements for lookouts along the roads?"

"That won't be necessary, but thanks."

He looked surprised. "Now I must ask you the same question you asked me, Brodie. Are you sure? There are only a few roads in or out."

"Which is why we don't need any lookouts."

"That seems . . . unusual."

Unusual, I agreed, but practical. I explained my reasoning. We were in the DMZ. The number of entry points could be counted on one hand. No unaccompanied civilians were granted access to the DMZ. Anyone who came through would be instantly visible. We could cover the ground if we split into two groups. Extra lookouts meant extra risk. I didn't want to spook them. What I wanted to do was let them come to us, then swing in behind them and trap them between our position and the minefields at the border. Simple, clean, and limited risk.

"All good points, sir. But wouldn't lookouts be a precaution worth taking?"

"Young soldiers against experienced spies or special ops from the North? I don't think so?"

"Okay, sir. You are in charge."

"Then it's settled. Can I trust you to pass that on?"

"Affirmative, sir." Robert Kim saluted, and marched off.

"They probably won't show before nightfall," KC said. "*I* wouldn't."

"I agree," I said. "But it's safer to set up as early as we can. Nothing about this abduction has followed the usual patterns."

Wilson-Yun scratched the stubble on his cheek. "Going to be a long night, then."

"And tough," KC said.

I nodded and Noda grunted.

KC's comment echoed what we were all thinking. Anything to do with the tunnels spelled trouble. And by far the most ominous of North Korea's underground ventures was Tunnel Number Three.

CHAPTER 63

OLLECTIVELY, the four officially recognized shafts dug under the DMZ from the North are known as "infiltration tunnels." When the first was discovered in 1974, the North and the South were in the midst of on-again, off-again peace talks, which could explain Seoul's mild-mannered approach to the naming of what was meant to be one leg of an invasion strategy.

Four years later, the unearthing of Tunnel Number Three sent chills down the spines of South Korean military and civilian leaders. Why? Because this newest underground passage was a leap forward for the North: it was nothing less than a full-on portal to invasion.

At the time of its discovery, the tunnel was nearly a mile long and had penetrated a quarter of a mile into southern territory. With its installed ventilation system, the subterranean passageway had the capacity to delivery thirty thousand armed troops per hour across the border—to within thirty miles of the capital city of Seoul.

And most frightening of all was this: until the defection of a North Korean army surveyor, the South Koreans had had no clue as to the existence of the incursion.

———

Night had fallen.

Noda, KC, Wilson-Yun, and I were ensconced in a blind with a view—through night-vision binoculars—of the territory around Infiltration Tunnel Three. The remainder of the team was in a secondary blind overlooking the rest of the targeted territory. We were in radio contact. KC's crew had brought their own weapons: M4 carbines and Beretta M9s in belt holsters, as well as extra handguns for Noda and me. Robert provided coffee, water, and double portions of *bibimbap*, the Korean dish of seasoned vegetables and meat over hot rice, which turned out to be everyone's favorite.

"Here's a question for you, Brodie," Wilson-Yun said.

We spoke in whispers. After the sun had set, our voices carried farther. Who knew what kind of ears—human or electronic—might be approaching, or listening in on the other side of the border.

"I'm all ears."

"Any of our targets terrorists or insurgents?"

"More like spies."

"Sounds like an easy takedown."

From behind his field glasses, Noda growled.

Wilson-Yun turned his attention to the chief detective, but Noda uttered no further sound, so the Marine looked at me. "You have a translation for that?"

I said, "My partner's saying spies are anything but easy. Different world, different bag of tricks."

Nodding, Wilson-Yun dropped into a Marine's combat stillness as he considered this new point of view. Eventually he said, "Roger that."

Time passed. Night sounds emerged. Cricket song welled up on all sides. In the nearby forested area, the long, subdued growl of something large and feral rode the low register.

KC spoke softly into his radio. "Game time is approaching, boys. Wits sharp and eyes sharper." He pressed a hand to his ear to better hear the response. "Affirmative," he said. "We got room."

"For what?" I asked.

"Company. The South Koreans are sending over QRF soldiers."

Noda said, "Explain."

KC smothered the microphone in his fist. "Quick-reaction forces. One of the first-line-of-defense specialty units out here. Locked and loaded and ready to fight twenty-four hours a day, three hundred and sixty-five days a year. Each one is trained in antitank weaponry, which could be part of a push by the North. Their canteens are always full. They carry rations. The fighting starts, first responders won't have time to grab provisions, so close are North and South. So goes the theory."

"No tanks tonight," Noda said. "Tell them no."

KC looked my way and I nodded.

He relayed the message, listened, then covered his mike again. "They're saying if our targets run, these guys can hunt them down. They know the terrain like their own backyard."

"'Like their own backyard'? So where's the tunnel entrance?" I said.

"That your official reply?" KC said.

"No. Just tell them we have too many bodies as it is and we're not looking to attract attention."

KC relayed my reply, listened, then said, "Robert wants a word. Channel thirteen."

I adjusted my headset and said, "What's up?"

"QRF are the best, sir."

"I already heard but—"

"Don't need them," said Noda.

"You hear that?"

"I did, sir, but the men are already heading your way. Camp authorities insist."

———

Two QRF soldiers joined us—Daewoo assault rifles at their shoulders, Kevlar vests over their uniforms like us, and fully armed equipment belts at their waists. Pistols, combat knives, grenades. Neither of them spoke English or would admit to speaking English.

But with or without language ability, they were still watchdogs.

I was losing control of the operation.

"Think our targets could be a no-show?" KC asked, peering through night-vision binoculars, then cocking his head and raising them skyward.

"Could, but unlikely," I said, scanning the terrain with a pair of my own glasses.

KC spoke into the radio. "Got two large birds circling overhead. Anything we need to worry about?"

I raised my binoculars. Silhouettes with six-foot wingspans cruised the wind currents a hundred feet forward and eighty feet above our position.

"Black vultures," Robert replied. "They found something dead."

"Hopefully not human," I said.

"Out here you never know," Robert said.

"We'll check the site if they land." KC signed off and glanced my way. "Tell me how sure you are about this location again."

"I'm sure."

"Your source?"

We still held Habu and his men in a hidden location out in the Japanese countryside. Our men continued to press the gang leader on several fronts but he hadn't changed his answers, and nothing new had emerged since Jiro Jo forced the disclosure of the tunnel-under-tunnel gambit.

"Solid. We got the right intel."

KC lowered his binocs. "Not looking good."

"Then we keep looking," I said.

CHAPTER 64

TWO a.m. came and went. Then three. The moon dropped behind a mountain range and the night grew darker still.

Sunrise was at 5:19.

The sky would start to lighten around 4:20.

KC put his hand to his ear. "Roger that. Hold." He lifted his glasses and scanned the area to our left. "Nothing yet." Then to me: "They have something."

I switched the dial on my headset back to our secondary unit but the channel was silent.

"Who you talking to?" I asked.

"Not sure. Robert patched me through."

I glanced at our uninvited guests. The QRF soldiers were clearly tuned in. Which meant channel thirteen.

I flipped over. "Robert, you there?"

"Yes, sir."

"The second unit has a sighting?"

If so, Anna's captors were taking the long way around.

He hesitated. "Not exactly, sir."

"Who has eyes-on, then?"

Robert's voice flattened. "The QRF soldiers on the road."

"What soldiers on the road? Did you relay our earlier discussion about avoiding lookouts?"

"Word for word, sir. They said they would take it under consideration, sir."

"And you didn't think it useful to tell me that?"

"I was under orders not to, sir."

I exhaled loudly. Of course you were. Was this the South Korean army acting on its own, or were they being prodded by the American forces commander here, himself guided by the hand of someone above him? There was no way to tell, and this was the wrong time to sort it out.

KC said in an undertone. "Eight o'clock."

Our left flank, behind us. I looked. There were tiny figures in the far distance. I raised my field glasses—and saw a miracle.

From the shadowy green haze, three figures emerged and were coming our way.

————

In the faintest whisper, KC said in my ear. "Targeting Alpha One." Meaning the farthest-forward male.

"Got Alpha Two," Wilson-Yun said.

A light sheen of sweat prickled KC's forehead. We waited until the trio drew closer—two men in South Korean uniforms and Anna, head draped in a scarf to ward off the night chill. Alpha Two held her upper arm in a tight grip and urged her forward. The leader stopped to consult a scrap of paper in his hand and pointed left.

"Thirty yards," KC said, his voice no more than a soft exhale.

The group moved cautiously forward, heading toward terrain directly over Tunnel Three.

"Twenty yards."

One of the soldiers behind me shouted loudly in Korean, an incomprehensible command blasting in my ear. As I stood by, stunned, Alpha One pivoted, bringing up a firearm.

KC shot him.

Anna's minder dropped flat to the ground and raised a weapon. Wilson-Yun took him out with a headshot. The QRF soldiers hit him with multiple bursts.

Head lowered and staring at the body at her feet, Anna stood frozen in place, arms glued to her sides, quivering and muttering, "No, no, no. Don't shoot. No, no, no."

The six of us emerged from our hide and spread out. We advanced slowly, a step at a time, weapons raised.

Noda and I pointed our Berettas, which would be effective in another few yards. KC, Wilson-Yun, and the QRF boys targeted Anna with their weapons.

KC spoke loudly. "Ma'am, raise your hands. We need to see your hands."

KC and Wilson-Yun's carbines pivoted back and forth between Anna and their downed victims. The QRF troops focused exclusively on Anna.

"Do not shoot her," I said in clear, well-enunciated English. "Do you understand?"

Neither of the QRF soldiers responded.

"Do—you—understand?"

"We hear you, sir," the closest said.

So they did speak English.

"Ma'am," KC said, "we're not going to hurt you, but we need to see your hands."

One of the QRF soldiers repeated the phrase in Korean and I did the same in Japanese, using Anna's name and telling her she was safe.

She nodded, seeming to understand, but stood frozen in place. Emotionally paralyzed.

The QRF guns rose incrementally higher as we advanced.

"Do not shoot her," I said again.

Noda snapped at them in Japanese, and they reacted at his intensity if not his words. The scar slashing across his eyebrow burned a bright red.

When we'd come within ten feet, Alpha One stirred. He yelled something into a radio in his left hand, the gun in his other hand jumping. Two swift trigger pulls took down Wilson-Yun and a QRF soldier with leg shots. Both men crumpled as KC's M4 flashed, sending three rounds into the prone North Korean. His body jerked spasmodically, then lay still.

Anna squealed in fright. Her hands came up. Her head came around. Where I expected to see a frightened face or maybe a timid smile of gratitude I saw a twisted snarl.

She was a he.

With a gun rising fast.

I shot her. Him.

Damn, damn, damn.

Decoys.

Or a test run.

CHAPTER 65

"TELL me!" I yelled into my headset.

"Sir?" Robert said for the third time.

"You heard me. The soldiers on the road—did they see anyone else?"

"No."

"Did the three men here do anything else?"

"They were in radio contact with someone."

I covered my microphone and said to KC, who was searching the bodies, "What's the range of their radios?"

"These pieces of crap? In this terrain, maybe half a mile. A mile, tops."

"Any other communication gear?"

"No. Cell phone transmissions would have been picked up."

So Anna's minders had been close, waiting for the go-ahead. If we'd been able to sneak up on the advance party, as was the plan, we might have scooped them up before they called the others. Once we'd unmasked the fake Anna, we might have been able to lure Anna and her real minders out here.

Too late for that.

I had to get to China. Fast.

Wilson-Yun and the injured QRF soldier were rushed to the base hospital, while KC, Noda, and I headed back to the Joint Security Area. The remaining QRF soldier and Marines stayed behind with the bodies, and others soon joined them.

I was furious, my mind reeling at the possibilities. I leapt from the jeep.

Robert hustled up, saluted, and said, "Sirs, you are wanted for immediate debriefing." Robert pointed to a nondescript white building, where no doubt top brass would be waiting.

"Get the hell away from me," I said.

"Sir, I must insist."

KC's hand went to his carbine. "Stand down, soldier."

Robert backed off and waited.

I stalked off to the far corner of the lot, out of earshot, and called a friend in Tokyo. Time was short and Anna's captors were on the move again. Let the base authorities listen in if they could.

When he picked up, I said, "I wake you or are you out on a shoot?"

"Hey, JB. On-site now. What's up?"

"I remember hearing you snagged a big Korean account. That true?"

I was on the phone to Ben Simmons, a longtime American expat photographer based in Tokyo who specialized in Japan and Asia. On a workday, Simmons rose before first light, because light is what he chased.

"Shoot twice a month. Setting up as we speak. Why?"

"You're in-country now?"

"Do Koreans barbecue?"

"Seoul?"

"Yep. Center of the world, south of the DMZ. Where are you?"

"The DMZ."

Simmons paused. "Gotcha."

He'd suddenly grown less talkative. He understood there might be ears.

I made my pitch, keeping it vague. I told him about chasing kidnappers across international lines. I told him Noda and I needed his connections to get to North Korea's other border—the one it shared with China—before the abductors and their victim.

Simmons clucked his tongue. "Bad stuff all around. How urgent is this? I've got a couple pots set to boil over."

"Very."

"Scale of one to ten?"

"Higher."

"And you can't tell me any more?"

"Hands are tied."

I didn't see so much as hear the wry smile on the other end. "There's a rumor circulating over the expat grapevine in Tokyo that you were at the Kabuki gig in DC. None of the Japanese news mentioned you, though."

"Why would they?"

"You're a minor celeb in Japan since the Japantown murders, not to mention the Steam Walker incident a few months ago."

"I try to keep a low profile."

"Uh-huh. Same grapevine says the second victim after the Tanaka woman was a friend of yours from San Francisco. I don't pay much attention to rumors, but since you're based in the City by the Bay I figure that particular tale might have some meat on its bones. Does it?"

"Yeah."

"Good friend?"

"The best."

Ben Simmons was a six-foot-four Georgian out of Columbus, with cool-hazel eyes, a slow Southern grin, and a sharp visual sense. Apparently he had a talent for reading between headlines as well.

"So why aren't you on your friend's case instead of tooling around K-country?"

On my end of the line I remained quiet.

Simmons cleared his throat. "I see. I'm setting up right now for an early morning shoot at the Statue of Brothers. You know it? At the War Memorial? In the old half of the city, north of the river?"

"I do," I said.

I'd been there. There are larger statues at the memorial but none as poignant as the Statue of Brothers. On top of a sixty-foot-wide half dome, two brothers meet on the battlefield and embrace. The larger one is armed and wears the uniform of the South, while the smaller one, unarmed and emaciated from the scarcity of food, wears that of the North. The statue is at once a symbol of the suffering of the Korean people and the unbearable separation of families when the country was split, as well as a beacon of hope for peace and reunification.

"Can you get here?"

"Can you talk and shoot at the same time?"

"I can talk, shoot, juggle, drink, and still catch the image I need. Most times."

"Fair enough."

"I'm going to ring someone who can make things happen."

"Stay away from anyone connected to spooks, special-ops guys, or government agencies, American or Korean, okay?"

"He's on the edge of some of those circles but he's discreet. Has to be."

"Just tell me he's not one of them."

"He's from a different mold. Let's leave it at that."

From a different mold. What the hell did that mean?

"Do you trust him?"

"With my life. And where you're going, you'll be doing the same, like it or not."

CHAPTER 66

DAY 8, SUNDAY, 5 A.M.
THE JOINT SECURITY AREA, DMZ

THE Korean authorities tried to detain Noda and me for debriefing, but I pulled rank and KC backed me up. We resisted on two fronts: first, my assignment was ongoing and I couldn't afford the time; and second, KC's testimony plus that of the remaining men involved in the shooting should be more than sufficient. KC would conduct me to my next meet, then return for his men and an interview.

Noda and I headed down Highway 77 to Seoul in a covered jeep with KC at the wheel. His presence was insurance against a follow-up attempt to detain us.

"Good to leave the barbarians behind," Noda said in Japanese three miles into the ride, a reference to everything to do with the North.

"Agreed," I said.

An endless stretch of fencing shadowed the highway. On the other side of the wire barrier was a vast expanse of military-controlled no-man's-land and, beyond that, North Korea. The fence was topped with a V-shaped wedge of barbed wire. Watchtowers flew by every three or four hundred yards. They were either manned or equipped with cameras and sensors and other state-of-the-art surveillance equipment.

"What he say?" KC asked. I repeated Noda's sentiment in English and the Marine waved the comment aside. "He's got it wrong."

"How so?" I asked.

"You don't see it but the Norker shadow is everywhere. Especially in

Seoul. Norkers make the Grim Reaper look like the Tooth Fairy. That's the genius of their dictatorship."

Norker was local shorthand for North Korean or a person from the North. It was a neutral, nonbiased term.

"You're talking about the saber rattling?"

"No, much more than that. They never let the South forget them. There's the nuclear tests and missile launches and the artillery north of the border buried in the hills. The Southers are good people. They're nice. They work hard. But thirty miles away is a rogue regime with massive guns trained on them. The Norker artillery could turn Seoul into a pile of rubble to rival a Middle Eastern city under siege. Try living with that day and night."

KC was talking about the psychological impact of the hostile North. The pressure had to be immense for the faint of heart.

He went on. "The rants and raves of the Supreme Leader keep the international community on edge. Think what that does to the people living in his shadow. Tonight we saw Norkers up close and personal. They were under orders not to be taken alive and threw their lives away for their country without hesitation. That's the State's hard-core ultra-patriotism. Many of the low-level Norkers don't follow that line in private, but in public, and among the elite, it's alive and well. Imagine dealing with that level of crazy every single day of the year."

I couldn't, but I might soon be forced to do just that.

We rolled into the center of town, then over the Wonhyu Bridge. High-rise apartment towers gathered like mushroom clusters along the Han River. The waterway was wide and swift and, today, unrelentingly gray. Up ahead, the hills of the old quarter sprouted with a blend of modern houses and *hanok*, the traditional homes.

A few minutes later KC pulled up to the curb in front of the War Memorial Museum, behind a wide-bodied taxi with its warning lights flashing.

Simmons was framing shots in front of the Statue of Brothers, which glowed ruby red in the warm morning light. At the sound of our approach, his head swiveled in our direction. The lensman jabbed a long finger at the cab with the emergency lights, then snatched up a daypack with a tripod anchored to the back and sprinted in our direction.

Noda and I made our good-byes to KC and followed Simmons into the backseat of the waiting vehicle.

"Got great light and wrapped up early," the cameraman said, as our driver eased into traffic.

"Good. So we can talk."

"No, need to dash across the river." He flipped through the thumbnails of the shoot, then dug around in one of the pockets of his khaki photographer's vest. "Where we're going next they have sculpture attached to the buildings, JB. Cool stuff."

"Sounds like it."

Simmons came up with a new memory card and swapped out the full one in his camera. "My guy's eager to meet you, because, and I quote, 'Your friend he hotter than sun. Maybe I can no say yes to him.' The guy's English is creative, but he doesn't miss much."

Noda and I exchanged an alarmed glance.

Word of our visit to the DMZ had already spread. How far had it traveled and whose ears had it reached?

CHAPTER 67

SIMMONS wasn't exaggerating.

We pulled up to the Hyundai I-Park Tower, a large fifteen-story black-glassed edifice with a mammoth silver ring on the façade. Inside the ring were bright red rectangles and threads plus a trio of silver bars. The effect was a pleasing abstract sculpture suggestive of a giant clockwork or something more symbolic that might have been conceived by Paul Klee if he were alive today.

"Cool, right?" my photographer friend said, glancing first at the building then across the street.

"Very," I said.

Simmons pointed to the other side of the road. "I can start from there." Then he was off with long-legged strides, heading for the corner.

"This place and Bear Hall around the corner blew me away," he called back over his shoulder. "When I mentioned them to the editor, he proposed I shoot them as a follow-up to a piece on the city's sculpture he assigned last month."

"I can see why."

Architecture fascinated Simmons, and his photography of the fluid, ever-changing Tokyo cityscape was stunning, one-of-a-kind images you could hang on your wall. He haunted the streets of the Japanese capital, always looking for a new angle, the decisive moment, *the* shot. "You want a fresh take on Tokyo, you go to Domon Ben," a gallery owner once told me, a play on the name of the iconic Japanese lensman Domon Ken. Of late, Simmons had been shooting Kyoto and Zen gardens, serene counterparts to his forays into architecture and city life. His years of work in Japan had spawned a number of books.

Once across the street, Simmons set down his daypack and began taking pictures. "The light's just right. I'll catch the glass of the building as a black sheet and the ring sculpture in hyper-focus. If I get the light I need, the red will give off a kind of Zen-like quality."

He was composing sans tripod, both hands gripping the camera. Behind us were a public square and the main entrance to the COEX Mall, a sprawling underground complex with shops, theaters, an aquarium, and more. A deep-throated bell from a nearby Buddhist temple made the air quiver.

"There's a copy of the *Korea Herald* in my pack," Simmons said, his eye glued to the viewfinder. "Amuse yourself. I'm going to be a few minutes. Plenty of places behind us to sit."

Right. I squatted down in front of the daypack, slipped an envelope from my pocket between the pages of the *Herald*, then freed the newspaper from its roost. Tucking the publication under my arm, I turned to scan the stone-tiled plaza behind us.

There were benches in the sun and under some shade trees. There were pedestrians rushing through the quad on their way to work. There were people lounging about on the benches.

On the far end of a long winding cement bench, a young couple was lost in each other's eyes. On the opposite end twenty feet away, a withered old man with a bad haircut sat reading a Korean news rag. Under one of the trees, two kids in school uniforms tussled with a Game Boy. One tree over, a suited businessman with sharp eyes drank coffee out of a tall paper cup while reading a glossy financial magazine. He glanced twice at Simmons as the American photographer bobbed and weaved on the sidewalk, camera in hand.

The bad haircut. I strolled over to the cement bench, took a seat a couple feet from the poorly groomed old guy, and opened the *Herald*. Even bathed in the morning light, the cement bench was cold.

"You smart man," Haircut said without lowering his paper. "Pick me first time try. How?"

"The hair. Unfashionable in Seoul but blends right in parts of China."

He nodded. "Okay. Thas good. My name Pak Ji-hyung. You call me Pak."

"Brodie," I said without looking his way.

We continued reading. My eyes roamed over an op-ed piece about the dire need to preserve the winding alleyways of the traditional neighborhoods and the classic Korean homes that roosted there. After a while Pak set his paper on the bench and began rummaging through a white vinyl bag at his side. He came up with a large, round golden-skinned Asian pear. It resembled an apple. Next he produced a small paring knife. He began rotating the fruit. In no time he had removed the skin in one curling snakelike strip.

I turned the page of the newspaper and found an article about the suicide of a top executive at one of the Big Five Korean companies in the wake of an embezzlement inquiry.

Glancing my way, Pak appeared genuinely startled to be sitting near a foreigner.

"Where you are from?" he asked in a louder voice than before.

"San Francisco."

"America. Thas nice place. You want fruit?" he said, offering a wedge he'd sliced from the peeled pear.

"That's very kind of you, thanks." I scooted closer and set my paper down on the bench between us. I plucked the segment of fruit from between the knife blade and his thumb. I took a bite. "Delicious," I said.

To any observer it would look like the man was striking up a conversation with a random foreigner and offering a slice of a local favorite as an icebreaker.

"You know what is Korean *bae*?"

"No," I said, but I did.

The fruit was called *nashi* in Japan and went by that name in specialty shops in the States. It was fragrant, crunchy, succulent, and, at its best, nectarlike in its sweetness.

"Best bae in world is a here in South Korea."

"Good to know," I said, waving the last mouthful at him in a gesture of thanks before popping it into my mouth.

"Ben tell about me?" he asked, lowering his voice.

"No."

"Thas good."

Pak liked his secrecy. A promising sign.

"Agreed," I said.

Up close, his age unwound before my eyes. The "withered old man" appeared closer to forty. An abundance of wrinkles flocked around the corners of his eyes and mouth. He had the pale papery yellow complexion of someone who led a nocturnal existence or spent large stretches of time indoors.

"Ben say you are for good friend."

"True."

"Thas very good to me."

I met his gaze. "People you can trust are hard to come by."

His murky chestnut-brown eyes roamed over me in a thoughtful manner. "We Koreans afraid just three things in this life. North Korea, bad friends, bad drivers. Seoul street crossing more dangerous than border crossing."

A signal.

"Some risks are acceptable for the right reason," I said.

He offered me another piece of fruit, and I accepted.

"You two people?" he asked.

"Yes, we need to get to the Chinese–North Korean border before nightfall. To find a woman."

"Where friend?"

"At our hotel, sleeping."

"No having visa?"

"No."

We'd braced Habu, the yakuza boss, less than thirty-six hours ago and had been on the go ever since. There'd been no time for niceties like official paperwork then, and there wasn't now. Japanese nationals could get visas on landing in China. Americans had to apply in advance. Approval could take two weeks or two months.

"I fix two hours. I need passports."

"In the newspaper," I said without looking down at it.

"Need woman picture."

"Also in the paper."

He considered me with an appraising gaze, his eyes digging deep into mine. They were the muddy brown of troubled water, and yet his look was honest and open.

Eventually he said, "You smart smart, maybe danger to some."

"Not to Simmons, not to you."

He ate another wedge of the pear. "Share friend, share trust. Thas good. Where you stay?" I told him and he said, "You buy three ticket to Jilin. Thas closest Changbai. Twelve o'clock, one o'clock, we fly, you know?"

"The sooner the better."

"I meet you three hour."

"Okay. Where? The hotel?"

He shook his head. "Hotel no good. Too much seeing place. Starbuck next next next your hotel."

"Three doors down?"

He said yes, then repeated the phrase a couple of times until he'd memorized it. "South Korea small small country but many Starbuck. More Starbuck than Milky Highway star."

He pointed at the sky. There was nothing to be seen overhead but a cloudless blue sky, so I didn't look. He stared at me, thinking.

"You watch danger point, which is me. Smart smart. Maybe I like you if you no danger point to me. You go now. No forget Starbuck."

"Starbucks it is," I said.

"Also, you no speak about me, Jilin, nothing to no any person. New danger point start now."

CHAPTER 68

STOOD, stretched, and meandered back toward Simmons, who stopped working as soon as I approached.

"About time," he said. "Need to get to the last location. Mind grabbing the tripod?"

"Not at all."

Simmons let his camera fall and it bounced lightly against his chest, held in place by a strap around his neck. He closed his daypack, snapped a couple of vest pockets shut, then flagged down a taxi.

"It's only four blocks, but the good light's disappearing fast. Sorry for the rush."

"No problem. Impressive guy, your friend."

"He take you on?"

"Yeah."

"Must have liked what he saw."

"He dangerous?"

Simmons gave me a wry look. "He's a survivor. Like you."

Which I took as a yes. Out of the corner of my eye, I saw Pak casually sweep up my newspaper with his and push both into his vinyl bag.

"Tell me about him. There's got to be a good story there."

"There is, but I need to get to the next shoot first."

"How about a hint?"

"You ever see *Seoul Train*? And I'm not talking about the music show."

"The film about activists bringing North Korean defectors out through the underground railroad? Yeah, sure."

It was a spellbinding and sometimes heartbreaking documentary about escapees from the North, relentless Chinese authorities, and the volunteers who dressed, fed, and coached the fleeing refugees so they would have a chance at passing through the maze of obstacles in China to safety in the South. Escaping the North was only the first step in a harrowing journey.

"That's the one. Pak is one of those guys. He's not shown in the movie. Might not even be with the same organization, but does the same work."

While Simmons checked the thumbnails on his camera, I thought about Pak's haircut. He lived and breathed the part. But more important was what he could do: if he could spirit people out of North Korea and China, he would know how they might be snuck in.

———

Simmons photographed the Bear Hall in record time.

"Shooting two more serious sites this afternoon," he said. "This is the whimsical one of the lot."

A family of four fashioned from what might have been giant nuts and bolts sat on a shelf two stories up. All of them dangled their feet in the air. One of the children was perched on the shoulders of a parent. Sitting on the roof six stories above us was a single parent with child, legs dangling, arms raised in exuberance or greeting.

"Maybe not an earth-shattering work but, like I said, the sculpture's on the building." Simmons fired away.

He was right. There was nothing profound about the Bear Hall ornamentation. Nothing as monumental as the I-Park Tower abstract. And yet, the playful sculptures would jar passersby, if only for a moment.

And maybe that was the point.

The seated figures were simple and approachable and immediately understood. Earth-shattering no, but in their unexpected locations they could startle a viewer into a new awareness so that he or she might give the next work of art encountered the extra moment of consideration it deserved. I was all for that.

Simmons finished up swiftly, then looked at his watch. "You all set?"

"Yeah."

"You need anything more from me?"

"No. Looks like we're in good hands."

"Pak knows everything there is to know. Just don't cross him."

"Wouldn't think of it."

"Then you'll be fine. He's one of the best. He's a defector himself, you know. Crossed over with his parents when he was only twelve. Their Chinese broker double-dipped. He took their money, then once they were in China he turned in the father for a reward and sold Pak's mother to a farmer's collective in the east, as a wife or something worse." He shuddered. "Hard to get my head around that. What kind of person makes a living selling other people? The broker planned to sell Pak as slave labor to some factory owner, but Pak escaped, hid out, and learned Chinese while he worked his way around the country and searched for his mother. He never found her. Nine years later he made it to the south, joined up with a refugee rescue group, and has been with them ever since. He's one of the leaders now."

"What happened to the father?"

"Executed by the North for trying to escape."

I shook my head. "Man, that's tough. But Pak seems to have come through it okay. And he looks to know his stuff. I owe you."

Simmons signaled for a taxi. "A couple of rounds of saké back in Tokyo ought to cover it."

"Done deal."

A glimmer of concern flickered across his features. "You be careful over there."

"Always am."

"World's different in northern China. Changbai is what they call an autonomous Korean county. It's part of China but surrounded by North Korea on three sides. It's tightly controlled. Some damn good folks up-country but also a lot of smuggling, so a lot of police and a lot of scum. Gangs, smugglers, traffickers. Some of them will kill you for your smartphone. Is Anna Tanaka pretty?"

"Yes."

"Then she's in play. Her minders drop their guard, they'll lose her to traffickers. So if you do find her, watch her back. And watch *your* back."

"Got it."

"No, I mean watch your own back too. You're also trophy meat up there. Americans are a big prize. If North Korean agents sandbag you, or even the wrong kind of Chinese trafficker, you'll wake up in the Hermit Kingdom. They'll put you on display as a morality lesson, carve you up some, then execute you in a public square. You'll disappear off the face of the earth."

"That kind of stuff actually happens?"

"Yeah. I'm your wake-up call. Make sure you get your carcass back to Japan in one piece so you can buy me that saké you promised."

CHAPTER 69

10 P.M.
CHANGBAI, CHINA, ON THE NORTH KOREAN BORDER

WHEN moonlight caught the ripples on the Yalu River, it looked like the flash of silk—a soft glowing wink, there one moment, gone the next.

We peered into the night, with and without night-vision goggles. On the North Korean side of the water, the town of Hyesan was steeped in darkness. And yet, in the darkness, there was life.

"In front your eyes three black shadow, you see?" Pak said.

The river separated China from North Korea. In Hyesan, under the cover of night, people darted through the streets. Along the river were the silhouettes of watchtowers. They had broad tented roofs and long rectangular bases. They had no lights, which would blind their occupants. Occasionally there was movement inside. Soldiers on watch. Pak was referring to three forms at the edge of the river, on the North Korean side.

"Yes."

"Two women carry rubber boat to come China side. Trading for black market. All women, you know?"

"I've heard the stories."

We lay in a doorway a half a block beyond the Dandong Noodle Shop, waiting for plan C to unfold. Once again darkness had fallen. Once again Noda and I had night-vision binoculars strung around our necks. Once again we were in a blind. Only this time it was the deep doorway of a neighborhood grocery closed for the evening with a view of the noodle shop, the name of which Habu had reluctantly disgorged at knifepoint back in Tokyo.

We were hidden behind the shop gate, peering through a six-inch gap at the bottom. We'd been there since nightfall, after walking right off the plane in Jilin with forged visas that passed the squinty-eyed scrutiny at Chinese passport control, then taking a Chinese wreck of a car Pak had waiting and arriving around four in the afternoon.

I pointed to another pair huddled in conference a hundred yards downriver on the Chinese side. "What about them?"

"Korea woman and China man, also trading."

"So the reports are true, then?"

"Yes, yes, all women all trading all true."

His voice was a whisper brushing my ear.

"Survival economics," I said.

"Yes, yes. Otherwise just starving their bellies."

Which is exactly how the horror stories began. The great socialist experiment of the North faltered when the Soviet Union collapsed and was no longer able to subsidize its communist offspring. North Korea didn't grow enough crops on its own. Government food rations dried up. The elite closed ranks. Everyone else scavenged for scraps. Dogs, cats, squirrels, frogs, and anything else on four feet were devoured.

Next, grasshoppers, moths, ants, and cockroaches disappeared. The hunger persisted. Tens of thousands starved to death. In increments. Slowly, painfully, irreversibly. Some collapsed in shame in their homes, often leaving death notes and farewells addressed to relatives in other towns. Others collapsed on the streets while begging or hunting for any scrap of nourishment. People clawed the bark off trees. Shrubs and weeds were harvested, chopped, and boiled. For their juices and nourishment, roots and leaves were chewed to a pulp.

Tens of thousands more died.

Survivors sifted the dirt for worms and decaying vegetation. In the end upward of three million people died, according to high-end estimates. Low-end calculations put the total at a third of that number or less, none of which were a consolation to anyone.

While husbands held down their mandatory government day jobs with their increasingly shrinking inflation-depleted salaries, the wives began to barter among themselves: trinkets and furniture and any spare scrap of nourishment they could find—anything that brought in a few extra pennies. Some clawed their way out. Many others did not.

Enterprising survivors slowly grew their businesses. They bought goods from the haves. A few pears, a couple of eggs, a half pound of meat. And piled up a few more pennies as their stomachs growled. They got by on one meal a day. When they had a stake, they began to buy goods from repatriated Koreans with relatives on the Chinese side of the border, then cut out the middlemen and ventured across the water themselves, doling out scraps of food, then monetary bribes to the guards, whose own families also needed to eat.

So was born North Korea's black-market economy, which popped up everywhere and disappeared in an instant at the first sign of authority. Additional bribes found their way into the pockets of local officials—and the markets stayed open longer and sold more. As the food supply stabilized, minor necessities were next. An extra pair of socks, a winter jacket, good shoes. Then luxuries like CDs and DVDs surfaced. The unsanctioned markets evolved into a conspiracy of survival.

Which is how the ruling elite found themselves trapped in a catch-22, North Korean style. The burgeoning black markets represented the most basic form of capitalism. They went against everything the Supreme Leader preached and everything the State's system stood for, but the government could not stamp out this wave of private entrepreneurs without sending the whole country back into another downward spiral of extreme poverty and famine, which could in turn lead to the collapse of the regime.

So top officials turned a blind eye—after accepting bribes of their own. As they saw the small traders grow more prosperous, they dipped into the practice themselves and expanded it.

"What about the Chinese guards on this side?"

Pak rubbed his thumb across the index and middle fingers of the same hand. "Money speak."

"We're looking at a well-oiled machine, then?"

"No, no. Many problem. Some China men steal Korea trading women when they cross river. Thas very bad. I see China men take woman, I kill."

Their Chinese broker double-dipped. He took their money, then once they were in China he turned in the father for a reward and sold Pak's mother to a farmer's collective in the east, as a wife or something worse . . . He never found her.

I said, "Anyone who traffics in women deserves what they get."

The selling of North Korean women was an open secret in China. Escapees arrived with little money, no language ability, and no path outward from the sprawling country into which they had fled. Unless they met an honest broker, they were easy prey. In China, Koreans were fourth-class citizens at best, and Korean women lower still.

Pak's face was red. "Stealing Korea woman big shocking for Korea people. Why so many China men stealing North Korea woman, you know? Why China government know what trafficker man's doing but they no stop?"

Pak was venting. He knew as well as I did what the reason was. China's one-child policy had changed behavior. Couples wanted male heirs to support them in their old age and continue the line in order to take care of the ancestors. So female babies were "erased." As a result, during its nearly four-decade run, the now-defunct policy had created a surplus of thirty million bachelors, leading to a huge black market for marriageable women. Mail-order brides from poorer countries filled only a fraction of the need. Eligible Asian women of any nationality were in demand by these "broken branches" that made up the "biological dead ends" of family trees.

"Trafficker men sell Korea women to farmer or they do rape and sell for sex shop. When I see those men I can no speak any my words."

"I'm sure," I said.

Pak's whisper turned heated. "They dirty China animal. I find, I kill, you know? I kill every time. I kill all them."

"Can't say I blame you," I said.

We spoke in hushed voices as we watched customers enter and leave the Dandong Noodle Shop. A red-and-yellow neon sign announced the store's presence. Black pillars on either side of the door made the place look bigger than it was. Red dragons flew up the pillars, their tails undulating behind them, their toothy maws open and threatening to swallow the stars.

Dandong was a thriving Chinese port city six hundred miles away. It too was a border town, squatting proudly at the mouth of the Yalu River where the waterway flowed into the Yellow Sea. Dandong's namesake a half block down the road was a twenty-four-hour operation and the only one in Changbai serving Dandong-style chow, according to Pak.

So we had the right place. The question was, would the kidnappers come?

Anna's abduction had been sanctioned by North Korea, but her crossing into the North would be clandestine, since official entry points were monitored, and the North knew it.

The rest of the world could not know Anna had made the crossing.

Her passage must be secret and undocumented.

So this was the spot, the Dandong Noodle Shop the portal.

So we watched and waited.

CHAPTER 70

"Y OU can tell?"

Pak nodded in answer to my question. He'd just claimed body language would give the North Korean contact away in an instant. Whoever brought Anna to Changbai would need a contact to usher her over the border unharmed.

"A man or a woman?" I asked.

"Always man."

"How will you know him?" I asked.

"You know what is North Korea Central Party cadre?"

"Yes."

"They travel foreign land for government business. They do special performing like tonight. They carry big head and big greed for power. You know?"

"I've got a pretty good idea."

"Thas how you find them. Look for double stink."

———

Next, Pak cautioned us about the secret police, the militia, and the regular duty cops. Tonight, he told us, hazards were many.

"All police hunting trafficker and gang and Korea defector. Secret police coming later in night. They biggest danger. Most power."

Our guide warned us for the fifth time to keep our voices low and conversation to a minimum after nine o'clock.

Then he explained why.

While the militia and regular cops simply patrolled the streets and would sweep up any suspicious character unless they'd received a bribe in advance, the secret police were harder to bribe, wanted bigger game, and possessed a heady bag of tricks. They wore civilian clothing and could appear at any time, from any direction. Even from the narrow passage two feet away, between our building and the next.

"They surprise our eye," Pak said in his stealth whisper. "We are in safety from their eye but not from their ear, so careful careful with your word. Keeping word soft."

Appearing unannounced was a popular technique. They might pop out from a hiding place or they could stumble forth from one of the bars, acting like drunken customers. Some patrolled the water's edge at night. They didn't like to soil their footwear, and only ranged near the riverbank when ordered by a superior or during a special crackdown.

Also on the prowl were smugglers who traded with the North Korean women, brokers who smuggled defectors out of the country, and traffickers who sold women and children. All of the nocturnal racketeers received protection by coughing up a steady stream of bribes. The police would corner the rest. We resided at the bottom of the food chain: any of the night creatures—police or criminal—would come after us.

"Criminal maybe sell us or give us like gift to secret police, so quiet quiet."

We'd stepped into a nightmare.

————

As it turned out, the stretch of the street we'd burrowed into held a modest standing as a nightspot.

Which meant, Pak said, we should expect more security than usual.

Aside from the all-night noodle shop, there were high-end eateries for the dine-and-date set, flashy discos for the energetic, and a handful of bars up and down the spectrum. We'd taken our position in the closed courtyard of the grocery at seven. The night owls began to surface around nine, and by eleven thirty activity swung into overdrive.

Canteens and watering holes flung open their windows. Celebratory noises poured into the night. Two of the bars owned karaoke setups and competed for customers' attention by rupturing the peace with Chinese ballads and pop numbers. There were homes nearby but no one complained. The police on patrol had received ample inducement to "close their ear," Pak explained.

We dug in for the long haul. Surprisingly, the occasional K-pop tune surfaced in the song rotation. Or maybe not so surprisingly. K-pop—all out of South Korea, of course—had taken the infectious three-minute pop melody to new heights of irresistibility, claiming legions of fans around the world. Most converts had no inkling of what the hook-laden lyrics actually meant. But it didn't matter. The music spoke for itself.

As the district came to life, cricket song along the banks of the Yalu River succumbed to the raucous vocal noodlings of amateur karaoke singers. The hours passed, then the trend reversed itself. Revelry dwindled. Crickets sent out tentative chirps. Customers staggered from bars and discos and eateries, climbed aboard rickety bicycles, and wobbled away. Owners of cars parked along the riverside trundled out, flopped down behind the wheel, and wove drunkenly into the night.

We prepared ourselves. We'd dozed on and off, watching in shifts, but from here on in the three of us would be on full alert. It hadn't taken us but a moment to determine that Anna's abductors would not show themselves until the precinct settled down.

Which is exactly how it played out.

CHAPTER 71

THEY surfaced in the darkest hour.

But before they appeared, another barometer confirmed their imminent arrival.

"Coming soon," Pak said.

"How do you know?"

Our guide pointed across the river, into the darkness. "I seeing moving there."

I squinted into the blackness. "What do you see? And how can you see without your binoculars?"

"You must finding shiny bouncy spot. Dark like night but shiny soft. Like a there. You see?"

He pointed to something on the North Korean side, about a hundred yards off. Four dark-green spots bobbed and flickered and trailed along the edge of the river about five feet off the ground with muted effervescence. They might have been fireflies with hangovers, if such a thing were biologically possible. Their movement was erratic. They stopped and started, drew closer then separated.

"What are they?"

"KPA guard."

Soldiers from the Korean People's Army who guarded the border. I trained night-vision binoculars taken from the trunk of Pak's car on the group. Two more soldiers came up over a rise and the four became six.

"They have side pieces in covered holsters but no rifles," I said.

"Rifle metal making big flash."

I continued to stare through the glasses at the cluster of guards patrolling the riverbank, wondering what had caused the firefly effect. I finally caught a gentle wink in the green field before me.

"Got it," I said. "The top button of their coats catches the light." *A gleam so mild you wouldn't pick it up unless you knew to look for it.*

Pak nodded. "They are coming together for waiting."

"For Anna?"

"For crossing."

————

"Thas the one," Pak said. "You see big Party head walking?"

"Yes."

"His greedy power wanting?"

"Yes, that too."

And I did. It was all there in his body language. A supremely confident stride he made no attempt to disguise. Accompanied by a haughty look of self-satisfaction. Moist lips and plump cheeks at once sensuous and full told me he ate well, and better than most of his compatriots. But the face was also tempered with shrewdness and caution.

Tailored garments hung on his well-fed frame as if he'd been born to them. They were elegant and stylish and in direct contrast to the coarse outfits worn by nearly everyone else we'd seen tonight. A pair of tassels bounced gaily on each shoe.

Pak said, "Thas guide. He high-up North Korea. He taking girl across. Now we waiting kidnapper group."

Five minutes later a guy in a shabby coat, bad hair, and shifty eyes turned the corner a block away and entered the noodle shop. The coat was as local as they come.

Pak stiffened. "Thas trafficker I know. Why he here is maybe for our business. But also maybe for other business."

If Anna had been handed off to traffickers for the last leg of her journey, that could pose a problem.

"Why don't I go for a bowl of noodles and see if they're sitting together?" I said

I started to rise, but Pak put a hand on my shoulder.

"You cannot. You America. Everyone looking you if you go."

He was right, of course.

Pak pointed at Noda. "We two go. Eat noodle. Talk. Speaking just only China in there, you know? Soft so people no hear Japan accent floating in air."

It was a good strategy. Pak had taken a scissors to Noda's hair and hacked away until the chief detective's straight glossy locks looked like a field of knee-high barley that kids had trampled through. Pak had followed his hairdressing feat by clothing Noda like a poorer cousin, in a cheap Chinese getup purchased from a secondhand store in Jilin.

They shoved their night-vision binocs into our supply bag, eased open the shop gate, then walked away, Pak mumbling softly to Noda in Chinese and Noda grunting like he usually did but in a distinctly Chinese vein.

Thirty yards on, they turned into the noodle shop, passing between the black pillars with the dragons—and leaving me alone with the night and the crickets.

CHAPTER 72

PAK shot from the noodle shop like ketchup from a plugged squeeze bottle suddenly unblocked—inexplicably and far faster than advisable. He turned away from me and disappeared around the closest corner.

What the hell?

Next, our two targets emerged from the shop, arguing. The North Korean Party cadre snapped and snarled and threatened in the imperiously arrogant manner of one used to getting his way. The Chinese trafficker whined and backed away, ceding ground but clearly not handing over what the Korean wanted.

Noda exited next, two yards behind them, giving the bickering men a wide berth and what could pass for a worried look. He turned toward me. They ignored him. The chief detective nodded me over. I jammed my night-vision binocs into the supply bag, shouldered the sack, and joined Noda on the street, staying in the shadows under the eaves.

"The Chinese guy wants a bonus," Noda told me in a low voice.

When the trafficker tried to turn away, the Korean grabbed his shoulder and jerked him around. The North Korean was big, and in his fury looked suddenly taller and bulkier and more powerful. He swung at the Chinese man, who stared dumbfounded as he took the blow full on the chin, folding up with a startled bleat of protest. The Korean began kicking him.

A second Chinese man appeared at the corner around which Pak had vanished, looking not unlike the downed man in dress and appearance. Threadbare garments, bad hair, five years younger. A brother or a cousin. He pushed a placid and confused woman before him, a blade to her neck, her left arm twisted behind her.

My heart leapt. It was Anna, and this time the miracle was no mirage.

The second man yelled at the Party cadre, who stopped in mid-kick and glared at the speaker. The Korean's features were distorted in anger, his brown complexion a fiery red. He aimed a furious last blow at the downed trafficker's ribs, cracking at least one of them, then advanced on the partner, shouting and alternately flailing and jabbing his hands in the air at Anna. Her captor grew nervous and backpedaled, dragging his dazed captive with him. The Korean stomped forward, bull-like and oblivious to the threat of the knife. He bellowed at the Chinese man, who shook his head, brandished the weapon in the air, then touched the point to Anna's carotid artery.

Over the commotion I yelled in English, "She's no good to anyone dead."

Both men froze and turned to stare in my direction. The North Korean's mouth fell open. The Chinese trafficker said, "Who you are?"

"Her friend."

"Go away. I kill her."

"You won't kill her."

He sneered and ran the back side of the blade across her cheek. Anna whimpered.

I took a step forward and he said, "Stop or I mark her. We still get double yuan for her. Japanese very valuable. Exotic."

I turned to Noda. "How much money do we have?"

"Enough."

"We'll double the price," I said.

He shook his head. "You trouble. Go away. This China."

"Triple the money," I said.

"Go away."

"That's not going to happen."

"What?"

"No going away."

With the look of consternation, the North Korean eyes bounced back and forth between Anna's captor and me.

The trafficker said, "You go now. Far away or I kill and find new woman tomorrow. Always many many woman." He rubbed his pelvis against Anna's thigh in a lewd manner, leering at me and showing a partial set of black, rotting teeth.

A shadow slipped up behind him. The light caught a glimmer of steel an instant before a blade slid across the trafficker's throat, leaving a thin red trail that, a heartbeat later, parted and gushed a waterfall of blood. The black-toothed trafficker deflated without a sound. Behind him stood Pak. Anna seemed not to notice the change in her situation. She gazed at us but didn't see us.

Pak pointed the soiled blade in the North Korean's direction and said in accented Chinese English, "You want, mister?"

The man raised his hands palm-out in the universal sign of surrender, then backed into Noda, who let out a low feral growl. The Korean shrunk away from the chief detective, pivoted, and ran off into the night.

The beaten trafficker groaned and stirred. Calling out in Chinese, he dragged himself upright. Pak was on him in two steps and made a second pass with the knife. The man grabbed at his throat, eyes staring in shock at Pak as blood oozed between his fingers. He tried to speak but his lips succeeded only in forming a bubble of blood. He toppled back against the wall of the shuttered shop behind him and sank to a sitting position, still clutching his throat.

"What are you doing?" I said. "The first one I get but—"

"Doing is for my mother. For all mother." Pak spit on his second victim. "Dirty China trafficker like this sell my mother maybe fifty dollar to farmer. I see, I kill. I kill all them."

I opened my mouth to respond but in Pak's eyes I saw a pain so raw, so all-consuming, I closed it again. The shrewd, world-weary rescuer of North Korean refugees had vanished. In his stead was the twelve-year-old child he had once been, with the bottomless anguish and uncomprehending agony he was to carry for decades to come.

Pak's first target no longer stirred. Ten feet away, hidden in the shadows under the eaves, the second mark continued to bleed out. His body twitched. Color drained from his face in pronounced increments.

Anna stood where her captor had left her, staring straight ahead in a vague unseeing manner. She took no notice of Pak's shouting or the fallen bodies.

Nodding at Pak's first takedown, Noda said, "Move him into the alley. I'll handle Ms. Tanaka."

Our luck ran out as I was dragging the dead trafficker into the closest alleyway.

CHAPTER 73

A T the end of the street a whistle blew. From four long blocks away, three sharp blasts cut through the night like an experimental jet through the ozone: swift, shrill, and with razor-sharp clarity.

"We need to leave," Noda said.

But it wasn't to be.

Anna Tanaka stood motionless before us, her expression one of placid compliance. Her black hair was greasy and tangled. She'd been drugged and registered nothing. She had no idea of what was unfolding around her. No idea whether she was free or in the hands of new captors.

I suspected it wasn't the drugs alone. She'd gone through too much that was too alien to everything she knew. She'd been brutally seized at her mother's funeral and trundled across Japan from one coast to the other, probably bound and gagged and tossed in the back of a van or the trunk of a car. Or possibly just heavily drugged and transported in a catatonic state from one point to the next. After her overland journey, she'd been thrown aboard a small watercraft and carted over the choppy, windswept waters to the coast of South Korea. Tossed into another vehicle and trucked through the back roads to the DMZ, or close to it, before her captors, warned by their confederates, reversed course, headed to the airport, and bundled her onto a plane to northern China. After countless hours in a drug-induced trance, she would be semiconscious at best. The only upside would have been a hands-off policy. There would be no molestation of such a highly valued prize.

Anna was staring at me. "Do . . . I know you?"

"You do. I'm a friend of your mother's."

But Sharon's daughter hadn't heard me. Or if she had, my response was funneled through a heavily medicated filter, emerging at the other end a distorted unrecognizable echo of the original. She stood on one spot, pale and silent and uncomprehending. Her eyes funneled into mine, dull and unblinking. There was no light of recognition. There was no light at all.

The whistle sounded again, three blocks away. A solitary policeman dashed in our direction at a sharp clip, shouting in Chinese and brandishing a wooden police baton.

Pak's gaze leapt up the street at the advancing badge. "We going now. Do greeting later."

In Japanese, Noda gently took Anna's arm. "We saw your father and your grandmother two nights ago."

With a reference to her family, the head detective hoped to prod her back to the present, but his words had no effect. She merely smiled and said, "Oh, Japanese. I love Japanese. It's so musical."

Another miracle drug abused. Long-term, two things gave me hope: her posture and her complexion. She stood straight and loose-limbed and unencumbered by injury or stress or any other overbearing trauma, and her skin was clear and glowed with the same creamy near translucence her mother had possessed. But short-term Anna was a liability. She couldn't run. She could only be led, and even then only at a slow methodical pace.

The policeman was two and half blocks away and closing.

Pak dragged the body of his second victim into an alleyway, then pointed farther into the passage. "Bringing Tanaka woman here."

I turned to Noda. "You three go on ahead. I'll slow the cop down and follow."

"You remembering place?" Pak asked, grabbing the bag of supplies.

"Yes."

We'd camped out at a safe house five blocks away until sunset before setting up our stakeout of the noodle shop. A van, battered and road-tested and unremarkable, was parked in a nearby garage. Pak would pilot it from Changbai to Ulaanbaatar, the capital of Mongolia, a thousand-mile journey as the crow flies. The last leg of the trek was through the

Gobi Desert. His people had worked up a South Korean passport for Anna as well, so documents weren't a problem.

Noda shook his head. "I'll stay. Pak can take her."

"No," I said, an eye on the advancing badge. "Pak can't handle her alone in this state. You go. I'll catch up, don't worry."

"I don't leave people."

"There's no choice. All of us can't leave without the police following. Go."

Noda's scar flared. "Bad idea."

"It's the only idea."

A block and a half and closing.

Noda cast an unhappy look at the cop.

I said, "Anna comes first."

He growled at his lack of options. "I'll be back."

"I'll be right behind you."

Reluctantly, Noda turned away, made a hurried bow to Anna, then hoisted her over his shoulder and trotted after Pak. Anna made giggling noises.

"The eaves," my detective friend called back as he disappeared into the darkness.

CHAPTER 74

I TURNED to face the policeman.

He was fifty yards away and moving in steadily now. Not too fast, not too slow. He still flourished the nightstick in a threatening manner, but I found the club reassuring. If he'd witnessed the murders, he'd be brandishing a gun.

Conditions worked in our favor. Streetlamps were few and dim. He'd been four blocks away. For all he knew, we were dragging drunks off the roadway. Or he'd witnessed the tail end of a street brawl. Both were probably the norm for the district. Undesirable, yet neither was irregular nor life-threatening. But once he understood he was dealing with murder, the firearm would come out. I needed to prevent the discovery at all costs. Which meant I needed to distract and then disable him. That was the scenario necessary for me to rejoin my friends.

I stepped into the street and raised my hands.

———

The cop was young but he wasn't dumb.

He approached with caution. Like any experienced officer would when confronted with a civilian, possibly a drunk civilian, not to mention a foreigner, in a scrimmage involving violence.

I drew up and waited for him to come to me. *Take all the time you want. I only need to stall enough for my friends to get to the safe house five blocks away.*

And then I changed my mind. Noda had had a better idea.

The perfect idea for the time and place.

The eaves.

———

During our stakeout, we'd watched an amorous couple shelter from prying eyes under the deep overhang of one of the traditional buildings, in a nearly impenetrable darkness. The lovers were a short distance away, and yet, under the concealing cover of the eaves, they were nothing more than an indistinct bundle. They could have been a stack of barrels or a pile of firewood. Their embrace was an inky slow-moving mass within a midnight black field. That was all.

So, with the advancing cop fewer than twenty yards away, I retreated to the protective shadows of the shop overhang behind me. The badge stopped five yards out and squinted into the darkness. I edged sideways. He shouted at me in Chinese. I didn't answer.

I wondered if he could see me with any clarity, and confirmed in the next instant that he couldn't. His searching look roamed over the side of the blackened storefront, his eyes unable to find mine. In the cloistered entry of the grocery we'd used for our stakeout, our eyes had long been accustomed to the night and we'd still been unable to make out details of the passionate goings-on. My current adversary was under a heavier handicap.

The safe house was only a short five blocks away.

I could confuse the issue.

To stall for time.

I eased closer to the wall, then shifted sideways, away from the policeman, careful to maneuver within the shielding shadows of the man-made canopy. Then a step forward. Then back. My movements were slow, fluid, and random.

I mapped out a square. Then a rectangle. I moved diagonally. I bent at the waist as I shifted positions. I raised and lowered my arms. As if I were but one person among several. Indecision clouded the policeman's features. His youthful confidence faded. He yelled out to me—or us—to step forward. At least, I presumed that's what he said. His tone was demanding, presumptuous, yet wavered at the end.

I switched to circles. A small, tight one. A longish oval one. Sticking carefully to the confines of the eaves, I added counterclockwise circles. I cut across the diameter of each ring. The cop opted for containment.

He roared at me again, frustration edging into his voice, then spoke into his shoulder radio. I'd stalled his advance. All time gained for my fleeing friends.

I kept in constant, slow, and random motion. Shadows have density. Layers. Shades. Like seawater at different depths. Within that density, I hoped to replicate the indistinct mass of the lovers we had glimpsed. We'd known there had been only the twosome, but as they shuffled about in their impassioned caresses it looked like more.

His annoyance rising, the policeman commanded me to show myself. I said nothing. What was he going to do? Shoot us all? I continued my charade. Tight steps. Up and back. Circular, straight lines, diagonals. Leaning left and right. Bending at right angles.

If nothing more came out of my probe into Sharon's and Mikey's deaths, we would get Sharon's daughter safely out of China.

I would accept nothing less.

A hard-fought and worthy victory.

At a cost yet to be determined.

CHAPTER 75

THE policeman's patience was unraveling. He inched closer. His eyes would soon adjust to the darkness and I would be unmasked.

I saw him straighten and gain confidence. His squint vanished.

Time to make my exit.

Five short blocks.

Noda and company would be indoors by now, or only a few steps short of the threshold. Unknowingly, the cop had stationed himself near my intended escape route—the same passage between buildings Noda and Pak had taken. He was close enough to fully penetrate the shadows and intercept me, so I'd have to use the far pathway. I edged toward the alternate route. I could slip around the corner without leaving the protective confines of the eaves. Maybe without the cop realizing I'd left him behind.

But the second option turned out to be gated and locked. I'd assumed that all the alleyways would be accessible.

Resigned, I had only one other choice. I stepped from cover and waved my passport at him. I raised my empty hand above my head and swung the passport arm in a wide, unthreatening arc straight out in front of me. The cop cocked his wrist, his club at the ready.

Fortunately, he was still only a force of one. A number I could overcome.

Five short blocks.

Then the odds changed drastically. His shoulder radio chirped. He hit the reply button and reeled off a short string of words. I heard loud chatter on the other end, then a disconnect, then running footsteps and two more uniforms rolled into view. Eyes locked onto my position, the cop backed up two paces to join them. One-on-one had morphed into three-on-one. They moved quickly into a tight V formation, senior officer on point, an underling on each flank.

I scanned their equipment belts. Flashlights, handcuffs, billy clubs, interphones, tear-gas canisters, Chinese revolvers. The guns were holstered and locked in place with leather straps and chains connected to their belts. Clearly a measure to prevent the weapons from being grabbed in a crowd situation, which was a common occurrence in China. The upside for me was that a rapid draw was not possible.

The three advanced as one. The leader issued commands in a loud voice meant to intimidate. The trio was still four paces away. I didn't move. The first cop, the youngest by far, gestured with his club at the black area behind me. He thought more people might be crouching in the dark.

At four paces, they determined that the shadows held no secrets and they pressed forward with renewed confidence.

In what I hoped looked like a peace offering, I held out my passport with my left hand.

The senior by age and probably rank said something in Chinese and they spread out, the first cop to his left and a more experienced one to the right. They inched forward in a straight line, coming within four feet and stopping.

I stood stock still, passport extended.

Raising his arm, the youngest took a step closer.

I let the passport drop.

Reflexively, he bent to retrieve the falling document. His training kicked in a fraction of a second later—but not soon enough. As his torso bounced back up, I drove a fist into his solar plexus, pivoted, and slammed the heel of my right shoe into the kneecap of the leader. My first target went down gasping for breath, the second howled as his leg collapsed under him.

Two blows. Two down. And both out of commission for the foreseeable future.

I whirled and faced the last cop. If I could take him out in short order, I could fade into the warren of backstreets and rejoin my group.

The third man had his truncheon out. Knowing I could jump him before he could release his firearm, he'd gone for the club. Then he surprised me. He shifted into a Chinese martial arts pose with all the calm of an experienced fighter. He wove the baton in a complex pattern in the air between us, then charged.

I backpedaled and dodged left toward the center of the street. I circled, giving myself time to gauge his speed, skill, and confidence. He followed with supreme assurance. His glance swept over my limbs and torso, scouting vulnerable strike zones.

Then, unexpectedly, he began to whirl. The movement soon became hypnotic. Which may have been the point, at least partially. He spun around in a complete three-sixty. He kicked out a leg long before I was within range, extending it fully, his thigh nearly parallel to the ground. Then, bending his knee, he gathered the limb back in, and in some sort of ballet-like move continued to spin, keeping his momentum going with a series of leg extensions and retractions, kicking out again and again.

He was tireless. He gained speed. He edged forward in my wake. With each rotation he kept a fierce stare locked on my features until, at the last possible moment, his sharp-angled features would whip around. I'd see the back of his head for the briefest instant, then his livid brown oval face would come around again and glare.

I'd never seen anything like it.

Not in real life. Not in this combination.

The next revolution brought him within range. I backed off. His club rose and fell in a pattern independent of his leg thrusts. He had two lines of attack going on simultaneously. His leg shot out and was withdrawn, but not always at the same height. I could no more fathom a way to approach than I could guess how to grapple with a porcupine with its quills raised.

The gambit was of a piece and I was alert for some hidden trigger. The move required phenomenal stamina and training. It was gymnastic in composition, operatic in appearance, and either as deadly as a cobra or as harmless as a garden snake.

After a few more cycles, I came up with an idea: the glare. It was meant to intimidate and it did, but in a curious way he was not its master. No more than he was a master of his own strikes. Once in motion, they controlled him more than he controlled them. They were rhythmic and predetermined. He was committed to each rotation, each kick, until he brought himself out of his continuous spin.

His body twirled away before his threatening visage, which stayed glued to my position. The leg and the truncheon were in the lead. They retreated first. The next time around, as soon as the kick and club swept past, I leapt forward. He strained his neck to keep his head in place and his eyes locked on my advance.

But he couldn't change the physics of the move.

His face was yanked away. I struck with the same bent-knuckle jab I'd used against Habu's knife attack in the Dragon Skin. The cop's head whipped around and his face came back into rotation. My jab met his nose perfectly. I rolled the rest of my body into his. I heard his nose crack and felt it begin to collapse as the nightstick and leg swung around yet again. His upper thigh banged harmlessly into my thigh, and the truncheon struck my hip, the power of each stroke partially blunted by my proximity. His head bounced off my knuckles and his body stopped as if it had slammed into a tree. He staggered back, then toppled over.

The final exchange had taken less than a minute, but it had eaten up too much time. I needed to vacate the area. The trio was sprawled across the pavement in various stages of hurt. Where the twirling dervish had connected—hip and thigh—my body pulsed with pain. I took a step and stumbled. My hip revolted. The blow from the club had caused more damage than anticipated.

I sucked up the pain and lurched toward the narrow passage Noda vanished into with Anna.

Behind me, I heard a weapon being cocked.

"No bouncy bouncy bullets today, mister."

I understood the reference and froze.

Instantly and clearly so there could be no mistake.

He was talking about his police-issue, Chinese-made 9mm revolver. The guns were specially designed for the patrolling badges. They carried proprietary ammunition, meaning bullets unique to them and sold only through government channels. They also shot rubber bullets. The "bouncy bouncy" was his way of telling me his weapon was loaded with lead. Not rubber facsimiles.

"Hand high up, mister."

He'd come from around the corner and snuck up on my blind side. I was only two paces from the exit passage and its protective cover. If I could find a way to distract the newcomer, or overcome him, I could still manage an escape.

I turned to face him, raising my hands and taking a step in his direction.

"No move, mister."

"Not an inch," I said.

Then I heard a commotion from the lane that was to be my escape route. The barrel of a firearm pressed against my spine.

"Step into street, mister."

I did as I was told, glancing behind me as I did so. Three militiamen had arrived, with rifles leveled. To the left and right, other passageways erupted with life. Uniforms poured forth. In seconds there were upward of ten officers, a pair of secret police among them. All had weapons drawn and aimed my way.

I heard the click of hard wood on a steel casing, then the length of a baton crashed against the backs of my knees. I grunted in pain and my legs buckled. My kneecaps slammed into the ground. I grimaced and fell sideways. The point of a polished boot slammed into my stomach. I curled into a protective ball as the pounding started from all sides.

In the near distance, tires screeched to a halt. A command was bellowed. The kicking stopped. Heels slapped the blacktop. I opened one eye. My attackers had snapped to attention. A tangerine-colored hatchback with tinted windows stood some ten yards off. The vehicle was compact and primitive and ugly. But relief in any form was a welcome sight.

An iron-toed boot prodded me in the ribs. "Stand up, mister. Now."

I dragged myself to my feet.

"Hand high up."

I did as I was told.

Five short blocks were now as good as five long miles. There would be no safe house for me.

A tangerine door swung wide and Zhou stepped onto the street, wearing a stylish knee-length beige overcoat and a look of extreme annoyance. He ran a jaded eye over the scene. Over the bristling array of weapons pointed my way. Over the bodies on the ground. Two of them struggling to stand, my final conquest unconscious and immobile.

The master spy's smile was sad. "This, my friend, is one reunion you should have avoided."

CHAPTER 76

ZHOU'S gaze lingered on the men on the ground. "It looks like I missed a fine display of talent."

I looked from the fallen men to the circle of weaponry pointed in my direction. Rifles, revolvers, and more revolvers. Fifteen and rising as police and militia continued to arrive.

I shrugged. "Are you planning to help?"

"Are you planning to tell me where the girl is?"

The master spy was speaking only English now. Being as open and transparent for the others as he could, given my lack of Chinese.

"No."

"Then you've answered you own question."

I nodded, got down on my knees, and clasped my hands behind my head.

––––––

"How did you find me?" I asked.

We sat in the rear seat of the orange hatchback. A Geely GC5. It had a black interior with chrome-colored highlights. Mostly silver painted over plastic. Manufactured by Geely, one of a nearly uncountable number of Chinese carmakers.

Zhou said, "It's my business to know everything and be where I must."

"That's not an answer."

"I don't owe you an answer. Give up the girl's travel route and they will go easier on you. I can guarantee you that much."

"That's all you're offering?"

The inside of the vehicle was immaculate. The seats were stiff and new. The padding underneath was buoyant and responsive. A new-car smell was prominent. In contrast, the exterior was dented and dusty and noticeably smudged. Two policemen occupied the bucket seats up front. The one on the passenger side leveled his revolver at my chest.

"That is all I am able to offer."

I gave no reply and Zhou said, "The girl, Brodie. Just point me in the right direction."

"She's long gone."

Zhou snorted. "She has gone to ground is what you mean. Hiding in some hole. The police are already swarming into the district. Roadblocks are being set. Your friend Noda and the other gentleman won't get ten blocks. They certainly cannot get a woman out of China."

"I'm sure you're right," I said, a response that only angered him further.

I thought of Sharon's husband, distraught and disheveled and shut up in his home. There was no way I was going to allow anyone to get their hands on another member of the Tanaka family, least of all Zhou.

With the authorities' attention focused on me, Pak and Noda would gain the time they needed to spirit Anna out of the country. And they needed the time. After Pak's double takedown, they would be running a tougher gauntlet, and it was going to take all of Pak's resources to cross over into Mongolia.

"Who was the third man?"

Anna Tanaka's ticket out of the country. "I have no idea what you're talking about."

"Don't toy with me, Brodie. Not now. The man's name."

"There was only Noda."

"Do not bother to lie, Brodie. There are witnesses."

I shrugged. "More of a denial, less of a lie."

"With or without your cooperation, the People's Police will find her. However, without your cooperation, your cause will go from bad to worse. Be careful, my friend."

"How much worse could it get?"

The Geely moved down dark paved roadways. The streets were empty of life.

Zhou spoke Japanese for the first time. "You should think carefully before refusing my offer. The People's . . . technicians are capable of cracking even the most stubborn minds."

There was a new solemnity to his words.

"I see," I said eventually.

"I do not think that you do. But you will."

I twisted my cuffed wrists behind me. There was no give in the manacles. No flexibility in the chain.

The movement did not escape Zhou's notice. "Let me point out that the ugly officer with the gun has orders to shoot should you attempt to escape."

Again in Japanese.

"I'll keep it in mind."

Zhou gave me a look I couldn't decipher. "For all the good it will do you. Their kind has a habit of defining escape in a creative manner."

"We hit a bad bump in this tin can, it could happen sooner. His finger is riding the trigger."

"That's a chance they are willing to take."

Not a promising avenue. I changed the subject. "How'd you find me?" I asked again.

Zhou gazed out into the night. "It is there, more than anyplace else, where you disappoint, Brodie. Passenger manifest. Even the most amateur among us travels under a false passport when an assignment requires it. Perhaps, after all, you are only an art dealer."

"It was a false passport."

"A *known* false passport ceases to be false. I red-flagged your name and known aliases after our meal in San Francisco. I never expected one of them to trigger."

Brodie Security ran on a tight budget, and we thought we could stretch the passport for a while longer. Clearly we'd misjudged.

The car reached the edge of the Changbai urban sprawl. All signs of opulence had vanished. The homes had turned scruffy. They were squat and flimsy and patched with scrap wood and corrugated plastic.

"Nice car," I said, still in Japanese.

"It is Chinese-made. I am a patriot and a humble servant of the People's Republic."

"Not your usual style."

"There is a time for everything."

"It's an eyesore."

"Eye of the beholder, my friend." He nodded once at my knees pressed into the back of the front seat. "Try not to punch a hole in the upholstery. You will only anger our traveling companions, and where you are going they are sure to extract repayment for any breach."

"Where am I going?"

"The end of the world. To our worst hospitality suite. Reserved for top criminals."

"I'm a criminal now?"

Once more, for an instant, I got the unreadable look. But there was no gloating. No satisfaction. Only dark eyes inexplicably growing darker.

"No, my friend, you have distinguished yourself yet again, I'm sorry to say. You have risen above the masses. You have become an enemy of the State."

CHAPTER 77

W E drove in silence for more than thirty minutes.

An enemy of the State.

With those words, a coldness swept through my entire body. Practically speaking, I wondered what the designation meant. It occurred to me that of the hundreds of people I was privileged to call an associate, acquaintance, or friend, not one of them knew where I was. Not even Noda, my usual fallback. And probably not Pak, our guide through this hostile land. Nor could anyone find me electronically. The first thing Zhou had done was deactivate my cell phone. I was isolated, anchorless, and more vulnerable than I had ever been.

We came down off the edge of the Changbai mountain range and onto a high flat plain of scrub. Early signs of dawn had turned the sky from black to navy. On the horizon a thin cobalt line glowed.

The end of the world.

An escalating sense of dread crept into my nervous system. Physically and geographically, I was in uncharted territory. Adrift in a vast expanse of rural China. I looked over at Zhou. The master spy had closed his eyes. He dozed.

I turned back to the scenery for a clue to our destination. The shadowy mountains that had accompanied us at the start of the ride had given way to hunched loping hills, which gradually flattened to dusty highlands. Farther on, crops appeared briefly, with endless rows of bright green sprouts. But the land looked anything but fertile and the tilled fields were short-lived. The last blue-gray hues of the night succumbed to the first yellow rays of dawn, which bathed the brittle brown scrublands in a pale flax-colored wash.

At the DMZ, I'd seen a vision of the end of the world, Korean-style. Was I getting my first hint of the Chinese version?

_____

The driver sped by a manned tollbooth with a nod.

Without slowing.

We rolled onto an expressway stretching like an endless pathway into an unforeseeable future. We drove for two hours at a reckless 120 miles an hour.

The Geely shook and rattled and protested but didn't come apart, which I chalked up more to luck than a miracle of modern technology. The car was designed for country folk to tool along country lanes and for suburbanites of modest means to totter along on an outing to the local public pool. That it was the current police vehicle of choice was so outlandish as to alarm me—it was too far removed from the norm.

When we finally exited the highway, Zhou stirred, stretched, and looked my way. "You did not sleep?"

"What are you charging me with?" I asked.

Zhou smirked. "Surely you know better than that. This is China. First we lock you up, then we find a charge."

"Of course."

"So, one last time, where is she?"

"Long gone."

"The route, then."

On the flight to Jilin, Pak had said the trip to the Mongolian border would take at least four days and conceivably as long as six. The journey would be roundabout and its length would depend on how smoothly the extraction had gone. In anyone's book, bodies in the street did not constitute a smooth extraction.

I said, "You never told me why you are chasing after the North Koreans. You guys despise them."

"How well you know us. Our neighbors to the east are indeed churlish, but that does not mean we would not pay attention should they stumble onto a toy we think we might enjoy."

"So you always knew about Anna?"

"We discovered they had found a backdoor into the NSA data centers the day before the Kennedy Center killings, but not their way in. When Anna Tanaka was taken, we had the means."

"Which is why you showed up in San Francisco and Tokyo."

"Yes. When you gave me the tattoo and the gang name, I knew where to start looking. But you beat us to the gang leader, so we sat on you. The Tanaka woman is the whole game. Always has been. Now it is your turn."

"Haven't I given you enough?"

"Not nearly. It's time to play or pay. I strongly suggest the former. The alternative is not pleasant."

CHAPTER 78

ZHOU was right.

Where they were taking me looked like the end of the world.

A confinement center rose up in front of us, massive and daunting. There was a mile of containment wall on each side. Rows of multistory cellblocks paraded in long straight columns within. I was looking at a warehouse of human bondage on a colossal scale. A penitentiary behind high stone walls with double-stacked coils of razor wire and lit up from above by countless spotlights.

"What do you think?" Zhou asked.

I didn't bother to answer.

Zhou shrugged. "It doesn't really matter. The People's Police have other plans for you."

The black ribbon of asphalt narrowed from two lanes to one as we approached the compound. As if to say, *Beyond this outpost nothing of import exists. Life itself comes to an end.* The road continued on for three hundred yards to the entrance of the prison complex, where it dead-ended. A minor branch, probably a maintenance road, swept off to the right.

The driver surprised me by veering onto the fork.

"This is unexpected," I said.

"If you only knew."

Paved roadway gave way to an unpaved track. The small Geely did not take well to the dirt path. It rocked and roiled. Its chassis protested with groans. The suspension screeched.

"Where we are headed is off the map," Zhou said.

I pointed upward. "Nothing's off the map these days."

Zhou cut me a narrow look. "You sure about that?"

"What's that mean?"

In the distance, I could make out the looming shadows of a new set of hills. To the rear, the penitentiary dropped from view.

"Our destination appears on no map. Not in China or anywhere in the world. It is absent from even the best satellite photographs your intelligence agencies have gathered."

In the days of orbiting eye-in-the-sky spy technology, his was an exceptional claim. Even when underground facilities existed—in Iran, Russia, North Korea, and elsewhere—we knew they existed from the aboveground activity and reports. Was it possible the Chinese could have a complex completely off the radar? I doubted it.

The dirt path grew rougher. The tangerine hatchback bounced and swayed. It emitted a new range of mechanical groans and creaks. The drive became a constant dance around ever-larger ruts and rocks. A film of new dust settled on the old.

The car had been here before.

The cop with the gun said something to Zhou, who nodded. The weapon disappeared.

"What'd he say?"

"He asked for permission to holster his firearm, because out here, even if you escaped, there is no place for you to go."

The jostling continued. The organs under my ribs began to ache. Some ruts had grown so large they could not be avoided. And volleyball-size rocks now pocked the roadway. One or two every minute needed to be swerved around. Not enough to make the road impassable, but enough so the neglected route appeared to be of little importance. As if the dirt trail we were on was so infrequently used, it was not worth clearing.

"Not my favorite part," Zhou said.

"So you've done this before?"

"As seldom as possible, and never by choice."

"So this is an international detention center?" Zhou specialized in overseas operations.

"On occasion, as needed. It's a kind of one-way clearinghouse for undesirables. Do not the volume of potholes and stones speak to you?"

" 'One way'?"

"Yes."

Off the map . . . a one-way clearinghouse . . . A chill gripped the back of my neck. The dusty sidetrack was not neglected. Nor lacking in maintenance. Nor scheduled for a paving. An upgrade would never be ordered. Because it was an access road meant to draw as little attention as possible—leading to a prison beyond a prison. For people who will cease to exist. Zhou had not been exaggerating for effect.

He said, "I see you have figured out our little puzzle."

"A black site."

The master spy grimaced. "The blackest."

The road began to rise.

CHAPTER 79

THE Geely did not like inclines.

It huffed and strained as the pitted dirt drive rose steadily. The peaks of the hills drew closer and reared up. Then the tops of two silos split the sky. The terrain topped out on a high plain.

"Are those cows?" I said, taking in the scene a quarter of a mile down the road.

"Yes."

"On a working farm?"

"Yes, my friend. That is precisely what your satellites see, and that is precisely what it is not."

———

Two minutes later we rolled to a halt in a farmyard.

"Welcome to the Farmhouse," Zhou said.

"What does that mean?"

"You'll see soon enough."

I looked around and didn't see much of anything. A squat stone farmhouse stood in front of us, and a weathered barn to the rear. The house was built of the same stone scattered over land and road. It was tucked up against the hills, which stretched back in waves in progressively taller mounds, like children lined up by age from youngest to oldest, one head higher than the last.

I looked toward the barn. Seated on an ancient Chinese tractor was an ancient Chinese farmer. The tractor was red and boxy and rusted where the paint had fallen away. The old man was shriveled and weather-toughened and wore a frayed straw hat.

"Lean forward," Zhou said, and when I did he removed the cuffs. "For the eye in the sky."

"They might still know."

The master spy reached into the cargo bay behind the seat, came up with a battered straw hat, and jammed it on my head. In the front, the police guards slipped out of their uniforms. Underneath they wore indigo farmers' overalls.

"Last chance to tell me where she is," Zhou said, reverting to Japanese, which clearly, unlike English, our escort in the front could not follow.

"Not going to happen. Tell me how you found out about her so soon."

"That is not important. What is important is that Anna Tanaka can engineer entry to all of America's secrets. It's as simple as that. Since you Americans are foolish enough to allow domestic spying, why shouldn't we take advantage of it as well?"

"I could think of a few reasons."

Zhou sneered. "You Americans are a careless people."

"Is that so?"

"You have forgotten how good you have it. Tens of thousands of Chinese have demonstrated and died over the centuries in attempts to gain a fraction of the freedoms you enjoy. Even now, demonstrations take place weekly, though the incidents are not reported. People are beaten or imprisoned or killed fighting for a sliver of the liberty you take for granted. Your founders created unprecedented freedoms, but today leaders in Washington are in the process of snatching them all away to 'protect America from terrorism.' The NSA has been given the power to spy on all Americans. Your country is turning into what China has been for decades: a surveillance state. Communism was the ideal, surveillance is the reality. Surveillance means control. That is a bad road to travel, my friend."

"Hello, Mr. Brodie," the secretary of Homeland Security had said. *"What's your personal opinion of the NSA?"*

"Do they have information on me, my daughter, and my friends?"

"I imagine they do."

"Then I hate it. I want my private life to remain private."

In effect, from the other side of the fence, I'd expressed a similar thought only a few days ago.

The driver said something in Chinese, and Zhou turned to me. "It's time to go. You have your own road to travel. Last chance to tell me where the girl is headed."

"The answer's the same."

Zhou sank into himself, seeming to grow smaller, which for him was saying a lot. Silence spread deep and dark between us. After a long moment, in an uncharacteristically subdued voice, the master spy said:

"Then this is good-bye. Allow me to give you a piece of advice before we part. Give them what they want."

" 'They'? Don't you mean you?"

"No. I don't. I wanted the girl, not you. Give them what they ask and I will . . . push to mitigate . . . what is to follow. Meanwhile, I will work on a story to spare our mutual friend the pain."

"What pain is that?"

"You were caught red-handed at a murder scene, Brodie. A policeman saw you drag a dead body into the shadows. For that you must pay."

CHAPTER 80

WE stepped from the car.

On the tractor the old man swiveled in his elevated perch to watch.

The farmhouse door, painted forest green, creaked open. We stepped through into a large rectangular room. A woman as ancient and as browned as the old man stood just inside. She bowed but did not speak. In a modest kitchen along the right wall was a wood-fired stove made of brick, and next to it a decades-old refrigerator with rounded corners and stilt legs. A sagging black vinyl couch was positioned in front of a boxy black-and-white TV, the picture running without sound. Alongside the couch stood six prison guards, with weapons drawn.

No more pretense.

My new and expanded guard detail now numbered eight.

They marched me into the basement. Zhou waited in the car. The farmer's wife stayed upstairs. In the basement was a second forest-green door. A guard swung it wide to reveal a long dimly lit tunnel—and the entrance to a secret subterranean complex built under the hills behind the farmhouse.

The Farmhouse.

No eye in the sky here.

With a fleet of guns at my back, I stepped into the long, unpainted cement entryway. It stretched for some two hundred yards and smelled of bleach and mildew. A cloying dampness hung in the air.

Solitary sixty-watt bulbs set in the ceiling fixtures every twenty yards punctured the darkness of the passage. At the other end, an iron grille, painted institution white, blocked our way. The bars of the grille were a crosshatch of horizontal and vertical pieces, the ends embedded in the cement.

I was looking at an indestructible door to an unknowable cage.

A pair of guards, pale and bored, stepped from an office on the other side. The older of the two unlocked the gate. The younger thrust a prison uniform into my hands and with gestures ordered me to change in a small chamber behind the office. The garments were blue and made of cotton. The jersey had long sleeves and two pockets. The pants had an elastic band and no pockets.

The beatings began as soon as the preliminaries were finished.

———————

A guard detail of two led me through a labyrinth of cement corridors into a torture chamber two levels down.

As we descended, the dampness increased. Mold and mildew had conquered the lower corridors. The torture chamber was a cement cell with brackish streaks of fungi on the walls and a drain in the center of a cement floor. From all sides, the floor slanted downward toward the drain.

At gunpoint, my guards gestured for me to lie on a large steel table, then shackled my wrists and ankles. Each manacle was attached to a chain, which was threaded through an iron loop at the corner of the table and pulled tight until I lay stretched out in a taut X.

The guards exited and thirty seconds later two men in their forties entered. They were pale and stringy and tense. One was tall and angular and grinning, the other short and hunched and morose.

The tall one said, "Today is beginning fun between us. We start simple. See how smart you be, mister."

While he talked, the morose short one went over to a three-tiered shelf stocked with tools of the trade and came back with an electric prod.

"You are called Brodie Jim," the taller one said. "This is right, I think."

Giving my name in the Asian order, last name first.

I nodded.

"You speak when question come. Okay?"

I glared at him and said nothing. His partner fired up the electric baton. It came to life with a buzz. A blue light danced at its tip.

"Okay," I said.

"Where going girl?"

I shook my head. Which earned me a jab with prod. My body bucked and convulsed. The jolt raced through every nerve in my body. I held back the scream that rose in my throat.

"No screaming sound. You strong. For now. You want another poke for dessert?"

His partner raised the weapon and I said no.

"You learning. I say question, you say answer. Always say answer. This simple asking is rule number one. Your name Brodie Jim?"

"Yes."

"Where going girl?"

"I don't know."

"Rule number two. No lie. Speaking lie bringing shock. Where girl going?"

"I don't know."

With the next charge, my bones seemed to rattle as my body thrashed about on the steel tabletop, straining against the shackles. Still I didn't scream.

The tall spokesman grinned. "You strong strong man. We changing that soon. Where going girl?"

"I'm not sure."

"Clever answer. Maybe true one. But no answer I like. You know name this table?"

"No."

"Death Bed. Why you think it call Death Bed?"

"It's not friendly, like you."

His perpetual grin stretched. "You give much clever answer, Brodie Jim. For that I tell you. Many men die on it. Even strong men."

"I see."

"Soon you see more."

He nodded at his shorter companion, who touched the prod between my ribs and held it there. My eyes bulged. Consciousness flickered. Then the electricity was withdrawn and the questioning began in earnest. They asked about how I'd arrived in China. What time? What airline? How many of us? Then they backed off and asked about previous trips. When, where, how. They were training me. Coaxing me into the habit of answering.

The tall one nodded and grinned as I answered. The grin never fully disappeared. It shrank or lengthened, like a rubber band between a child's fingers.

The stream of questions continued. As long as I supplied an answer, they spared the baton. Initially they didn't call me on my answers. They were establishing what passes for a rapport in their world. But inevitably the questioning circled back around to Anna Tanaka and her escape route. Inevitably I gave them answers they didn't like and received shocks that sent my body into spasms. The manacles carved rings into my wrist and ankles.

Still I swallowed the pain and again my grinning torturer said, "You strong man."

The appraising gleam in his eye caused me to revise my strategy.

I was in peak physical condition, my core strength firm. They would work to break it down. My pain threshold was high, but I decided I could hide behind the illusion of pain. When they came at me again, I started with low moans I seemed unable to contain, then gradually worked myself into screaming mode. My dramatics lowered the bar of my perceived pain threshold, which pleased the morose one and gave the pair a sense of progress. Which meant they were less likely to amp up the power of the juice stick. So far the shocks only jarred my nervous system. There were no burns or blisters. Which gave me a buffer zone. But, even so, I eventually sank into unconsciousness.

On the second day they doubled down and my buffer zone vanished.

Whenever I threatened to fade away, they slapped me back to consciousness. When brute force stopped working, they brought out smelling salts, then sharp needles. They continued to pummel me with questions about Anna, which meant the authorities had yet to find her.

The thought sustained me even as the continual electric treatment depleted my strength.

They upped the voltage and the smell of burning flesh seeped out from under my prison garb. Now the blisters would come. In stages, every nerve ending in my body went numb. My insides seemed to hollow out. Eventually my mind emptied out. I went to a place I'd never been. A place none of my previous trials had ever taken me.

I'd found a way station. A place where torture victims went to hide. I grew delusional. They carried on. Questions, shocks, slaps, needles, repeat. But their efforts penetrated less and less. Hallucinations began to dominate my conscious moments.

This was my mind seeking to cope. Clawing about desperately in an effort to protect me. Playing tricks to mask the pain. It had shifted into survival mode in the hope of whisking me off to a place my torturers couldn't reach.

They found it.

———

I woke in my cell, on a one-inch-thick mattress with a blanket draped over my legs. The mattress was bare and stained with blood. Only some of it was mine.

A cracked plastic tray rested on the cement floor next to the bed. It offered up half a bowl of white rice and a cup of weak green tea.

The room was a replica of the torture room, down to the drain in the center. A low steel bed frame replaced the torture table, and a slop bucket stood in for the shelving. In a back corner a hand towel hung on a nail, over a water bucket. That was all.

I ate the rice and drank the tea and relieved myself, then crawled back into bed and slept. Soon after, I heard the cover of the peephole in the iron door slide back and snap shut. Then they came for me.

It had been a mistake to eat.

They strapped me on to the Death Bed and pounded me with questions about Anna. About our arrival, about our escape route, about the clothes she wore. The questioning was incessant and grew more insistent. The rice came up during the second round of shock treatment. Both men laughed. The tall one leered at me. His grinning countenance hovered over me. He began a new round of questions, rephrasing them, approaching the same subjects from different angles. I gave a verbal response each time and yelled with each dispensation of pain—whether electric or needle.

As long as they kept asking about Anna, I knew she, Pak, and Noda had not been captured. At least four days and conceivably as long as six, Pak had said.

Anna Tanaka was a highly desired target, so Pak had activated a plan usually reserved to extract top-level North Korean political defectors. The strategy would get her out of Changbai, even during a period of high alert, but from that point forward the length of her extraction from China depended on the intensity of the search.

When I next woke, I was back in my room, with no memory of being moved. I'd lost all sense of time and place and being. A bright display of high-intensity lights had dragged me back to consciousness. The original sixty-watt bulb was now outflanked by three rows of corn-yellow floodlights. They robbed the room of darkness and robbed me of the comforting blanket of blackness behind closed eyelids. I lost the ability to sleep soundly.

My days were filled with torture sessions and restless intervals in my cell followed by feverish stretches of sleep. I fought a constant battle with fatigue. My mind deserted me for increasingly longer periods. Every time I woke, my body throbbed in new places, some of them places I didn't know could hurt.

By my count, Anna needed at least one more day.

Three at most.

I wasn't sure I could hold out.

CHAPTER 81

O N day four, they deprived me of all food and drink.

There were no windows in the underground complex, and no clocks. But I'd figured out a way to count the days. Or, more precisely, the mornings. I knew another twenty hours had passed when my torturers arrived clean-shaven.

I needed to make it to six days . . .

They stripped off my jersey. They pulled the chains anchoring the ankle and wrist irons tighter so that when I thrashed around after a shock treatment, the steel manacles cut deeper. I was weakening. I passed out more frequently, often self-induced. Something in my decreased capacity allowed me to flip the switch.

My captors had seen the trick before, and when their initial revival methods yielded diminishing returns, the injections began—a series of ever-stronger stimulants to jump-start the heart and jolt me awake.

My physical stamina slid downhill. The floodlights in my cell stayed on around the clock. The temperature in the room hovered around ninety-five degrees. Sweat poured out of me. Which increased my thirst. Water was withheld. So was food. They woke me at odd hours, dragged me into the torture chamber, then threw me back in my cell. Then the routine changed. They marched me to a new interrogation chamber and threw me in a chair. A glass of water and a plate of food sat on a table just out of reach.

While the morose one hovered nearby, the tall one pointed at the meal. "Your salvation, Brodie Jim. Where going girl?"

"I don't know."

They tossed me back into my cell with force. The moment I dropped off to sleep, they hauled me back to the interrogation room. The glass of water remained but the food had been removed.

"Food no more, Brodie Jim. Where going girl?"

"I don't know."

The perpetual grinner stepped aside. I expected the prod but his moody partner held a knife in his hand.

"Girl?" he asked. His English was limited.

"No."

He pushed the knifepoint into my right thigh maybe an eighth of an inch and I grunted in pain.

"Girl?"

"No."

He inserted the blade an additional quarter of an inch and I howled.

"Girl?"

"No."

When the morose one flashed me a grin for the first time, I knew trouble was coming. The knife went deeper, then he rotated the blade in the wound. My scream rose to decibels I'd never before reached. My leg jerked up and knocked the knife from his grasp. I passed out. I woke up in my cell, lying on the cement floor. The mattress, bed frame, and blanket had been removed.

The glaring floodlights above baked me, while below the cement leeched all the heat from my body. Curling up for warmth, I dropped into a fitful sleep. Next, the door banged open and a strong spray of water hit my body, then the walls and floor were hosed down. The floodlights were extinguished and the dousing continued all around me until the temperature dropped. They trucked in wheelbarrows of ice and dumped them over me. Whenever I crawled out from under one pile, they brought in another. The room temperature plunged. The iron door creaked shut. In the darkness and the cold, I began to shiver. As I drifted away, I wondered where Anna was now. Consciousness faded.

At least four days and conceivably as long as six . . .

Pak's plan was ingenious. Anna would be given a chest wrap for "bosom flattening."

"Was mother big in front her chest?" he'd asked.

"No, typically proportioned," I said.

"Thas good."

From the photo I'd passed over to him in Seoul, an artist sketched her as a man, without makeup, long lashes, and shaped eyebrows, then they sought and found a male look-alike. They paid him a fee, applied light makeup, trimmed his eyebrows, and took passport photographs. In the safe house, Pak would cut Anna's hair and dress her in secondhand men's clothing from Seoul. He'd named a price for the passport, the model, and the services he and his organization would supply from beginning to end and I agreed without hesitation.

Replaying Pak's plan gave me some comfort in my more lucid moments, which grew infrequent. More often I was delusional. The earlier hallucinations came on more vividly. Thirst cracked my lips. My throat grew parched and brittle. Somewhere in the back of my mind I recalled that a person can live without food for up to three weeks, but only a week without water. Before I passed out yet again I remembered I was surrounded by melting ice. With what little strength remained, I licked up the water trickling over the cement toward the drain. I passed out before my thirst was sated.

Nightmares and flashbacks and fragments of dreams appeared in a whirlwind of disconnected images and voices. Jenny and Renna and Noda and Rie spoke in turns. I heard Jenny triumphant over her victory in the judo dojo. Renna grumbling about spooks. Noda reluctant to leave me behind. Rie begging me not to go.

I woke up with Rie's plea ringing in my ears and my teeth chattering.

Was this what she'd seen in her nightmare?

The chill of the room grabbed hold of me. I was shivering and dizzy. I lay in a small pool of my own blood from the wound in my thigh. Some of it mingled with the water trickling toward the drain. I lapped up more water and tasted blood and grit. I looked down at my leg. Untreated, the gash still bled.

My captors had been sloppy or lazy.

I reached for my blanket before remembering it had been carted away with the mattress. The towel hanging over the water bucket had vanished with the water supply. My shirt had disappeared earlier. At some moment I couldn't recall, I'd been stripped of my pants as well. I peeled off the plain white boxers I wore. With my teeth, I tore them in half and knotted one part above the cut to suppress the circulation. I gritted my teeth against the pain as I positioned the second piece over the wound, losing consciousness when I started to draw it tight.

When I next woke, I was still naked on the wet cement floor. The water coming off the melting piles of ice sluiced around me. My body convulsed. I developed the shakes. The bleeding had lessened but not stopped. Gingerly, and with trembling fingers, I adjusted the wrap and managed to stem the leakage without losing consciousness.

The mattress . . . the blanket . . . the towel . . .

Fading body heat . . . cold cement floor . . . blood loss . . .

"Lazy" was not part of the equation.

Letting me bleed out had been added to the agenda.

Someone had decided it was time for me to die.

CHAPTER 82

THEN the torture ceased.

The questions about Anna ceased.

The ice was hauled away and my bed and blanket were restored.

My wounds were treated.

Ointment was applied and bandages affixed.

I outlasted them, I thought.

But the idea turned out to be another delusion.

They were readying me for the next stage.

Two guards escorted me to the shower room, gave me a bar of grainy soap and a ragged towel with faded bloodstains, and informed me I had five minutes to clean up.

I washed and scrubbed every uninjured area thoroughly, then soaped up my hands and ran them gingerly over the tender spots, which constituted most of my body. Next, I lathered up the soap and shampooed my hair with the suds. I was soaping up my legs for a second time when the spray stopped.

"Not done yet," I called.

"Time is done. This no hotel."

"Too bad. I wouldn't mind checking out."

"You funny man, Brodie Jim. You no checkout." They laughed. "Is one-way only."

"For some."

"No no, Brodie Jim. You here, you stay. Joining Bone Room is end."

Bone Room?

They led me to a new chamber.

It had carpeting and air-conditioning. They nodded me toward a table and chair in the center of the room. The chair was padded. Not hardwood or steel. Sinking into the cushioned comfort felt like heaven. After days of trotting barefoot on hard cement, the soft carpeting underfoot felt like a massage against my soles. The cool air brushed across my skin with the gentleness of a cat against my leg. I wanted to stay there forever.

"Nice room," I said.

"Yes, good treatment for you. You lucky."

My eyes darted to a glass of water and a plate of vegetables on a desk beyond reach but plainly visible. The sauce looked like oyster.

"Nice view too."

My stomach growled. I could no more stop the reaction than I could prevent my glance from straying toward the victuals.

"You see food?"

"Of course."

"You want?"

"Of course."

"You sign, you eat. All go easy. You be free."

He slid a paper in front of me and set down a pen beside it. I squinted at the sheet with my one good eye. The other had closed up during the last beating. I wondered what my captor's definition of *free* was. He didn't say in his butchered English *You'll go free* or *You'll be free to go.* The phrase he used could include death by firing squad or hanging. Or execution in any form. In some people's minds, that was a kind of freedom.

"What happens after?"

"First eat."

"After that?"

"You drink."

I tried a different approach. "What does the paper say?"

"You know what it say."

"I don't read Chinese."

"You read Japanese and they are many similar. Japanese stole Chinese writing system, you know."

He was right, up to a point. Centuries ago the Japanese adapted the Chinese system to their own purposes. They selected the characters that suited their way of life, then, over time, refined and simplified them. They devised new compounds and characters to express Japanese concepts. They developed two additional alphabets to be used in combination with the characters. The end result was two writing systems that were more like distant cousins living in distant lands: they shared an ancestry of some fifty generations past but were distinct and independent of one another.

"*Stole* might not be the right word."

"It is."

"I can't read it."

"In your heart you know what it say because you guilty."

"Of what?"

"You American spy. You conspire to People Republic of China. You guilty, you sign."

"So it's a confession?"

"It is your truth giving. Just give your name and you can eat and drink."

Throughout China, police routinely force confessions with repeated torture sessions. By law, or the inference of the law, confession proves guilt. After signing, the downhill slide is swift and irreversible. It starts with a trial behind closed doors. Without press or reportage of any kind. The right to a lawyer is not automatic, especially to an outsider like me.

"How about I tell you where the girl is heading instead?"

He waved the idea away. "We no more want."

I hid my excitement. Pak had succeeded in spiriting Anna safely away.

His expression softening, the grinning one said, "You must repent. Sign and all go easy."

"I repent."

"Good. You sign, you eat."

He nudged the pen closer.

"I repent. Tell your boss."

"You must sign."

"And then?"

"You eat and drink."

"I know that."

"You are spy."

"I'm not a spy."

"You are spy."

"Does it say I'm a spy?"

"Yes, of course."

"And if I sign?"

"You have trial."

"So I'll get a lawyer?"

"Why you need lawyer? You spy. You guilty. Paper say you guilty, so all finish."

"That doesn't sound easier to me. You promised easier."

"You can eat."

"Not a fair deal."

"You get no more torture."

"That's a start. I need to know how I get out of here."

"You get out but no checkout. We already say."

"I don't understand."

"You are spy."

"I am *not* a spy."

"You are spy. We shoot you soon."

"I don't think so. You stopped the torture. You treated my wounds. You allowed me to shower."

The grinning man translated my last volley for his moody partner, which led to a long round of shared merriment. It was several minutes before their laughter subsided.

"You funny man, Brodie Jim. I think time we visit you Bone Room."

CHAPTER 83

I WAS lost for words.

Behind a floor-to-ceiling wall of glass was an unending stockpile of human skulls and ribs and legs and hands and all the remaining parts of the skeleton. Bones filled every square inch of the chamber to the top. They were bare and bleached with age. They had long ago been separated, either naturally or forcibly, from any restraining ligament, tendon, or other tissue that had once held them together.

"This oldest room," my captor said in my ear, his eyes bright, the grin as wide as it could stretch.

He shoved me toward the next full-length window. Another room as densely packed as the first. In all, we visited twenty-three rooms of human remains—underground chambers the world knew nothing about. Room after room of a grotesque hoard, each gruesome collection a shade darker in tone than the last, as if the chain of chambers represented a march from absolute death toward life, but stopping cruelly short.

"What think Brodie Jim?"

I shook my head. No words would come. Viewing the secret storehouse drained me. How many thousands had been dragged off to this underground house of horrors before me? My captors intended the visit to crush my spirit, if not my will. I wouldn't fall prey to their ploy, but the effect of the Bone Room, with the cumulative impact of the torture and pain and unending circular conversations I'd endured, took its toll. I'd guessed wrong. My jailers' persecution had not ceased. The attack simply came from a different angle.

"You lucky man, Brodie Jim. Because your bone go in special room at end. You want see?"

"No, thanks." There was a thick, gravelly texture to my words.

He shrugged. "No matter. Bone Room is your resting home."

"There will be calls for my release."

The White House would apply pressure, as well as the State Department and the American embassy in Beijing. And Brodie Security would bring heat through Japanese channels.

"Already many call about you but you no checkout."

"Then your bosses haven't gotten the big call yet."

"We got many big call. We got call from your Slater Joe, American president."

"Good, so we're done here."

"Yes, Brodie Jim. You sign. All done. All go easy."

"You just said—"

"Is true, you friend with your America president?"

"Yes."

"So you spy."

"No."

"Why you know Slater Joe?"

"I just do. It doesn't matter. But if the White House contacted your government, then you will be releasing me soon. That's why you cleaned me up. That's why you stopped the torture. Getting me to sign a confession is a last-minute trick."

Over his ever-present grin, the tall one's eyes began to dance. He translated my latest comments and the two men fell into another fit of mutual laughter.

"Your spirit is high, Brodie Jim. Very good for spy but no help you."

"I'm not a spy."

"All was heard from your American president Slater Joe and all rejected by our president."

"That's impossible."

"It is truth giving."

"Your bluff has no meat."

The two men huddled, whispered between themselves, then separated. "We no understand 'no meat.' Sign confession and all go easy. You can eat and drink and die. We feed you beef too. I give pain pill. Bonus for you because I like you, Brodie Jim. Your spirit is high. With pain pill you no feel death visit. But you must no tell about pill. They secret."

"You can't hold me. Anna Tanaka has left the country. I freed a kidnapped woman your people wanted to abduct again. The story is out there now."

"Girl no matter no more."

"This is revenge for what you couldn't get."

The tall one cocked his head and huddled again with his partner. After a brief exchange he said, "Revenge not for missing girl. Revenge for two honorable Chinese family."

"You're making no sense."

"You pretend no guilty again. No matter. You die. You eat and drink and die, or just die. No matter."

"Why? I haven't done anything."

"Two honorable Chinese people dead in Changbai."

I froze. He was talking about the pair of traffickers whose throats Pak had slit with such precision. Zhou had mentioned them but I'd assumed his comments were meant as leverage to get me to reveal Anna's location.

"You can't tie me to them."

"You crazy man, Brodie Jim. Your group kill them. Your Slater Joe no can help murder of two honorable Chinese people. You go Bone Room. No checkout."

"You're lying. You allowed me to shower. You bandaged me up. What's really going on?"

He tapped the glass again. "No lying. You spy, you guilty, we shoot. You go in special Bone Room for foreigner. Party decide yesterday. We send fake bone for America."

"No trial?"

"Yes, trial. But you spy, you guilty, you go bye-bye. We make you clean for killing photography. We send photo and fake bone to embassy. You cannot look messy when we make photo. You see? You dead but you *clean* dead. You lucky."

CHAPTER 84

THE next morning a pair of guards I'd never seen led me back to the old interrogation room. For a brief moment I held out hope for a shift change, but the grinning man strolled in on the heels of the guards, shaking his head. "You no lucky like I thought, Brodie Jim."

"Why's that?"

"Beijing want your signing. You sign now?"

"No."

"You sign, we shoot, all over. No more pain. Better for you, you sign."

"No."

His morose partner produced the blade he'd used to carve a hole in my leg and at knifepoint backed me up until my heels hit the cement wall. He gestured for me to face the wall, and when I did, he leapt forward and with a snicker planted the point of his blade against the base of my neck while his taller partner fit my wrists into shackles hanging overhead.

"See? No lucky." His breath was laced with ginger and fennel.

I said, "I thought you needed me clean."

"You sign now?"

"No."

Morose walked over to the shelves and pulled a long stick off the top shelf, returned, and shoved the end of the implement under my nose. I craned my neck for a better look. It was a six-foot-long, three-inch-thick wooden rod encased in a quarter inch of black rubber.

"You know?" the tall one said.

"No."

"Hurting much but no mark leaving. Clean hurting, so clean picture. You sign now? I give pain pill."

"I don't think so."

"Beijing want sign. You unlucky, Brodie Jim."

They started from the bottom and worked their way up. Calves, thighs, buttocks, back, shoulders. No bones, no joints. Just tissue and muscle and sinew, over and over, as if pounding out the toughness in bad beef.

I lost consciousness in the middle of round three, when the moody one, mumbling something uncomplimentary in Chinese, took out his frustration with a home-run swing to my upper thighs.

This time, I thought as the blackness swooped in, *I might not make it back.*

———

Hardened heels stormed down the concrete corridor outside my door. A loud, insistent voice broke through my death sleep. Keys jangled in the hall. The next instant the barrier was flung open.

Five men swept into the room, among them a new figure in a navy suit, red tie, and highly polished black patent leather shoes with the rock-like heels I'd heard. Gathered around him were my two tormentors and a pair of guards. The grinning one snapped at the suited man in the red tie, who brushed the comment away with a disdainful wave. My tormentors stomped out. The man in the suit issued a sharp order and the two guards bowed and scurried away.

I was alone with the stranger.

He nudged me with the tip of a shiny black leather shoe. "Stand up, prisoner. I am here to escort you to the execution grounds."

When I didn't move, he poked me harder. "You are able to stand, are you not?"

"For the right reasons."

"I could have you beaten some more. How would that do?"

"If I am to be shot, what do I care?"

"There is ample time between now and tomorrow morning to inflict so much more pain, you will march gratefully to your own death. Do not tempt me."

His English was impeccable, with a European accent I couldn't place.

"The same answer applies. Besides, I haven't signed anything."

"I have orders. No more waiting. Your signature will be forged."

"Hard to do."

"A sample has been found."

"The president's people will know."

"The Western signature is a flighty, inconsistent thing."

This was an educated man. His English was grammatical and nuanced and had flair. I'd narrowed the accent to Swedish or Swiss.

"American experts will come down on the negative side."

He shrugged. "Then the games begin. Our experts will deny and qualify. There will be talk of stress and other contributing factors. But since the document will not be produced until long after you have been executed, the verbal tug-of-war will be pointless. Your politicians will soon lose interest. They will move on. They always do."

Which, unfortunately, was true, especially when it came to overseas negotiations.

"I won't go easily."

"Do as you wish. Nothing would give my superiors and myself more pleasure than to levy additional punishment on an enemy of the State." The man reached into his jacket and pulled out a Chinese-made Norinco pistol. "Or I may just shoot you myself, here and now. Then we will film the execution of another prisoner who resembles you from a distance. The film will be grainy, the camera unsteady."

"You've thought of everything."

"More than you will ever know. So listen to me carefully and do exactly as I say and we will both survive this process with far fewer irritants. When they bring you a fresh prison outfit, you will change and allow yourself to be handcuffed. And then we shall leave for the execution grounds."

"And if I should refuse to budge?"

The man stiffened. Towering over my bent and battered form, he fell seriously silent. Eventually he said, "I was warned you might be feisty."

"Good for you."

He cocked an ear toward the exterior passage. He heard no approaching footfalls. Maybe he would shoot me now and claim assault or a misfire.

Instead he amazed me by doing the unexpected.

Careful to stay beyond striking distance, he crouched down and said in a low voice, "I was given a message for you. A certain mutual acquaintance requests that you join me without delay or he may never have the pleasure of sitting down at Gary Danko with you for a full-course meal."

CHAPTER 85

THE guards returned with fresh prison garb.

I dressed, succumbing to a fit of dizziness with the effort and falling back against the cell wall for support. The three men looked on without comment. One of the guards told me to stop fooling around.

I was handcuffed and directed to a conference room with eight chairs around an oblong table and a framed photograph of the president of China. The man in the suit snapped out another order. The guards produced a second pair of manacles and secured my ankles to the legs of the chair. Tea for one was brought and I watched my self-proclaimed patron drink it.

As soon as the guards left, the man checked his watch. "Now we wait."

"For?"

I still had no absolute proof the new player seated across from me was on my side. A reference to a San Francisco restaurant did not suffice as sufficient credentials.

He looked at me for a long moment, then sighed. "The deputy warden here belongs to Chen, the man I am impersonating."

"You're impersonating someone?"

His brow darkened. "The guards may return any second, so listen, don't talk. My disguise has one flaw. The look is perfect but I could not maintain a conversation with the deputy warden for long, so we must not meet face-to-face. Fortunately, he is systematic and predictable, and we've been able to keep my visit a secret, though he could still hear of it." Zhou's emissary glanced at his timepiece again. "Duty comes first. He finishes his rounds in eight minutes and will receive a call in ten minutes.

The call should keep him occupied until we have left and before he can come looking for me."

"Will he be arrested?"

"If this plays out successfully, most certainly."

"He will protest."

Zhou's supposed surrogate smiled. "The more the better. Everyone is guilty in China once they are accused, especially those who protest the loudest."

"The innocent ones."

"You know our system well."

"Your English is excellent."

"I studied in Switzerland."

"You studied well."

"I accomplished many things there," he said, giving me a cryptic look. Then he changed course: "Can you act?"

"Passably."

"I need you to try to escape. Two times would be preferable. Once in the hall near the gate, and a second time when we return to the surface. Never mind about the feasibility. You should resist in a convincing manner. Can you do that for me?"

"That kind of acting comes naturally."

His look turned grave. "Now the hard part. I need you to resist in such a way as you are . . . punished severely."

"Are you serious?"

"Yes. Our lives may depend on your performance. The better your acting the less our departure will be questioned or examined later. I wish my story to hold until we are well out of range."

After the beating with the rubberized rod, I wasn't sure how much more pain I could stand. No bones had been broken or fractured, but the muscles and tendons were approaching dysfunctional.

"Is that really necessary? You look the part. You sound convincing."

"Attempted escapes will allay the doubts of the skeptical. Your effort will be an additional layer of obfuscation to this charade."

"Was I really to be executed tomorrow?"

"You still are."

———

We made our way up to the upper level of the prison.

The heady mildew scent lessened noticeably. Ahead stood the white iron grille I'd seen on the first day and the long tunnel leading to the basement of the farmhouse. My nostrils flared in anticipation of breathing untainted air.

"Chen" took the lead position. His crisp steps echoed down the corridor. The senior-most guard followed a pace behind, then me, with two young guards bringing up the rear. There were too many of them. The idea of a staged escape attempt was a bad one. My hands were still handcuffed behind my back. Favoring the leg with the knife wound, my limp was prominent.

Chen paused and said something to the guard detail, then he turned to me. "Deport yourself with dignity, Mr. Brodie, and your last hours shall be handled with equal decorum."

I flashed him a look of unbridled disdain.

At the gate, Chen accompanied the senior guard into the office, where papers and a red ink pad were produced. Chen pulled a cloth pouch from his pocket, extracted a marble chop, inked it, and stamped the document. I inched forward. Chen lingered to talk with the gateman while he wiped the residual ink from the end of his chop with a tissue. The senior guard unlocked the iron barrier in preparation for our departure. I stepped forward, rammed an elbow into his ribs, and took off.

I envisioned racing to the end of the hall and possibly as far as the basement steps, but my injured leg only made it five paces before it began to liquefy. Shouts rose up behind me. Footsteps pounded the concrete in my wake. Five seconds later one of the pursuers brought me down with a flying tackle. In the distance, the brisk footfalls of Chen's patent leathers clacked on the cement.

The next instant he loomed over me, his face a ball of fury. He aimed his gun at my head. Had I been played? Had I just given him a reason to put a bullet in my skull?

He was cursing in Chinese. A long, fluid string. Some of which I understood. Then he began flinging orders. The guards jumped up and saluted.

They pulled me to my feet. Chen snapped out another order and the closest guard plowed a fist into my stomach. I doubled over and hit the floor again. They began kicking me as the police in Changbai had done. Only then I hadn't previously sustained a systematic pummeling with a rubber-coated bat. When I curled up in a protective ball this time, the blows struck the sensitive areas along my back and legs. A wave of unbearable pain subsumed me. I howled. No acting required.

I waited for my newfound benefactor to step in but he never did.

———

I regained consciousness as they were lugging me across the farmyard. For the trek to the car, my restraints had been removed. They dragged me forward like a sack of rice, a guard in farmer's garb at each arm, the tops of my bare feet scraping the dirt.

They flung me into the back of another tangerine-orange Geely GC5 as battered and dusty as the one I'd arrived in. The eye in the sky would see it as the same car. Very clever. Same model, same plate number, different machine. Matching vehicles gave the Chinese authorities the ability to send prisoners from locations around the country with ease. As long as the traffic to and from the Farmhouse was regulated to avoid suspicion.

My escort slipped in beside me. He slapped shackles around my ankles and handcuffs on my wrists, then we hit the road. Once more the car shook and rattled and wove its way between rocks and potholes. Zhou's representative began speaking in a soft voice that didn't carry above the racket. "You were convincing."

"I missed the second act."

"You did such a good job, an encore performance was not required."

"If it gives us some extra time, it will be worth it. Why is our mutual acquaintance doing this?"

"He has his reasons and will explain when he is ready."

"When might that be?"

"The timing is delicate." He nodded toward the police radio in the console. "As you can see, we can still be called back at any moment."

"And if we are?"

"Assuming we are not shot where we sit, I will be detained and you will be returned to the prison and executed tomorrow morning, on schedule."

CHAPTER 86

WE returned down the same dusty dirt road, no doubt rolling over many of the same potholes.

The jostling sent stabbing pains to the tender parts of my body, the number of which could not be counted on the fingers of two hands. I closed my eyes and bore the suffering in silence as the car bucked and bobbed. I drew substantial comfort from the knowledge that every bump in the road took us farther from the Farmhouse.

The car radio crackled and my eyes flew open. I glanced sideways at Chen. He wouldn't meet my gaze.

The rattling of the chassis and the gritty rumble of the tires prevented us from hearing what was said. Would Chen use his gun if the tide turned? No, I decided, but I would, if given the chance to grab it. I was not going back.

The cop in the driver's seat said something to Chen, whose retort was acerbic and accompanied by a wry smile. The three of them laughed.

"What?" I said.

"The prison staff is asking about the personal effects you left behind. I told them an enemy of the State had no right to any possessions and they should burn them and send the ashes to America.

"Will they?"

"Of course not. They will sell everything and divide the cash."

In front of the colossal penitentiary with the mile-long walls we rejoined the paved roadway. The ride evened out and the constant stabbing aches from the rocking car gave way to a dull throbbing of muscles and nerves too frequently abused of late.

Forty-five minutes later we entered a small town, pulled into a lot next to a gas station, and stopped alongside an official-looking black sedan with a government license plate. Chen affixed his chop to a second set of papers and thanked the policemen in overalls. Before driving off, the most senior of them noted the license plate on our ride, nodded a last time at Chen, then dropped behind the wheel, and guided the Geely out of the lot. We stepped into the waiting vehicle and hit the road.

"Aren't they worried about leaving you without a guard?"

"You are cuffed hand and foot, and I have a gun."

"What about the car plates? The cop took a good look."

He gave me a tight grin. "They are copies of Chen's plates."

"So we're safe?"

"No. We have a long way to go."

"China Rules?"

"Unhappily, yes."

We rode in silence until we reached the highway. Meanwhile, I considered the idea of China Rules inside China and felt nearly as vulnerable as I had in prison. *If you want to live a long life, trust no one or no thing. Not Party, country, friend, or sky.*

"What is it you do normally?" I asked.

Outside, endless high-plains scrubland stretched to the horizon in every direction.

"Oh, I am a mere cog."

"What kind of cog?"

"A humble servant of the people. Of no importance."

"And your day job?"

"I work for the Chinese post office." My face collapsed. Chen caught my disappointment and said, "I clean up pretty good, don't you think? I am a manager and supervise seventeen people. Does that reassure you?"

"That depends. Have you ever fired that gun you have under your coat?"

"On a range, yes."

"Ever shoot anyone?"

"No."

"And if we were, say, pulled over by a patrol that had orders to take us back to the Farmhouse, would you shoot them?"

"Certainly not. Weren't you listening? I work for the post office."

As we drove, the stark high-plains emptiness gradually gave way to swaying fields of rice, corn, and soy. With hours yet to go before we reached the Mongolian border, I slept through the first roadside stop.

When I woke an hour later, I noticed my escort looked different. He had re-combed his hair. No, that wasn't right. His hair broke differently and it was of a coarser texture. He'd removed a wig.

But that wasn't the end of his transformation. I was looking at the same man who was somehow not the same at all, but I didn't understand why.

"Aside from the hair, what else has changed?" I asked.

Chen smiled at me via the rearview mirror. "Good, isn't it?"

"Yes, but why?"

"I took off makeup."

"You weren't wearing any."

"Oh, but I was. Light and subtle and hard to detect in normal situations, impossible in poorly lit places like the Farmhouse. I studied for six months under an expert."

Unmasked, he bore only the faintest resemblance to the man he had impersonated. I searched with diligence to uncover similarities. The building blocks were there but needed to be assembled in a precise fashion to be effective. Diabolical and clever beyond belief.

"Why are you doing this?" I asked, still concerned about his trustworthiness and the master spy's ultimate plan.

"I am helping my cousin."

"Zhou?"

"Yes."

"Why?"

"I owe him."

"How?"

Skepticism guided my questioning. I worried about our direction.

Were we really headed toward the border? Town names came up on the road signage, in Chinese and occasionally in English, but—this being China—no mention of Mongolia appeared anywhere. We could be en route to the execution ground, for all I knew.

"Ten years ago my cousin happened to notice I bore a similar facial structure to one of his most dangerous opponents. I also had a cleft palate. Even without the deformity, I was an ugly man. Zhou offered to pay for an operation."

"And for your education in Switzerland?"

His look grew cautious. "You are a thoughtful man, but yes."

"Why would you allow him to change you like that? Fixing the cleft palate I understand, but do you look anything like you used to?"

"There is a hint of my heritage. He first sent me to South Korea, where some of the best plastic surgeons in Asia practice. Then to Switzerland. Now I have a beautiful wife. Before the operation, I never once dated a woman or was considered eligible material for matchmaking. Women could not stand to look at me."

"So you wanted a wife?"

"Having a normal family life was all I asked for, but over the years my cousin provided three million more reasons in an overseas bank account in my name. American reasons."

"Very generous."

"He can be that way."

I thought about the time frame. "This was ten years ago?"

"There is a Chinese saying: 'The best time to plant a tree was twenty years ago. The second best time is now.'"

"I know it."

"We Chinese always plan ahead."

His comment only served to increase my disquiet.

Chen swung onto an exit ramp. "We are making a slight detour."

"Anything you want to tell me?"

My ears popped. We'd climbed to a higher altitude. Grazing lands had dislodged tilled fields.

"You are in for some changes."

I stiffened but said nothing.

At the top of the ramp, the road curled to the left. We drove for a mile. A forest of Mongolian oak and pine sprang up on both sides of the road. Chen slid the sedan behind an abandoned cabin, beckoned me to follow, and stepped crisply from the car. I trailed after him with caution. Practically speaking, I remained a prisoner. Chen had removed my restraints once we'd left our police escort behind, but that meant nothing. As he had pointed out, I couldn't make it far on my own.

We entered through a back door. The cabin was old and drafty and unoccupied. Sweeping up a box of matches on a countertop, Chen lit a candle in the center of a rickety wooden table. The candle illuminated a kitchen strung with cobwebs and a faded photograph of Chairman Mao pinned to a wall.

"No electricity," my guide said.

Two brown bags awaited us on the table. Chen passed one to me. "Blond hair dye. Mix the two tubes in equal amounts, work it into your hair, then rinse in twenty minutes. There is a false moustache in there too. Dye it as well."

"All right."

"In the shower room you will find three buckets of water. That's all we have. I will have a set of clean clothes waiting."

"And what will you do in the meantime?"

He rubbed his cheeks. "I will certainly shave, for one. Now you must go. Time is short."

So I went and did as instructed. When I returned, slung over the back of a chair I found a pair of generic jeans and a knockoff powder-blue Ralph Lauren polo shirt with the apricot-orange logo over the left breast.

Chen wore a new suit. Black with a pressed white shirt and a pewter-gray tie. His hair was oiled, parted on the opposite side, and brushed back at the front. On the table rested a chauffeur's hat and a pair of pearl-white gloves.

Just outside the circle of candlelight sat another man.

"Blond works," a familiar voice said. "Get dressed. We have much to discuss and little time to do so."

CHAPTER 87

WE returned to the road.

Zhou and I settled into the backseat. Chen, in a second transformation, had slipped on the hat and gloves then slid behind the wheel.

The master spy checked his watch. "My alibi needs maintaining and we need to finalize your disappearance."

He was again speaking Japanese.

"A minor detour before we begin," I said. "Convince me you aren't carting me off to put a bullet in my head elsewhere. Not that you'd be able to pull it off."

Zhou nodded. "'An enemy well regarded is better than a friend you doubt.' Do you remember that?"

"Yes, a favorite of yours."

"An original."

"I stand corrected. What about it?"

"You, my friend, are the enemy."

My eyebrows shot up but I said nothing. Rather, I took a moment to consider his pet phrase in my current situation. Put another way, the slogan laid claim to the idea that a principled enemy could be more reliable than a friend or acquaintance easily tempted. Zhou's axiom was about paranoia versus trust. About loyalty and virtue on the other side of the fence. It was about the political sharks in the political pool in which the master spy swam and made his living. It was about his eternal search for solid ground in a land of too much quicksand. If he actually meant what he said, it might just well be the most backhanded of backhanded praise.

"You're serious?"

"I am."

"I don't know what to say."

His smile was distracted. "Give it time. It is a compliment. Now can we move on?"

Once in a great while, among enemies, a meeting of minds can be reached. It is a rare thing. It happens when, beneath seemingly insurmountable differences in language or learning or history or culture, a human connection is made.

Zhou's expression was open and yielding. His words sounded heartfelt. But words are cheap. Free, in fact. Too many times people say one thing but do another. History is filled with victims who listened and accepted and lost.

If I made it to the border without him or one of his minions attempting to put a gun to my head, I would know he was sincere. And if he was sincere, I would be honored. That said, he had dropped me into the bottomless pit that was the Farmhouse. Then again, he'd pulled me out too. Flip it once more, and the turnabout was a brilliant way to recruit a reluctant asset. After all, Zhou was a trickster by trade.

Was this spycraft at its most sophisticated, or an olive branch?

It could swing either way, so I chose neutral ground.

"I'm all ears," I said.

The master spy had waited with impatience, his face taut, his eyes focused. "Excellent. Now, listen carefully. You will cross the border with Chen as your driver in five hours. Officially, Jim Brodie is on his way to a new execution site. All the right paperwork has been distributed. By tomorrow morning, when the execution does not take place, the news will be out. Until then, each prison thinks the other has you."

A vision of the Bone Room rose up in my mind and an involuntary shudder rattled me.

Zhou's glance was curious. "Are you okay?"

"Yes. Any problems ahead?"

"One. Someone or something could trigger an alarm. If this happens, then border guards will stop all Americans."

I stared at him. That seemed a major flaw in his escape plan, which was unlike the master manipulator I knew. "So you have a work-around?"

"Of course. You, my friend, are not American." Zhou handed me an Italian passport. "I think I came pretty close on short notice. I would prefer you a bit more swarthy. If they notice, just say your Mediterranean tan faded."

I opened the passport and was confronted with a thirty-something face of an Italian native by the name of Mario Fabbri. Zhou had indeed found a reasonable likeness. Six foot to my six-one. Broad shouldered, chiseled cheeks, high nose—all were a match. Or close enough.

Unfortunately, there were two glaring obstacles.

"The blond hair we took care of," I said. "The moustache I could have shaved, but he has steel-gray eyes and I have bruises and scabs on my face and an eye that is only half-open."

Zhou picked up a manila envelope on the seat between us. "Hospital reports of treatment for a minor accident you were involved in, in Beijing. Plus receipts. Chen will bandage the worst of your wounds. As for the gray eyes, you will find colored contacts in there as well."

"You've been thorough."

He ignored the comment. "A few last details and we are done here. Can you speak Italian?"

Alarm shot through me. "No."

"Say a few things in Italian, then?"

"A few phrases, sure. Will the border guards know some?"

"No more than 'Good afternoon' or 'Thank you,' which you can handle with a smile. Throw out an Italian word or two, then switch to English. But you must speak English with an Italian accent. *That* they will listen for. Drop the *h*'s and add *a*'s to the end of your words. Talk in a singsong voice. You must sound like this"—a light hum rose in his throat—"'Beijing was-a 'eavenly place-a.' Can you do that?"

"I'll manage."

"Manage or you will be back where you started. Now for the genius of the plan. You must not 'shave' your moustache. You must wear it and flaunt it. Display it proudly."

"Because?"

"We Chinese are fascinated by a full Western moustache. It is your true passport to safety."

"How so?"

"You'll see, trust me."

I nodded unhappily. I had little choice.

"So, finally, we are done," Zhou said, pleased at what he saw when he checked his watch.

"Far from it," I said.

WHY did you really get me out of prison?"

Zhou's brow darkened. "I told you. 'An enemy well regarded . . .'"

I waved my hand at his re-suited cousin in the front seat. "All this is elaborate. You didn't put it together overnight. What's changed?"

His eyes flared, angry at being caught out. "Again you see too much. I had planned to tell you later, but now will work if we hurry. I am fighting for survival and you are part of the solution."

Like China itself, the man across the seat from me possessed a strategic and complex way of thinking and was, at times, unfathomable.

"I need more."

"Three simple reasons. First, the man my cousin impersonated has attacked my faction but, with your escape, he is about to find himself taking your place. Second, you Americans need help, and in my modest way I am about to offer some. I live in a twisted world where everyone is a marionette controlled by a puppet master, who is controlled by another puppet master, all the way to the top."

"An interesting way to put it."

"It's the truth, though no one speaks it."

"I believe you."

"You already know my views about your people taking their freedom for granted. Losing freedom is losing half of the American dream. It is a dream people everywhere dream, including Chinese people. We are a good people, our government less so."

Coming from an insider within the Chinese governmental apparatus, that was quite a statement.

I said, "And you're going to help how?"

Dark, troubled eyes held mine. "You Americans are too cavalier about your freedoms. You are also too cavalier about China. That is my third reason. Have you heard about China's Hundred-Year Marathon?"

"I've heard the theory."

It is the alarming belief among some China watchers that the country, rather than seeking the "peaceful rise" it claims it wants, is actually engaged in a clandestine hundred-year plan to supplant all Western powers, especially American power, then replace them as number one and "harmonize" the world according to "superior" Chinese ideals. Key among the plan's components is a display of humility and complacency while China engages in an all-out grab for Western technological, military, and economic intelligence.

The plan also states that China can eventually achieve dominance when it has accumulated enough money, intel, and power. China watchers claim Chinese leaders are working toward this goal in hundreds of different ways with programs funded by the State, including cybertheft, the purchasing of industrial and technological secrets it can't steal, cornering the market on rare minerals and other valuable resources, buying influence in as many third-world countries as possible, and on and on.

The master spy wagged his head in disapproval. "You disappoint me, Brodie. It is no theory. It is operational."

"And you know this how?"

"Because a lot of it involves espionage."

The fire in his eyes was impossible to ignore. I was no longer looking into the hypnotizing orbs of a rattlesnake. Or the cold, dead beads of a shark on the prowl. For the first time in our many encounters, I was seeing the unadulterated passion of the man behind the spy.

"By the whole government or just a faction?"

"You ask the right question. It is being pushed by our *ying pai*. The right-wing nationalists. They have their hooks in some of the top leadership. Many others follow them willingly or are dragged along. It is not absolute but momentum is strong."

"I see."

"My point is simple. My country is moving chess pieces and your people do not even know they are in the game."

This last was a powerful image, hints of which I'd encountered on my Asian travels over the years.

"Okay," I said, "I'll give you that. And so?"

"Some of your leaders are aware of this. But they are not moving as fast as they should."

I nodded. "All good points I find easy to believe."

Zhou's look was triumphant. "Do you know why it is easy to believe? Because you and others in your government can sense it in your gut. They feel it, but they are confused because our leaders smile and bow and give in on the small things. Our leaders are clever. When an American or Western dignitary visits, my people often make small concessions, giving the visitor some minor triumph to take back home and wave in front of the people. These actions pull your instinctive feeling the other way. The Hundred-Year Marathon is why they wanted access to the NSA data. It would have cut ten years off the hundred. Now for a fourth reason, which I believe is the worst of all."

"Let's hear it."

"There's a dirty secret that frightens us Chinese to death."

Just then Zhou's cell phone rang. He looked at the screen, said he had to take the call, asked Chen to pull over, and stepped urgently from the car.

———

Chen and I looked at each other as we watched his cousin pace back and forth in front of a roadside rice paddy, out of earshot.

"What do you think it is?" I said.

"I don't know. We can only wait."

Which we did. The spy's voice grew louder but the words remained indistinct. Then he was finished and trotted back to the vehicle and jumped in.

"Is everything okay?" I asked.

"No." He turned to Chen, speaking in English for my benefit. "I have to get to a local government office to plug a leak if you two are going to make it to the border. How far are we from my car?"

"Less than fifteen minutes," Chen said.

"Get me there as fast as you can." The master spy turned to me. "We have until then. Where was I?"

"You were talking about the worst reason of all."

"Yes, that's right." His eyes clouded over. "There can be no China as number one."

I shot the master spy a skeptical look. "You have always struck me as a patriot."

"I am a thinking patriot, not a blind one. I love my country and my people and I want what most of my people want. Which is freedom. Our living standard is rising and people are living better. We are making more money than ever before. But I come from the inside and have seen behind the mask. The dark, dirty secret is that we Chinese do not trust our leaders, and neither should you. Our leaders encourage the wishful thinking of the West that China will move to democracy or a semi-democratic system once Western-style capitalization takes hold, but this will never happen, because it means the Party would have to give up control and all the 'goodwill' money its members siphon off from State enterprises, which are cash cows."

I nodded. "The money's too good and it's there for the picking."

"Yes, and the power gives them a free way in, with discretion. The State runs forty percent of all Chinese 'free enterprises.' That is a lot of money and power. What they do is wheedle and blackmail and steal everything they can from Western companies to make State companies stronger, feeding off the outside companies as much as they can. But they know that is not endless. The Party has played out the leash, that is all. And when complaints grow too loud at home or abroad, it stages an anti-corruption campaign or something similar, and chooses a few victims. To those of us in the system, this is laughable. But when the mask comes off, the Party will yank back the leash. Then they will be ruthless and none of us will be laughing."

"Okay, I've got that. But what does this have to do with me?"

"I need you to convey all of this directly to your President Slater."

I looked at Zhou in surprise. "You know about that?"

"I am a spy. It is my job. Why must I keep telling you that?"

I conceded the point with a shrug. "Then you know I have no clout, aside from my work to find Anna."

"It is enough to whisper in his ear. He will consider your source. Whispers are powerful."

I studied the man before me. He knew the power of intrigue. He knew the power of lies and secrets and deception. So it stood to reason he knew the power of rumors and whispers on the wind. Perhaps the most powerful tool of them all. A word in the president's ear and Zhou's message would surely spread.

"That I can do."

"Good. Now for a bonus reason."

"And what might that be?"

"I never meant for you to be executed."

I stared at him, dumbfounded. I couldn't imagine a scenario where that played out as he said. Could this be the first of a new set of tricks? Was the landscape about to shift again? If so, I wasn't buying.

"That makes no sense," I said. "You let them torture me."

"You need to keep things in perspective."

I was on the edge of my seat. "I think I'm doing pretty well, all things considered."

"No, you are not. The torture was simply business."

I opened my mouth to speak, then shut it, stunned yet again.

In the grander scheme of things, he was right. Whether you condoned torture or condemned it.

CHAPTER 89

A S soon as Zhou left, I fell into a bottomless pit until we reached the Mongolian border and Chen called my name. I'd decided the master spy had arranged for my escape for the reasons he said, and they were strong and numerous enough to discount a double cross.

"You ready, Mr. Fabbri?"

I woke in an instant. "Yes."

Chen straightened his hat. We'd arrived at the border crossing. Two entry lanes. Six or seven cars in each, engines idling, waiting to be processed.

The last barrier to freedom.

The Chinese section came first. A guard approached Chen in the front, questioned him but soon lost interest, and signaled me to roll down my window.

"Passport, please."

"*Ciao,*" I said, and handed over my Italian document. The burgundy booklet was stamped with the emblem of Italy in the middle, UNIONE EUROPEA, REPUBBLICA ITALIANA in gold lettering above, and the obvious label PASSAPORTO below.

"Your visit to China was good, Mr. Fabbri?"

"I 'ad a 'appy time. Is good-a country, no?"

Nodding, he asked me a series of innocuous questions, including one about my accident in Beijing, which Chen must have mentioned. He flipped through the pages of my passport and glanced from the pages to me, or rather to my moustache, obliquely. None of the passport pages arrested his interest as much as my facial hair.

"Now you visit Mongolia?"

His first unnecessary query. He made eye contact, then his gaze dropped back to the document in his hand by way of my blond upper-lip ornament.

"Yes-a," I said, and he nodded abstractly.

"Enjoy the rest of your trip."

He stamped my passport, then handed it through the open window, his eyes lingering one last time on the moustache.

Chen put the sedan into gear and drove up to the Mongolian check-point, which we cleared in another few minutes, then drove on. Zhou had been right. The moustache had engaged most of the guard's attention.

Relief rolled through me as we drove away.

I'd escaped China.

Which left one last hurdle on the other end and I saw no way around it.

—————

I hurt all over.

My body throbbed and twitched and jiggled as I took my seat aboard the Turkish Airlines flight to Tokyo. Zhou had supplied a crutch along with a suitcase full of clothing I could check in. Passengers without baggage triggered alarms. I surrendered the crutch to the flight attendant and asked not to be disturbed for anything less than an emergency.

The attendant nodded politely, noted my seat number, and stole a furtive glance at the bandages on my face.

My body had become sensitive to any movement beyond the ordinary. The unavoidable bumps as the plane gathered speed on the tarmac, the gravity pressing my body back against the seat, the sudden lifts and drops as the plane rose and tried to break free—all of them tormented me in fresh and inexplicable ways.

Why?

Because the rubber-coated bat had pounded the flesh at my back into something approaching a jelly-like consistency. My skin and muscles and every other tissue of my being that was wrapped around bone from calves to shoulders seemed to flex and shift in unfamiliar ways. Every little tick, twitch, and throb of pain rippled through the jelly like a wave over the ocean, moving rhythmically, evenly, kinetically. And that was before the burns and blisters from the two sessions in which they'd jacked up the juice of the electric prod.

Despite the distress, or perhaps because of it, I was asleep in seconds, but—unlike my respite in the car—my slumber was fitful rather than deep. Images and voices wafted by, as they had done back in the prison cell, but without any of the subconscious panic.

Jenny floated by, chatting gaily about judo and soccer and her favorite movies. I reached out for her hand but she faded from sight in the way that people in dreams do. She was followed by Renna and Noda and, finally, Rie. My girlfriend exited to the shadowy perimeters of my dreams far sooner than the others, with the same desolate look on her face I'd witnessed at our parting in Tokyo.

After landing at Narita Airport, I declined the offer of a wheelchair. I deboarded with a crutch under one arm and hobbled down the series of hallways toward Passport Control, wondering how long the process would take before officials pounced.

Once I stepped up to the inspector's booth, I could see downstairs to the luggage area. At the far end were the Customs lanes and beyond them the charcoal-tinted exit doors leading to the arrival terminal, where Rie and Noda waited. I'd called them collect from the Mongolian airport.

The expression on the inspector's face told me it was only a matter of moments now.

Minutes or seconds, then the how.

He wore a starched white shirt, a blue tie, and security ID on a long neck strap. I looked at his ID. He was who his ID claimed he was. The problem was his computer screen told him I was not who the Italian passport said I was.

I waited, resigned.

I found my mind straying back to Zhou's last reason for masterminding my escape and, oddly enough, found some comfort there:

Zhou had repeated his claim. "I never meant for you to be sent to the executioner's."

Which is when my long-contained rage finally broke free. "My re-mains were scheduled to be displayed in the Bone Room. Have you seen that place?"

"I had the distinct displeasure of being given a guided tour by a very pompous local official."

I shook my head, unconvinced. "Why should I believe you?"

"We are here, for one."

I frowned. "That's not enough."

The master spy seemed disappointed. "It should be."

I pushed on stubbornly. "So all this talk about the hundred-year plan is true, but the murder charge you saddled me with when you left me at the Farmhouse was a bluff?"

"Of course it was a bluff. I wanted Anna Tanaka's escape route before it was too late. I was a touch saddened by what you would have to go through, but I saw no way around it. It is partly your fault, you know."

"My fault?"

"Because of who and what you are. I knew from our very first encoun-ter five months ago when you refused both of my bribes to give up the Chinese agitator that you would be hard to break, so I threw everything at you."

Unfortunately, a credible comment. He'd initially offered me fifty thousand dollars to give up an old Chinese reformer hiding in Yokohama Chinatown. When I'd refused, he offered me an impressive chunk of real estate in San Francisco to "give my daughter a permanent home." I had no doubt that he would have delivered, but I'd turned him down flat.

"So what changed your mind?" I asked.

"I never changed my mind. My plan was to drag the escape route from you, catch Anna Tanaka, and eventually release you to your embassy, with our bureaucrats voicing loud complaints about your subversive activities in China. That was my assignment. It was simply business. The problem was my plan was hijacked."

"Hijacked how?"

He shrugged, as if to say some things were unavoidable. "I am re-quired to file a report detailing my strategy. An idiot puppet master up the line decided that actually executing you for the traffickers' deaths would be a good finger in the eye of your country. Of course, the plan would also earn him points with his bosses while doing almost nothing himself. He made a strong case and his proposal was approved."

"Did you go along with it?"

"It is above my pay grade. But the idiot's plan is just the sort I despise. If I were asked, I would have agreed to it and done just as I have done. I knew you did not slit those men's throats. It is not your style."

"Thanks for that."

"Do not thank me. It is my job to know my adversaries."

"Thanks, then, for getting me out."

He turned away to look out the window, embarrassed. "Do not be so grateful. I nearly got you killed."

His reaction pointed to what went unspoken but what we both knew to be a core truth. He hadn't left me to die. Yes, he also used my escape to frame a political enemy, but he could have saved the Chen ruse for another time and place and left me at the Farmhouse, for the Bone Room. Inaction was the safer choice. It meant far less risk to him personally, not to mention his career. All he had to do was look the other way. Many men would have done just that.

He hadn't.

My reverie was interrupted by a voice at my back.

"Would you mind coming with us?" it said.

CHAPTER 90

T HE last phase had started.

I turned to find three immigration officers standing behind me in buttoned-down navy blazers. They ushered me into a small room with walls the color of a gravel pit. My fingerprints disgorged a name from their system that contradicted the one on the Italian passport, as I knew it would. Before Japanese officials could haul me off to some dark cell, I played my get-out-of-jail-free card: Ambassador Tattersill. The irritable diplomat would be indignant but would follow the president's mandate and send an underling to vouch for me, after which the nightmare would be over. I'd be back with my friends and colleagues. Back in Rie's arms.

My new minders nodded, listened, and left. Two hours later they returned with a command to follow them.

In Japanese. No apology. No English. No Italian.

I limped after the lead uniform, with the remaining two at the rear, cutting off any retreat. We traipsed down a long hallway and into another room with the same gravel pit walls but a new welcoming committee.

"Surprise, surprise," said Thomas R. Swelley, Homeland Security agent and professional bastard. He wore a grin tight enough to crack a molar.

"Since when are you Tattersill's errand boy?"

"Since never."

"Then what are you doing here?"

"I had an alert out for you, so your return was routed through Homeland. I made an executive decision not to bother the ambassador with something so . . . inconsequential. You're all ours."

Two of Swelley's goons from Washington, DC, leaned against a far wall. They wore black leather jackets far too hot for late May in Tokyo. The pair watched the exchange with undisguised glee. Their eyes glistened. Next to Swelley stood one of the Japanese-American undercover agents sent to Sharon Tanaka's funeral. One of the ones who had watched without protest while Anna was taken away by Habu's gang. My anger began to rise.

Swelley fixated on my battered features. "It looks like someone started the party without us."

"It does, doesn't it?" the Japanese-American said.

My police escort had not followed me into the room, which was unfortunate. Instead, after listening from the threshold, one of them cleared his throat, made a comment about passing the baton, and closed us in.

Swelley turned to his Japanese subordinate. "What'd he say?"

"They gave us Brodie with no strings."

"Nothing about the embassy or the ambassador?"

"Not a word."

Rubbing his hands together, Swelley's grin grew.

I didn't waste another second. The crutch flew from under my arm. With a flick of the wrist, I grabbed the narrow end, hopped forward, and looped the shaft out and up and into the side of Swelley's skull. Emitting no more than a clipped chirp of surprise, he crashed into his Japanese-American underling.

While the agent tried to steady his boss, I rocked back half a step and rammed the end of the crutch into the stomach of the errant agent. He released Swelley and grabbed his midsection, then sprung up in a howl of rage. By that time the crutch was coming around again. It caught him on the side of the head as it had Swelley. He crumpled in a heap alongside his boss.

As expected, the two goons in the leather jackets bounded off the wall across the room. But I'd calculated the distance between us beforehand. Now, I pivoted to meet their charge.

Or, rather, I gave the command to pivot. In my mind's eye, my body had already begun the turn. I'd devised the next two moves and envisioned how I'd take down Swelley's leather-jacketed backup.

But the pivot never happened.

Nor did the crutch swing around.

I'd exhausted my reserve and my body had shut down.

The largest of the pair connected with a brutal but predictable blow to my jaw. The full force of the punch flung me against the wall. I'd conceived a way of blocking the strike, but my arms dangled motionless at my sides like cut branches hanging by a last strip of bark.

I sagged to the floor.

The pair piled on.

What had I been thinking? I couldn't summon up the strength to recall my reasoning. But whatever it had been, I'd turned a no-win situation into the perfect loss.

———

I woke up on the floor of a windowless van. Swelley's Washington gorillas sat side by side on a bench, rocking gently with the movement of the vehicle.

"Where's your boss?"

"Getting an X-ray as we speak. He's going to want to work you over personally when he's back."

They'd hog-tied my arms and legs behind me. "Did he say that or is that your interpretation?"

The two men exchanged a look.

"He didn't regain consciousness, did he?"

Neither man replied.

"Good," I said.

Ah, that's what I'd been thinking. Dumb. It seemed my reflexes weren't the only one of my faculties to have suffered a setback. All my frustration about Swelley's slick moves had snuck in behind my fury over the Japanese-American agent's inaction at Sharon's funeral and ambushed me.

"You won't be saying that for much longer," the man who had thrown the first punch said.

But that's where the chatter stopped. Neither of Swelley's pit bulls rose to extract another pinch of retribution. Nor did they insult me, curse me, or abuse me in any way. They just swayed with the van and watched me.

I'd have felt better if they'd flung some personal threats of their own. Or swore or taken another swipe at me. That was normal.

A silent vigil was not.

————

"Is he awake?"

"Was before, Mr. Haggis."

"You give him anything? Meds, another beating?"

"No, sir. Hands off, just like you ordered."

"Good job, boys." A toe nudged me.

I wasn't asleep, just resting. I stirred and opened my eyes. Swelley's thugs had dumped me on my side, still hog-tied. My cheek rested on cold concrete. More cement, but of the consistency of a serious building pour, not the coarse mix of an underground dungeon to house people the government wanted to forget.

The ground was crazed with the hairline cracks small Japanese buildings accumulate over decades of being subjected to routine tremors and quakes. So I lay in an older structure. The floor did not slant toward the middle of the room and yet it had a drain. So the place didn't originally serve as a lockup. The metal on the drain sparkled. So I was dealing with a recently repurposed site. Up close, the faint smell of gasoline product and even fainter shadows of long straight lines presented themselves. So I'd been brought to a converted parking garage. And the room was much cooler than it should be for this time of year. So I was in a basement two or three floors down. Maybe more.

My situation had not improved but my mental faculties had resurfaced.

"There you are, Mr. Brodie," the man called Haggis said. Swelley's two watchdogs stood nearby, attentive. "You put my main man out of commission for a spell."

"How about that."

"You don't seem too shook up."

"Should I be?"

"Yes, because what you visited upon him we are going to visit upon you tenfold."

"Sounds biblical."

A tightness threaded its way into his voice. "Oh, it is. We will be sending you to your maker."

"For taking a swipe at Swelley?"

"No, he's a pro. He'll take his lumps."

"What, then?"

"For what you did to Anna Tanaka."

"Are you insane? I saved her."

"You scuttled a top secret op. Strap him in, boys."

"Wall or chair?" one of the leather jackets asked.

CHAPTER 91

IRON manacles bolted to a metal chair, itself bolted to the cement floor, secured my wrists and ankles. After locking me down, Swelley's boys left me alone with their boss's boss.

"This is the armpit of hell," Haggis said. "But don't worry. You're only here for a short time, then you will disappear. Uh, let me correct that. You have already disappeared."

Haggis paced back and forth in front of me. He was a pale man in his forties, with a well-shaped head of prematurely gray hair. The hair lent him dignity, and his large burly frame lent him a commanding air. He had a tall forehead, which gave him an intelligent look, but at the moment his brow was furrowed with a curious mix of anger and elation.

"There must be some mistake," I said.

"There's no mistake. You're a traitor."

The official reason I'd been dragged here. Wherever "here" was.

"Again, there's got to be a mix-up."

Haggis's eyes filled with fury. They were dark and predatory. "The only blunder was mine. I should have eliminated you much earlier."

"What is it you think I did to Anna?"

His eyes blazed. "You scuttled a sanctioned op."

"That wasn't my question."

"That damn well is the answer." He brought an inflamed face to within inches of mine. "Anna Tanaka was in play. The North Koreans were *supposed* to take her."

"*What?*"

"Think way back, Brodie. I sent Swelley and his team to warn you off in DC. We tried to take you down at the ambassador's and at the airstrip, but you escaped and managed to totally screw up the operation."

So Haggis, not Swelley, was the mastermind behind all the attacks.

"I saved Anna's life."

"No, you signed your own death warrant. Which I am going to enjoy fulfilling. It's just you and me. No cameras, no microphones."

Then his right fist slammed into my ribs. Followed by the left. With my arms and legs strapped in place, I was helpless. He continued to pound away. In my weakened state I immediately began to fade.

I was still trying to get my head around *supposed to take her* when my body went into protection mode and shut down.

———

My eyes flickered open and I tasted blood.

Haggis strutted in a moment later. He'd said no electronics, so he had a peephole in the door I couldn't see.

"That's right," Haggis said, reading my look. "Old school. What screws you in the end is recorded evidence. You figure out the score yet, Brodie?"

"Sure. It's not rocket science. Sanctioned by who?"

His eyes narrowed. "Wrong question again. The correct one is why."

He waited with mock expectation.

"All right, fine. 'Why?' "

"To establish a channel of disinformation that would keep North Korea and its allies heading down the wrong path. The plan would have set back their spying capabilities years."

"China was after it too."

"The original target was North Korea, but China forced its way in and they are a bigger fish. The op would have been huge either way. I'd be looking at assistant deputy director in a few years. That's what you screwed up."

I stared at him, my mind working furiously. *Supposed to take her . . . There's no mistake. . . . Supposed to take her . . . Anna Tanaka was in play . . .*

I finally understood. "I can't believe what I'm hearing."

Haggis spread his arms. "What you see is what you get."

"You put Anna out there as bait. You set her up."

"I just tweaked the original op a bit."

"You call it a tweak? It wasn't the North Koreans at the Kennedy Center, was it? You killed Anna's mother so Anna would be forced to come out of hiding to attend the funeral."

"Yep, a tweak to end all tweaks. You're a clever man."

"But not as clever as Swelley?"

"God, no. No smarts there. Just a loyal soldier, not another brain." Then Haggis turned indignant. "But you don't get to ask questions. All you get to do is die. No more beatings. All that's left for you is a shoot-and-dump."

"You're serious?"

"Yes. From the beginning, you've been the only problem. You have the president's ear. I couldn't risk some small comment triggering a White House probe. The others I could handle. Swelley and his crew know nothing but the original plan. Anna doesn't either. Your people, it'll be their word against ours, if they even figure it out. Once you're gone, no one can point a finger. The official version will be that North Korea sent an assassin after Sharon Tanaka."

"He spoke Spanish."

"You think I'd send one that spoke Korean? Even the North wouldn't do that. They'd hire a freelancer, just as they contracted out Anna's kidnapping to the Japanese. End of story. End of you. 'Last meal' time, Brodie. Steak or sushi? Lucky for you I'm a traditionalist. A token display of humanity goes a long way toward pacifying the staff."

I studied the man before me. His face had closed up. There was a sudden aloofness to his manner. He'd made his decision and was in the process of washing his hands of me. I constituted the only loose end. Everyone else—from the Tanaka family to Zhou to the national security establishment to the American president—believed North Korea was behind all of it.

"Others will learn I was killed here."

"For reasons of national security. It's routine and no one will speak of it. Ever. Steak or sushi?"

His comment was spot on. The clandestine services community was as close-lipped as they come.

"Steak and fries," I said. "Ketchup, full salad, with good tomatoes, croutons, oil and vinegar. I'm a traditionalist too."

CHAPTER 92

THIS wasn't the Farmhouse, but it might as well have been.

    I was in another windowless room. There was another dim light-bulb on a string overhead. There was another drain in the floor. And I was once again underground. Not below a range of anonymous hills, but in the subbasement of an anonymous building in Tokyo, repurposed by an American government agency. In a building that, to pedestrians strolling by, didn't exist.

No, that wasn't right.

In a place that didn't look like what it actually was.

Just like the Farmhouse.

How was it that two governments with such opposing belief systems and opposing styles of rule could come up with such similar detention facilities? I didn't know, but I knew my last meal was on its way down, after which Haggis wanted me dead.

And he might succeed. I had no fight left in me.

No, again my thought was slightly off-center.

In spirit, I had plenty of fight left. It was my body that couldn't take or give any more. Everything had been pounded out of me at the Farmhouse. In the confrontation with Swelley out at the airport, three swings of the crutch in less than ten seconds had drained my reserves. Under Haggis's pummeling, I'd lasted only a few punches. With nothing left to draw on, my body had shut down both times.

I would need a week to recuperate before I could fight my way out of this place, but I wasn't going to get a week.

I heard footsteps in the hall. The door swung open and Swelley's leather-bound hooligans crossed the threshold. One stationed himself by the exit and drew his weapon. The other set a tray on a table near the door.

"Here you go. Steak and fries and a salad. Don't get it, though."

"What's that?" I asked.

"This is Japan, man. Great sushi is everywhere. Why not go for the best for your last?"

"So Haggis is sticking with the final meal ploy?"

"No ploy. That's what it is."

"Am I really supposed to believe that?"

He shrugged, bored and ready to leave. "Believe what you want."

"Not sure I can do that."

The man sighed. "Let me lay it out. Do we need anything from you?"

"No."

"There you go then."

He had a point.

"But why?"

"You stuck your nose where it don't belong. You mess with national security, it messes with you. You people got to learn that."

I shot him a sharp look. "You don't know why."

He fired back a smirk. " 'Need to know.' We *know* you're a traitor and that's all we *need*."

Traitor, like *terrorist*, was a loaded word. Wield it in the right way and it became an all-purpose excuse.

"You going to do it?"

"Nah. The big boss. Now I'm going to uncuff you. Try anything at all and my partner will put you down."

The man at the door tightened his grip on his piece.

"I'm not going to give you any trouble."

"Don't think you can, man. Don't know what they did to you out in China, but they emptied your tank."

"That they did."

"So we'll be doing you a favor, putting you out of your misery."

"I wouldn't go that far."

"You got an hour to eat, and if you're of the persuasion, say your prayers."

Then he backed away. Two pairs of eyes and one gun were trained on me until the door slammed shut.

Time to eat.

CHAPTER 93

*Y*OU *got an hour.*

I ate my last meal. The steak was marbled Japanese beef and melt-in-your-mouth tender. It disappeared far too quickly. The fries and salad were fries and salad with nothing much to recommend them, but I polished them off as well. My body, not surprisingly, craved the calories.

I stood and stretched. My muscles ached and my nerve endings twitched and buzzed and sent little warning charges throughout my body that sparked and fizzed and said don't do too much. Anything beyond ordinary movement would unleash waves of pain.

I settled gingerly back in the metal chair and closed my eyes. What else could I do but wait for Haggis? I found the overhead lighting annoying. Since I was free to roam, I shuffled over to the table, picked up the ceramic dinner plate, and flung it at the lightbulb. The bulb shattered and the room went dark.

"Much better," I said aloud.

I retook my seat and closed my eyes.

———

The door banged open and Haggis stood on the threshold.

"Your hour's up, Brodie. Smashed lightbulb's not going to buy you any time. Stand up, hands in the air. I'm going to enjoy this. I think I'll start with a leg. Maybe a kneecap. Stretch things out."

The Homeland agent's large silhouette filled the doorway. He aimed a firearm with one hand and held a flashlight over the top of the gun with the other, the way he'd been taught in training.

I stood and raised my hands.

Haggis took a step into the room and his feet flew out from under him. They went up and his head came down on the cement with a stomach-churning smack. The weapon and flashlight tumbled away into the darkness. I rushed forward, wincing with the sudden movement but not slowing. However this played out, I would not go down without a fight.

The fall had stunned Haggis, so I hobbled past him and stuck my head out the door. There was no one in the hall. Behind me, Haggis groaned. He tried to rise and couldn't. He tried to lift his head and couldn't. Saved me the trouble of supplying the knockout punch, which even in my weakened condition I could manage against a stationary target.

In a groggy voice, Haggis said, "What the hell just happened?"

"Oil and vinegar just happened," I said.

———

Quickly I retrieved the flashlight and used it to search for the errant gun, a Beretta 92FS, which I examined then shoved in the front of my waistband.

I relieved Haggis of the key ring hooked to his belt. When I searched him, I found a conceal-carry Glock 27 in an ankle holster and a pair of brass knuckles in his pocket. He carried no extra magazines for either gun. I hated brass knuckles and tossed them aside. I shoved the Glock in the back of my waistband.

Haggis said, "I need a doctor. I can't move."

"You're talking to the wrong guy."

"Call on the radio."

I looked down and saw I'd missed a two-way transceiver, which had come loose from his belt and skidded away. I flipped it to listening mode but heard no chatter. I stepped away and shook it. Tapped it a couple of times on the table.

"Broke in the fall," I told Haggis, and set it on the table.

Haggis said, "You're not getting out of here without my say-so."

"Not buying today, sorry."

"We're four levels down. Each level is locked. For security purposes, none of the key rings carries more than two keys. That's two floors. You get the next ring from a guard on the other side of a gate. You see? You're trapped."

I lifted the ring and studied the keys. There was a different tooth pattern on each key. Which meant two different locks. No master key, otherwise I'd be staring at a single piece of dangling metal.

"Give it up," Haggis said. "You can't get past my men."

He lay on the chilly cement floor, stiff and wooden. He was flat on his back. When I moved, his eyes followed me but his neck did not. Paralysis was a possibility. He could slide his arms up and down over the floor—like a snow angel spreading fresh powder—but the movement took effort and looked painful.

"I'll take my chances."

"Won't work."

"What you mean to say is that if I get out, your secret gets out."

He was silent for a beat. "Losing proposition, Brodie. The men have standing orders to shoot."

"Guess I'm going to test those orders."

I pulled the Glock out and considered it. I had fifteen rounds in the Beretta. I was either going to escape shot-free or after firing a round or two. Either scenario would require luck and maybe some deft maneuvering. If I needed anywhere near fifteen bullets, I wouldn't be leaving of my own volition. Which made the Glock deadweight.

I popped the clip, dropped eight of the nine bullets, then slammed the mag home and set the subcompact down at the edge of Haggis's reach. His fingers could scramble over the cool cement and wrap themselves around the gun in a minute or two, but no sooner. What little he could move was moving at a glacial pace.

"A going-away present," I said.

Haggis snorted but said nothing. I stepped from the cell into the dim amber light of the hall and silently locked him in.

It was time to go home—if I could.

CHAPTER 94

THERE were five other cells on my floor, all of them empty.

An iron gate blocked the stairway leading up. One of the keys on the ring opened it. The passage had the impenetrable brackish look of tarnished silver. A light switch beckoned, but I left it alone. I started up, silently, with gun drawn, a stair at a time. With the knife wound in my leg throbbing, I leaned heavily on the rail.

I paused on a landing at the halfway mark where the staircase doubled back and peered up around the bend. Another barred gate. I climbed the second set of steps at the same cautious pace. My ribs began to ache, courtesy of the beating I took from Haggis. A blue *3* was painted on the wall next to the gate. The second key unlocked the grille, and I let myself onto the third level.

The hallway was empty. The floor again housed six rooms, but this time interrogation chambers. A light box had been positioned above each door that, when engaged, read IN USE. None of them were lit, but even so somewhere inside of me anger flared. *Stay focused, Brodie. Get out of here first.* I wanted to take a match to the whole place. Maybe I would.

I limped toward the staircase to the second level and was confronted with another gate, but it took the same third-floor key. The staircase doubled back as the other had. At the top I found the number *2* and another gate.

There was no guard in sight. I approached. I tried both keys but neither worked.

Haggis had been telling the truth. I was trapped.

———

Embedded in the wall was a call button. Above it a panel with a digital clock read 11:13 P.M. The reading unsettled me. I thought it was closer to six in the evening. I pressed the button, sheltered behind the rising stairwell wall, and pulled out the Beretta, wrapping my palm around its cool steel grip.

Nothing happened.

I waited three minutes. No one answered my call. I hobbled from my hiding place, hit the button again, then scrambled back into the shadows.

Nothing.

After three more minutes I approached the grille and ran the barrel of the Beretta across the bars, which produced a loud metal-on-metal racket that echoed down the hall. Then I called out in my best imitation of Haggis's voice.

From my hide in the stairwell, I waited. A minute later I heard footsteps. Two sets. The leather-jacket boys. Keys jangled. I raised the gun. This would be tricky. I couldn't show myself or shoot until the keys were within range.

A familiar voice said, "Looking for these?"

Shooter Watanabe, Brodie Security's military-trained asset who had watched our back at the airfield, held up a key ring, grinning. Behind him stood Noda, a look of relief on his face.

They let me out in short order.

"Where are the guards?" I asked.

Shooter pointed at the ceiling. "Going nowhere fast. Got all three of them corralled in a holding cell one floor up."

"Glad to hear it. How did you find me?"

His answer brought the second surprise of the night. "Your cop friend, Rie."

"Really?"

"Yeah. She dug out the location from her PSIA buddy."

The Public Security Intelligence Agency again. Japan's counterespionage group. The "buddy" was no doubt Ibata, the oily agent with the surgically enhanced dimples Mari and I had gone to see. Why would he help now when he'd refused earlier?

"An obnoxious fellow," I said, "but I may have to cut him a little slack."

"Don't be in too much of a hurry. Your woman gave big to get the intel on this place, and some kind of bad came down with the good."

An uneasiness chilled the back of my neck. "What kind of bad?"

Shooter shook his head, perplexed. "She was vague."

We'd climbed to the first basement. The next floor up led to street level, and freedom. At the end of the hall, two Brodie Security staff stood guard in front of the locked cell housing the captured personnel.

"No matter," I said. "We'll pay it back. Whatever it takes."

Shooter frowned. "That's just it. I don't think you can."

My mind went blank as I fished for possibilities. What had Rie done?

Then I refocused. "One thing at a time. Let's finish here first."

———

I stepped out into the night.

I inhaled deeply. Fresh, untainted air filled my lungs. I breathed freely for the first time in days. I took in another lungful of the cool night air and enjoyed the way it coursed through my nasal passages and into my lungs. The simplest of acts. One I'd always taken for granted, but never would again.

I gazed at the scene before me. I stood on a street no different from a thousand others in Japan. Ma-and-pa shops and small family businesses lined the avenue. A twenty-four-hour convenience store was open on the next block. Within walking distance I saw a steak house, a sushi restaurant, and a ramen shop.

Noda eased up behind me. "You ready?"

"There's one more thing."

The chief detective grunted as if he expected as much. "Make it quick."

We returned to the first basement, which contained a locker room with showers, a guard station, the holding cell, and an office.

"Where's the items you took off the guards?"

"In the office."

"That's where we're going, then."

The office contained six desks and looked like any other office cluttered with paperwork and computers. I hobbled over to the confiscated equipment—guns, cuffs, knives, radios, cell phones, wallets. I picked up one of three multiband, two-way radio transceivers identical to the one I'd taken from Haggis. I dropped into a chair. Noda and Shooter sat on either side of me. I flicked on the radio. I heard a light scraping sound. Haggis's arms moving along the floor.

I said, "You there, Haggis?"

I'd set his transceiver to universal mode. That meant the mechanism itself switched between the speaking and listening settings automatically, sensing the sound on either end and transmitting whatever it picked up in real time.

Silence, then: "Yeah. Radio's not broke?"

"Guess not."

I'd lied about the condition of his two-way. I thought I might want to talk to him again, but I didn't want to retrace my steps, nor did I want him using the radio to call for help. I'd bluffed and it worked.

"I see they got you. Boys, come get me. I'm down."

"They're not coming, Haggis. I've been outside. It's nice tonight. A lot of stars, the moon's nearly full, no clouds."

"You're lying. Too many gates. Too many guards. There is no way out without going through my guys."

"There was a way and I found it. Or it found me."

Silence.

"Good-bye, Haggis."

"Proof of life," he said.

He was asking for an irrefutable sign of my escape. *Proof of life* was the phrase sometimes used in abduction cases to prove the hostage was still alive. It usually amounted to a live conversation or a photograph of the captive holding up a copy of the day's newspaper.

"There's a convenience store on the corner and a steak house just in front of it. That where you got my meal?"

Silence.

"Haggis?"

No answer.

Then we heard the unmistakable crack of a .40-caliber bullet and gunmetal clattering on cement.

"Time to go," Noda said.

I nodded.

We stood and headed for the stairs.

As I made the climb, favoring my sore ribs and leg, it wasn't the sound of the Glock that echoed in my ears but Shooter's words on the second-floor landing: *Your woman gave big to get the intel on this place, and some kind of bad came down with the good.*

The emergency room doctor gave me an encouraging prognosis, but qualified his assessment with more caveats than a Hollywood contract. For starters, I needed to stay with them for five to ten days for treatment and monitoring, after which I would be an outpatient for at least a month.

He and his staff did not know what to make of some of what they saw. Apparently the whole back side of my body was one giant bruise. They were stunned by the sight, and when the doctor asked what had happened, I told him about the rubberized stick but not the who or the where.

An additional catalog of my injuries showed raw red skin where I'd been tapped with the electric prod, and blisters where my captors had dialed up the charge. Rounding out the list were a deep knife wound in my thigh, abrasions on my face, and two cracked ribs. I was also suffering from malnourishment and dehydration.

All injuries were dressed, after which a concerned nurse led me into a clean white room with clean white walls and fresh, sanitized air. There was a bed with clean sheets and a clean cotton blanket. No mildew, no bloodstains, no drain in the floor. In my current frame of mind, this constituted heaven on earth.

The hospital staff attached sensors all over my body that fed data to sophisticated monitors stationed around the room. The process seemed complicated. It took fifteen minutes to connect the sensors and confirm they were working. Last, the staff hung intravenous drips for rehydration, nourishment, and medication. The sacks of liquid were endearing in their simplicity.

After Noda and Shooter completed the necessary paperwork, I told them to go home, because all I was going to do was sleep for a few hours.

They went home and I slept.

The "few hours" turned into eighteen.

When I woke up, Rie was sitting in a chair next to my bed, in her police uniform.

———

"Hello," I said, working myself into a sitting position, careful not to dislodge any of the sensors or IV feeds. "You don't know how happy I am to see you."

Her lower lip quivered.

I said, "I am actually fine this time. Especially now that I'm back in Tokyo."

I smiled, and received a troubled look in return.

I tried again. "Even with the number of injuries, the doctor said there's nothing time and rest won't heal."

She nodded like I wasn't telling her anything new.

"What is it?" I said. "The nightmare you saw—it's over."

"No," Rie said, both lips trembling now. "It's not."

$\mathbf{R}$IE walked over to the window and closed the curtain. Brodie Security had sprung for a private room, with a window alongside the door. The curtain was to remain open except when privacy was required.

"You know, it's after visiting hours." Rie's voice was soft. "I had to claim police business to get in here."

Disconcerted, I sat up a little straighter. Rie never let her career spill over into her personal life. The practice had been almost a religion with her.

"What's happened, Rie?"

She reclaimed her seat. Her hands fluttered around indecisively before settling, tightly clasped, in her lap. "You know, it's a miracle we lasted as long as we did."

I stared at her, as confused as Shooter had been. Rie had expressed the same sentiment less than two weeks ago, only then it had been in bed and accompanied by a celebratory bottle of champagne. And couched in the present tense.

"What's that mean?"

Affection and sadness mingled in her look. "It's been nothing but thrilling for me, but . . . but . . . it's over . . . between us."

"You're talking about breaking up? Right this minute?"

"Yes. I'm sorry."

"That's what you really want?"

"Of course not."

My bewilderment redoubled.

"There are circumstances," she said.

I dismissed the idea with a shake of my head. "If we don't want it to happen, then it's not going to happen."

"It has to. I gave my word."

"What are you talking about?"

Her eyes teared up. "In the long run, it wouldn't have worked anyway. You and I lead full and busy lives in two different countries. You're an art dealer and a private badge. I'm public. I come from a very conservative law enforcement family. It's a miracle we survived this long?"

"Stop saying that."

"Well, it's true. Things could have fallen apart any number of ways. Clashes over culture or career or family. We had a good run."

"None of those tripped us up."

"Which is why," she said, blinking away tears, "it's a miracle. But this is the end."

"It isn't if we don't say so."

She lowered her head, and from under tumbling black locks she said, "I say so."

I was stunned.

I thought I had heard her incorrectly but she kept her head down and her eyes averted. I scrambled to decode the meaning behind the words. I stared at the woman whom I'd spent time with on and off for the last eight months. Who had worked with me on three cases, and supplied vital insights into all of them. I could come up with no explanation for her behavior other than that something had shifted. Something big. I was willing to fight through it, but Rie, it seemed, had already capitulated. I fell back against the headboard and waited for clarification.

Finally, with great reluctance, Rie spoke. "I told you not to go."

"I remember. But I'm back. In one piece."

She hesitated. "It's not that."

"What else could it be?"

"I . . . read my nightmare wrong. I told you I saw something terrible happen in a dream. I saw you suffering in a dark place and saw myself suffering too. I thought I was suffering for you. But I wasn't. I was suffering for us. The end of us."

Could you see that in a dream? I wasn't sure, but I said, "If I don't see an end, why should you?"

She shifted uncomfortably in her seat. "I am honored that you want to fight for me, but it is too late."

My throat went dry. "'Honored'?"

Her tone had turned cool and distant.

"You made a choice to go after Anna Tanaka. I don't blame you for that. If I were in the same position, and brave enough, I would have made the same choice. You almost didn't come back to me, though."

"But I did."

She looked up. Tears shimmered at the edge of her eyes. And from behind them, a deep sorrow emerged. "Yes, and for that I am grateful. It is another miracle, and it's wonderful."

We were talking at cross-purposes. What was I missing?

"But," I said carefully, as if tiptoeing around a child, "we're past that."

With even more care, she said, "I'm engaged, Brodie."

The non sequitur threw me. "What are you talking about?"

Had she thought I wasn't coming back after Noda and Anna returned from China without me? Did she think I had died? Was she so insecure, she immediately threw herself into another relationship? I considered each scenario and instantly discarded them in quick succession. Rie wasn't flighty. She was tough, sensible, loyal. And yet, when I looked into her eyes, I saw the truth of what she had done.

I started to speak but she raised a hand to silence me. "Shhh. It's okay, Brodie. Don't say anything."

"How could I not—"

Resignation consumed her. "Without you there would have been no light in my world. Now the light will simply be farther away. I can live with that because the . . . alternative is unthinkable."

She was making less sense with each passing minute.

"I don't understand how you could be engaged."

"Well, I am. To Ibata-san."

I nearly jumped from my bed. "The creep from the PSIA? I don't believe it."

"He's always had a crush on me."

Had Rie blindsided me? Had I misread every sign between us for the last eight months? Did she have some on-again, off-again relationship with the guy?

I didn't see how that was possible. "He's not your type." I thought of Mari's aversion to him. "I'm not sure the man is capable of affection."

"He is, just in a more . . . irregular . . . fashion."

"And that's okay with you?"

"Of course not. But I saw no other way."

"No other way for what?"

Rie hesitated. "Brodie, this is very hard for me to talk about."

Which was evident. She'd been circling around something I couldn't see since the start.

She said, "Just let it go, Brodie. We're over. I gave my word. I've made my decision."

"Why?"

"Like you, I made a choice."

"Why?"

She bit her lower lip. "Just accept it, please. I don't wish to talk about it."

I grew very still. We were approaching a precipice. I could sense it even if I couldn't see it. I was puzzled and frustrated, and yet wary to the point of near paralysis. An inner voice told me to reverse course, but I couldn't. Instead, I tried a different approach, which gave me a shock to rival anything the Farmhouse had slung my way.

"And," I said, "if you had refused Ibata?"

"Then you would have died."

CHAPTER 96

HER answer left me speechless.

Her features softened. "So, you see, my 'choice' was no choice at all."

"No, that can't have been your only option."

Rie nodded sadly. "It was. It is. How do you think Noda found you?"

Icy fingers clawed at my heart. "Shooter told me it was you, through Ibata."

"That's right."

"Did you even try anyone else first?"

"Are you kidding? I tried everyone else first. And not just me. Noda and I were both waiting for you at the airport. Once you didn't appear, we knew something had happened. Noda was searching for you. Brodie Security was searching for you. I was searching for you. We found out very quickly you had had passport trouble and had asked for the American ambassador. Then we learned Swelley had taken you away. Once we knew that, we knew time was short. Were we wrong?"

"No."

"So there was a panic. Everyone was calling in markers but you had disappeared. It was as if you weren't even in Japan anymore. We only knew, instinctively, that we had to move quickly." She looked to me for confirmation and I nodded. "I tried everyone I could think of. My colleagues at work. My boss and his boss. I even went to my father and his cop buddies. My father was my last resort. Him, and Ibata-san. You know I've always tried to avoid Ibata-san."

"True," I said.

From my first mention of the PSIA, she had sidestepped the issue of using him. It was only after I pressed her that she acquiesced with a reluctance so great I wanted to retract my request, but hadn't. Had my visit to the PSIA put her back on his radar?

"I'm not sure how but Ibata-san found you. He and his family have high-powered government connections."

"What about Noda's friend at the PSIA?"

"He came up with nothing. Ibata-san told me you were going to die."

My brow darkened. "He *knew* that? Are you saying Ibata would have let me die?"

"*Let* has nothing to do with it. He had no control over what happened. There are treaties and secret agreements between our government and yours. You may have been on Japanese soil, but you were in American hands. Ibata couldn't interfere. The PSIA *wouldn't* interfere. We were lucky to find you. Ibata mentioned someone by the name of Haggis. Are you sure there was no mistake?"

Even among secret agencies, not all secrets stayed secret.

"I'm sure," I said.

Rie's shoulders sunk. "Then I do owe Ibata-san."

"No, *I* owe him."

"You weren't in a position to bargain with him. Only I was."

"And his price for locating me was you?"

"Yes. I was the only thing he would accept."

———

A bleak silence welled up between us. I hunted for a way out of her bind, and Rie watched me struggle.

"Why didn't you call his bluff?" I asked eventually.

"There was no bluff. I either accepted or you died."

"What about money?"

"He comes from a wealthy family."

"He couldn't let me die once he told you. He'd know you would know."

Resignation flooded her features. "Even if he had had the power to save you or sound an alarm, he wouldn't have. Because as long as you were alive, he knew I was lost to him."

"So you agreed?"

She twisted her hands. "It boiled down to whether you lived or died, which was no choice at all, so I asked for traditional *omiai* conditions. A Japanese arranged marriage in a year's time."

"And he agreed?"

"He's from the countryside. He loved the idea."

"I bet. So what happens now?"

"We'll meet for coffee, the occasional light date, but nothing heavy or intimate."

Completely traditional and even a step back from what is practiced in most places today. She could keep him at arm's length for twelve months.

"I hate this guy."

"Don't say that."

Her defense of him devastated me. It meant the hook had been set.

––––––––

We stewed in yet another uncomfortable silence until I said, "You sacrificed yourself to save me."

Her smile was crooked. "I saved myself too. If you . . . had . . . had . . . died . . . when it was within my power to prevent it, I don't know what I would have done. It would have destroyed me. At least I know you are alive. And knowing that will warm me on cold days. Even if it must be from a distance."

I was lost for words.

She said, "One last thing."

"What's that?"

"Remember the message I gave you to deliver to your daughter?"

"Every word."

"Don't forget to pass it on to her."

"Of course not."

"There might be something in there for you too."

With that, Rie rose, bent over the bed, and kissed me. A light, feathery kiss. Her lips floated over mine, brushing them, drifting away, then pressing forward with a feverish passion.

After a long moment she pulled away.

"Please save that for a bad day," she said. "That's what I'm going to do."

Rie straightened and smoothed out her uniform. I tried to rise too but she waved me back. She drew open the curtains, then the door, then she was gone.

Around me, the monitors beeped and flashed and showed no indications of flagging vital signs.

Physically, I was on the mend.

CHAPTER 97

AGENT Haggis's account of the NSA op turned out to be accurate on a number of levels, several of them unsettling.

The NSA and Homeland Security had developed a joint disinformation operation housed in the NSA's massive data center. Hundreds of false files and so-called sanctioned ops were ladled into separate servers. For the NSA, the massive disinformation plan would distract cyberattackers from the agency's real data banks and could hamstring enemy spying activity. For the DHS, it was a proactive plan to undermine potential espionage or terrorist plots from North Korea before they were conceived, or misdirect any that might be activated. Since the success of the scheme depended on keeping its true nature a secret, the number of people who knew of its existence was severely restricted. For that reason, I was kept out of the loop.

Anna Tanaka was one of the key operators. She layered in the information in any number of convincing ways and wrote programs to capture the hackers' data and trace them back to their home bases. She was strictly behind-the-scenes, stashed securely away at Fort Meade, where she applied her talents to various other projects as well.

The data banks were located inside one of the NSA's operational centers at Fort Meade. A DHS hub in Japan handled the on-ground aspects in Asia. When the program went operational, the NSA baited hooks and North Korea nibbled.

The project was Haggis's brainchild, inspired by his years in the field as an agent for the CIA in Europe and Asia before he moved over to the DHS. He held the overall managerial lead, and it was understood a successful launch would result in a decent though not stellar promotion.

But he wanted into the upper ranks of the DHS, and only a spectacular success could propel him as high as his ambition reached.

So he came up with his "tweak": he attached Anna's name to the project in a place where North Korea would stumble on it, then drew her from the protective cocoon at Fort Meade to Japan by having her mother killed.

If the North Koreans got their hands on Anna, they could get into the system that much faster. The NSA-DHS team could then reel out more disinformation in a speedier fashion. North Korea would share some of the stolen data with its allies, including China, in return for favors or lucrative payments. The disinformation would spread. The possibilities were nearly endless and the project promised to contain, cripple, or mislead the spying and/or terrorist activities of some of America's enemies for years, if not decades.

Just as he'd claimed, Haggis had managed to keep his tweak a secret. As soon as Anna was kidnapped, he made preparations to scuttle investigations into her whereabouts, then grew alarmed at the unexpected involvement of the first lady and my subsequent recruitment. He sent Swelley to block me at every juncture.

Simultaneously, Haggis turned his attention to laying the groundwork within the agencies for the worst-case scenario. If Anna vanished into the North before she could be found, the DHS and the NSA might be better advised to hold back for six months to a year before making an official protest. The North Koreans wouldn't release her immediately in any event, if ever, and on no account until they'd siphoned off all of what she knew.

Since that was the case, Haggis argued, they might as well take advantage of the unfortunate situation to ramp up the disinformation project as rapidly as possible. Haggis promoted this not-altogether-unattractive alternative with such exuberance, while maintaining the proper amount of anguish over Anna's dilemma, that both agencies saw the efficacy of using their tech whiz from the other side of the border if they couldn't get her back. After all, Haggis pointed out, she would be a prized prisoner and would not be mistreated. Further, they needed to keep up the pretense of the disinformation project as an authentic cache of NSA files, or Anna would be labeled a plant and executed as a spy.

In short, Haggis had gone rogue in an extremely clever and unconventional manner.

Had he pulled off the feat of getting Anna into North Korea or China and boosting his disinformation program, three events would have followed in short order. First, the success would be considered, off the record, a home run. Second, in the corridors of the DHS, Haggis's status would have skyrocketed for his ingenuity in creating the program, and for his back-end leadership in salvaging the mishap for the agency, if not for Anna. Third, Haggis would have been in line for a major promotion.

More than one official expressed shock at how close Haggis had come to realizing his goal. I supplied one more piece of the puzzle by furnishing the description of the Kennedy Center shooter to the DHS. A review of Haggis's CIA career turned up the identity of the asset he had used to kill Sharon and Mikey. Interviewed on his home turf in an unnamed South American country, the gunman confirmed the assignment. Haggis had led him to believe it was a CIA-backed operation, which, apparently, was not beyond the realm of possibility, despite the CIA's clear mandate to operate exclusively on foreign soil. Not that the assassin cared either way, as long as he collected his fee.

The Japanese government was intent on extraditing the assassin to Tokyo to stand trial for Sharon's murder. In the United States, one arm of the government urged the same course of action, while the clandestine branches believed that a trial would set a bad precedent. An anonymous third party settled the issue by making the problem go away.

———

A joint DHS-NSA team flew to Tokyo to debrief Anna, who wished to stay with her family for the immediate future. Normally, an interviewee would be sequestered until the debriefing was concluded, but considering the emotional elements of the case an exception was made.

Her American husband had voluntarily stayed away from his mother-in-law's funeral in order to avoid drawing attention to his wife's secret departure, but now he could be found by Anna's side every moment she was not locked in with the debriefing team. She wound up her testimony, and despite her traumatic experience at the hands of the kidnappers she steered toward a swift and steady recovery, which, according to Mari, was to be expected of someone of Spiker13's caliber.

The same team debriefed Swelley and his Homeland crew. The probe confirmed that Haggis acted alone. Swelley recovered from my assault without any lingering effects, aside from an unquenchable desire for revenge. He was ordered to cease and desist, but whether the order would take root was questionable.

I heard through Margaret, the first lady's chief of staff, that Ambassador Tattersill had elected to take an early retirement from the diplomatic corps. Officially the decision was predicated on health issues, but unofficially his departure was the result of President Slater's displeasure with his actions over the whole affair. I lost no sleep over the dismissal. Overseers considered the inexperienced attaché Gerald Thornton-Cummings a small fish, so they threw him back, with a warning.

Trending in the opposite direction, Joan Slater saw to it that Jacobo Perez, the Marine who had helped us out at the ambassador's residence, received a presidential commendation and a sterling recommendation to the Marine Corps officer program. KC and his unit also received commendations.

As to the existence of a tunnel under the infamous Infiltration Tunnel Three, the South Korean government investigated the report but would neither confirm nor deny the existence of a new subterranean incursion.

I passed on what I knew about the black site in Tokyo to my Japanese journalist friend, Hiroshi "Tommy-gun" Tomita. His story led to the closure of the facility, assuring that I would not one day find myself an unwilling returnee. He and his gang of reporters next set their sights on the Farmhouse.

Several of my acquaintances in the American security services contacted me to express their displeasure with my role in exposing the facility. When I told them I had been an involuntary guest, they universally reversed their stance, with comments about better controls being needed.

On the art side of things, Dr. Kregg and her museum outbid two other contenders for the Kabuki robe. The costume became part of the permanent collection, and was currently on exhibit. Attached to the acquisition was a memorial plaque and an art intern program in memory of Sharon Tanaka and Michael C. Dillman, funded by a single anonymous donor. The unnamed benefactor was none other than the first lady. I had this firsthand.

Noda had lugged the shell-shocked Anna Tanaka to the safe house in Changbai, then returned for me. He arrived in time to see a cluster of police and the retreating taillights of the tangerine Geely hatchback. Having no means to follow the vehicle, he approached Pak with the task of tracking me down, offering the plate number of the Geely as a good place to begin. Pak's group could not field the resources for such an assignment, so Noda contacted an outfit in Hong Kong, which initially accepted the job but soon reversed itself. After informing him the plate number did not exist and I had vanished from the grid, the agency hurriedly refunded Noda's advance and dropped the case. Which is when the chief detective had dug in. He'd kept at it through various channels until I'd resurfaced in Mongolia.

During a celebratory evening of saké and sushi back in Tokyo, Noda let slip two new items. He and Jiro Jo, the Korean bodyguard, had been talking over a couple of beers about maybe working a case together if the right one came along. But despite their growing friendship, the Great Wall still wanted a piece of my hide. I rolled my eyes but said nothing.

Next, the chief detective told me it had been a mistake to let me out of his sight. I told him not to worry about it. He grumbled about my disappearance turning into a pain in the neck for him and the rest of Brodie Security. I apologized for the "inconvenience" I'd caused everyone—a very Japanese gesture—and Noda, in turn, offered his own platitude about not concerning myself since he'd found a solution should it ever happen again. When I expressed some curiosity, he said, "The plan next time is to shoot you myself. Put us all out of your misery."

————

The president caught me in my antiques shop on Lombard, arranging the stock.

In the three weeks since I'd escaped from the Tokyo black site, I'd talked to his wife four times and him twice. Now seemed like a good time to pass on Zhou's warning about his country's hundred-year game plan, so I did.

"All that from a high-ranking Chinese spy?" Joe Slater asked with some amazement when I'd finished.

"Yes."

"Why you?"

"As much as he trusts anyone, he trusts me."

"Again I'm forced to ask, why you?"

"He has an expression: 'An enemy well regarded is better than a friend you doubt.' "

"A well-turned phrase."

"Apparently, I fall under the 'enemy' category."

"Obviously, Mr. Zhou is an observant fellow."

"Obviously," I said, and we shared a laugh.

The next instant the president's tone turned reflective. "I will give your report serious consideration. There has been vague speculation about such matters but never anything this concrete."

"Do with it what you will. But if you want my opinion, Zhou was sincere and everything he says jibes with everything I've come across in my years of travel across Asia. Which is anecdotal, of course."

The president was quiet for a moment. "I will pass it through the White House bullshit detector, then run it by a few experts. If it holds up, I may want you to retell the story in person to several members of my cabinet as well as a handful of officials in several key posts. Would you mind?"

"Not at all."

Joe Slater gave a soft grunt of satisfaction, then said, "Once more, my wife and I wish to thank you for all you have done. There will be settlements with the Dillman and Tanaka families. We cannot replace what they lost, but the terms will be generous. I will see to that personally."

"Thank you."

"No, thank *you*, Jim. Sincerely. We could never put a monetary value on the torments you went through in China, but I hope my wife's remuneration will keep you in saké for a spell. Or in whatever your particular poison may be."

"You were more than generous. And thanks for covering the damaged camera too."

"We wouldn't have it any other way. Are you still seeing the doctor?"

"Three times a week until the end of the month, as an outpatient."

"And no complications?"

"Not yet."

"I'll pass that on to Joan. She asked."

"Please thank her again for the signed photographs for the staff in Tokyo. Your wife is quite popular on that side of the world."

"She's popular everywhere. At times, more so than her husband."

"Way of the world, maybe."

"And not a bad way."

After we finished, I leaned back in my office chair and stared at a framed ten-by-fourteen group photograph of about half of the Brodie Security staff holding up signed personalized photographs of the first lady of the United States.

Everyone in the shot looked happy.

———

I showed up at the Dillman eatery and pub down by the bay without calling ahead. They had a number of tempting local craft beers, but considering the place and the occasion I ordered a Guinness on tap, a personal favorite, even if the brew didn't measure up to its cousin across the pond. I carried my pint over to an empty booth in the back, polished off the first third in one go, then sat back to wait.

Which didn't take long.

Ian Dillman strolled up and said hello. I nodded. He looked me over. I no longer had any bandages on my face but there was still evidence of my Asian passage.

"Good to see you back in the city," he said.

"Good to be back."

"Looks like the trip had a few bumps."

"There were some rough patches."

He gestured at the opposite bench. "Mind if I sit?"

"I was counting on it."

He slid in across from me and signaled his bartender, who brought over a full bottle of Jameson Rarest Vintage Reserve, two shot glasses, two tumblers, water, and ice.

"Save the beer for later," Ian said.

I glanced at the Jameson. "I think I might."

"We'll start with a shot for Mikey, then move on. This stuff is too good to drink fast."

I nodded and he poured a stiff one for both of us. We raised our glasses. Ian made a toast to Mikey and we drank.

A second shot disappeared for good measure, then Ian laid out the tumblers and set down fresh pours. We touched glasses and sipped in silence for several long moments, giving Mikey his due. The Jameson was impossibly smooth, a complex mixture of fruit, nut, spice, and more. Mikey and Ian and I had sat in these booths on more occasions than I could count and it nearly felt like one of those times now.

Ian eventually got around to saying what I knew was coming. "You didn't give me a whack at the guy."

"I didn't forget. Just didn't work out that way."

"But you got him?"

"Big-time."

"So tell me how you did right by my brother."

And as we worked our way through the whisky, I did just that.

JENNY, of course, jumped all over me as soon as I returned home. She wanted her gifts, attention, and the special message from Rie.

Sitting in our small apartment with a view of the Golden Gate Bridge, we caught each other up on everything the other had missed, then I passed on Rie's message. After an exuberant congratulatory comment about Jenny's win and new belt, it went like this:

"Remember, you were strong at the tournament, but know you can be strong anytime. Tournaments are brief. The rest of life is ongoing. There's always—and I mean always—a way to win a fight. Never, never, never give up or give in."

Jenny thought about the message, asked me to repeat it, thought about it some more, then said, "She's not talking only about punching and kicking and throwing, is she, Daddy?"

"No, she's not."

"She's talking about what you and I always talk about. About the world spinning, sometimes in a good way and sometimes in a bad way, but always spinning and us always learning and always enjoying the good, which is gooder than the bad is badder."

"She is."

"Plus the never giving up part."

"You've got it, Jen."

She beamed up at me. "Tell her thank you. Can I go play with Lisa now? I need to take her her Totoro pajamas."

———

The call came a month after my initial exchange with Jenny.

We'd just finished reviewing some of my daughter's latest judo moves, and she was getting into her sleepwear following a shower. The caller ID was blocked. I picked up anyway and said hello.

"I see you made it home safely."

No return salutation. No names over an open line. But I had no trouble recognizing the voice. I never would.

"Yes. Where you calling from?"

"You don't want to know."

Jenny walked into the room in her pajamas, drying her hair with a hand towel. I pointed behind my ear and at my toes and she nodded. She'd washed both places.

Zhou said, "I heard there were complications in Tokyo."

Complications. "There was a minor inconvenience or two, now that you mention it."

"Good thing you made it out. I would have hated to see all my effort go to waste."

I took the roundabout sentiment for what it was worth. Which was a lot.

"Got a question for you," I said. "Who is the real Chen?"

Jenny flopped down on her pink-and-yellow-striped eyesore of a beanbag, smiled at me, and continued to dry her hair. I'd lobbied to throw out the anachronism a dozen times, but my daughter was having none of it. As a result, I'd been forced to patch up the beanbag more times than doctors had patched me.

"A former big wheel in the Ministry of Foreign Affairs now behind bars for helping you escape."

"And how did that come about?"

"Two days after your unfortunate breakout, he was found asleep in a hotel room with two lovely ladies from a local . . . pleasure institution. The celebration had been ongoing."

"Sounds like a honey trap."

"A variation. There was evidence to tie him to your jailbreak and a convincing amount of hard cash in the room safe with his fingerprints all over it. He and his confederates are now in custody. They will be interrogated and shot as traitors."

"Which is what they had in mind for you?"

"I don't know what you are talking about." *Yes.*

Clearly, crossing the master spy was suicidal.

"Are you in any more danger?"

"No. I am a hero. I captured you. The man who let you go is an enemy of the State."

"Remind me never to play chess with you."

Jenny stood, yawned, and, as was her habit of late, crawled onto my lap.

"You did quite well. Your one mistake was to show up in my territory and allow yourself to be outnumbered."

"Live and learn."

"You did at least one of those admirably without assistance."

A sobering thought.

Zhou said, "There are people in China who want to be able to do what you do every day, Brodie. Who want the freedom to sit down at a good meal in Tokyo or San Francisco without the Party looking over their shoulder. Who want the freedom to stroll across the Golden Gate without a burden of any kind. That's what you Americans have and we Chinese do not. That's what many Chinese think but can only say in private, among friends and family."

"Do many of them think that?"

"Millions."

"Not to mention you."

"I haven't the faintest idea what you are talking about." *Yes, of course.*

"I didn't think so," I said. "By the way, I passed on some of what I 'learned.'"

The president's chief of staff had contacted me about flying to Washington for half a dozen private briefings, and suggested I be prepared for more.

On the other end of the line Zhou seemed to settle into himself. "See, I was right about you. You *are* the enemy."

"I have no idea what you're on about," I said.

———

By the time we hung up, Jenny had fallen asleep in my arms.

I settled into my seat and just held her. Her breathing was faint and feathery, her features calm. She looked at peace with the world.

I had yet to mention my forced separation from Rie because it would break her heart. But that was only the first of two reasons. Recalling the conversation in the hospital room, I had an inkling the feisty police-woman had passed me yet another coded message.

If I was not mistaken, Rie had, if not a trick up her sleeve, plenty of fight left.

ABOUT AUTHENTICITY

BRODIE'S story ranges over five countries this time around. Here's what's true, country by country.

JAPAN

I start with the elements in the novel from my adopted home of more than twenty years, the always intriguing and often enigmatic Japan.

Kabuki theater traces its roots back hundreds of years. The historical facts about the Japanese performing art presented in the story are all true. That said, the opening Kabuki sequence at the Kennedy Center is a composite of many performances I have seen over the years and not drawn from one particular play. The fireworks are a nod to a variation known as Super Kabuki.

The pair of Kabuki costumes Brodie finds for his client actually exist, and the descriptions and histories in the book are faithful to the originals. The first robe belongs to a private collection in western Japan. The second, which, in the story, found a home in the museum of Brodie's curator-client actually resides in just such a depository, the Tokyo National Museum. It was donated to the museum by Kyo Takagi in 1901. Takagi was the daughter of a one-time maid to the daughter of the eleventh shogun Ienari Tokugawa, who ruled from 1787 to 1837.

Although Kabuki evolved into an all-male activity, Japan is also home to the Takarazuka Revue, an all-female musical theatrical troupe with a history dating back more than a hundred years.

Eating in Japan falls into the category of a national pastime, and is part of the adventure, whether it's one of the many specialties of the native cuisine or a Japanese variation of, say, Italian fare or the classic Western oyster bar. The Ostrea Oyster Bar and Restaurant is tucked away on a brick-lined lane in the Akasaka district of Tokyo. The menu lists forty-five types of Japanese oysters, although the offerings appear seasonally. The two specimens Brodie and Zhou sample are winners, and the oyster risotto a brilliant finish.

Yakuza gangs can be found throughout Japan. While they understandably keep a low profile most of the time, they have their hands in a number of enterprises, and are known to provide third-party muscle. The Chongryon is a functioning group in Japan that has supported the North Korean regime for decades.

While I have been to the American ambassador's residence in Tokyo and to the Yokota Air Base on a number of occasions, for security and plot reasons the details about both locations have been altered.

As for the rest of the Japanese sites and activities, the funerary practices described are true to form. The PSIA counterterrorist agency is located in Tokyo's Kasumigaseki district. Shinjuku Ni-chome is in fact Tokyo's largest gay quarter, home to some three hundred bars, though the Dragon Skin is fictional. The Japanese bath, so unlike its Western counterpart, is indeed restorative.

And last, the poisonous snake known as the habu, from which one character takes his nickname, inhabits the islands of Okinawa. Like its namesake in the story, it is best avoided.

SOUTH KOREA * NORTH KOREA

For this novel, I visited Seoul for the fourth time, and the DMZ for the first time. I also dipped into dozens of sources of all types to confirm the information presented in these pages, including *Seoul Train*, the documentary mentioned by one of the characters.

Three books with distinctive voices that left an impression because of their unflinching determination to look at the real situation in North

Korea and China today, as well as their desire to debunk the old stereotypes and clichés about the countries, are *North Korea Confidential: Private Markets, Fashion Trends, Prison Camps, Dissenters and Defectors* by Daniel Tudor and James Pearson; *The Real North Korea: Life and Politics in the Failed Stalinist Utopia* by Andrei Lankov; and *The Girl with Seven Names: A North Korean Defector's Story* by Hyeonseo Lee.

But nothing in the books could compare to my unsettling visit to the DMZ. Guards from the North and South face off on a daily basis, sometimes only a handful of yards from one another. I worked hard to make my descriptions of the highly secure area as accurate as possible. While there, my passport was scrutinized no less than five times, and on each occasion I was instructed to hold it alongside my face for comparison. A South Korean solider was required to ride along for portions of the visit, and when I arrived in the Joint Security Area, I was required to sign a waiver absolving the joint government commission of all responsibility in case of a sudden outbreak of hostilities.

The village of Daeseong-dong exists and is located within the DMZ. The special privileges and protections accorded its residents as mentioned in the story are all true, as are the restrictions.

The South Korean soldier "Robert" Kim, who assists Brodie's team at the JSA, took his nickname from US Navy commander Robert M. Ballinger. Commander Ballinger and ROK Marine Corps major Kim Hah-Cheol were killed in an explosion in 1975 while investigating the first infiltration tunnel.

The account about the attempted attack on South Korea's presidential residence, known as the Blue House, by North Korean special commandos is true, as are the casualty numbers.

The Statue of Brothers at the War Memorial of Korea in central Seoul may be visited, as may the Hyundai I-Park Tower and Bear Hall. Both have sculpture attached to the buildings as depicted.

The North Koreans did employ a malware called DarkSeoul against the South. Cyberattacks by North Korea continue apace, another making international headlines the same week I compiled these notes.

Two photographers appear in this book. Ben Simmons, the lensman

Brodie meets in Seoul, is a portrait of an actual expat American photographer of the same name out of Columbus, Georgia. Based near Tokyo, Simmons has made a career of shooting Japan and Asia. He also took the author photo for this book. Karen Stokely, who appears in the San Francisco sequence with Zhou, is fictional but not unlike a number of talented expat female photographers I've met over the years.

The plight of defectors fleeing North Korea for a better life is dangerous, with police and human traffickers in China ready to pounce on the unsuspecting refugee every step of the way.

The history of North Korea's kidnapping program is true. Many Japanese fell victim to it in the 1970s and '80s, as did citizens of more than a dozen other nations. While only seventeen Japanese have been officially recognized as kidnapped, by some accounts the number runs into the hundreds. There is talk of new kidnappings even now, making Anna's plight all the more frightening.

In the 1990s, a famine spread across North Korea and hundreds of thousands perished, with some estimates rising as high as three million. The lack of food was so dramatic, pervasive, and enduring, it is said to have stunted the growth of an entire generation of North Koreans.

This was a tragic period, and it changed the mindset of the North Korean people as they realized they could no longer rely on the government to provide them with all of the basic necessities to live. This has led to a thriving underground black market as described in these pages, and to an even newer generation of entrepreneurs, many of them in the upper echelons of North Korean society.

CHINA

Before I was a full-time author, I was an editor. Among the many books I acquired were a few on China. Several of the books involve the classic strategies of deception and battle, and another was on contemporary business practices. Not surprisingly, I drew on these works for the novel. I also turned to Michael Pillsbury's *The Hundred-Year Marathon: China's*

Secret Strategy to Replace America as the Global Superpower. The views of the Chinese character Zhou in the present piece of fiction are an amalgamation of much of what I gleaned in discussions, other sources, and Pillsbury's work.

As for the locales in the novel, Dandong and Jilin are actual Chinese cities, while Changbai is technically a county with an urban center also called Changbai. Dandong and the urban area of Changbai sit on the Yalu River, which also defines a portion of the border China shares with North Korea. North Korea is clearly visible on the other side of the river. I took some liberties with the layout of the streets and shops in Changbai.

The selling of North Korean women defectors "captured" by Chinese human traffickers is an ongoing problem in China, and is only inflamed by the huge "surplus" of males to the tune of thirty million, courtesy of the one-child policy, which has been brought to a close.

China's practice of repatriating North Korean escapees while knowing that returnees will face execution, or in the best-case scenario life imprisonment, is, from any angle, unconscionable. On the other hand, the country hardly treats its own citizens who fall into disfavor much better.

China justifies its actions with a verbal sleight of hand, labeling all escapees "economic refugees" rather than "defectors," thus technically circumventing international law even though people from all levels of society leave for a variety of reasons. Further, while some North Koreans wouldn't mind settling in China, and historically a number of them have, the vast majority would prefer going to South Korea or somewhere else if offered the choice.

Torture in China remains widespread. The torture sequence involving Brodie was hard to write but harder to research. Chinese officials deny all such incidents, citing statutes on the law books that prohibit acts of torture. But the flood of testimony from Chinese defectors, activists, and others tells another story. The Death Bed is one of many means of torture practiced in China. However, the bone-crushing technique Zhou proposes to use on Brodie's friend in San Francisco is fictional.

On a lighter note, the Geely GC5 is an actual car manufactured in China and does, happily, come in tangerine orange.

UNITED STATES

Brodie frequented two places in the United States this time around, San Francisco and Washington, DC, I grew up in California and spent a great deal of time in San Francisco and the Bay Area, and return there for visits and book tours every chance I get. As for DC, I've made many research trips to the nation's capital, and have been aided by insiders on the finer points of the city. I am fond of both places and tried to do them justice.

On the San Francisco food front, the pair of restaurants featured in these pages are real and have a loyal patronage. Gary Danko is a stalwart on most "best restaurant" lists and a San Francisco institution. And Mr. Pollo is a true hidden gem and perennial favorite among locals in the know, and now one of mine. It actually does seat only twelve at any one time, give or take the occasional chair squeezed in for a larger party. Fortunately, it has three seatings on most nights. And since I know many readers like to visit places in the books, let me just add that a reservation for either restaurant is recommended.

The Cathedral of Saint Mary of the Assumption, known locally as Saint Mary's Cathedral, can be found at Geary and Gough and is an impressive piece of San Francisco architecture. Not to be confused with the Old Saint Mary's Cathedral.

The sculpture by Bay Area artist Peter Voulkos can be found on the corner of Bryant and Seventh Streets.

As for Washington, DC, the Freer Gallery of Art is a branch of the Smithsonian museum group and has a number of exemplary pieces of Japanese art. Its collection, in tandem with that of the Arthur M. Sackler Gallery, is varied, extensive, and intriguing. The museum is on my short list of must-sees every time I'm in town. A visit offers an exotic trip through the cultures of many countries, all under a single roof.

The Kennedy Center hosts dozens of events each year, and has had Kabuki-related events as well as exhibitions of Japanese art. While the exterior description of the Center is accurate, I took some liberties with the layout of the theater.

At the White House, the practice of borrowing paintings from the National Gallery of Art, also in Washington, DC, is one way for those in residence to live with art from recognized masters.

One of the irresistible things about being a writer is having a built-in reason to visit so many great places, with the added benefit of meeting so many interesting people. All these are experiences I find endlessly fascinating, and I am extremely grateful to be able to have them. Attempting to bring to life some of what I encounter for readers around the world is, for me, a great pleasure. I hope you enjoyed the ride.

ACKNOWLEDGMENTS

FIRST and foremost, I wish to thank Robert Gottlieb, my agent at Trident Media Group, for his stout support. Also at Trident, I am grateful for the efforts of Erica Silverman, Mark Gottlieb, and the rest of the staff.

At Simon & Schuster my editor, Amar Deol, immediately embraced the book with enthusiasm and sincerity. And my thanks to the rest of the staff, including Kathryn Higuchi, Carly Loman, and Beth Maglione, as well as freelancers David Chesanow and James Walsh.

A number of other people provided access, insights, or assistance. For a behind-the-scenes look at stage design for television, and for filling me in on some of the differences between television and theater backdrops, my heartfelt gratitude goes out to Jill Haber, assistant paint foreman. The same for Gerald Gates, the paint foreman on-site. Both Jill and Gerald have long-running careers in Hollywood.

For recommending the restaurant Mr. Pollo after I explained the culinary and espionage needs of the ever-cautious Zhou, I am indebted to Susan Tunis, mystery fan, event coordinator, and bookseller at BookShop West Portal in San Francisco. And an additional nod for suggesting I add Saint Mary's Cathedral to my list of potential church sites.

For assisting in my search for admirable Kabuki robes, thanks are due to Shigeyoshi Suzuki.

For finding the time to read a first draft of this book during a sometimes impossibly hectic schedule and for then giving above and beyond, my thanks to friend and fellow author Anthony Franze.

For reading behind me on the cultural front, thanks are due to longtime Japanese-to-English translator and friend Gavin Frew.

For making sure all was clear and stowed away on the Marine front, my gratitude to Colonel Joseph N. Mueller (USMC, Ret.). And additional thanks to Boyd Davis, owner of Next Chapter Books in Canoga Park, California, for introducing me to Joe.

For guiding me through the intricacies and technicalities of an operating airport, I am indebted to Ken Babione, airport operations supervisor at Bishop Airport, in California.

For providing transporation, entertaining conversation, and a near visionary instinct for finding parking in San Francisco on my romp through the city for this book, my thanks to Mike Salo.

For hours of general conversation about good food, drink, and more, a tip of the hat to Robb Satterwhite, longtime American expat and proprietor of Bento.com.

For invaluable additional guidance on the ground in Seoul, a special shout-out to Sungkil "Peter" Ahn.

For giving me a line and a hint of youthful "attitude" from her young niece that worked perfectly for Jenny, I wish to thank Catherine Diann of Southwest Airlines.

For help along the way, I also wish to express my gratitude to Jeff Stern, Wade Huntley, Susan Rogers Chikuba, Mio Urata, Marc Lancet, Annette DeBow, and the rest of my family scattered throughout California, Hawaii, and Japan.

And last, and equally appreciated, for generously offering to travel around his adopted city of Kyoto and photograph sites where scenes in the third Brodie book, *Pacific Burn*, unfolded, my deepest gratitude to expat Irishman and writer Michael Lambe.

ABOUT THE AUTHOR

Barry Lancet's *Japantown*, an international thriller, won the prestigious Barry Award for Best First Mystery Novel and was selected by both *Suspense Magazine* and mystery critic Oline Cogdill as one of the Best Debuts of the Year. His second book, *Tokyo Kill*, was a finalist for a Shamus Award for Best P.I. Novel of the Year. The third entry in the Jim Brodie series, *Pacific Burn*, explored, among other things, the tragic aftermath of the Fukushima quake-tsunami disaster and the subsequent cover-up. Although there are recurring characters, the books are independent of each other and can be read in any order.

Lancet moved from California to Tokyo in his twenties, where he has lived for more than two decades. He spent twenty-five years working for one of the country's largest publishers, developing books on dozens of Japanese subjects from art to Zen—all in English and all distributed in the United States, Europe, and the rest of the world.

His unique position gave him access to many inner circles in cultural, business, and traditional fields most outsiders are never granted. Early in his tenure in the Japanese capital, he was hauled in by the police for a noncriminal infraction and interrogated for three hours, one of the most heated psychological encounters he had faced in Japan to that point. The run-in fascinated him and sparked the idea for a mystery-thriller series based on his growing number of unusual experiences in Japan.

Lancet is based in Japan but makes frequent trips to the United States.

For more information, please visit **http://barrylancet.com** or look for Barry on Facebook and Twitter (@barrylancet).